A RUSH OF PASSION

"Just tell me when you want to leave, and I'll be ready," Kora said.

"Oh, no, not *we*." Mace frowned. "I'm going by myself. I'm not going to put you in any more danger, and that's that."

In the small, dimly lit room, he towered over her, strength emanating from his lean figure, but she refused to be intimidated.

"How do you know I'll be in any more danger on the trail with you than sitting here in this hotel room, where anyone can find me?" she asked.

Mace grabbed her shoulders and she thought he meant to shake her, but instead he sighed and softened his grip.

"You're right, of course," he said. "And stubborn as hell." A grin tugged at the corner of his mouth.

Kora glanced at him, but she couldn't really be angry. When he reached out to brush the hair away from her face, she felt a tremor run through her. Mace must have felt it, too, for his eyes darkened and he brushed his thumb across her lips.

In the silence of the night, Kora thought she could hear their hearts beating.

Hearts
of
Gold

⋈ MARTHA LONGSHORE ⋈

HarperPaperbacks
A Division of HarperCollins*Publishers*

This is a work of fiction. The characters, incidents, and dialogues are products of the author's imagination and are not to be construed as real. Any resemblance to actual events or persons, living or dead, is entirely coincidental.

HarperPaperbacks   *A Division of* HarperCollins*Publishers*
10 East 53rd Street, New York, N.Y. 10022

Cover illustration by Vittorio

First printing: October 1994

Printed in the United States of America

HarperPaperbacks, HarperMonogram, and colophon are trademarks of HarperCollins*Publishers*

❖ 10 9 8 7 6 5 4 3 2 1

For Chris:
Without your faith and constant support,
this would never have been written. Your memory
inspires me; your love lives in my heart.

ACKNOWLEDGMENTS

Many thanks to all my friends and family who believed, even more than I did, that I could write a book. To Judy Longshore, for her sharp eyes and merciless pencil. To my editor, Abigail Kamen, for her understanding and patience. And to the Sacramento County Historical Society for their dedication to researching and promoting the history of their vibrant city—any factual errors are mine alone.

1

"And best of all, we won't be rivals any-more." Jared gave Kora a conspiratorial wink and leaned over their clasped hands to brush her lips with his.

"You don't think I'll come work for the *Union* just because we're married, do you?" Kora Hunter asked playfully, her heart still skipping from his proposal. "Papa might be willing to lose a daughter, but I don't think he'd take kindly to your stealing one of his reporters."

Jared rose to sit beside her on the sofa, fastidiously brushing off the knees of his tweed trousers. "Kora, honey, what did I just ask you to do?"

"To marry you, silly. Or are you trying to back out already?"

A lock of black hair curled down his temple as Jared shook his head in amusement. Kora wondered if he knew how condescending his chuckle sounded.

"Yes, to marry me. You don't think I'd let Mrs. Jared Davies work for a newspaper? Once we're married, you'll be too busy to put pencil to paper."

"Oh, I don't think I'll ever be too busy for writing. Besides, when Papa retires, Troy'll need me. You just want to eliminate the competition." She smiled at the familiar joke. Jared didn't smile back.

"Kora, come now. Think about what you're saying. You can't seriously mean to work after we're married. It's time to give up your scribbling for good. I'm going to give my wife a life of ease." He leaned toward her with a dazzling smile. "And if you really need to keep busy, I think I can find a way to keep you occupied."

Kora jumped to her feet and moved to the parlor window, pulling aside the heavy curtains in the hope that sunlight would ease her darkening mood. She had dreamed of Jared's proposing for so long, so why wasn't she more excited now that the moment had come? And why hadn't she realized that he would expect her to quit writing for her father's paper?

"Jared . . ." She didn't know what to say. Shock and a slow burn of anger stole away the words. "Scribbling?" was all she could manage.

Jared came up behind her. "It's bad enough now, listening to people talk about how unseemly it is for a woman to write for a newspaper. I won't have them saying such things about my wife." The firmness of his voice brooked no argument.

Kora looked out the window. A newly planted apple tree graced the yard of the house across the street. Next door, construction had begun on yet another new building. Her father had come to Sacramento seeking opportunity, determined to forge a better life in a growing land. The true wealth of California lay in its possibilities. And here, Kora had discovered that even women could dream.

She turned to Jared. "Things are changing. Don't you read the news you print? Because of the war, more and more women are taking jobs. While their men fight to bring the country back together, they're keeping the economy from disintegrating."

Jared put his hands on her shoulders, scowling down at her. "This is California, Kora, not Virginia or New York. If your father and I get drafted to fight the Confederacy, maybe we'll need you to keep the news flowing. But I don't think that's going to happen."

She bit back a hasty reply. He was right. She should have been prepared for this. If not for her father, she would never have gotten the chance to be a reporter at all. But she loved what she did at the *Valley Times.* Surely another reporter could understand that.

She looked imploringly into Jared's brown eyes, eyes that grew more distant even as she spoke. "I know I won't have as much time once we're married, but surely I could do an occasional article. That wouldn't hurt anything, Jared. Writing is in my blood."

"Then you'll just have to get it out," he replied with finality. He stepped away from her, leaving her feeling cold and alone.

"Please listen to me, Jared. Can't we discuss this reasonably? My father . . ."

"You needn't worry about your father. There must be fifty hacks in this town he could hire to cover the society round. He won't even miss you."

Icy tendrils of anger and pain curled around Kora's

heart as she stared at him. "That shows what you know, Jared Davies. I write a lot more than society pieces."

"Kora, women simply don't have the objectivity or the shrewdness to cover hard news."

"Then why in hell did you ask a woman reporter to marry you?"

Kora bolted from the parlor into the hall and threw open the front door. Blinded by tears, she didn't notice her father coming up the steps.

"Kora, watch where you're going!" He dodged her nimbly, one hand on his Panama hat. Sharp hazel eyes peered down at her.

"Sorry." She ducked her head as she stepped around him, not wanting him to see her distress.

"Shouldn't you be down at the riverfront, Kora? You're supposed to meet Chester McDougall's steamer, remember?"

She paused, her hand on the railing, trying to stop the whirling in her head long enough to understand her father's words. She'd completely forgotten that his old friend was arriving from Boston today.

"I'm just on my way, Papa," she stammered, glad for an excuse to escape the house. She ran down the steps and hurried up the street, praying that Jared wouldn't follow.

After three blocks, she slowed and risked a glance over her shoulder. No one. After the cruel things he'd said, Jared didn't even have the grace to come after her. Anger and regret roiled in her stomach.

She hurried on toward the embarcadero, impatiently brushing a wisp of blond hair from her eyes. She'd run out of the house without hat or coat, but if she turned back now, she'd never make it to the riverfront before the steamer docked. She sighed and went on.

Breathless from heat and exertion, Kora reached the embarcadero just before the *California* was due to arrive from San Francisco. She picked a spot in the shadow of a warehouse to wait, certain she already felt the beginning of a sunburn on her nose.

Minutes stretched out slowly in the steamy afternoon. Two o'clock came and went with no sign of the *California.* As her hair, her clothing, her very muscles succumbed to the humidity, Kora's frustration rose.

Normally the bustle along the riverfront would have intrigued her, each load of goods, each important merchant or lowly dock hand suggesting a potential story. Front Street's warehouses and storefronts gave visitors their first impression of vibrant, commercial Sacramento. Today Kora would have traded the whole exciting scene for a hard iron bench to sit on. She considered moving to the Central Pacific Railroad passenger platform nearby, but she might miss McDougall from there.

Why couldn't Troy meet the old newspaper man? Somehow he always managed to get out of doing anything tedious. Even as a child, her twin brother had displayed an uncanny knack for being busy or absent just when the dishes needed washing or the garden needed weeding.

Kora wasn't really angry with Troy, though. She was looking forward to seeing Chester McDougall again. If she played it right, she could learn a great deal from him during his stay in Sacramento. Besides, her brother wasn't the one who had ruined what should have been one of the happiest days of her life.

She pulled her watch from her pocket. Nearly an

hour late. She rubbed the small of her back. Maybe the steamer had run aground on a sandbar. It had happened before. She could be here all afternoon.

A shout from the levee caught her attention. Finally the *California* eased into sight down the river, wheels churning against the powerful current. Kora scanned the deck as the passengers' faces came into view. No McDougall. He must be belowdecks. Some people could get seasick even on the river.

As the steamer moved toward its berth with agonizing slowness, Kora's mind wandered again to Jared. Her anger drained by the heat, she mulled over his demand that she quit reporting. If he caught her now, hot and miserable, with an aching back and burning nose, she might even give in without a fight.

She imagined herself sitting in the cool front parlor of Jared's parents' house, drinking a refreshing cup of tea. Chatting with Jared's mother. Entertaining his mother's guests.

Bored to death.

A nudge against her hip brought Kora back to the present.

"Oh, excuse me, ma'am." A young girl of perhaps nine or ten looked up at her with startling blue eyes behind long, dark lashes.

"That's quite all right," Kora replied, smiling at the child's careful good manners. The steamer had docked while she'd been deep in her reverie, and other passengers were jostling past with much less courtesy than displayed by this little girl.

Kora searched for McDougall's wispy white hair and round, cheerful face. Could she have missed him? No, he would have seen her, even if she'd been too busy worrying about Jared to notice him.

A hand tugged on her blue gingham skirt. Kora glanced down to see the dark-haired, blue-eyed girl still beside her. The child's face was tight with worry.

"Is there something the matter?" Kora asked, trying to keep an eye on the crowd while she spoke.

"I can't find my father."

"Your father?" Kora repeated distractedly. The last of the passengers from San Francisco were straggling by. McDougall hadn't gotten off the steamer while she'd been watching. He must have passed her in the crowd. She sighed. This just wasn't her day.

"I was holding his coat, but I had to let go to pick up my hat."

Kora looked down again. The girl's voice remained steady, but tears were forming in the corners of her eyes. Kora fought a smile. She felt the way this child looked.

"It seems we're in the same predicament. I don't see my friend either," she said. "Maybe if we stick together we can find them both. What's your name?"

"Jessica," the girl answered, suddenly a bit shy.

"I'm Kora," Kora told her, offering the child her hand. Jessica shook it politely. "Now, what's your father's name?"

"Mason Fielding. We're from Boston," Jessica answered, more forthcoming now that they were introduced. "I've never been to California before. Papa says it's awfully wild."

Kora laughed. "Oh, it's not so wild as all that." But glancing around, she saw the scene before her with new eyes. Although Sacramento was a thriving city by Californian standards, the empty plain of the Sacramento River valley stretched endlessly to the north and south. To the west, where the sun hung

hotly above the cottonwoods across the river, lay the
outriders of the Coast Range. To the east, framed by
the buildings of K Street, she could make out the purple smudge of the lonely foothills of the Sierra
Nevada, that great mountain chain lost in the haze of
the afternoon sky.

Around her, passengers from the steamer chatted
with their friends, many dressed in the finest San
Francisco fashions, but among them were rough-looking miners and rancheros with untrimmed beards and
fingernails caked with dirt, wearing colorful shirts
and old, beat-up hats. Chinese laborers dressed in
blue cotton tunics and broad-brimmed hats and a few
wary Maidu Indians moved through the crowd. The
whole effect must have been overwhelming to a well-
bred girl from proper Boston society.

"Perhaps California is a little rough yet," Kora
admitted. "But that's what makes it so exciting. Where
else can you make and lose a fortune in gold or silver
stocks in a single day? Or sleep out with panthers and
grizzly bears one night and go to a fancy ball the
next?"

"Do you really think I'll see a grizzly bear?" Jessica
asked eagerly. "I saw a panther and some monkeys
from the train in Panama. I liked the jungle. Papa says
there isn't any jungle in California."

"No, no jungle," Kora agreed, glad to see some of
the fear leave the girl's face. She took Jessica's hand,
giving it a squeeze, and led her toward the railroad
ticket office across the street where a knot of steamer
passengers appeared to be congregating. "But we do
have some of the biggest trees in the world. They
felled one that was so big they made a dance floor out
of the stump."

"After we find Papa, can you take us there and show us?" Jessica asked, her taste for adventure winning out over her skepticism that a tree could really be so big.

Kora laughed. "I'm afraid it's pretty far away. Let's find your father before we make any plans."

Mace Fielding stood on the levee with his back to the river, fighting down his growing panic. He searched the crowd for a glimpse of green cotton or a small straw hat. A moment ago his daughter had been right by his side. Now she had disappeared.

He glanced toward the steamer. Perhaps she'd forgotten something on board. He hurried along the levee toward the gangplank.

A lone steamboat employee leaned against one of the posts securing the *California* to the shore.

"Hey, you can't board yet!" the man said, stepping in front of Mace. "It'll be near an hour."

"I just got off this ship," Mace explained, trying to keep his voice calm. "I want to make sure my daughter didn't get back on."

"Ain't nobody gone back to that boat. I been here the whole time."

"Thanks," Mace muttered, turning away.

His gaze fell on a stovepipe hat that towered above the people milling about the embarcadero. Mace's heart jumped. Earvil Berry. Jessica had made fast friends with the Berrys' daughter, Alice, on the trip from Boston. She'd probably gone to find them and say good-bye.

Returning to street level, Mace pushed through the crowd toward Earvil Berry's hat, relief warring in his mind with the tongue-lashing he'd give Jessica for scaring him this way.

"Berry!" he called.

A wide smile split Earvil Berry's long, thin face. "Mason! There you are, man. We've been looking for you. Alice refuses to leave until she gets a chance to say good-bye to your Jessica."

Mace's smile froze as he glanced at Rebecca Berry and down at little Alice. "You haven't seen Jessica?"

Earvil frowned. "No. She isn't with you?"

Mace's heart numbed. "We were separated. I thought she'd run off to find you."

He turned away, once more scanning the river-front. Small groups lingered along the embarcadero, saying their good-byes. There was no sign of Jessica.

Through the thundering in his head, Mace dimly heard Rebecca Berry saying they'd watch for Jessica and keep her with them if they found her. More clearly, he heard the memory of his mother's voice, sharp and hard.

"You can't take the child with you to California, Mason," she'd told him imperiously. "It's just not safe. Even if she doesn't die of malaria in Panama or get kidnapped by Mexican bandits, you can't have her associating with those loose western women. She'll end up a wanton just like her mother."

And now, twenty minutes after arriving in Sacramento, he'd lost Jessica just as his mother had warned. Lost the one joy left in his life.

As cold fear threatened to overwhelm him, he spotted a familiar small figure hurrying across Front Street. For a moment, relief weakened Mace's legs so he couldn't move. Then he was running across the street, dodging a team of oxen, his eyes never leaving his daughter.

Not until he'd almost reached her did his mind register the woman beside her. A tall, slim blond clasped Jessica's hand, leading her away with purposeful strides. He took in her disheveled appearance, her dusty skirts.

He glanced up the street in the direction she was leading his daughter. "Imperial Saloon" proclaimed the awning of a building not far away. Mace froze. A woman of questionable character was kidnapping his daughter in broad daylight right before his eyes.

The last of his ebbing fear spurred him forward.

"Where do you think you're going with my daughter?"

Kora whirled, finding herself eye-to-eye—or rather eye-to-chin—with a grim-faced man whose startling dark blue eyes, the echo of Jessica's, were made even darker by his anger. Kora stepped back, shocked by his sharp question.

"Papa!" Jessica cried joyfully, brushing past Kora to wrap her arms about her father's waist.

For a moment, Mason Fielding's eyes left Kora as he knelt to crush his daughter to his chest.

"Thank God you're all right," he muttered, his choking voice barely loud enough for Kora to hear.

"Just a little scared," Kora put in, glad to see Jessica so relieved.

Abruptly, Mace's attention snapped back to her. He rose to his full height, leaving a hand resting protectively on Jessica's shoulder.

"Jessica, I thought I told you not to talk to strangers," he said sternly, eyeing Kora.

"Kora was going to help me find you. I was lost, Papa," Jessica informed him before Kora could say anything at all. "She's a nice lady."

"This isn't Boston," Mace told his daughter. "Many of the pretty young ladies here aren't nice at all. And I don't want you talking to anyone you haven't been introduced to."

The man's sharp gaze remained on Kora, and she felt the color rise in her cheeks as she realized what he was implying.

Mace turned Jessica back to face the steamer. "See the Berrys standing over there? Why don't you run and say good-bye? Alice won't go home without seeing you. I have a few things to say to this lady, and then I'll join you."

"Okay, Papa. Thank you, Kora. Good-bye," Jessica said, glancing at her father's unreadable face before making her way toward the small group waiting near the steamer landing.

"The ladies of Sacramento are just as respectable as those of Boston," Kora said once Jessica was out of earshot. "And we're always ready to help those who need it. Perhaps if you took better care of your daughter, she wouldn't have been lost and frightened and wouldn't have needed to ask me for aid at all."

"And do the respectable ladies of Sacramento often wander the riverfront alone, letting their noses burn?"

The man's caustic tone reminded Kora that she was indeed without hat or coat. She also discovered that her hair had shaken loose of its pins to fall wildly about her shoulders.

She blushed again, but anger overrode her embarrassment. "If I were not a respectable woman, I would hardly have stopped to help your daughter."

"And just how were you planning on helping her? I suppose you were going to offer her a drink to soothe her nerves?"

"What?" Kora stared at him. The man had obviously lost his mind.

"You can't be surprised at my wondering why you were taking a nine-year-old girl to a saloon."

Kora glanced over her shoulder. Past the railroad office, she saw the saloon. The faint sound of piano music came through an open door. She looked back at the tall, dark man standing before her. The suspicion lingering in his eyes was just too much for her to tolerate.

"I have never met such an ungrateful, uncivil, unreasonable man in all my life! Anyone else would thank me for what I've done, but I'd settle for not being insulted."

"I am quite grateful to have my daughter back safely." Some of the tension eased from his stance, and Kora let herself relax in response. "I won't pursue the incident any further. You're free to go."

"You arrogant dandy!" Kora snapped, spinning on her heel.

As she whirled away, Mace saw a youth rushing toward them carrying a large wooden crate. Instinctively, he grabbed Kora's arm to pull her out of the boy's path. She turned on him, fury sparking in her eyes, which were now only inches below his. He held her shoulders, partly for her protection, partly for his.

"Let go of me!" she cried, her face red with anger and embarrassment.

Now up close, Mace took in the appearance of the woman before him—the modest cut of her dress; the smoothness of her skin, unblemished by paint; the blush of ruffled dignity that stained her cheeks. Her eyes—what color were they? A pale brown, almost gold. Like cat's eyes, and burning with indignation.

Slowly it occurred to him that he might have just made a colossal fool of himself.

"Oh, hell. You are . . . I mean, you really . . ." He didn't have any idea how to continue. His own cheeks heated slightly. "What I mean to say is . . ."

"Let go of me, you . . . you . . ." She choked on the word she wanted to use.

Mace almost laughed, the utter absurdity of the situation suddenly clear to him. "I just kept you from being run over," he informed the fury in his arms. "Now give me a chance to apol—"

"I'd rather be flat on the ground than this close to you!"

"Here now, hold still. Let me thank you properly for helping my daughter."

The woman froze. Catching the sudden alarm in her eyes as she focused on his mouth, he realized what she thought he intended.

For a moment Kora felt with dizzy certainty that he did indeed intend to kiss her. His lips, curled almost to a smile, were so close that she could feel the brush of his breath on her cheek.

Her own breathing had all but stopped. She knew how warm those lips would feel on hers.

Then her mind raced in compensation for her immobile body. *How dare he!* She'd slap that half-smile right off his handsome face. She'd . . .

His grip on her shoulders loosened, and he stepped back. "Don't be silly. I'd like to oblige you, but I wouldn't want to damage such a respectable lady's reputation."

"Oblige me? You don't want to . . ." Kora sputtered, her fury heightened by the crimson heat she felt spreading over her face. "How dare you, you self-

important, presumptuous, conceited son-of-a . . .
Jessica would have been better off staying lost."

She stomped the heel of her boot down on his toes,
wrenched free of his grasp, and stalked away without
another word, her head spinning.

When she caught her breath enough to think at all,
she consoled herself with the knowledge that
Californians were not the sort to put up with such a
pompous ass. He'd be running for home with his tail
between his legs before the week was out. She almost
regretted she wouldn't be there to see it.

Mace watched the tall, slender woman march
away, her back stiff with indignation. He flexed his
toes, wincing. He'd certainly managed to ruffle her
respectability.

A chuckle escaped him. She could hardly have
been more offended if he'd actually kissed her, and
he couldn't say those fiery eyes and soft pink lips
hadn't tempted him. He thought about following
her to attempt one more apology for his unfounded
suspicions, but he didn't think she'd stick around
to listen to an explanation, even if he had one to
give.

He couldn't properly explain his fear of losing
Jessica. The thought of her alone and frightened in
this strange place made Mace's stomach churn.

He looked toward where his daughter was finishing her good-byes to Alice Berry. The Berrys were
headed for Shasta City; it was unlikely they'd meet
again. The way the two girls were hugging and crying,
one might think they had known each other for years
instead of the few months that the trip from New
York had taken.

Jessica glanced over and saw Mace. She gave Alice

one last hug as Mace strode across Front Street to meet her.

His mother had told him it was his duty to leave Jessica with her, where she'd be well provided for if anything happened to him—always speaking as though he'd never return from California, that savage land to the west. He supposed it was part of her campaign to convince him to stay in Boston. Ever since the death of Mace's younger brother, Jesse, their mother had urged him to settle down and produce some proper heirs. Sophia and Eugene Fielding firmly believed in duty and were determined to do theirs by Jessica, but after nine years, it was hopeless to wish they'd ever love her.

They'd never liked Jessica's mother, which had been partly Cecilia's own fault; she'd loved to tweak the elder Fieldings' stiff sense of propriety. And they had never believed Mace's story that he had managed to marry Cecilia before Jessica's birth. Luckily Jessica's dark hair, blue eyes, and stubborn chin marked her as a Fielding, even though the mahogany tint to her tresses and her full, smiling lips came undeniably from her mother. His parents had never guessed the real truth.

Mace reached out to pull his daughter into his arms, smoothing her dark hair, relief surging through him once again.

"Papa, you weren't very nice to Kora," she said accusingly before he could speak.

"No, I wasn't, kitten. I was so worried about you that I wasn't thinking straight. Maybe we'll see her again, and I'll get another chance to try to apologize. Do you agree with her that your Papa is a terrible father? I have to warn you that if you say yes, I'll be forced to lock you in a garret with only a big rat for company and feed you nothing but bread and water for a week."

Jessica giggled and gave her father a hug.

"If that's settled, maybe we should see if we can find our host."

Mace looked up and down the embarcadero. Chester McDougall had described Ellis Hunter as a middle-aged man, somewhat tall and slender, with thinning sandy-brown hair. He saw no one fitting that description, and most of the people down to meet the steamer had already wandered away. It wasn't surprising they'd missed each other in all the excitement. Mace would just have to ask directions to Hunter's house and introduce himself there.

He caught himself glancing around once more in hopes of catching a glimpse of Jessica's newfound friend. After the riverbank he scanned the street, but she had disappeared. He attempted to compose a proper apology in his head, but the memory of those cat eyes, just a shade deeper than her honey-colored hair, distracted him.

Of course, blonds weren't really his type.

For a moment Cecilia's bright red hair and laughing green eyes danced before him and he felt again his double loss of her, only slightly muted by the years. Perhaps the man he had come to California hoping to find could give him some answers that would help put those memories to rest.

2

Kora poured water from a pitcher into the bowl on her washstand, then splashed some on her face. She studied herself in the mirror to see if it was still obvious she'd been crying. She wished she could cry ladylike droplets that sparkled on her cheeks instead of these rivulets of water that left her eyes puffy and red. She patted her face with a towel and decided she looked almost presentable.

Then she walked over to her bed and smoothed it. Dodge, deciding the storm was over, leaped back onto the bed, but he eyed her warily when she sat next to him.

"Silly cat," Kora murmured, ruffling his gray fur. Dodge accepted the peace offering and closed one yellow eye.

"I'll be more careful next time I throw myself on the bed, I promise."

The cat's whiskers twitched, and the other eye drooped shut.

Kora's father's voice came from downstairs. "Kora! Supper's ready!"

Kora rose reluctantly and checked the mirror again. She didn't feel like eating, but if she refused to come to supper, it would only mean more explaining to do. Her parents were sure to question her anyway about her odd behavior earlier. She hadn't meant them to see her dejection, but when Papa had become cross with her for losing Chester McDougall at the riverfront, and Mama had rebuked her for running out on Jared this afternoon, Kora's control had snapped, and she had run to her room.

She still had to decide what to do about Jared. Her anger had cooled since their fight, but that didn't lessen her confusion. The morning had begun so well, but from the moment Jared proposed, everything had gone wrong.

Right down to that awful man at the steamer, whose attitude still made her burn with anger. How dare he treat her like that? And the way he'd cast aspersions on her character just because she was a Californian and he came from Boston! His manners certainly were no better than hers, and his fancy clothes hadn't hidden his obvious defects.

Even as that thought crossed her mind, Kora had to admit to herself that other than his glaring personality problem, Mason Fielding's defects were very few. His clothes, of the finest English cloth and cut, accentuated the hard lines of his torso, thighs, and shoulders and they had remained clean and neat despite his long journey, adding to the impression of self-confidence he gave. And those compelling blue eyes, sparkling behind thick lashes. . . .

Fielding had probably been quite a peacock back

east, and as far as Kora was concerned, Boston could have him back. That conceited stuffed shirt wouldn't last a day in California; he'd probably be on a steamer home within the week. It was too bad poor Jessica was stuck with him. She seemed like a lovely girl.

Kora wondered where Jessica's mother was and why she hadn't come to Sacramento with them. The poor woman probably couldn't stand being around such an obnoxious husband, despite his citified good looks. He probably wasn't as handsome as Kora remembered, anyway.

"Kora! It's ready *now,* not a year from now."

"Coming, Papa."

She took a deep breath and hurried down the stairs. Her father waited at the bottom.

"You all right, sweetie?"

"Just fine, Papa," Kora said, attempting a cheerful smile. "I just hope Chester McDougall isn't wandering lost around the streets of Sacramento."

Her father patted her shoulder. "I'm sorry I snapped at you earlier, honey. Don't worry, he'll make his way to us eventually. He probably got stuck in San Francisco, or maybe he decided to take the train up to avoid getting on another boat. Anyway, I shouldn't have assumed he'd be able to stick to his schedule and arrive today."

Kora's reply stuck in her throat as she entered the dining room and saw Jared leaning against the sideboard, chatting with Troy. Her brother flashed her an encouraging grin.

Her mother gave Kora a meaningful glance as she set down a steaming bowl of German potato salad. "Kora, there you are. I invited Jared to have supper with us after you ran off to the riverfront this afternoon."

"You should have told me where you were going. I could have kept you company." Jared's formal tone told Kora he was still angry. Pulling out her chair for her, he took care not to touch her.

"No point in your afternoon being as boring and futile as mine," she told him, trying to keep her voice light.

"You weren't out kidnapping our Mr. McDougall, now, were you, Jared?" Troy teased. "Why else would you waste your time on Kora if not to keep tabs on the competition and steal our big stories?"

Kora made a face at her brother but couldn't think of a snappy reply. After all, Jared had probably lost all interest in her after today. But he *had* come to supper. She glanced at him as he scooped out a helping of potato salad.

Jared's face expressed the same single-minded concentration that he put into everything he did. His dark eyes focused on his plate, avoiding her gaze, and his lips were tight with irritation.

She had fallen in love with Jared Davies when she was thirteen and he was, at sixteen, a young, determined apprentice at the *Sacramento Union.* He had seemed so much older and more mature than the other boys she knew, aloof and uninterested in a tomboyish little schoolgirl like her. She had decided then and there she would marry him some day.

As she grew older, she gave up on ever getting him to notice her, though when she saw him at church or on the street, her heart still fluttered. Then, that glorious night last fall, she'd gone to a dance at Lily Marshall's house. Jared was there, just back from a year in San Francisco. And instead of looking past her or asking how it was going with his favorite little "cub reporter," he had asked her to dance, and dance again, and they had spent the whole evening together, much to the amusement of their friends.

She began to dream again of being Jared's wife. And now he had asked her, just this morning.

Kora picked at her cold chicken, glancing once more to her right. Jared's black hair accentuated the dramatic lines of his face, making him look more handsome than ever. She had wanted him for so long. She should simply have said yes. He couldn't have meant all the angry words he'd spoken. And surely she could make him see that she didn't have to give up writing altogether in order to be a good wife. . . .

After supper, they retired to the back sitting room. Kora's mother had already come to the conclusion that Jared would be a member of the family before too long and no longer felt compelled to offer him the more formal, but less comfortable, hospitality of the front parlor. Kora took a seat on the flowered sofa, leaving room for Jared, but he wandered over to the window. With a flash of irritation, she wondered if he intended to punish her by making her uncomfortable for the entire evening.

Just then the bell at the front door jangled, interrupting her thoughts.

Startled, Kora's mother looked up from the pillow cover she was embroidering. "Heavens, who could that be at this hour?"

"Maybe it's Grandpa, home from the hills," Troy said. He went to answer the door.

"Jared, would you like a glass of brandy?" Ellis Hunter asked, opening the cabinet that held his small store of liquor.

Jared shook his head. "No, thank you. It's such a

warm night, I was wondering if perhaps Kora would like to take a short stroll with me?"

"What a lovely idea," Anna Hunter said with an encouraging smile at her daughter.

"I'd love a walk." Kora glanced gratefully at Jared, but his brooding expression didn't change. Perhaps she had upset him so much he wanted to withdraw his proposal.

"I've solved the mystery of the missing McDougall," Troy announced as he burst back into the sitting room. He grinned at his sister. "You couldn't find him, because he didn't come. Allow me to introduce his replacement, Mr. Mason Fielding."

Mace stopped short in the doorway to the Hunters' sitting room. *My God. It couldn't be.* There on the sofa sat the girl from the docks this afternoon, her gold eyes wide with surprise, a flush creeping up her cheeks.

"This is my father, Ellis Hunter," Troy said, gesturing toward the older man in the room. Now that he knew why he hadn't seen the man at the riverfront, Mace noted that Chester's description had been accurate. Ellis Hunter was tall and sandy-haired, though perhaps a little less slender and a little more gray than when Chester had last seen him.

Mace shook his hand firmly, forcing himself to continue smiling. No easy task, considering the sudden revelation that he'd offended the daughter of the man he'd come here to work for. If she made a fuss about it, Ellis Hunter might send him packing on the next steamer to Boston, and he'd have no chance to do what he'd come here for. She wouldn't hold a little misunderstanding against him, would she?

He felt those gold eyes boring into him from

across the room and groaned inwardly. Of course she would.

"Welcome, Fielding," Ellis Hunter said. "Let me introduce my family. Troy you've already met. This is my wife, Anna, my daughter, Kora, and Jared Davies, a business rival, but a friend of the family."

"How do you do, Mr. Fielding," Anna Hunter said, slightly flustered at having such a well-dressed gentleman from Boston shown into her comfortably worn back room. "You must have had a long day. May I get you anything? Something to eat?"

"No, thank you. Please don't go to any trouble," Mace said. "I shouldn't have intruded on you so late without warning, but I had to find a boarding house and get my daughter settled. I thought I'd come by tonight, so you wouldn't worry about Chester when he didn't arrive."

He offered the envelope he held to Ellis. "A letter from McDougall," he explained. "It introduces me and describes why he couldn't come himself. Ches didn't trust the mail to get it to you safely."

"Please have a seat, Mr. Fielding, and rest yourself," Anna insisted.

"Just call me Mason, or Mace. We may have just met, but we're all newspaper people."

"Well then, take a seat, Mason, and tell us about yourself," Troy said with a smile. "All the pertinent facts—who, where, when, and why."

"First . . ." Mace turned his most charming smile on the golden girl on the sofa, wondering why she hadn't yet had him thrown out of the house. "I must apologize to your sister. We had an unfortunate misunderstanding down at the riverfront today. I'm sorry for offending you, Miss Hunter. I appreciate your befriending Jess. I was terribly worried about her, and I reacted inappropriately."

Her expression remained fierce, but to his immense relief she nodded, albeit stiffly. "That's all right, Mr. Fielding."

"Call me Mace, please."

She didn't respond to that but admitted, "I can understand your concern. Jessica is a lovely girl."

"Thank you." Mace tried a grin. "To think we got to know each other so well, and I never got your name. That might have saved us a bit of trouble."

Her frown indicated she didn't share his amusement, and Mace chided himself again for acting like an idiot earlier. Concern for Jessica had clouded his first impression of Kora, and then something about the challenge in her eyes had made him unable to resist ruffling her some more. But worst of all, he'd let his mother's paranoid fantasies get to him.

Ellis Hunter put the letter down on top of the liquor cabinet and tucked his reading glasses back into his pocket. "How was Chester when you left him?" he asked Mace. "Pneumonia at his age is no small thing."

"Pneumonia? How awful!" Anna exclaimed.

"Is he all right?" Kora asked.

Mace nodded and took the seat that Troy had offered him across from the sofa. "By the time I left, he was over the worst of it. He should be just fine, but he was too weak to travel."

"Brandy?" Ellis offered.

"Please." Mace took the glass handed him and sipped the amber liquid. "Jeffrey Westcott, the senior editor at the *Bay News,* was distressed that McDougall's illness might cost him his stories from California, especially since he'd already advertised them in the paper, so I volunteered to take Ches's place."

"Doing what?" Jared asked abruptly. "You've hired another reporter, Ellis?"

Mace glanced at the young, wary-looking man in the corner. Hunter had called him a business rival but a friend of the family. Considering his age, he was more likely a friend of Troy's . . . or Kora's.

"I guess it's no secret now," Ellis said, only a slight smile betraying the satisfaction he felt at surprising the competition. "It was McDougall's idea originally. Fielding is here to write pieces on California for the *Bay News* back in Boston. We'll be paying part of his salary and publishing some of his stories right here in the *Valley Times.*"

Mace noticed Jared's glance at Kora, who was looking guiltily at her hands. Yes, the man was a beau of Kora's and she hadn't told him that Mace—McDougall, rather—was coming to California. She glanced up suddenly, her eyes flashing with hostility. The more he saw those eyes, the more they fascinated him. Just what color were they, anyway?

Some devilish impulse made him wink at her. He was rewarded with a shocked glare and a pretty pinkening of her cheeks. He should thank heaven for the restraint that had kept him from giving in to the impulse to kiss her, but when she blushed like that he couldn't quite stifle a perverse twinge of regret.

"He came all the way out here for that?" Jared asked incredulously. "Why not just send out some pieces by local writers?"

Mace noticed that Jared directed his question not to him but to Ellis. He wasn't sure he liked this young man's belligerent attitude. "Ches thought our readers would like to see California through a Bostonian's eyes. The stories will offer them some distraction from the war news," Mace explained. "The editors want the stories to be exotic, to play on the readers' idea of this young state as wild and slightly dangerous."

"Not to mention barbaric and crude," Kora interjected, an edge to her voice.

Mace acknowledged her barb with a smile, still wondering when and if she were going to tell her father about their unfortunate encounter. He could only wait and see. He took another sip of brandy, rose, and turned back to Ellis. "I've taken enough of your time this evening. I walked past the *Valley Times* office earlier, so I know where it is. When should I come by tomorrow morning to meet the rest of your staff?"

Troy laughed outright and Ellis chuckled, explaining, "You've just met most of us. We're a pretty small outfit. I do most of the editing and handle the business end of things. Troy here not only writes but is in charge of running the press, making sure the paper is ready on time. Dan Larsen, our senior reporter, takes care of the rest of the Sacramento news, with some help from Kora. Other than that, we have Mitch Breck covering San Francisco. He sends us all that's fit to print from there. And there's a fellow who writes for the *Territorial Enterprise* in Virginia City who keeps us up to date on what's happening in Washoe. And then we've got a couple of folks who do the typesetting and some boys to take the papers around. I guess it doesn't seem like much after working for the *Bay News,* but we work hard enough to keep the competition on its toes."

Ellis winked at Jared.

"In any case, there's no need to rush into work tomorrow. Get a good night's sleep and come in when you like. We can put your nose to the grindstone later."

Mace handed his glass to Ellis, then shook his hand again. "Thanks," he said, and meant it. He needed some time to see about getting Jessica into a school. "I'll see you tomorrow, then. It was a pleasure meeting all of you."

He glanced around the room. Jared Davies still glowered in his corner. Kora hadn't yet attempted a smile at him. Mace wagered she would be even more striking when she smiled. Not that he was ever likely to see it.

"Mr. Fielding—Mason—please won't you come to supper tomorrow night? And, of course, you must bring your wife and daughter. It will give us all a chance to get to know each other better."

Anna Hunter's invitation caught Mace off-guard. "Thank you. I'd like that. I'm sure Jess would be happy to spend time with people other than me. But her mother—my wife—isn't with us. She died soon after Jess was born."

"Oh, I'm so sorry."

"No, really, that's all right."

Looking into the older woman's concerned face, Mace's mind involuntarily flashed back to his mother's reaction to Cecilia's death. True, it was before she knew of his brother's death, before she knew about Jessica, but he would never forgive her for that cold, hard "Good riddance." Suddenly Mace needed to get out of this warm, inviting room, out of the whole comfortable, cheerful little house.

"Good evening, everyone," he said, managing what

he hoped was a charming smile. He nodded to host and hostess and escaped down the hall, stopping only to grab his hat and coat before rushing out into the street to breathe the cool, dry evening air. He shook his head to clear it. He'd been too abrupt, he thought, possibly offending the Hunters. But the bitterness and the questions flooded back to him at the strangest times. He had to put his past to rest. He had to find Booth Garrett.

He was close now. Garrett was here, somewhere, in California. And he would have the answers Mace was looking for.

As she walked down Eighth Street with Jared, Kora glanced up at the stars. She found the Big Dipper and followed it to the North Star, wishing briefly for a beacon as steady to guide her through life. But then the light from the street lamp they were passing blotted out the stars, and she brought her gaze back down to earth.

"Your father's scheming sure backfired on him this time," Jared said. "That Fielding fellow, what a coup. His brand of eastern snobbery should go over real well in Sacramento."

"Papa couldn't foresee McDougall's getting sick," Kora pointed out, not appreciating Jared's glee at what she had to admit would probably turn into a disaster. "And Chester must think highly of Fielding or he wouldn't have sent him in his place."

"'Call me Mace, please,'" Jared simpered in an exaggerated Boston accent. "'We are all newspaper people, after all.'"

She couldn't help giggling. "I suppose his first

piece will compare California to Ireland and himself to Saint Patrick, bringing civilization to the heathen."

Jared's smile faded. "And I didn't like the way he kept looking at you."

"What do you mean?" Kora asked, his tone making her oddly defensive. She'd glanced up more than once that evening to find Fielding's dark blue eyes on her, but behind the intensity of his gaze, there had been a detachment that left her feeling more awkward than frank admiration would have done.

She wasn't sure what Jared had seen to make an issue of it. Besides, she had done nothing to encourage such scrutiny. The memory of her strange paralysis in his arms this afternoon made her distinctly uncomfortable, but once she'd recovered from his shocking rudeness, she'd let him know exactly what she thought of him.

Jared stopped walking and took Kora's arm to turn her toward him. "I mean, Kora, that you're a beautiful woman, and I'm tired of watching other men look at you the way Mason Fielding looked at you tonight. I want you waiting safely at home for me when I come back from work, and I want you on my arm when I go out in the evening. I want you to be my wife."

"You make me sound like a pair of diamond cufflinks," Kora snapped, then bit her lip. She didn't want to start another fight. "I don't want to be your ornament, Jared. I want to be your wife. I want to share your life, not give up my own."

He dropped her arm and stepped back, the scowl reappearing on his face. "What do you mean by that? Is this still about reporting? I thought we settled that."

Once again he'd closed her out of the discussion;

she could almost see the shutters behind his eyes. He looked at her, but couldn't see her. "*You* settled it, Jared."

"Kora, be practical. I know you like to play at reporting, but I'm tired of seeing you with your clothes covered with dust and your hands black with print, not that you aren't still darned attractive." She didn't share his teasing smile. "Part of the reason I'm asking you to marry me is so I don't have to put up with that any more."

"Jared, listen to me—"

"I don't know why you're being so mule headed about this, Kora."

And what about you? she wanted to cry, but she held her tongue. She couldn't explain to him that it wasn't about reporting anymore. It was about her sudden fear that in all the time she'd thought she loved Jared, perhaps she hadn't gotten to know him very well.

"Jared, I'm sorry. I'm not trying to be stubborn. I just . . . I do love writing, and your proposal caught me off-guard. Let me think about it for a few days. Please?"

He shrugged, but a small victorious smile curved his lips. "Of course. I understand. It's charming to see a crack of irrationality in that practical exterior of yours, and most women are a bit nervous at the prospect of accepting a marriage proposal. You take all the time you need. But I know what your answer will be."

Kora let him lean over to give her a kiss, but she pulled away before he could take her in his arms.

"I think you'd better take me home now," she said as calmly as she could. The thought that Jared believed her reluctance to be some sort of female fickleness made her wince, but she didn't want to argue any more tonight. She needed to work out for herself how she felt about all this before she could make him understand.

"Fine," Jared said, the satisfied smile staying on his lips, "but don't make me wait too long until I can take you home with me at night. It's a lonely feeling leaving you at your door and going home to an empty bed."

In bed that night, Kora stared at the canopy above her, unable to prevent her mind from running through the same unresolvable circles over and over again. It wasn't as though she really had a choice. Marriage to Jared was the right thing for her to do now. She wanted a husband and a family. Maybe his assessment was correct, and the sudden distance she felt from him indicated merely a case of cold feet on her part.

After all, if she'd thought about it, she'd have known he'd expect her to quit working for her father when they married. At only twenty-three, Jared was already one of the *Union*'s top reporters, and he didn't plan to stop there. He studied law in his spare time and would probably move into state politics in the future. State senators' wives gave garden parties, smiled prettily, and attended political rallies; they didn't write for newspapers. It wasn't proper. And besides, no good wife ever minded making sacrifices for her husband's career.

But what hurt so badly was that Jared didn't recognize that it would be a sacrifice. He'd always treated her reporting as a little hobby, never commending her for the stories she wrote. *He* was a reporter. And this morning he'd been downright insulting, implying that anyone with a pencil—any *man* with a pencil—could write her column better than she did.

What if he's right. . . . Kora halted that thought abruptly. Her pieces on the people and places that gave Sacramento its character helped the *Valley Times* compete with the large daily papers like the *Union* and the *Bee.* She was proud of her work, and even if Jared didn't know about the stories she wrote under Troy's name, even if she'd never shared her secret dream of becoming a first-rate investigative reporter, he should be able to recognize her ability. And how much she loved to write.

Though, truth be told, she was not eager to go to work tomorrow. She knew she was being selfish, but she wished Chester McDougall had waited until he got well and come out himself. Why did he have to send that Mason Fielding?

The man was simply insufferable, and as much as she hated to admit it, Jared's prediction that Fielding's writing for the *Sacramento Valley Times* would back-fire probably would be fulfilled if his writing style was as annoying as his person. And Kora didn't even want to think about having to work with him, or being civil to him at supper tomorrow night.

It annoyed her, too, that her parents and her brother had taken an instant liking to the man. Of course, he did have a certain self-confident charm, and she supposed he was attractive, physically at least—his patrician nose and strong chin; the way his dark hair waved back from his temples; his lean, muscular frame; that maddening half-smile; those piercing deep blue eyes. . . . All right, he was handsome enough. But he was also arrogant, rude, and impossible.

The way he had treated her this afternoon at the riverfront left her smoldering with embarrassment and anger. It would take more than a brief apology to make up for that. Still, he *had* bothered to apologize and even sounded as though he had meant it. And his concern for his daughter and his pain in talking about his wife's death suggested that a real person lurked beneath his mannered veneer. She'd find out soon enough.

But what was she going to do about Jared?

Kora pulled the pillow over her head and growled in frustration. If she didn't get any sleep, tomorrow would be even worse than she expected.

One sheep . . . two sheep . . . three sheep . . .

3

"I think Jessica will get along just fine in my class, Mr. Fielding," Berta Nash said as they stepped out of the schoolhouse into the dazzle of the early morning Sacramento sun.

"I'm sure she will," Mace agreed, smiling at Jess to reassure her. A plain young woman with mousy brown hair, Miss Nash displayed a warm smile and an air of self-assurance that Mace liked.

"You be a good girl, kitten, and don't cause Miss Nash any trouble." He bent down to give his daughter a kiss.

"I'll see you tonight, Papa," Jessica said bravely, but her tight hug told him she didn't want him to go.

"Melissa!" Miss Nash called over Mace's shoulder. He turned to see a little girl about Jessica's age distinguished by a pug nose crowded with freckles and a head of curly brown hair.

Miss Nash introduced the two girls. "Melissa

O'Connor, this is Jessica Fielding. Jessica is starting school with us today. Why don't you show her around before class begins?"

"Come on, let's go get the swings before anybody else gets here," Melissa urged. "Do you like licorice?"

Jessica nodded.

"Here."

Mace cringed as his daughter took the piece of black candy that Melissa pulled from a pocket of her skirt. *A little lint never hurt anyone,* he told himself as Jess popped it into her mouth.

"My pa runs the store down the street there," Melissa told Jessica as they went off. "He says licorice is good for digestion, but I hate it. I like lemon drops best."

"I like lemon drops, too," Mace heard Jessica tell her newfound friend as the two of them began trotting across the hard-packed dirt of the yard toward a live oak tree from which hung two wooden swings.

"Your daughter seems bright and quite charming. I know I'll enjoy having her here," Miss Nash said. Mace recognized that now she was attempting to put him, the nervous father, at ease, and decided it was time to leave.

"Thank you for taking her today. I thought it was best to get her into school before she had a chance to worry about it too much."

Miss Nash nodded. "Please feel free to drop by anytime before or after school if you have any questions or concerns."

Mace thanked her again and waved to Jessica. She was too busy chatting with Melissa as they bobbed back and forth on the swings to notice that he was leaving. He smiled and turned down the road toward downtown Sacramento.

He nodded with satisfaction as he passed his boarding house. Mrs. Johnson, the elderly widow who ran the house, had told him about Tucker School right down the road. She'd recommended both the school and Miss Nash highly, as five of her many grandchildren had prospered there at one time or another.

And she had taken an instant liking to Jessica, offering to keep an eye on her when the girl came back from school in the afternoons. Jessica was used to looking out for herself, but it eased Mace's mind to know she'd have company if she needed it.

He chuckled to himself. No doubt Jessica would have all the company she could use soon enough if little Melissa O'Connor lived nearby. Jessica gave and accepted friendship with an easy grace that Mace envied. He had always been adept at charming the people he knew, but he found it hard to give his heart to anyone.

A memory rose unbidden. He was eighteen, lying in the shade on the soft green grass by a little pond near Watertown. Cecilia's naked legs were entwined with his as he stroked the red curls lying against his chest.

She looked up at him with a smile as she ran her fingernails across his stomach.

"Everyone is so eager to be Mason Fielding's friend," she purred, stretching against him in a way that made him want her again, with that desperate hunger she inspired in him. "But none of them know you like I do, my sweet darling."

And damn her, no one had ever hurt him like she had, either. Since then he'd vowed that no one would ever get that close to him again.

Mace's pleasure in this bright California morning evaporated. What had seemed, moments before, an eager, bustling city, now appeared a drab little town with too much dust and too few trees. The very birds mocked him for getting himself stuck out here at the end of the earth on some fool's errand.

He pulled out his pocket watch. It was only eight-forty-five. Still plenty of time before he had to meet Ellis Hunter at the newspaper. He might as well start his search for Booth Garrett this very morning.

He'd considered his options the night before and decided that the first place to look would be a surveyor's office. Garrett had plenty of money, and what would a smart man do with money in California? Undoubtedly buy land, for either mining or ranching. All Mace needed to find him was a little patience and a little luck.

Kora sat in her father's swivel chair behind the front desk, staring at the familiar backward letters on the window. Read from the outside, they spelled in a large arc "Hunter's Print Shop." Underneath, in smaller letters, "Office of the *Sacramento Valley Times*." It felt good to be a Hunter, part of the family enterprise. Why couldn't she feel that way about starting a family with Jared?

"If you intend to do some work today, maybe you could come in and give Max a hand with the typesetting," Troy said, interrupting her thoughts.

Kora dropped her pencil onto the piece of paper before her. "I just can't come up with a headline for this story," she said.

"What story?" Troy moved forward from the doorway of the printing room to look over her shoulder.

"The one about Señor Sanchez's escaped bull running amok down by the courthouse. It's a humorous piece."

Or at least she'd thought so when she'd written it Monday afternoon. In her present mood the light tone seemed annoyingly frivolous. Kora turned the page so her brother could read it more easily.

"'Monday morning saw even more bull attending the state government than usual. Nearly half a ton more to be exact. Passersby speculated about the beefy new state rep.' . . ." Troy chuckled. "Don't look so down, Kora. This isn't half bad. Why not head it 'Senator Toro' or 'Capitol on Horns of Dilemma' or 'New Budget Cruncher'?"

Kora shook her head at her brother with a smile. "No wonder you prefer printing to writing. But that last suggestion isn't bad."

She penciled it in above her story.

"I don't need to see my name in a byline to enjoy my work," Troy said.

"Luckily I don't either, since it's your name that's attached to some of my best stories."

"Shh!" Troy glanced over his shoulder. "Pa will put a quick end to that if you don't keep your voice down."

The two conspirators leaned closer together. "Anything more on Assemblyman Bond's ties to that fraudulent silver stock?"

Kora shook her head. "As much as I hate to admit it, I think he's clean."

"Too bad. Keep an eye on that one, kid. He's rotten somewhere; I can smell it."

She laughed. "You're starting to sound just like Papa."

"Give me that." Troy tugged the bull article out of her hand. "Now leave me alone to work my magic on this thing, and go help Max. It will be a miracle if the paper gets out at all this Friday, much less if it's on time."

"Every week you turn out to be a miracle worker," Kora said impudently. She hurried into the printing room before he could reply.

The large back room served as both workroom and storeroom for the print shop. The newspaper press filled the right side of the room, bounded by shelves laden with paper and ink and boxes of extra type. By the left window stood the smaller press Ellis Hunter used for notices, playbills, and various legal forms he printed on commission. Ellis was currently peering under this machine with a wrench in one hand and a bottle of lubricating oil in the other.

Along the back wall of the shop ran a slanted counter. Above it were displayed the blocks of carved pictures used in advertisements or to fill space. Beside the counter stood a cupboard of shallow drawers that opened to reveal boxes of print type. From these a short, elderly man was picking tiny letters and marks of punctuation, creating lines of type by placing them from right to left on the frame in front of him.

"Max," Kora said. "Troy said you could use some help."

Max Logan smiled up at her, wiping his fingers on an ink-stained apron.

"Sure could, missy. I'm workin' on this here story, line eight. Right after 'said the governor.'"

Max pushed the piece at her while he took off his

glasses and stuck them in his apron pocket. Kora found the place he had indicated. As she began to read slowly from the sheet she held, Max's hands flew among the boxes in front of him, whisking the pieces of type into their proper order.

Max could read the stories and set the type by himself, but it meant squinting through his glasses at the handwritten story, reading a small bit at a time, and then doing the typesetting. With someone reading to him, he typeset at an even pace without worrying about being able to see, since his fingers knew the positioning of the type boxes by heart.

The old miner was a friend of Kora's grandfather. He was too advanced in years to be able to cope with the rigors of panning gold anymore, but he had a capable mind that couldn't stand the idea of sitting idly at home when he could be doing something productive.

"How's that Davies fella?" he asked Kora when she paused in her reading to let him catch up. He shot a sharp glance at her before returning to the type. "Seems like he might git around to makin' his intentions known one o' these days."

Glad he was too busy to see her blush, Kora didn't answer. Instead, she read the next sentence to be typeset.

"I must admit, I don't like the idear of him takin' you away from us," Max continued, undeterred. "He rubs me the wrong way. But then, mebbe it's none of my business."

"It's not," Kora said firmly. Max didn't like anyone who worked for rival papers. "Besides, don't assume I won't be back just because you marry me off. You can't get rid of me that easily."

He turned to her with a wry look on his wrinkled face. "Married women got better things to do with their time than breathin' ink all day long."

"What?" Troy asked incredulously from behind them. "What could be better than working here? Max, you shouldn't even think such things, especially around our new help. Let me introduce you to a bona fide eastern newsman, Mace Fielding."

Kora's blush crept further up her face as she turned to find herself once again subjected to the scrutiny of those deep blue eyes. She wondered how much of her conversation with Max he and Troy had overheard. He acknowledged her glance with a smile.

"Good morning, Miss Hunter. How nice to see you again. And it's a pleasure to meet you, Mr. Logan," Mace added in response to Troy's introductions.

"Just Max," Max told him, shaking his hand firmly.

"Fielding! I see you've found our humble shop," Ellis Hunter called, coming across the room to greet his new reporter. "I guess it seems quiet compared to what you're used to, but this is home to us."

"Bigger and more mechanized is not always better," Mace said. Kora searched his tone for any trace of condescension but found none.

"But don't get the idea that because we don't have steam engines whirring and flocks of newsboys running about, we have time to waste," Troy warned him. "Papa keeps us busy."

"And Troy's the slavedriver-in-training," Kora added. She expected the punch in the arm from her brother, but Mace's laugh surprised her. Maybe he could act halfway human when he wanted to.

"Well, this slave's eager to get to work," Mace said. He turned to Ellis. "Where should I start?"

"I thought you might like to get a feel for Sacramento and the sorts of things that go on here before we send you off on your own, so I'm going to send you out with Kora for a few days to learn the beat, so to speak."

Startled, Kora gaped at her father but he seemed completely unaware of the unpleasant shock he'd just given her. Of course, she'd assumed she would be working closely with Chester McDougall when he arrived, but Mason Fielding's coming in his stead had changed everything, or so she'd thought. Apparently her father thought differently.

She couldn't possibly work with this man, not after yesterday. But before she had a chance to object, Mace did it for her.

"I'm sorry," he said, "but I was hoping to get working on some real stories right away. I don't think the readers of the *Bay News* will be too interested in the latest round of Sacramento balls and social affairs."

"Pardon me?" Kora said in disbelief. Her dismay at her father's orders was quickly giving way to a creeping anger in the pit of her stomach.

"Not that such things aren't important locally," Mace said quickly with a smile at Kora, "but I think my editors are expecting more colorful stories—mining and ranching, fortunes won and lost, exotic scenery, maybe a political scandal here and there."

What had she just been thinking about him being nearly human? Indignation nearly choked her, but Kora managed to get out her words almost sweetly. "Then I guess my little sewing bees and bake sales wouldn't interest you. That's too bad. Perhaps Dan Larsen will have time to show you around when he gets back from whatever exciting, world-shaking story he's chasing now."

She moved toward the door to the office, but her father caught her arm and pulled her back.

"Nice try," he said. "Mason, my daughter is not a half-bad reporter. It's true she doesn't cover the hard news, but no one knows Sacramento better. She'll give you the feel for the city you'll need to get started. I'm not saying you two have to work cheek by jowl for the next year, but let's see how it goes for the next couple of days, okay?"

"Of course, Papa," Kora said tightly. She glanced at Mace Fielding, pleased to find him looking uncomfortable. If she couldn't get out of this unpleasant situation, she could at least ruffle his feathers a good deal more before the day was out. "We might as well get started now, Mr. Fielding. Come on."

She turned on her heel and walked to the door. After a brief hesitation, she heard his footsteps follow her.

Ellis called after them, "Don't forget, Mason, you're invited to supper. Make sure you're home in time today, Kora."

Without stopping to reply, Kora burst through the front door into the street. She turned right, walking swiftly past the neighboring storefronts.

"Hey, slow down." Mace soon caught up with her, and it only annoyed her more that his long strides kept pace effortlessly with her furious rush. She slowed, turning her head to glare at her companion.

"I thought we'd head for the dressmaker's shop first to find out what wild new fashions are brewing for the governor's ball," she said.

"Perfect. Perhaps we can frighten her into confessing which ladies have eaten their way out of their last dress size and cause a real scandal. I'll hold her down, you threaten her with a hat pin. Right now you look wild enough to terrify anyone."

But Kora was too incensed to be teased into good humor. She stopped and spun to face him head on.

"Look, Mr. Mason Fielding, Esquire," she began, her frustration and anger spilling off her tongue in a torrent, "I don't know why you bothered to come out to California if you think it's so uncivilized or why you find it impossible to drop that arrogant attitude of yours and act with common courtesy and I don't really care, but I'm tired of being insulted by you. I may not be a man, but I've got a good mind and I work hard. I'm good at what I do, and I'm not about to feel ashamed of it just because you or anyone else think it's silly or unladylike."

Mace raised one eyebrow. "Miss Hunter, I don't believe I ever said a word about you being silly or—"

"And that's another thing. You keep calling me Miss Hunter as though I don't count as one of your old-boy newspaper people."

As she finished speaking, Kora noticed passersby beginning to stare at the two of them. She made a move to cross the street, but Mace caught her arm and pulled her back so that she stood only inches from him as he glared down at her, his blue eyes dark as they bored into hers.

"I just can't do anything right with you, can I?" he asked. "I admit my behavior was questionable yesterday, but I rather hoped you'd give me the chance to start fresh today. But obviously you've made up your mind about me, and nothing I do is going to change it."

He suddenly let go of her arm as though he'd just realized he was touching her, but Kora didn't step back. His eyes dared her to hold her ground.

"And as for what I should call you . . ." He paused to let possibilities suggest themselves to her. "If I hadn't addressed you as Miss Hunter this morning, you would have charged me with being forward."

She wanted to protest, but she knew she had been unreasonable to attack him for merely being polite, especially since she *would* have been infuriated by anything less after his all-too-familiar actions of the evening before. And once again she found herself standing much too close to him. She noticed he smelled faintly of lemons and tobacco. Irrationally, she wondered just why he hadn't kissed her yesterday. She could have sworn he had wanted to.

Then his mouth quirked in a slight grin. She noticed he had a deep dimple when he smiled like that. "Now that you have let me know how you prefer to be addressed, it would be my pleasure to use your first name, Kora."

The sound of her name in those deep, masculine tones sent a shiver through her. She stepped back quickly, as though suddenly aware of an undefined danger. That voice, as magnetic as his grin, melted her ability to stay angry with him.

"Thank you." She struggled to regain her composure. "I have no more desire to be stuck working with you than you with me, but as long as we're going to have to spend time together, I'm willing to put aside any differences we've had so far."

"It's a deal. If you're as good a reporter as you say you are, I look forward to the partnership."

"You'll see that I am," Kora replied confidently.

She recognized the skepticism in his statement but didn't allow it to rekindle her anger. After all, she remained just as skeptical of his abilities. He knew nothing about her. It had been natural for him to assume she was merely a society watcher. Perhaps, just perhaps, she had been a little unfair to him because of her anger at Jared. . . .

She shook Mace's proffered hand, returning his infectious smile despite herself.

"That's better," he said. "You're rather charming when you smile."

So are you, Kora thought, but recognized the absurdity of the comment before it could leave her mouth. She reached into her pocket, pulled her watch out by the fob, and studied its face carefully while sternly advising herself to start acting like a reporter and not an impressionable country cousin. Mason Fielding was an arrogant snob who didn't take her seriously, and she wasn't going to let herself be charmed into forgetting it.

"What time is it?"

Kora started. She'd been staring at her watch without seeing it. She checked it again.

"Almost twelve-fifteen," she answered, careful to avoid Mace's eyes. She looked up and down the cross street they faced. "Are you hungry? There's a restaurant just a few blocks from here where we can get some lunch before we get down to work."

Mace shrugged. "I could eat."

They crossed the street and turned right. Passing a livery stable and a small law office, they turned left, and in two more blocks arrived at the Golden Arrow Restaurant.

Inside it was dark and cool compared to the bright

heat of the early afternoon. Gleaming wood tables and chairs occupied the front area of the restaurant, while a marble counter with red upholstered stools ran parallel to the back wall. The Golden Arrow did a brisk business among laborers, clerks, and unmarried businessmen who had neither the time nor the inclination to go home for a proper dinner.

Today the restaurant was buzzing as usual. Men and a few women downed sandwiches or stew, while one or two junior lawyers leaned back in their chairs reading contracts or stock reports, hoping they looked impressive in their carefully creased new tweed suits.

"Kora! We haven't seen you in a while!"

"Hi, Andy," Kora greeted the large man behind the counter who was serving a bowl of thick soup to one of his customers. "Do you have room for us today?"

Anderson Morgan laughed. "Of course, there's always room for the city's most beautiful reporter." He waved down the counter toward an empty table in the corner. "I'll be there in just one minute."

"You rate special treatment," Mace commented as he pulled out a chair for Kora, noting the two hardworking waitresses that took the other customers' orders.

"I wrote a piece on Andy and the Arrow last year," Kora told him. "Didn't hurt his business any."

"He doesn't exactly look the part of a restaurateur," said Mace, examining Morgan's huge frame and curly black beard. "I rather picture Grizzly Adams as looking something like that."

"Well, I don't think Andy has wrastled any grizzlies lately," Kora said, laughing at the image. "He came out here to be a miner. He was smart enough to realize that catering to the miners' needs was a more reliable source of income than mining itself, so he started up a restaurant."

"And a mighty successful one at that," boomed Morgan as he approached their table. "What'll it be today, darlin'?"

"The corned beef," Kora replied, adding to Mace, "Andy makes an outstanding corned beef sandwich."

Morgan wrote down Kora's order on a small pad, even though her order was always the same.

"Two, then," Mace said.

"They'll be ready in no time," Morgan said.

Within a few minutes their sandwiches arrived as promised. Mace sampled his, then nodded approval. "You're right, this really is good."

"I may not be used to dining in the finest French restaurants," Kora said, defensive again, "but I do know a good corned beef sandwich when I eat one."

Mace's eyebrow quirked. "Must you take everything I say as a personal criticism? I'm sorry you felt I wasn't taking you seriously earlier, but I've never run across a female reporter before. I would think it's difficult. I mean, you can't just have a round of drinks with the politicians in their favorite bar or wander around alone in the more unsavory parts of town. How do you come up with stories?"

Kora glanced at him sharply, but he seemed honestly curious. "I have my sources," she replied. "There are times when being a woman actually has certain advantages." Kora thought of the many politicians who had made the mistake of letting down their guard in front of what they took to be a sweet, harmless little lady who claimed to be doing groundwork for her brother.

"But how did you get started writing in the first place?"

Kora shrugged. "When Troy and I were little, our favorite game was to pretend to be reporters like Papa. We interviewed friends and family, and made up thefts and murders and things to investigate. No one ever bothered to tell me that little girls couldn't grow up to work for a newspaper."

She looked to see if Mace thought this sounded silly, but he gestured for her to continue.

"When I was about eight we came to California, and Papa started his own paper. Troy began working as a reporter when we were fourteen, though he prefers the business end of things. Anyway, I was jealous, so Papa let me do some pieces on church bazaars and other social functions. He thought it was harmless enough, but I was sure I could be just as good a reporter as my brother."

She glanced at Mace again and found him still studying her with that disconcertingly intense gaze.

"Were you right?"

"Troy has a great head for numbers and organization. Papa taught him everything he knew about running a paper, and Troy's even better at it than he is. But I have a better eye for the news, and I'm a better writer."

Kora remembered then that this statement would not be borne out if Mace bothered to compare articles printed under the byline of Kora Hunter with those of Troy Hunter. In fact, he'd find the quality very much the same. She clamped her mouth shut so fast she almost bit her tongue. This man must have put her under a spell to make her talk so freely. She'd been right in her feelings earlier. He could be dangerous.

"I guess your father couldn't argue with that kind of talent."

"Mama did for a while," she told him, relieved to turn the conversation in a less perilous direction. "Despite Papa's assurances I'd only do dignified, genteel pieces, she insisted reporting wasn't a proper occupation for a lady." Kora still remembered the awful feeling of her mother's disapproval hanging between them. That was the only time she could recall feeling so isolated from either one of her parents. But the strain between them had worn Anna Hunter down, too.

"I won't tell you that you can't write for your father," she had relented at last. "Just don't do anything to make me regret it. I guess I shouldn't be surprised, considering the blood running in your veins." And Kora suspected that her strong-willed mother hadn't just been referring to her father's influence.

"What about you?" Kora asked Mace. "What inspired you to become a reporter? I wouldn't think someone of your good breeding would be interested in the sordid streets journalists have to walk."

He grinned at her, letting her barb go by. "It's true I was expected to do something suitably useless and ornamental when I grew up. My mother was horrified at the idea of my writing for a newspaper. It seems we have something in common after all. I guess it started out as a lark, and then I found I just couldn't stop."

Kora considered this as she watched him finish the last of his sandwich. He'd managed to answer her question politely without telling her much at all. She'd noticed the night before that he said very little about himself, as though he'd put up a wall between himself and the rest of the world. She found herself curious about what might lie behind that wall.

"Miss Hunter! Miss Hunter!"

She looked up to see a boy of about twelve dressed in ragged denims and a dirty white shirt standing in the doorway. He hurried to her table.

"What is it, Timmy?" she asked. The boy struggled to catch his breath, his eyes shining in excitement beneath his tousled hair. One of her cadre of street urchins, Timmy Johnson knew Kora Hunter would part with a quarter for a good story tip.

"It's a murder, Miss Hunter! They found a woman killed back of the liv'ry stable."

"You sure of this?" Mace asked skeptically.

After a suspicious glance Mace's way, Timmy decided to ignore him. "Hurry, Miss Hunter. It's not far. You'll be the first one there. Come on, I'll show you."

Mace arched an eyebrow at Kora. "I see you do have your sources. How much do we owe Mr. Morgan for lunch?"

"He'll put it on my tab," Kora told him, already on her feet. "Let's go."

They followed Timmy outside. As they hurried up the street, turning right at a familiar corner, Kora suddenly realized that the livery stable Timmy had mentioned must be the one just down K Street from her father's print shop. And indeed, a small crowd was forming in front of the large, drab building that was Hampton's Livery Stable.

"They found 'er down here." Timmy pointed to the alley that ran between the stable and the neighboring building. He slipped into the crowd of onlookers and moved toward the alley. Kora and Mace followed.

A uniformed policeman blocked the entrance to the alley. Beyond him, Kora could see two other policemen and a man she recognized as an assistant to the coroner standing by what looked like a pile of rags.

"No one gets any closer," warned the policeman before them. He was trying studiously to look bored, as though murder was all in a day's work for him.

"We're reporters," Kora informed him. "We'd like to speak to the officer in charge."

"Sure you are," he scoffed, letting his gaze travel openly over Kora's trim figure.

She bit back a sharp reply. Although she often encountered such treatment, she had never grown used to it. But she wasn't going to antagonize this officer. She'd never had the opportunity to cover a homicide before. Murders always had the potential to be big news, and she couldn't afford to lose her first chance at a headline story.

And she wasn't going to let Mace know she was nervous. If she convinced him that such investigation was routine to her, he couldn't very well tell her to go wait for him back at the office as her father would have done.

"We work for the *Sacramento Valley Times*," Mace was telling the officer. "I understand that you don't want to interrupt the investigation, so perhaps you could give us some of the details yourself. What's your name?"

He pulled out his notepad and pencil, watching the policeman expectantly. Kora appreciated his technique as she watched the officer swell noticeably with self-importance.

"Officer Luke Hensley," he replied.

"So what's going on here? Some gambler get himself killed?"

"The corpse is female," Hensley corrected him,

now eager to demonstrate his knowledge of the event. "Some squaw. Cheating on her lover most likely or caught stealing by a client, if you know what I mean."

"Indeed," Mace said. "And how was she killed?"

"Knife in the back. Clean, not a lot of mess."

"And did you find the body, Officer?" Kora asked in a honey-sweet tone, her wide eyes fixed on Hensley. She'd let Mason Fielding know he wasn't the only one who could get information out of a witness.

Officer Hensley had now relaxed enough to smile at her indulgently. "The proprietor of the stable, a Mr. Hampton, found her out behind those boxes there."

He pointed to some crates stacked by the wall of the stable. Kora saw that the other two officers had rolled the dead woman onto a stretcher. She caught a glimpse of long black hair before they draped a sheet over the body.

"That's where Mr. Hampton leaves water for the stable cat," Hensley explained.

The coroner's assistant came up behind him. "We're moving it out now," he told Hensley, frowning at Kora and Mace.

"All right, folks, make way," Hensley called loudly. "Just stand back, there's nothing to see. Make way."

Mace worked his way toward the street, and Kora stepped back, almost colliding with the man behind her. "Pardon me," she said, catching a glimpse of the man's faded denims and heeled boots. He smelled like horses. *Must work here,* she concluded distractedly, her concentration focused on the small procession now exiting the alley.

Just as the first officer passed her, the coroner's assistant accidentally stepped on a corner of the sheet hanging from the stretcher. The continued movement of the stretcher pulled the sheet from the body, leaving Kora looking directly down at the dead woman's face. Someone had closed her lids and she looked peaceful, as though merely asleep. Her thick black hair was tangled behind her, strands of it falling across a smooth brown cheek. Even dressed in simple brown muslin, she was a beautiful woman.

Kora had seen dead bodies before, a hazard of living in a town hardly removed from the frontier, but those had been old men—dead from too much whiskey and too little food—or desperate men, shot by other desperate men over money or women. This woman couldn't have been much older than Kora herself and, at least in death, she looked terribly innocent.

"Oh, God," Kora whispered, suddenly stripped of her customary objectivity. "I hope they get the man who did this."

"They won't. What do the police care? She's just an Indian, just a Digger." The derogatory term hung bitterly in the hot, still air.

Kora started at this sudden outburst from the stable worker next to her.

"How can you say that?" she began as she turned to face him, but she stopped when she took in his entire appearance.

The middle-aged man beside her was an Indian himself, hardly taller than Kora. The dark skin of his face was feathered with lines that deepened around his set jaw and his dark eyes. His eyes silenced Kora. A deep pain filled those eyes.

But his voice held no emotion except disdain when

he said, "You say you are a reporter. If so, you know what I say is true."

He stepped around her toward the alley.

"Wait!" Kora called after him, but he turned behind the stable building and was gone. Kora tried to shake off the creepy feeling his words had engendered in her. The man was obviously bitter about something, but that didn't change the fact that the police would be interested in catching any killer as soon as possible.

Behind her she heard the rattle of the coroner's wagon as it moved slowly down the street.

"They're taking her to the morgue," Mace said. Kora jumped. She hadn't noticed him come up beside her.

"Do they have any idea who might have done it?"

Mace looked at her closely, and Kora wondered if she sounded as upset as she felt.

"I don't think so. I gather he didn't leave a business card with the body."

Kora glared at him. "That isn't something to joke about," she snapped. He hadn't seen the woman's face as she had.

At that moment she saw Officer Hensley standing near the street, urging passersby on horseback and in buggies to continue on their way and not stop traffic. She brushed past Mace and tapped Hensley on the shoulder.

"What?" he said, annoyed, but he grinned when he saw Kora. "Can I do something for you, miss?"

"Do the police have any clues as to who that woman was, Officer?" she asked.

"Well, yes," Hensley answered, but Kora's initial eagerness was dashed when he continued, "She's most likely the kind of woman a lady like you doesn't know much about, and that's just as well. Don't you worry about her. She probably deserved what she got."

"Deserved to be stabbed in the back?" Kora asked incredulously.

She felt a hand on her arm. It was Mace.

"Let's let Officer Hensley get back to work, Kora. We've taken up enough of his time."

But she shook him off, venting her fury on Hensley. "How could you even think such a thing? She can hardly have deserved to be murdered!"

Hensley sighed a practiced, world-weary sigh and shook his head sadly. "You'd be surprised."

"But it's your job to catch whoever did this and make sure he pays for it."

Hensley smiled. "Oh, don't you worry about that. These Diggers aren't too clever. It's probably a lover or jealous husband. We'll find him drinking and bragging about the whole thing with the bloody knife still on him. And even if we don't, it's nothing for you to worry your pretty little head over. She was nobody important."

Kora bit her lip to keep herself from telling Officer Hensley what a smug, brainless fool he was. Instead, she marched out into the street.

"Kora!" Mace's voice called out a warning.

She looked up to see a hansom cab hurtling down the street much too fast, coming right at her. She could see the whites of the horse's eyes as the animal reared its head back, trying to swerve around her. For a split second Kora's feet froze to the ground and she couldn't move.

The blow came from behind, throwing her to the

hard dirt of the street, out of the path of the onrushing vehicle. Kora lay gasping on the ground, the breath knocked from her body.

"Are you okay?" Mace Fielding's rough, anxious voice came from beside her.

Other voices rustled above her.

"Is she all right?"

"That driver didn't even stop."

"Did you see her step right out in front of him?"

She managed to sit up. Her dress had torn above one knee.

"Kora?"

She looked up into Mace's face, which was crumpled with worry as his eyes searched hers intently. A shiver ran through her at the thought of the sharp hooves and remorseless wheels that could have crushed her.

"You saved my life," she whispered.

A slight, wry smile touched Mace's lips. "Then maybe I've made up for any past callousness on my part?"

"Maybe." Kora smiled weakly. Her stomach still churned from the scare.

"Can you stand?" He reached for her hand to help her up, and she suddenly realized how much it stung. She looked down to see bits of rock and dust rubbed into the scrapes on her palms.

Mace noticed them, too. He took her elbow and pulled her to her feet.

"We'd better find some water and rinse these off." He pulled a handkerchief from his pocket and wrapped it around her right hand, which had begun to bleed slightly. Kora let him put an arm around her shoulders and lead her to the side of the street.

Officer Hensley's voice made her glance up for a moment. "Are you going to be all right? You should really be more careful crossing the street."

His look managed to combine a pedantic self-satisfaction with fatherly concern, but Kora was too exhausted to get angry with him again. Instead she simply nodded and turned away.

"He's right you know. You gave me quite a scare. Don't you ever watch where you're going?"

Kora looked up at Mace. His hand still rested on her arm, steadying her. She had recovered enough now to notice the scrapes on his knuckles. Dust covered the sleeves of his coat, and his hair was tousled.

She felt a flash of guilt for all the nasty things she'd thought about him. This dandified, stuffed-shirt New Englander had risked his own safety to rescue a cantankerous young woman he'd known for less than a day.

And standing there beside her, frowning in concern, without his usual mask of detached politeness, he was even more handsome than she had thought possible. Kora caught herself searching his face to see if she could see into him, discover the man he really was. His eyes held hers for a moment, and she thought she felt a spark jump between them. She found herself blushing, surprised at herself for being so silly.

"Thank you," she murmured, dropping her gaze from his, hoping he wouldn't notice her confusion.

"That's quite all right," he replied lightly, taking his hand from her arm. "I wouldn't want to lose my boss's daughter my first day here; it wouldn't be good for my career. Now let's go do something about your hands."

Kora smiled at his joke but felt a pang of disappointment. The mask of polite efficiency had returned. But she could still feel the warmth of his hand on her arm.

For heaven's sake, Kora, get hold of yourself. You're practically engaged. She needed a glass of water. That near accident had really rattled her.

4

As Kora entered the cool front hall of the house, she breathed a sigh of relief. Even now, in late May, the sun could be unbearable, and it had seemed a long walk home from the newspaper office today.

"Kora, is that you?" her mother called.

"Yes, Mama. I'm just going upstairs to change; I'll be right down."

"Wait a moment. I want to speak with you." Anna Hunter entered the hall from the dining room. She had dressed for company, her fair hair pulled back in a black-netted chignon and topped with a tiny brown-ribboned cap that matched her black-on-brown printed calico dress. The effect set off her figure and complexion to perfection.

She opened her mouth to speak and then paused when she noticed Kora's disheveled appearance.

"Kora, what happened to you? Are you hurt?"

Kora looked down at her torn and dirty dress and

wished she'd managed to escape upstairs before her mother had seen it.

"I'm fine, Mama," she assured her, trying vainly to brush some of the dust from her skirt. "I took a spill dodging a runaway cab. Mace—Mason Fielding—pushed me to safety. It wasn't really as bad as it looks."

Her mother frowned. "This occurred while you were showing Mason around Sacramento for your father?"

"A woman was killed down by Hampton's Livery Stable," Kora said. "Mace and I just happened to be in the area when her body was discovered. It upset me a bit. I guess I wasn't watching where I was going."

"Hmph." Her mother's lips pursed tighter, telling Kora she'd said exactly the wrong thing.

"Kora," Anna began, choosing her own words with care. "Kora, I know you've enjoyed writing for your father, and I've put up with a great deal of disapproval from my friends for allowing it, even though I don't necessarily like it myself."

"I know. You've been wonderful about the whole thing."

"Yes, I have," her mother said sternly, refusing to be detoured. "I thought that once the novelty wore off, you'd realize how tedious and exasperating working for a newspaper is. Then, when you and Jared began spending so much time together, I assumed you were starting to think about a family of your own."

"I am thinking about it, Mama," she answered, feeling guilty for a moment until she remembered that she really *was* considering Jared's proposal. That is, she was planning on considering it. Soon.

Her mother's expression didn't soften. "I hope

you'll do more than think about it. Just look at you, dirty and hot, completely unladylike. And you could have been killed today. What kind of life is that for a young woman? I wish Jared had asked you to give it up sooner."

"What?"

Anna set her jaw tighter. "Jared came by at dinnertime looking for you. He wanted to tell you he's been sent to San Francisco for a couple of days, and he told your father and me that he'd asked you to marry him. He wanted our blessings. I would have thought you'd have accepted at once. He told us you actually want to continue reporting after you're married. I find that hard to believe, but if it's true, then I think it's gone far enough."

Kora flushed in anger and embarrassment. "Jared had no right to talk to you about this without my knowledge."

"But we're your parents. Of course we should know. And why didn't you tell us yourself? You don't usually keep things from me."

"Why didn't I tell you? Because I knew you'd react this way. Couldn't you even have supported me in front of Jared? He hasn't even tried to understand why writing is important to me. And Papa needs me, at least until he can hire a replacement. Surely he must see how unfair Jared is being."

"Your father agrees with me."

Kora felt as though she'd had all the breath knocked out of her. "That's not true!"

"Why don't you ask him," her mother said, tight-lipped. "He's in his study."

Kora turned and threw open the study door. She could not believe that her father would betray her this way until she saw the guilty look on his face as he glanced up from behind his desk. He must have heard every word she and her mother had spoken in the hall.

"Papa, how could you?"

"Honey, be reasonable. Your mother and I have talked about this, and we agree that this hobby of yours shouldn't come in the way of your happiness."

"Hobby?" Kora cried. "Hobby? Is that all the newspaper is to you?"

"Of course not. I run the *Valley Times* to make money to take care of this family. But, Kora, you don't need to spend your life making money. Jared, or any man you decide to marry, will take care of that for you."

"So you don't enjoy what you do?" she challenged him, managing to get the words around the lump in her throat. "You wouldn't do it if you didn't have to?"

"Don't use that tone with me, young lady," her father responded, his voice rising. "We're not talking about me, we're talking about you, and I hardly think at your age you know what you want, much less what's good for you."

Tears threatened behind Kora's eyes, but she held them back. She knew she couldn't sway her father that way.

"I'm twenty years old," she said softly, "and I'm a reporter. You gave me the chance to try to be what I'd dreamed of since I was a little girl, and now you expect it to be easy to give up. I want to be a wife and mother, but I don't see why that means I can't do something I love so much."

She paused, then asked the question she couldn't

avoid any longer, "Are you telling me that I can't work for your paper anymore?"

Her father looked away from her toward the window. "No."

Kora's muscles eased in relief, even as she felt her mother's silent disapproval behind her.

Ellis Hunter turned back toward her and his eyes caught hers. "No, I'm not firing you, Kora. This is your decision to make." He glanced at his wife for support. "If we made this decision for you, you'd be resentful, and I doubt you'd see the wisdom in it. However, I think you know which is the mature and sensible path to follow, and I hope you choose to accept it."

Kora nodded, biting her lower lip to prevent another outburst. She couldn't afford to appear childish now. But as she turned to leave the room, she couldn't help saying, "Papa, I don't believe that if your parents had thought reporting wasn't right for you, it would have been enough to make you give it up."

Her father stood, leaning his palms against his desktop. "Maybe not, but if I'd had to choose between reporting and your mother, I would never have hesitated to leave the newspaper business for good."

Kora glanced up at her mother. Anna's fingertips rested on her lips and her eyes glistened as she looked at her husband with love. Kora said nothing, but simply slipped past her and hurried up the stairs to her room.

She closed the door softly. "Hey, Dodge," she whispered, lowering herself to the bed and pulling the cat's warm, purring body against the ache in her heart.

*   *   *

When she came back downstairs twenty minutes later, Kora had changed into a clean lilac princess frock. Her hair was pulled back in a neat chignon with a few fashionable stray curls, and her eyes were dry. She couldn't pretend that nothing had happened, but she was determined to show her parents that she intended to make her decisions rationally, calmly, and on her own.

If her mother wondered what she was thinking, she didn't ask as Kora helped her set the table and chop celery sticks to go with the dinner of roast chicken, stuffing, boiled cabbage, and apple pie. Because of the odd hours Kora, Troy, and Ellis kept at the newspaper office, Anna usually planned the large family meal for supper instead of the noon dinner hour.

As Kora folded the last napkin and laid it on the table, her mother placed a hand on her shoulder. "Kora, you know that women can't just flout society's rules. You have to learn to accept that. According to those rules, Jared isn't being at all unreasonable."

Her eyes searched her daughter's face, compassion softening her firm tone. Kora couldn't be angry with her. She knew her mother only wanted what was best for her, but Kora's heart couldn't accept her advice.

"Maybe it's time to change society's rules," she answered softly, meeting her mother's gaze.

The front door slammed and long strides hurried down the hall toward them.

"Hey, Kora," Troy called as he stuck his head into the dining room, grinning in his usual irrepressible way. "That story you and Mace whipped up on the

murder down at Hampton's Stable looks good, but
you need more facts."

He blanched as he suddenly noticed Anna standing
in the pantry doorway. "Hullo, Ma."

"I'm going to take Mason down to the police station tomorrow morning so we can see if they've iden-
tified the body and if they have any suspects," Kora
said, letting him know their mother already knew
about her involvement in the story.

"Troy, go wash up for supper," Anna said, shaking
her head affectionately at her son. "You've been
working too hard. You look awful."

"I just need a good home-cooked meal." The jaunty
smile was back as Troy winked at Kora to thank her
for covering his slip.

The front door slammed again. Troy turned to look
down the hall.

"Grandpa!" he yelled. "Are we rich yet?"

"I met your guests at the door," Kora's grandfather
announced in his heavy German accent as he entered
the dining room, followed by Mason Fielding and
Jessica. "Will you have left enough food for a weary
old man?"

"Hello, Papa," Anna said. "We weren't expecting
you until Saturday."

"So I eat at a restaurant tonight?"

"*Ach*, Papa," Anna scolded him, hugging the weath-
ered old man and kissing his cheek. "Sit down. Dinner's
ready as soon as Kora can set another place. Troy, go
run a comb through your hair."

She smiled at the young girl. "You must be Jessica."

"Yes, ma'am." Jessica edged closer to her father.

"Jessica is a lovely name," Anna continued, trying
to put her at ease.

"I was named for my Uncle Jesse," Jessica told her proudly.

"Well, Jessica and Mason Fielding, this is my father, Friedrich Kraus."

"Fritz," the old man insisted.

"Mason is a reporter from Boston. He's here in Sacramento to write some stories for Ellis."

When her mother had finished the introductions, Kora gave her grandfather a hug, then turned to Jessica. "Hello, Jessica," she said warmly. "I'm glad to see you again. I've set you a place next to me so you can tell me what you think of California so far. Is it as wild as you were expecting?" She shot Mace a side-long glance.

"It's nicer than home," Jessica said, causing her father to glance down at her in surprise.

"Why do you say that, Jess?" he asked, but she shrugged and looked away.

"Oh, I don't know. It just is."

Kora motioned Jessica to the chair next to hers, then hurriedly set another place for her grandfather on the girl's other side. Mace sat across from his daughter next to Troy. Ellis arrived from his study and sat at the end of the table, across from his wife.

Her nerves were too frayed from the earlier conversation with her parents to do much more than pick at the food before her, but Kora noticed that Mace had a hearty appetite.

"This is delicious," he told her mother. "I haven't tasted chicken this good since—well, I don't know how long."

"Thank you, Mason," Anna answered with a smile. "Usually, the only way I can tell if my family enjoys my meals is by how much they consume."

Troy laughed. "In that case, would you please pass me the stuffing?"

"So, Mason," Kora's grandfather began between bites of cabbage, "you are an easterner. What do you think of the war news? Is the North going to win?"

Mace nodded. "I don't think there's much question about it. The Confederacy just doesn't have the resources to continue much longer. They got by for a long time on talented leadership, but you can't have an army without ammunition, food, clothes, and medicine. Of course, before the first Battle of Bull Run, I thought the war wouldn't last more than a month."

"Chester McDougall's letter of introduction said you had been a war correspondent," Ellis said.

"Yes." Mace's shrug indicated he didn't particularly want to discuss it.

Kora glanced up in surprise. They'd spent most of the day together, and he'd never mentioned reporting the war. For some reason that hurt her. Was he regarding her more as a source of information about Sacramento than as a co-worker and potential friend?

"One reason I like California better than Boston is that Papa could take me with him," Jessica said.

Kora sympathized. "It must have been hard to wait at home while your father was away at the war."

"I wasn't at home," Jessica answered with what sounded almost like defiance. "I stayed with my grandparents."

Kora's brow furrowed as she watched Jessica lean over her plate to avoid looking at her father. She must really have resented him when he left her to follow the war. But then, Kora thought, that was understandable, considering the danger he must have been in and the fact that he was the only parent she had.

"You're pretty lucky, then," she said, trying to lighten the girl's mood. "Grandpa always used to spoil Troy and me rotten when Mama and Papa left us with him."

"I knew it!" Anna cried at the same moment Fritz protested, "Never!"

"It's true," Troy said. "Grandpa used to let Kora dress up in my clothes and we'd go bet on the horses over at the Louisiana racetrack."

"Papa!" Anna exclaimed, horrified, but everyone else laughed.

So only Kora and Mace heard Jessica's quiet reply: "Grandmother said Papa had turned me into a spoiled brat already, and if I didn't watch myself I'd end up killed just like Uncle Jesse."

Kora didn't know what to reply to that, but she saw Mace's jaw tense.

"Eat your cabbage," he told Jessica curtly, but he seemed to have lost his appetite for his own food.

Kora saw Jessica's hurt at her father's tone but wasn't sure that he'd meant his anger to be directed at the girl. Mace had withdrawn again, lost in thought.

"Kora, would you help me serve the pie?"

"Hm? Sure, Mama."

During dessert and while helping her mother clear the table, Kora wondered about Mason Fielding. Why was he so reluctant to talk about his past and himself? Why had he come out to California anyway? It seemed to her that any sort of travel-diary work would appear silly and trivial after writing about the Civil War.

She observed that he had impeccable manners, a

very different impression from the one she had first formed on the riverfront yesterday. But he seemed to hold himself aloof from any genuine interaction with the rest of the company. As they moved from the dining room to the sitting room—Anna had obviously taken a liking to her guests to offer them comfort over formality—Kora caught herself feeling frustrated. Though Mace had smiled at her several times during dinner, he treated her no differently from the rest of her family.

It's not as though I want him to fall in love with me, she told herself somewhat guiltily. She had enough trouble with Jared. But Mace had saved her life today, and she'd thought they were getting along pretty well when they had returned to the print shop.

As they entered the sitting room, Mace stepped back beside her.

"Are you angry with me about something?" he asked quietly.

Kora felt his breath brush the side of her face. Her spirits rose, even as his low tone made her nerves jump. He had made an excuse to talk with her semiprivately. Perhaps he didn't regard her as merely part of the furniture after all.

"No, of course not. Why do you ask?" She hoped she sounded perplexed rather than coy.

"You've been staring at me all evening."

Kora's cheeks began to burn. "I was not!" She was surprised by his tactlessness. Had she been?

He shrugged, but to her embarrassment his lips curled in an amused grin. "All right. I just wondered if I'd offended you again. Or maybe you've realized I'm not so hard to look at after all?"

With that, he moved past her into the sitting room.

For one moment all Kora wanted was for the floor to open up and let her sink out of sight into oblivion, but her chagrin sparked a touch of anger that spread through her like wildfire. If only that spark could jump the space between herself and that obnoxious Boston dandy and incinerate him!

She stalked to an uncomfortable straight-backed chair behind her mother's easy chair. Staring at him, indeed! All she'd done was wonder if he wanted her for a friend. Now she knew.

The fact that her face remained red only increased her anger. Did he think she had some sort of school-girl crush on him? After his rudeness yesterday, he was lucky she even spoke to him! Maybe proper Boston maidens found his good looks irresistible, but she'd lived long enough in California to know that what counted in the Far West wasn't a handsome face, an established family name, or a good suit, but character and compassion. Obviously, Mason Fielding had little enough of either.

She vowed to herself that she'd show him just how little she cared about what he thought of her. *And make him sorry that I don't care,* she added to herself with a slight toss of her head. Maybe she wasn't as ladylike as the women in Boston, but plenty of men found her attractive, and it would take more than Mace's rudeness to crush her self-esteem.

But despite her resolve to ignore him, she couldn't help feeling hurt and puzzled by the way Mace had acted this evening.

"So, Fritz," Ellis was saying as he packed tobacco into his favorite meerschaum pipe, "We weren't expecting you for a couple of days. Is everything going all right up in the hills?"

"Is that *Gott* damn mule—pardon me, ladies," Kora's grandfather responded. "I was exploring for possibly a new claim. I leave the mule alone for one minute and he get spooked and run home. I get back hours later and he's there waiting, looking at me so to say, 'Where have you been?' His bridle is broken, so I take the excuse to come to Sacramento early to surprise my family and have it fixed."

"You're a miner?" Jessica asked. "Like a Miner Forty-niner?"

"We came to California in '52, but it doesn't rhyme so good," he told her with a smile. "And I don't have such an operation as the folk in Placerville or Washoe, but I pan enough to earn my keep."

He pulled a small glass vial from the pocket of his red laborer's shirt and handed it to her.

"See there? That is the first gold I took from my claim."

Jessica shook the vial and watched the shiny flakes swirl for a moment in the water, then sink back to the bottom.

"I'd love to see a real gold claim," she said wistfully as she handed the vial back to the old man.

"Come see mine!" Fritz suggested, obviously pleased by her interest. He turned to Mace. "My cabin is not far from Placerville. If you come with me on the stage Monday, I will show you everything for you to know about gold. That would be something to write up for your eastern paper."

Though she had been pointedly ignoring him during this conversation, Kora now glanced at Mace to see what he would make of this offer. She saw his eyes light up. Had he come to California out of simple gold lust, like so many others?

"That's very generous of you, Fritz," he replied, smiling at Jessica. "We'd love to have you show us what a miner's life is like, if we wouldn't be putting you out. And if it's all right with my boss."

Ellis shrugged. "Stories about salty old miners will make good copy until they've taken every bit of gold from the ground. Besides, it would give you a feel for more of the state than just Sacramento."

"*Ach, gut!*" Fritz said. "It will be nice to have company. Kora often comes up for a few weeks in the summer. Will you come with us then, *Liebchen?*"

"Oh, I don't know, Grandpa," Kora said, somewhat surprised at suddenly being included in the conversation.

"Do come, Kora," Jessica pleaded. "It'll be fun."

Kora looked from Jessica to Mace to find him gazing back at her. She hastily turned from him to her grandfather, fighting a surge of anger. Despite his earlier comment, Mace seemed to feel free to stare at *her* whenever he pleased.

She shook her head. "I don't think so, Grandpa. I've got quite a bit to do here in town. This isn't the best time."

Jessica and Fritz looked disappointed, but Kora thought she saw her parents exchange a speculative glance. If they thought she was staying on to consider Jared's proposal and get her feelings about reporting sorted out, they were right, in part.

It was also true that at this moment she didn't want Mace to think she was eager for him. But she wouldn't let a desire to avoid him keep her from a trip to her grandfather's cabin. She simply had too much on her mind to leave Sacramento right now.

"You'll visit me later, then?" Fritz asked her.

"When I can," she assured him.

"Anna, thank you for the wonderful dinner." Mace stretched his legs and rose with a grace surprising for his tall figure. "It's been a lovely evening, but I think I'd better get Jessica home so she can get some sleep. She's got another long day of school tomorrow, and I want her to get settled in as much as possible before we go traipsing off into the mountains."

"Of course," Anna agreed. "Jessica, it was lovely meeting you. I hope you continue to enjoy California."

"Thank you, Mrs. Hunter," Jessica answered, shy again.

As her father walked Mace down the hall, Kora took the opportunity to speak with Jessica. She might not be sure what to think of Mace, but she knew she liked this independent, inquisitive girl. And something told her Jessica might appreciate a sympathetic female ear.

"Jess, I just want you to know you're always welcome here. I'm sure you'll be making lots of friends at school, but I hope you'll consider me a friend, too."

A big smile rewarded her. "I'd like to be your friend, Kora. Are you sure you won't come with us to your grandfather's claim?"

Kora wavered for a moment. She did love the peace and beauty of the mountain cabin. Then the memory of Jared's ultimatum and her parents' decision to side with him rushed back to her. She wouldn't be able to enjoy the mountains until she resolved those issues.

"Sorry, Jess. This just isn't the right time. But we'll have plenty of time this year to do things together. All right?"

Jessica nodded. "All right. Bye, Kora."

"Good-bye."

They caught up with Mace and Ellis at the front door.

"You ready, Jess?" Mace asked, handing his daughter her dark blue cloak. He smiled his most charming smile for Kora. "Good night, partner, I'll see you tomorrow."

"Bright and early," she said, though her teeth clenched involuntarily. He had plenty of nerve, teasing her and then acting as if nothing had happened. "We've got to get to the police station and back tomorrow morning so we can get the paper run off tomorrow night."

"Bright and early," Mace agreed, then followed his daughter out.

As the door closed behind them, Kora suddenly realized how exhausted she was.

Her father noticed as well. "You look tired, sweetheart. Maybe you should get some rest. It's been a long day."

She looked up at him. She hated to be angry with either one of her parents, and she could see in his face that he wanted to make peace.

"Yes, it has," she said. "Good night, Papa."

He responded with a wan smile. "Night, Kora."

Wearily, Kora trudged up the stairs to her room. It *had* been an awfully long day. She'd been ordered to work with Mason Fielding, called to a murder scene, almost run over by a cab, had her parents tell her to do what Jared wanted without listening to her opinion, and then, after changing her mind once again about Mace, he'd made her feel like a fool for wanting his friendship.

If yesterday had been a terrible day, today had

been even worse. She didn't even want to think about tomorrow.

Mace strolled down the darkened Sacramento street, whistling "When Johnny Comes Marching Home," because Jess liked the song.

Jessica walked beside him, taking in all the sights of this new place. It had pleased Mace on the walk over to the Hunters' home to hear Jessica chatter cheerfully about her new school and the children she'd met. He still wasn't sure that coming to California had been the right choice, but it seemed good for her, which eased his mind considerably.

Still, he couldn't help the nagging feeling that she ought to be more homesick. He himself had missed his old Boston haunts and companions quite a bit during their journey here. But then, what did Jessica have to feel homesick for? He had left her alone with his parents a lot during the last few years. He hadn't wanted to, but covering the war had been important to him. He wondered what else his mother had called Jessica besides a spoiled brat, what other bitterness his daughter held inside her, and he felt a flash of protectiveness. He wished his family was different, wished he could shield her from the pain of the past.

Mace stopped whistling and pulled a cigarette from the pocket of his overcoat.

Jessica spoke up from his elbow, "See, Papa? You're practically a westerner already."

"How's that, kitten?" he asked, lighting his match. He breathed deeply, first that spark of sulfur, then the sharp smoke of the tobacco.

"Wearing boots and smoking a *cigarillo.*"

He looked down at his daughter's serious face and grinned. "But I did that before we left Boston, ever since I went off to the war."

Jessica simply shrugged, and Mace chuckled at her unspoken approval of his new habits.

They walked in companionable silence the rest of the way to Mrs. Johnson's boarding house, enjoying the cool breeze that waved away the warmth of the exercise.

In his room, Mace lit the lamp beside the one comfortable chair and sat down, opening the small *California Story Book* that a previous occupant had left behind. He flipped through it, coming to "The Maniac Mother and Child Angel."

He heard the door open and looked up to see Jessica in her nightgown, ready for bed. She came over to him and kissed him lightly on the cheek.

"Scratchy."

"Sorry, kitten." He returned the kiss. "You're sure school was all right today? They're not going too slowly for you?"

"It was fine. Melissa and her friends are nice."

"Good. Now hurry off to bed like a good girl. If you're cross and grumpy the next few days, Mr. Kraus may take back the invitation to visit his claim."

Jessica scrunched her nose. "I'm awfully sorry Kora won't be going with us."

"Well, she said she was busy. I'm sure you'll get to see plenty of her while we're here in California."

Mace turned to his book, but Jessica surprised him by adding, "You should be nicer to Kora, Papa."

He looked back at her with a sudden frown. "What do you mean?"

"You said something to her tonight that made her mad."

Mace stared at his daughter for a moment, startled by her perception, and by her impertinence in telling him what to do.

"If I did, I certainly didn't mean to," Mace responded in a voice that indicated this was the end of the discussion. "Now good night."

"Night, Papa," she answered, but paused once more to conclude, "She's not like Grandmother's friends, you know, Papa."

She was gone before Mace had a chance to respond, which was just as well, because he couldn't quite stifle the chuckle that rose to his lips.

"Grandmother's friends" referred to the parade of eligible young ladies that his mother had insisted on introducing to him at every dinner he ate at her house. Inevitably disastrous, these dinners ended with his father flirting genteelly with the young guests, his mother pointing out all their charms and connections, and the women themselves supposing that by acting like simpering fools, they'd manage to snare one of Boston's most elusive bachelors.

Then he recalled how he used to come home to Jessica and make her laugh with barely exaggerated caricatures of his mother's latest offering. He hated to admit that his mother might be right in any criticism of his parenting, but she could have had a point that he was too lenient with Jessica. It wasn't any of his daughter's business how he chose to conduct himself with women.

Still, Jessica was right: Kora was nothing like the daughters and nieces and granddaughters of his mother's friends. Her fresh, natural looks gave a glow to her smooth complexion and honey-colored hair, and the glint in her golden cat eyes made her seem more lovely than any woman he could remember . . . since Cecilia. More important than her appearance, though, was her refreshing honesty and openness. How long had it been since a woman had actually surprised him, the way she managed to every few minutes? She was not afraid to state her opinions to anyone. Nor had she been intimidated by him, even when he'd confronted her on the riverfront.

A female reporter. He shook his head. And from what he had seen today, she might just be a good one.

All of which was precisely why he had said what he had to her this evening. She *had* been staring at him, albeit surreptitiously, throughout dinner. He wanted to nip in the bud any chance that she might develop a more than professional interest in him. He had realized this afternoon that he liked her, and he didn't need her turning into a lovesick girl, interfering with either his work here or his personal reasons for coming to California.

And he didn't want to hurt her. He never intended to fall in love again. He enjoyed female company, but he hadn't met anyone who could make him forget Cecilia.

More than nine years had passed since Cecilia's death, yet the memory of her betrayal still sliced as cold and sharp as a scalpel through his stomach. The fact that at the end he had let her go without telling her he still loved her only made it worse.

Lodged beside that pain was his brother's death. Jesse had been the outgoing, generous Fielding brother, always ready to make you laugh or to commiserate with your sorrow.

Mace's parents loved him, expecting him to live up to the family's name and carry on the Fielding tradition. But they had doted on Jesse. After Jesse's death, his father had retreated from the world, taking companionship from his bottle of Scotch, and his mother's strictness had turned harsh and selfish.

Mace shook his head, trying to clear it of the ache he got from wondering about the past. If only his own feelings didn't cloud his memory so darkly. He might have had good reason to hate his brother, but no one could ever have hated Jesse, and certainly not Mace, who had been his best friend for so many years. Jesse had been a little spoiled, certainly impulsive. He had done some things Mace could never forgive him for, but Mace wouldn't believe that either his brother or Cecilia was capable of murder based solely on the word of that old man in Missouri.

He'd learn soon enough whether or not the old man's claims were valid. Booth Garrett would tell him what he knew, and Mace would be able to let it go, one way or the other.

He rubbed his forehead with his palm. His quest was going better than he'd hoped, and for some odd reason that made him nervous. He'd had no trouble locating property belonging to a Mr. Booth Garrett at the surveyor's office. Garrett owned a ranch and gold-mining operation near Placerville, and tonight Fritz Kraus had offered him the perfect excuse to travel to Placerville and find the truth.

No matter what the truth turned out to be, though, it would not change the pain he carried in his heart. Accustomed to being alone, he had no need to risk sowing or reaping any more pain. It would be better to push Kora away now than to hurt her later on.

But underneath this musing he had a nagging suspicion that he hadn't hurt that self-sufficient, intriguing young woman at all tonight, only annoyed her. She'd blushed when he confronted her, but she hadn't acted like one of his mother's prospects would have, giggling or pouting or having a fainting spell.

Mace's own cheeks warmed a little at the idea that he might have made an ass of himself for nothing. Perhaps she wasn't attracted to him at all.

Which was what he wanted, of course. So why was the thought keeping him awake now?

He stood and dropped his book on the little table by his chair. Then he stretched his back and his legs, stripped off his clothes, and rolled into bed. The cool sheets felt good against his skin, brushing the day's events from his mind.

In no time he slipped into a deep sleep. For once Cecilia's ghost stayed away, leaving his dreams to be haunted by flashing cat's eyes and hair of golden silk.

5

"*Good morning,* Officer Gant," Kora said to the dour policeman seated behind the scarred oak desk.

The officer's graying mustache twitched in what passed for him as a smile. He had little use for the press in general, but he always showed a grudging fondness for Kora.

"What can I do for you?" he asked, shuffling the papers on his desk to indicate how much work she was interrupting.

"We're following up on the murder of an Indian woman at Hampton's Livery Stable yesterday morning. We'd like to know if you have any information on who she is or who might have killed her."

Officer Gant glanced at Mace, who stood beside her, as though to get corroboration that they were, indeed, together. Mace's silence seemed to satisfy him.

"Yes, they've solved that one," he said, looking back down at his desk. "Give me a minute to find the paperwork."

Kora's heart began to beat a little faster, but she shushed Mace with a wave of her hand when he seemed about to question Gant further. She knew from experience that the old man moved more slowly if a reporter appeared too eager for information. And he refused to answer any questions without the appropriate written material before him.

As Gant rummaged through a cabinet behind his desk, Kora glanced around the police station, feeling awkward in her attempt to keep her eyes off Mace so he couldn't repeat his comments of the night before. She had considered telling her father she was sick this morning and unable to work, but she refused to let her parents' displeasure, or Jared's ultimatum, or Mace's odd behavior, prevent her from doing her job. Fortunately, neither her mother nor father had mentioned their discussion of the previous afternoon, and Mace seemed content to act as though nothing had happened between them last night.

"Here it is." Officer Gant positioned several sheets of paper on his desk as he sat back down. He put on a pair of spectacles.

To Kora's amusement, Mace was too frustrated to hold back any longer. "You said they'd solved the case?" he asked, looking as though he'd like to tear the papers from Gant's hands.

Gant glanced at him, then at Kora, then back down at the sheets he held. "Yes."

When he showed no inclination to proceed, Kora suppressed a grin and pulled out her notebook. "Do they have her name, Officer?"

"Hm, yes," Gant answered, rewarding her professional demeanor. "Relevant facts: The victim's name was Rosemarie Amado, age twenty-five. She worked as a maid for a lawyer named Miles Osborn. Her husband, Diego, has been arrested and is being held on suspicion of murder."

"What led them to the husband?" Mace asked.

Gant frowned. "I couldn't say."

"We'll have to talk with the officer in charge of the investigation." Kora's tone warned Mace not to push Gant any further.

Mace changed tactics. "May we interview the suspect?"

"Both of you?" Gant seemed surprised. Kora had built a comfortable working relationship with Gant, since she came by the station several times a week to glean information on crime and law enforcement "for her brother," but she'd never actually been inside the jail.

"Of course," Kora replied, trying to sound casual. She wasn't about to let this particular story slip through her fingers just because she wasn't a man.

"I don't know, Miss Hunter. . . ."

"You mean to say you're keeping reporters in the dark about his case?" Mace cut in, as if Gant's hesitation included them both. "Is there some sort of cover-up going on here?"

"Of course not, I . . ." Kora had never seen Gant flustered before, and it took him only a second to recover. "Officer Brady!" Gant called across the office to a group of officers standing around another desk.

A youthful, sandy-haired policeman hurried over to Gant's desk.

"Take these reporters back to see prisoner . . . ,"

Gant glanced at his papers again, "prisoner Amado, Diego."

"Sure. Follow me," Brady said.

Before Kora turned to follow Brady and Mace, she said, "Thank you, Officer Gant."

The black scowl he sent in Mace's direction twitched into another smile as he caught her eye, before he returned to the work on his desk.

Kora caught up with Mace and Brady in the hall leading from the offices to the jail cells. Housed in the city waterworks building, the police station occupied several "bays" on the first floor. Whenever she entered the building, Kora imagined she could feel the city's water pressing down on the roof far above her head.

As they walked, her skin prickled with excitement. She'd never spoken with a murderer before. Her mind flashed back to the sight of the dead woman. What sort of man could do such a thing?

Brady grinned at her. "I've heard about the girl reporter, but you're even prettier than they say."

Kora saw Mace's lips twist in amusement.

"I've also heard you're tougher than you look," Brady added, thinking Kora's scowl was directed toward him.

"Believe it," Mace said with a grin.

Kora ignored Mace's comment. "I'll take that as a compliment."

"Maybe the two of you will be able to get something out of this fellow, then," Brady said. "He hasn't said much of anything since we brought him in."

"You made the arrest?" Mace asked.

"Yes. I was there with the detective in charge."

"And he won't talk?" Kora prodded.

"Won't admit he did it, but he doesn't deny it either,"

Brady told her. "Usually the fellows we pick up are squawking about how they don't know anything, never saw nothing, even when we catch them with the gun still hot in their hands. Which, by the way, is practically how we caught this one. He works at the stable where the murder occurred, and we found the knife he used under an old blanket in an unused stall in the stable itself."

Kora felt a flutter of uneasiness. Would such circumstantial evidence be enough to convict the man of killing lovely young Rosemarie Amado? The vehemence of her desire to see this murderer brought to justice surprised her. "Is that all the evidence you have to go on?" she asked.

It was the wrong question. Brady straightened defensively.

"No, that's not all," he said, retreating into official reserve. "I can't really discuss much more of the case with you, but several people have given us statements about the man's odd behavior, before and after the murder. Mr. Hampton, who owns the stable, said he wasn't real surprised that this happened. He says he's thought for some time about firing Amado because he seemed dangerous."

Brady stopped to unlock the heavy door before him. He pulled it open, and beyond him Kora could see a corridor lined by a row of holding cells, dimly lit by barred, dirty windows.

Brady stepped aside so Kora and Mace could pass him. "Amado's in the end cell," he said, gesturing down the hall. "He's the only murderer we've got here right now. You've got fifteen minutes with him, then I'll be back to get you."

As she heard the door thud shut behind her and

Brady's key turn in the lock, Kora felt a flutter of anxiety. The dim light and unpleasant smells of this place told her more than she needed to know about the despair of being locked away, even for the short time prisoners usually remained here before their trials.

Her desire to interview Amado lost some of its fire. She'd never been face-to-face with a murderer before, with someone evil enough to commit such an act, with someone now facing the possibility that he would never enjoy another day of freedom.

"I can take this one by myself, if you'd rather," Mace said quietly beside her.

Kora's head snapped up, angry with herself for letting him see her hesitation. "I think I can manage, but the minute I need you to take over my story from me, I'll let you know."

"I thought it was *our* story," he told the back of her head as she walked down the corridor.

Their footsteps echoed off the cool, whitewashed walls of the cells, sounding a desolate rhythm to the snores of the two drunks in the second cell they passed. The city required prisoners to be segregated by gender and crime, and Kora tried not to wonder which crime each cell represented today.

Kora wanted to pause to gather her courage before she reached Amado's cell, but she wouldn't give Mace the satisfaction of seeing her nervousness. She stepped forward to look boldly through the bars, then caught her breath in surprise.

The man staring back at her from his seat on the crude canvas cot was the Indian who had spoken to her at the scene of the murder, the one who had said the police would never catch the murderer.

In the shock of recognition, she spoke the first

thought that rose in her mind. "You were wrong." Her words sounded cold in her ears.

"What?" Mace asked, startled.

Diego Amado's face remained impassive, as did his voice. "Wrong? About what?"

"You said the police wouldn't catch Rosemarie's murderer. And they have."

She wasn't sure if the quiver in her voice was reaction to the discovery that she had stood within a few feet of a cold-blooded killer without knowing it, or indignation at the man's audacity the previous afternoon. She found her surprise at Amado's identity being replaced with the burning anger that had begun in her the moment she had seen Rosemarie Amado's body, frozen forever by death.

Mace touched her arm. "Kora," he murmured. She shook him off.

"I said the police did not care who killed that Indian woman, my wife," Amado replied, unperturbed. "They do not."

"Mr. Amado, I presume?" Mace asked in a tone of brisk efficiency, touching his pencil to his notebook. He didn't look at Kora, but she knew he was telling her to get herself under control.

She already had. Her desire to see Rosemarie's killer brought to justice gave her the strength to face the murderer. Kora opened her own notebook, but her eyes remained on Amado.

"I am Diego Amado," the man affirmed. "And you are reporters who have come to ask me why I murdered my wife."

"*Did* you kill your wife?" Mace asked.

"The police think I did," Amado replied, glancing at Kora.

"That doesn't answer my question," Mace pointed out.

"It doesn't matter whether or not I killed Rosemarie," Amado said. His voice remained dispassionate, but his dark eyes sparked. "If I said I didn't do it, no one would believe me. The police have more than enough evidence to convict and hang me. The story they will give you, which you will print, is that my wife was a whore, or at least an adulteress, and that I killed her in a fit of rage."

"If you give us your story, we'll print that, too," Kora told him, fighting down her pique at the implication that she and Mace were mere mouthpieces for the police to control.

Amado's face showed momentary amusement.

"Yes?" he asked skeptically.

"Yes," she replied, expecting him to back down.

"Here is my story, then."

Amado leaned backward on the cot to rest against the wall behind him. His voice remained cool and steady.

"When I was only a baby, my parents were murdered by two drunken white men out looking for wild Indians to kill, hunting them like animals. But even they would not kill a baby, so they took me back to the ranch they worked at. The rancher's wife made her husband take me to a Catholic orphanage near San Juan. The padres there gave me a Christian name. They taught me to read and to write, and they taught me that my people were savages living in sin and that I was lucky that I was an orphan."

That explained his accent, Kora thought. His speech had the lilting flavor of Spanish, though his English was impeccable. She had to admit his manner impressed her. He was a far cry from the inarticulate, desperate drunk she had conjured in her mind on the way to his cell.

Amado glanced at her and went on. "When I left the orphanage, I looked for work. There wasn't much that white people would hire a Digger for, even an educated one, but I found jobs and worked hard. I built fences, roped cattle, even dug graves for a while.

"Then I came to Sacramento and found work at Hampton's Livery Stable. I met Rosemarie here. Her people were Indians, Nisenan, like my parents had been, but they were converted, 'civilized,' like me. Her family—Rosemarie, her parents, and her brother—had been taken from their home after refusing to go to the reservation. They went to work for a wealthy family not far from here as indentured servants. The man who owned them thought even such slaves as these should be Christians. So I didn't think of Rosemarie as a savage, and I married her."

Kora found herself resisting Amado's words, though she knew well enough that in a free state with some strong southern sympathies, indenturing Indians had been allowed as a compromise on slavery until the Emancipation Proclamation had led to the abolishment of the practice last year. It wasn't so much what Amado said as how he said it that disturbed her. The man telling this story did not fit her idea of the type of person who could viciously, cravenly stab his wife in the back.

"After we married, I worked harder than anyone else at the stables, longer hours for less pay. Rosemarie worked as a maid, cleaning the parlors of rich people who wouldn't stoop to pick up a mop. But we didn't care, because we were saving our money. Rose's brother and I were going to buy ourselves a ranch as soon as we had enough. We planned to raise cattle and make our livings like real men."

Amado stopped. It took Kora a moment to realize that he had finished his story.

"You going to print that?" he asked finally.

"Mr. Amado, that's not exactly what we're looking for," she said, frustrated because somehow Amado's tale had shaken her firm belief in his guilt and she didn't know why. "You obviously want us to believe that you didn't kill your wife. But if you didn't, who did?"

Finally Amado's voice showed his anger. "I don't really care what you believe, Miss Reporter," he said, leaning toward her. "You will believe what is easiest for you. I will tell you that I believed what those padres said about the pagan Diggers. I thought God had favored me to escape their degraded savagery.

"But now I have lived in your society long enough to know I don't believe that any more. My wife's people still have relatives on the reservation who try to keep to the Indian ways. They do not have all the material things that white people have, but they have their own ways, their own honor. I don't believe any more in a society that will hang an Indian for killing a white man in self-defense, but does not punish a white man for killing an Indian for amusement. I don't respect a people who say their God is better because he says 'Love your neighbor,' and then use their neighbors' godlessness as an excuse to annihilate them."

Amado shut his mouth sharply, as though he hadn't intended to say so much.

"I don't think that is right, either," Kora told him, because she didn't know what else to say.

Amado stood and walked forward, pausing just before the iron bars that separated them. His voice was calm again, and his face almost sympathetic as he looked at her.

"You asked if I knew who killed my wife. I can't say. But if I did know a reason that someone might want to kill her, and that person was a white man, by your laws I would be unable to give evidence against him. Because I am an Indian. So, as I said, it doesn't matter if I killed her or not. I am still guilty."

Amado turned away and slowly lowered himself to his cot. Kora stared at him, her mind turning over what he'd said, trying to see into his soul to find the truth.

"Mr. Amado," Mace said, his voice insistent, "what you have told us is intriguing but not very helpful. Can't you at least give us something to go on so we can investigate this case?"

"I have nothing more to say."

"Just a name, a hint."

Amado lay back on the cot, his eyes on the ceiling. "Please, leave me alone now."

"Mr. Amado?" Kora tried, but it was as though the man had closed a door and could no longer hear them. She felt a knot forming in the pit of her stomach. If he wanted justice served, he couldn't hold back from them in this way. "Mr. Amado! Please!"

"Come, let him be," Mace said, taking her elbow. "Our fifteen minutes must be up."

Kora stiffened, but she allowed Mace to lead her down the corridor to the door.

Officer Brady let them back out into the main hall. He seemed disappointed that they hadn't been able to wring a confession from Amado, or at least an out-right denial. Kora let Mace deal with Brady, too locked in her own thoughts to say much of anything until they had escaped from the police station.

In contrast to the humid heat of the day before, high clouds covered the California sky, and a cool breeze tugged at Kora's skirts as she ascended the few steps out of the sunken station house courtyard up to Front Street. She shivered, feeling as though she'd escaped from the underground to find the world changed.

During their interview with Amado, she had real-ized that he spoke at least a partial truth. Having a convenient prime suspect, the police were unlikely to dig deeper into Rosemarie Amado's murder. And that meant an almost sure conviction for Diego Amado unless someone other than the police took steps to investigate the case. But none of that made him inno-cent, she reminded herself.

"What did you think of Amado's statement?" she asked Mace, not bothering to hide her own uncer-tainty.

"I think there's some question about the case," he said, "though the police have a good story."

Kora shook her head, checking both directions carefully today before crossing J Street.

"I'm not so sure they do," she said. "They keep implying that Amado killed his wife because she was a prostitute, but I saw her body yesterday. Her dress was quite proper, and she wore no rouge or paint of any kind."

"Hm."

Kora couldn't quite read the hesitation in Mace's expression. Ignoring it, she went on. "I suppose we could look for Rosemarie's brother and question him, but he's probably long gone. He is sure to realize he's the next logical suspect if the police can't make a murder charge stick to Amado. How about the people she worked for? Did you get their names?"

Mace said nothing as she stopped and opened her notebook to check for herself. "Osborn. A lawyer."

"Kora?"

When he didn't continue, she looked up at him. "What? Is something wrong?"

"This murder has really gotten to you, hasn't it?"

"What do you mean?" she asked suspiciously.

"I mean, it's important to you that Rosemarie's murderer be punished. More than just professionally important. Personally."

"Are you saying I'm too involved in this story to approach it professionally?" she asked, struggling to keep her temper, frayed from two days of betrayals and self-doubt, under control. "Or are you saying that I'm too emotional to be a reporter at all?"

Mace raised one eyebrow, surprised by her outburst. Then he grinned that devastating grin. "Kora, if I didn't think you could handle being a reporter, I would have dumped you yesterday. I didn't come out to California to be a mother hen to some silly girl."

Her agitation evaporated at the unexpected compliment, and despite its backhanded bite, she knew that was how Mace intended it.

"I'm probably nine or ten years older than you are," he continued. "I have slightly more experience than you do, and I don't want you to make the same mistakes I did. Caring too much about a story can lead to trouble. I don't want to see you get hurt."

He paused, and she nodded for him to go on.

"You know I reported on the war before I came out here." Mace made the statement without reference to the fact that he hadn't told her that himself. "Well, the war's still going on, but my boss, the editor-in-chief of the *Bay News,* was more than happy to send me safely off to California. I had begun to get too involved in the lives of the people the war was affecting. I was allowing my hatred for the war to influence the stories I sent in. He thought they were bad publicity, were weakening the morale of our readers. He pulled me from the front. And he was right to do it."

Kora tried to assimilate this information, this revelation from a man who had taken such care not to reveal himself. Something in the way he spoke, something in the way those deep blue eyes studied her, said her understanding was important to him.

"But don't you think the North is in the right?" she asked. "After all, it was the South that asked for a fight. Not only is the war necessary to preserve the Union, but it has led to the Emancipation Proclamation, the abolition of slavery."

He nodded, and Kora could tell he'd thought about such things often. "Slavery is one of the most heinous crimes ever perpetrated by man against his fellow beings. In a hundred years, the abolition of slavery will be worth all the lives that have been lost in this war. But right now, each life lost is some family's tragedy, and it may just take us a hundred years to recover from so much horror.

"I was at Chickamauga," he said simply, his expression hardening. Kora sensed that he was not seeing her but the hazy smoke of gunfire, not hearing the rattle of passing carriages but the screams of injured men. "I wandered out onto the battlefield after the first day of fighting. It was evening, but the bodies stood out against the green. I came across a Union soldier, a private. He was going through the pockets of a dead Confederate, taking his watch, his tobacco, even the letters he'd been carrying in the pocket over his heart."

Mace's face twisted with the disgust he'd felt. "I asked him what he thought he was doing. How he could dishonor the dead like that."

His gaze came back from the past and found Kora's again. "The soldier—he couldn't have been older than seventeen—looked up at me and said, 'He's my brother, sir. My mother will want these things to remember him by.' And that was my last war story."

He glanced away from her, but Kora saw the sadness, the weariness from the weight of these horrors. She reached out tentatively to place a hand on his arm, not knowing what to say. The grimness in his tone had torn at her heart, but she also felt a sense of wonder that he had let down his defenses to share something that had affected him so greatly. Mace Fielding's polite reserve was only a front after all, and behind it lay a man who could feel, and feel deeply.

"I'm sorry," she whispered, wanting to comfort him somehow, wanting to let him know she understood what telling her this had cost him.

Mace looked at her then. She couldn't read the expression in his eyes. He seemed puzzled, or maybe surprised at himself for telling her that story, but she also saw gratitude for her response, and something else, something indefinable and fleeting.

"So will you at least consider my advice?" he asked, recovering.

"You're right, I am emotionally involved." Kora startled herself with her own confession, knowing she'd never admit such a thing to Jared or her parents. "But there's something about this story that has caught me. I won't let Rosemarie's murderer go free. She was so young, so innocent. I just can't give it up, Mace."

"No, I don't suppose you can," he said.

With a jolt of astonishment, Kora suddenly understood that Mace was expecting her to work on this story with him as an equal, a story neither her mother nor her father thought she was capable of covering. He hadn't called her unladylike; he'd called her a reporter.

"I guess . . . I mean, I should have thanked you sooner for getting me past Officer Gant to see Amado," she said.

"I'm not sure I did you any favors, but he annoyed me."

Mace's face softened, and he reached over to brush away a wisp of hair that had escaped from Kora's bun to blow in her eyes. His fingers grazed her cheek with surprising gentleness.

A completely unexpected electrifying shiver ran through her body.

"Are you cold?" he asked, his voice as gentle as his touch. Before she could answer, he took off his frock coat and placed it over her shoulders, leaving a hand resting on her back.

"Is that better?"

She pulled the coat around her, feeling the warmth of his body retained by the black worsted. The slightly musky scent of him surrounded her, affecting her strangely. If it had been cold that had made her shiver, now she flushed with an unaccountable heat. She swayed slightly, and Mace's arm tightened across her back, steadying her.

"Kora? Are you all right?" He leaned closer to look into her face, his eyes searching hers with concern. Something about the sight of her made him catch his breath. The folds of his coat engulfed her, and her honey-colored hair shimmered against the black fabric. But it was her face that struck him—the intractable wisps of gold falling about her soft rose cheeks, making her look so young and vulnerable, a contrast to those warm, tawny eyes touching him with such an odd expression.

He wanted to reach out and touch her cheek again, feel the softness of her skin, smell the fragrance of her hair.

The strength of the sensations that ran through him at these thoughts shocked him. The memory of holding her on the riverfront rose in his mind, and he wondered how a kiss from that soft, warm mouth would feel. The idea stirred a fire in him that surged through his veins, stunning him with its heat.

"Kora?" he asked again, cursing the unaccountable huskiness of his voice.

She nodded, suddenly not trusting herself to speak with those keen eyes studying her so closely. She broke contact with them and gazed at the strong line of his jaw. The slight twist of his sensuous mouth reminded her involuntarily of that moment on the riverfront when she'd thought he was going to kiss her. The memory did nothing to calm her runaway pulse. For a second she half-feared he might be considering it again. The thrill of excitement that thought sent through her shocked her back to reality.

"I guess we'd better get back," she managed to say, stepping forward down the street.

"Yes," Mace agreed, walking beside her, but not taking his hand from its place near her shoulder. He told himself it was to ensure she didn't stumble; he couldn't make himself let her go.

Kora concentrated on gaining control of her breathing, something she couldn't remember ever having so much difficulty with. Her mind refused to focus on anything other than the closeness of Mace's tall, strong body beside her.

This is ridiculous, she told herself. *You're just having a reaction to this murder investigation, that's all. You'd be better off deciding how to handle that.*

She thought over what they'd learned today, trying to come up with something to ask Mace, anything to distract herself from her body's unwelcome response to his nearness. But the question that came out of her mouth related instead to the story he had just told her.

"Did your brother—did Jesse—die in the war?"

As soon as the words were out she wished them back. Mace pulled his hand from her as if it had been burned and crossed his arms on his chest.

But to Kora's surprise, he answered her. "No, he died long before the war." The words were cool, but the pain in his eyes was not. "He was trying to make a go of it on a ranch out in Missouri. Indians attacked the place one night and burned it to the ground. When my brother tried to escape the flames, they shot him and scalped him.

"Or so they say," he added, so softly that Kora couldn't decide whether she'd heard him correctly.

"What?"

Mace didn't answer. Her mention of Jesse had caught him off-guard, sending his mind spinning back to that horrible moment when Cecilia had told him his brother was dead. He'd known it before she'd spoken the words, read it in those emerald eyes, wide and dark with fear.

She'd described the attackers: half-naked, their bodies painted black, yellow, and red, the patterns vivid and alive in the awful red glare of the fire. How she'd escaped their notice, crawling out the cellar door and into the high, dead grass beyond the house, even she couldn't say.

And Booth Garrett had escaped, too, the only other survivor. His letter had confirmed that the Indians had caught Jesse, and that his death had at least been quick.

But unbeknownst to Garrett or Cecilia, there *had* been another survivor—or so that old man, Jackson, had claimed when Mace ran into him in a bar in Calbert, Missouri, years later. Jackson, Garrett's sometime stable hand, had been sleeping in the barn, which for some reason the Indians had not burned. Jackson claimed he'd gotten a good look at the painted savages and they weren't Indians at all.

Mace shook his head. Nothing but alcohol-induced fantasies, that's all the old drunk's theories could be. But something about Jackson's stories, something about the old man himself, had been the spur that finally sent Mace out to California.

"I'm sorry. I shouldn't have asked."

Kora's voice startled him out of his reverie. He glanced at her, and what he thought he saw in her eyes brought back in a rush his startling desire to touch her.

He stopped his hand before it could raise itself to her face, thrusting it deep into his pocket. He stepped away from Kora, breathing deeply in hope that the air would cool this unexpected heat.

"That's all right," he said as calmly as he could, though he couldn't quite remember what she was apologizing for. "Don't worry about it."

He heard her quicken her pace to keep up with him, but he didn't slow down. What had gotten into her to look at him like that, as though she cared what he was feeling? She'd been furious at him just moments before when she imagined he'd criticized her reporting.

He couldn't believe he'd told her about Chickamauga. Even his own mother didn't know he hadn't come back from the front voluntarily. But something about Kora said she would listen. Even Amado must have felt it, to tell them all he had.

Still, that didn't explain why he, Mason Fielding, would open up to a woman he hardly knew. Not when he understood the risks of trusting another person.

Mace ground his jaw, furious with himself. Kora was young and beautiful; it made sense for him to be attracted to her, to want her. It had been a long time since he'd been with a woman, but this particular woman meant trouble he could do without.

She was impulsive, headstrong, impossibly touchy about her work, and besides all that, she had something going with that Davies fellow from the *Union*. Mace had better get his lust in control and damn quick, because Kora Hunter was not what he needed right now.

He didn't think about the concern he'd felt when

she'd shivered earlier, the impulse that had made him wrap her in his coat. He didn't consider the feeling that made him want to protect her from the pain that investigating Rosemarie's murder was bound to cause her.

And if his feelings toward this golden girl hurrying beside him went beyond simple lust, surprising him with their tenderness, he buried them deep in the back recesses of his mind.

6

After she and Mace finished rewriting and editing the short piece on Rosemarie Amado's murder that was to run in the next day's paper, Kora spent the rest of the afternoon helping Max Logan set type. She usually dreaded the monotonous tasks required to ready the paper for publication, but today she welcomed the chores, focusing her mind on type and ink and advertising to keep from brooding over the problem of Rosemarie Amado's death or, worse yet, her intense reaction to Mason Fielding's touch earlier in the day.

To her relief, her father sent Mace and Dan Larsen, the senior reporter, home early. Ellis and Troy had developed their own peculiar system of setting and printing that looked like chaos to outsiders, but they managed to get the paper out on time every week. They attacked the job single-mindedly and preferred to do things themselves rather than risk mistakes.

The daily papers, more mechanized and efficient, did this every night, but the scaled-down equipment Ellis Hunter owned made getting the *Sacramento Valley Times* out even once a week a major undertaking. But the quality showed, for the *Valley Times* had already outlasted many of the other papers started in Sacramento in the 1850s.

Kora and Max had hardly finished setting the last story before they too were rushed out the door so the actual printing could begin.

"Tell your mother not to wait supper for us," Ellis told Kora on her way out. "We'll eat something cold whenever we get in."

He sent this reminder home every week. If he and Troy ever arrived home for supper on a Thursday evening, Kora firmly believed her mother would faint dead away. On Thursdays, Anna and Kora ate soup and freshly baked bread and talked. Usually, Kora looked forward to these times alone with her mother, but this week she was grateful her grandfather was visiting. His presence would keep the conversation safely away from Jared and his proposal.

Kora entered the house quietly, feeling guilty for wanting to avoid her mother and another scene like yesterday's. She slipped upstairs to her room and took her time washing up. Dodge came in after her, stretching luxuriously while she scratched his back. When he tired of that and wandered away to find a spot of fading sunlight on her bed, Kora took a deep breath and steeled herself to head back downstairs.

She was relieved to hear voices coming from behind the dining-room door. Her grandfather must have already arrived for supper, making her safe for the moment.

Indeed, when she entered the room, she discovered the table fully set and her grandfather already buttering a slice of warm bread while talking animatedly with Clemency Tate, Kora's closest friend.

"*Ach! Liebchen,* you're finally home," he announced, seeing that as permission to take a large bite from his bread.

"Don't let Mama catch you eating that before supper," Kora warned him with a smile. "Hello, Clem."

Clemency grinned, deepening the dimples under her rosy cheeks. "'Lo, Kora. I hope you don't mind, but your mother said I could invite myself over for supper. Ma and Pa are at it again."

Kora made a sympathetic face, not needing to reply. Clemency knew she was always welcome at the Hunters' house, especially when her parents were having one of their fights. These periodic flare-ups were never about anything in particular and invariably blew over by the next morning, but they were acrimonious and loud. Kora had never heard anyone howl louder than Mrs. Tate, except for her husband.

"Oh, good. You're home," Anna Hunter greeted her daughter as she entered from the kitchen, carrying a tureen of hot, thick pea soup. "Your grandfather would have eaten the bowls if you'd been much longer."

Anna shot her father a stern look, but he only smiled back. Kora noticed his jaw working surreptitiously as he finished the last bit of evidence that he hadn't waited for supper after all.

Kora enjoyed the warm, soothing soup and listened contentedly while Clemency gossiped about mutual acquaintances and her grandfather tried to find out if Clemency had a beau.

"What? Are all the men here blind? Why have none of them made of you a wife yet?" he asked in outrage when Clemency told him there was no one special.

"Clem has lots of beaux," Kora assured him. "She just can't decide among them."

Clemency shrugged, tossing her cinnamon-colored curls in imitation of a heartless flirt. "I'm not ready to be serious about any of them yet. I'm leaving that to Kora and Jared."

"*Ach,* that is so serious?" Fritz asked. Kora wondered at the sharp look her grandfather sent her.

"I haven't seen Harriet Moffet lately," she said, abruptly changing the subject. "Do you know what she's been doing, Clem?"

Clemency winked at her and let the subject of Jared drop for the moment.

After supper, Kora and Clemency helped Anna clean up while Fritz retired to the sitting room to light his pipe. Anna remained in the kitchen to prepare some cold meats and slice the leftover bread for Troy and Ellis's return.

Kora followed Clemency out to the front porch and joined her on the wooden bench. The air was cool but fresh, and the sky had finally cleared, leaving the lowering sun to fringe the few remaining clouds in white.

The two young women sat in silence for a moment, watching an empty wagon rumble by, the driver obviously looking forward to getting home.

"Well?" Clemency said finally, turning to Kora, her voice conveying some impatience.

"Well, what?"

Clemency pursed her lips. "Don't you have anything you want to tell me?"

"About what?"

"About Jared, silly. I thought I was your best friend."

Kora's stomach clenched. "What exactly are you talking about, Clem?"

"Don't play coy with me, Kora Hunter." Clemency's reply was light, but Kora saw a flash of hurt in her eyes. "Jared told me he'd proposed to you."

"He told you?" Kora stared at her in disbelief. Of course, the Tate and the Davies families were the best of friends, and such news was bound to trickle between them eventually, but she wouldn't have thought Jared would mention it to Clemency. Then again, he'd also mentioned it to her parents without her knowledge or consent.

"He assumed you'd already told me," Clemency said testily. "I must say, I would have expected to hear it from you first. Is there some particular reason you didn't want me to know?"

Kora caught the glint of tears in Clemency's china blue eyes. She could have kicked Jared for his thoughtlessness.

"Oh, Clem, I would have told you, right after he asked me, but . . . well, we had a big fight, and I've been trying to decide what I ought to do, and I didn't really want to talk about it."

Clemency sounded somewhat mollified when she asked, "A fight? What about? Haven't you accepted his proposal yet?"

She shook her head.

"Why on earth not?"

Kora gritted her teeth. She really didn't want to have this conversation. "He told me I have to quit writing altogether once we're married."

Clemency obviously didn't see the problem with that request. "Well, won't you? I mean, you can't work and raise a family at the same time."

Kora sighed. "I don't know, Clem. Maybe not. I just think I ought to be the one to make that decision, not Jared. It made me wonder . . . how I really feel about him."

In her most no-nonsense tone, Clemency said, "Let me give you some advice, Miss Hunter. Accept Jared's proposal. Not only is he handsome, charming, and devoted to you, but he's going to be someone important. I'll bet he could become governor some day if he put his mind to it. If you marry him, you'll never have a care in the world except what you're going to serve at your next dinner party. What more could you want? If you let him go, you'll be sorry."

Kora looked at her friend and couldn't help thinking that Clemency fit the model for the perfect wife she described much better than Kora ever would. Clemency loved planning dinners, always dressed in refined style, never had a hair out of place. If only she could learn to be like Clemency, she could live happily ever after as Jared's wife.

"Why don't you get married, Clem?" she asked, trying to shift the focus from herself. "You've had enough offers. That Phil McKinney certainly seemed crazy about you."

Clemency shrugged. "I want to make sure I get the best." She laughed, but Kora thought she caught an odd sadness in Clemency's eyes before she looked away. Kora decided not to push her. After all, she didn't want to talk about her own private life right now, either.

"My, my, who is that gorgeous gentleman? I do believe he's looking at us, Kora," Clemency said, patting Kora's arm to get her attention.

Kora followed her friend's gaze. Walking toward them in a suit of dark brown cheviot, with his matching bowler tilted rakishly on his thick, wavy dark hair, was Mace Fielding. A little shiver ran down Kora's spine.

"That's Mason Fielding," she said, managing to keep her voice calm. Even from a block away those piercing eyes caught hers and wouldn't let them go. "He's a reporter from Boston. He's working for my father."

"Oh, dear!" Clemency sighed theatrically. "Please tell me that little girl with him is his sister or his niece."

"That's Jessica, his daughter," Kora told her, but at Clemency's woeful expression, she relented. "He's a widower."

"Mmm." Her friend's expression brightened once more.

"Stop staring, Clem," Kora said, looking down at her clenched hands to keep her own eyes off the approaching figures. The fact that Mace was walking up her street toward her house at this time of evening should not make her feel flushed and unsure of herself. After all, just yesterday evening she'd detested the man.

Despite what she told herself, she couldn't control the jump of her heartbeat when she heard him say her name in that deep, crisp voice.

"Good evening, Kora."

She glanced up to see him standing with one hand on the rail of the porch, his lips in a slight smile as he looked up at her. For a moment her voice failed her.

"Hello, Kora," Jessica piped up from beside her father.

"Hello, Jess," Kora said, relieved that the words came out. "Good evening, Mace. I'm afraid you won't find my father at home. He's still down at the print shop."

Clemency's elbow jabbed sharply into her side.

Kora started, but Clemency smiled at her innocently. "Mace, Jessica, this is my good friend, Clemency Tate. Clem, meet Mason and Jessica Fielding."

Mace stepped around the railing and up the stairs to take Clemency's proffered hand.

"Pleased to meet you, Miss Tate," he said, bestowing on her one of his pulse-quickening grins.

"Why, thank you," Clemency answered, her voice soft and sweet as lemon meringue. For some reason this annoyed Kora. "Mr. Hunter's loss is our gain. Why don't you stay and join us for a while?"

"We didn't come over to see Kora's papa," Jessica announced as she sat down between Kora and Clemency on the bench. "We came to see Kora."

"Oh?" Kora glanced at Mace in surprise.

He smiled wryly. "I got an address for that fellow Osborn, the lawyer who employed Mrs. Amado. Since you're so eager to talk to him, I thought we might go over there this evening and see if he's home."

Kora felt her pulse quicken again, this time with the familiar excitement of tracking down a story. She grinned.

"I hope you don't mind if Jessica comes along," Mace continued. "Mrs. Johnson is out at a church meeting, and I didn't want to leave her home alone."

"Jessica can stay here with me and Mrs. Hunter," Clemency volunteered, forgetting to flirt. "Would that be all right, Jessica?"

Jessica's face fell, and she looked down at her toes.

"It's up to you, kitten," Mace assured her.

"We could bake some cookies and maybe get Mr. Kraus to tell us mining stories," Clemency said.

Jessica looked at Clemency, then up at her father. "I'll stay here," she finally said.

"Cookies prevail over your father's company yet again," Mace said mournfully. He looked at Kora. "Ready to go? Or would you prefer cookies, too?"

Something in the tone of the question made Kora's breath catch oddly again.

"Just let me go in and get my coat." In no time she was back on the porch, adjusting her coat and saying quick good-byes to Clemency and Jessica.

"Good luck," Clemency called after them.

The sun was beginning to set now, and the few soft clouds above them blushed a pale orange-pink. Kora buttoned her coat against the cool evening breeze, pulling stray tendrils of hair from under the collar. She breathed deeply, enjoying the freshness of the air and the peace of the city as it slowed for a moment between the sober industry of the day and the raucous carousing of a western night.

Kora glanced at Mace, who had pulled a cigarette from a pocket of his coat and was now fishing around for his box of matches.

"I didn't think you were all that interested in following up on this story," she said.

He shrugged. "Rosemarie Amado's murder strikes me as the sort of case where if the most obvious suspect, her husband, didn't actually do it, then the real killer may never be found at all. It's possible the crime was committed by someone who was a stranger to everyone who knew Mrs. Amado, maybe a stranger to her as well, and in that case we have absolutely nothing to go on."

He found a match and lit his cigarette before continuing, "Of course, if there is any connection to her friends or family, don't worry, we'll find it."

He grinned broadly at Kora. Somehow his air of cocksure self-confidence didn't irritate her this evening, perhaps because of his confession this morning that he knew he had limitations after all.

They walked in companionable silence, finally turning down a street almost as familiar to Kora as her own. Two blocks down she could make out the house where Jared and his family lived, and across the street was the Tates' tasteful, spacious home.

"This is it," Mace announced, stopping before the wrought-iron gate of the house beside them. "The Osborn residence."

Kora quickly examined the sober, white two-story building with its well-kept garden in front and lacy curtains in the windows. The door sported a large brass knocker in the shape of a lion's head. Mace sharply rapped it twice.

They waited a moment. Mace was about to try the knocker again when the door opened.

"Hello?" A well-dressed middle-aged woman looked out at them curiously. The gray silk of her dress on her dainty form and the way she peered at them, as though she needed glasses but refused to wear them, gave her the look of a dove happily watching the world from the safety of its dovecote.

"Mrs. Miles Osborn?" Mace asked.

"Yes, that's me. May I help you?"

"We're reporters from the *Sacramento Valley Times*," Kora explained. She allowed a note of professional sympathy into her voice. "We've been follow-ing the investigation into the death of Rosemarie Amado. We understand she worked for you, and we'd like to ask you some questions."

"Oh." Mrs. Osborn shook her head in polite dis-tress. "What a horrible tragedy. Horrible. Why don't you come in and sit down."

They followed Mrs. Osborn, still sighing and shak-ing her head, into her front parlor, a lavish room fur-nished in mahogany and velvet, with a baby grand piano in one corner and a rosewood china cabinet in another.

Kora settled herself carefully on the brown velvet settee, and Mace sat beside her. Because they were crowded on the small seat, his thigh grazed Kora's. She attempted to move over, but even scrunched uncomfortably against the arm of the settee, she couldn't escape touching him. Focusing her attention on the woman before them, she tried not to let her arm brush against Mace as she pulled her notebook from her coat pocket, then scolded herself for being so oversensitive to his presence.

Mrs. Osborn fluttered into the chair opposite them. She looked Kora up and down several times as though she wondered how the young woman across from her had come to call herself a reporter, but she couldn't quite bring herself to ask.

"Would you like some tea?" she queried instead. "I'd offer you coffee, too, but Rosemarie always made the coffee, and I keep getting it wrong somehow."

Mace shook his head, and Kora said, "No, thank you. We're fine."

"How may I help you?" Mrs. Osborn asked. "The police say her husband killed her. I suppose you know that. It's so hard to believe. She was such a good maid, never a minute's trouble.

"I had people tell me, 'Oh, you can't trust Diggers. They'll as soon steal all your silver as look at you.' I never listened. 'Not my Rose,' I'd say. 'She's as honest as you or I.' But I guess you never know what your servants do when they leave your home."

"Mrs. Osborn, just because someone killed Rosemarie doesn't mean she'd done anything wrong," Kora reminded her.

"Oh, I know," the woman assured her, then added in a whisper that managed to combine horror, embarrassment, and an air of conspiracy: "They say she was a prostitute, you see."

"Do you believe that, Mrs. Osborn?" Mace asked.

"Why, I suppose." She fluttered her hands nervously. "I mean, I wouldn't have thought it of her, she seemed so well behaved, but you just don't know."

"When did Mrs. Amado begin working for you?" Kora interjected. Mrs. Osborn didn't seem able to form a stable opinion of her own, but perhaps she'd be more coherent relating dry facts.

"Rose's family was indentured to our friends the Shipmans," the woman answered. "They recommended her to us, and she worked here about three years."

"Did you ever have any trouble with her?"

Mrs. Osborn shook her head emphatically. "Oh, no. She was always punctual and worked hard, and she was never insolent or impolite. You don't expect Diggers to be quick witted, but Rose was. Do you know, she even knew how to read. Miles just couldn't believe it when he found that out recently. Not that it's really necessary in a maid, but I liked to have her read my mail to me. Oh, I just don't know how I'll ever replace her.

"I hired a woman temporarily today, but she refused to start work until tomorrow, and I've had to do everything about the house myself. Well, you know we have a cook, Hannah, but I mean, all the serving and cleaning and everything has fallen to me. It's awful!"

"I can imagine," Mace murmured sympathetically, while Kora bit her tongue to keep from saying something rude. The woman's attitude might be aggravating, but she seemed happy to part with any information she had. And while her information didn't appear terribly useful at the moment, Kora knew they couldn't afford to antagonize her.

Kora opened her mouth to ask another question, but a voice from the hallway interrupted her.

"Dimity! I thought I heard voices. Do we have company?"

As the owner of the voice stepped into the parlor, Kora guessed he must be the lawyer, Mr. Osborn. He was wearing a conservative but expensive black frock coat, slacks of black superfine, and a burgundy silk waistcoat. He had a long face, and the corners of his mouth turned down, giving him a gloomy look, but he scrutinized his wife's guests with sharp, clear eyes.

"Oh! Miles, dear, I didn't want to disturb your work. These are reporters; they're here about Rose." Dimity Osborn's eager smile faded at her husband's deepening frown.

"I was told the police had solved the case," he said to Mace and Kora, his tone indicating he thought it rude of them to bring up such an ugly episode after it had been satisfactorily resolved. "What are you doing here?"

"We're gathering background information on Mrs. Amado for our newspaper," Mace replied. "And we're not completely convinced that Mr. Amado was the one who killed his wife."

Dimity Osborn gasped.

Her husband's thin brows met in a *V* over his nose and he folded his arms across his chest. "Do you have any evidence of this?"

"The police seem to think Mr. Amado killed his wife in a jealous rage," Mace replied. "But they haven't uncovered any evidence that she was actually with another man. We just don't think they've done enough investigation into this crime."

Miles Osborn responded with sharp disapproval. "Sir, your hunch, or whatever it is, does not warrant your coming to my house and frightening my wife with the thought that our maid's killer might still be loose."

Kora shot a look at Mrs. Osborn and thought that the faint flush in her cheeks came rather from the thrill of being at the center of so much attention than any personal distress about whether or not the police had caught the right man.

Miles Osborn's frown deepened. "You reporters are always criticizing the police, the government, the very institutions that make this a free and law-abiding nation. Why don't you learn to mind your own business and let the police do their job? I personally believe Mr. Amado killed Rosemarie, but it is up to the court to decide. In any case, it has nothing more to do with me or Mrs. Osborn. If you will please excuse us now?"

This last was an order rather than a request.

Dimity Osborn rose with Kora and Mace, her face

showing displeasure at her husband's rude treatment of her guests.

"Good evening," she said. "I hope this whole thing is cleared up soon."

"Thank you, so do we," Kora assured her. She followed Mace around Mr. Osborn's stern figure to the front door. They let themselves out but heard the door closed firmly behind them.

"I hate to say it, but I think that was a waste of time," Kora said as they walked together back toward her house.

"Maybe so, although even negative information can be helpful. Despite Mrs. Osborn's acceptance of the police theory that her maid was a prostitute, Rosemarie obviously never gave her employers any reason to think she was anything but a hardworking, responsible, moral woman."

Kora sighed. "I have to admit, I was hoping Miles Osborn would have a fit of guilt and sob out a confession when you said you didn't think Diego Amado was the culprit. He's not a pleasant person."

Mace laughed, a deep, heartening sound. "Well, I don't know. Osborn doesn't strike me as a vicious killer. But he sure didn't like the thought of our investigating the case."

"He doesn't like reporters much," she agreed.

She didn't really want to talk about the interview they'd just conducted because she had a feeling they had learned only that they didn't know what to do next. Mace, too, let the conversation lapse. Discouragement made the air colder and the walk longer.

Mace ran their talk with Dimity Osborn over again in his mind, but his instinct told him they hadn't learned anything useful or, at least, not anything that meshed usefully with the information they already had.

He looked at Kora, whose arms were folded across her chest, her eyes focused inward, lost in thought.

"Do you have a suggestion of where we should go from here?" he asked.

She shook her head.

"There must be something we're overlooking," she muttered, but her voice lacked conviction.

"Maybe there's nothing to overlook, Kora," Mace said gently. "Maybe Diego Amado really did kill her. If not, chances are it was some crazy, drunk gambler or miner who's fled town and will never be found."

Kora's chin came up. She looked at him now, and he saw fear that he might be right mingling with determination in her eyes.

"I don't think Amado killed her."

"Why not?"

"It's just a feeling I have." Her lips set as she said it, daring him to laugh.

He didn't. Instead he reminded her, "The police found the murder weapon inside the stable where he worked."

"That's right, they did!" Kora's eyes brightened suddenly. She looked eagerly at Mace, but he didn't understand the reason for her newfound excitement.

"Don't you see?" she asked, walking faster as she talked. "Amado wouldn't have been so stupid as to hide a bloody knife in the place he worked. He's obviously too intelligent to make a mistake like that. So whoever killed her must have known her."

"Why? How does that follow?"

Kora gathered her thoughts before answering, "Whoever killed her, assuming for the moment it wasn't her husband, could have found a better place to dispose of the knife if he didn't want it found. Why not throw it in the river or just take it home and wash it? If he had panicked, he would simply have left it with the body or tossed it down the alley instead of going to the trouble of hiding it in the stable."

Mace understood now where her argument led. "You're saying the murderer knew Rosemarie's husband worked at Hampton's Stable, and he was trying to throw suspicion onto him."

"Yes. It has to be."

Mace liked the way she looked with her eyes shining like that, picking up the faint light of the spring night, seeming hopeful for the first time since they'd left the jail earlier in the day. He wished he could share her optimism.

"Kora," he cautioned, "it's still possible that the killer had no idea who Rosemarie was and that he left the knife in the stable to keep the police focused on Hampton's employees until he could get safely out of town. And it's also possible that Amado did kill her and simply panicked."

He watched the smile fade from her face. They had reached her house, and she placed a hand on the railing of the porch stairs for support.

"But it's a place to start, isn't it?" she asked, almost wistfully.

The light from the lamp by the front door caught her hair, making it glow from the inside, like a jar of honey with the sun shining through, but her face was pale and troubled. At that moment, all Mace wanted was to pull her to him and tell her everything would be all right, to hold her slim body in his arms and kiss her until she forgot about such things as murder and knew only his touch.

He reached out to touch her cheek again, her skin as smooth and soft as satin, as warm as a peach ripened in the sun.

"It's a place to start," he agreed, his voice low and husky. His hand slid down to her jawline. Those glowing gold eyes darkened beneath their glittering lashes, and he could see the faint pulse at the base of her throat.

Warning signals clamored through Kora's body, but she couldn't break the spell that froze her there. Her body no longer obeyed her but responded only to Mace, to the faint pressure of his fingers tracing her jaw, tilting her chin. The world had gone silent except for the beating of her heart.

Her lips parted slightly, but she couldn't speak. She couldn't tell him to stop because she didn't want him to. And she knew he knew it as his head tilted down toward hers.

Suddenly he stopped and stepped back. As though from a great distance, Kora heard the front door open. Jessica's voice sliced through the silent night.

"Papa? Kora? I thought I heard voices out here, but then you didn't come in. Did you find what you were looking for?" She skipped across the porch to look down at them.

Mace cleared his throat, fighting down a brief surge of anger at his daughter.

"Not really. The Osborns weren't much help," he told her. He glanced at Kora, but she didn't look at him as she swept past him up the stairs and into the house.

"Papa?"

Jessica's worried tone angered him even more, implying that every time he was alone with Kora he did something to hurt or upset her. But then, he almost had.

"She's upset about this story." He ruffled Jessica's hair as he passed her on the porch. For heaven's sake, he should be grateful to his daughter for preventing him from doing something he'd sorely regret.

After recognizing his attraction to Kora this morning, he'd promised himself that he would keep their relationship strictly professional. But that was damn hard to remember out here in the summer night, with her soft scent in the air and those tender lips turned up to his. He felt his stomach tighten at the memory. She was more temptation than a man should have to handle, but he had to learn to control himself around her, for her sake as well as for his.

Kora was standing in the hall when Mace entered, but she still refused to look at him, motioning instead to Jessica who entered on his heels.

"You'd better put on your coat to walk home," she told Jessica. "It's chilly out there despite being almost June."

Kora helped the girl into her cloak, trying to ignore the silent man standing near the door.

"There you are!" Clemency's cheerful voice rang down the hall as she came out of the dining room. She handed a package wrapped in brown paper to Mace, who looked at it in confusion.

"Cookies," she explained with a laugh. She turned to Kora. "We'd just about given up on you two. Jessica and I thought you'd run off and eloped."

Kora couldn't muster a response to that, but her friend didn't seem to notice.

"Troy's back to have some supper," Clemency continued. "I guess the printing is going well tonight. He's just run out to see if he can find me a cab. I don't really want to walk home by myself in the dark." She turned her most charming smile on Mace, but he didn't react to the hint. Clemency was undeterred. "I'm sorry you have to go already. I hope we'll get a chance to know each other better."

Kora could have sworn Clemency actually fluttered her eyelashes.

"It would be my pleasure," Mace said. Then his eyes sought Kora's. "Good night, Kora."

"Good night," Kora replied, glancing away to keep herself from flushing. "Good night, Jessica."

"G'night, Kora. G'night, Clemency."

Once they were gone, Clemency heaved a deep sigh and placed a hand over her heart.

"Kora, he's gorgeous! No wonder you've been keeping him all to yourself."

"Don't be fooled by his appearance," Kora told her curtly. "He's rude and he has an awfully high opinion of himself." She felt a twinge of guilt, because she knew that since this morning she no longer quite believed that was all there was to Mason Fielding.

Clemency gave her a knowing smile. "Oh, come on, Kora. He's charming. True, he has a daughter, but she's charming, too. She says he doesn't have a sweetheart back in Boston. He seems ripe for the plucking, if you ask me."

Kora turned to the hall mirror, pretending to fix her hair. She tried to soften the scowl she saw on her face, but it wouldn't go away.

"Quit smirking, Clem," she said, her tone only half-joking. "If you're that interested, good hunting. But remember, I warned you."

Clemency's face appeared next to hers in the mirror. "Touchy, aren't you?" she teased, gently twisting one of her curls back into place. "If I didn't know how you felt about Jared, I'd swear you . . ."

"Don't be ridiculous!" Kora exclaimed, turning to face her friend, but finding herself unable to maintain eye contact. "It's hard enough having to work with Mace. I have no desire to spend any more time with him than I have to. Now can we talk about something else?"

Clemency shrugged. "I'm glad to hear you say that, because from the way *he* looked at *you* . . . Well, I'd have to say you'd be pretty stiff competition."

"Clem!" Kora glared at her, feeling her cheeks pinken, but footsteps on the front porch precluded further discussion. Clemency only smiled and swished her skirts as she turned back toward the door and opened it abruptly, admitting a surprised Troy.

"Hey!" He caught the door frame for balance. "I guess you're ready to go, aren't you, Clem? Your cab is right out front."

"Thank you, Troy." Clemency pecked him on the cheek and then turned to wink at Kora. "I'll be seeing you soon, Kora. And with any luck, you'll have *him* in tow."

"Him?" Troy asked after Clemency left. "What poor fellow is she after now?"

Kora just shook her head and hurried up the stairs to her room, leaving Troy staring after her.

Kora undressed in the dark, throwing her dress over a chair and splashing cold water over her face. This time she managed to avoid Dodge when she threw herself on the bed, but he howled in complaint anyway, dropping to the floor with a thud.

Kora buried her face in her pillow, wanting to

block out the whole evening, to hide away in the inky blackness and never come out.

What had she been thinking of? Last night Mason Fielding had made it perfectly clear that if she had any sort of crush on him, he was not at all interested. And tonight she had just stood there and waited for him to kiss her. No, not just waited, *wanted.* Her breath caught at the mere memory. She had wanted him to kiss her, wanted to feel those strong arms pulling her close.

She blushed in shame, pushing her face harder into the pillow. She hadn't even tried to hide it. Mace was probably chuckling to himself over her silliness right now, all his self-satisfied assumptions about her confirmed.

And Clemency! She hadn't helped a bit. Kora rolled over onto her back. It had been a long time since she'd been as angry with Clemency as she'd been downstairs with her just now. Her friend was very popular with men, but rarely coy the way she'd been with Mace tonight. She'd virtually thrown herself at him.

And she'd all but accused Kora of being jealous. That really was ridiculous! Clemency was living proof that just because you wanted to kiss a man didn't mean you were in love with him or felt jealous about him.

"And I'm certainly not in love with Mace. I'm in love with Jared," Kora told herself. But remembering Jared didn't make her feel any better.

Anyway, if Clemency wanted Mace, she was welcome to him, but Kora didn't think she was his type. Clemency needed a man with ambition, someone whose career she could direct and support. Not someone like Mace who had shrugged off family expectations to become a reporter, who would drop everything to set off for California and write about the frontier. Mace needed a wife who wouldn't mind the hardships of traveling, who would care for his daughter as though she were her own. Someone who considered reporting politics as important as being a politician.

Sounds like you, a voice inside her head mocked her. "Oh, be quiet," she mumbled.

She got up long enough to pull back the covers on her bed. She rolled into them, drawing them up to her chin. Only then did Dodge jump back up beside her and take his place behind the small of her back.

She had to think about Jared. She'd not only made a fool of herself tonight; she'd almost done something to jeopardize their relationship. He'd be back from San Francisco soon, wanting an answer to his proposal. She'd said she loved him. She'd loved him for years. She ought to accept.

Kora felt a knot in her forehead ease. Why not? He was a good man. She could marry him, even if it meant giving up reporting. Right now, reporting was causing her nothing but frustration, anyway. He'd said some thoughtless things to her, but proposing to a woman would make any man nervous. That was probably all her own reservations amounted to. She was too intelligent to expect marriage to be a case of "happily ever after." She would have to put aside youthful fantasies and face reality.

She relaxed, feeling a great weight lift from her chest. Giving up writing wouldn't end the world. She'd have plenty to keep her busy.

And once Jared came back and she told him she'd

marry him, they'd be so happy that she could forget all about Mace, forget how his touch had made her blood rush and her knees weaken. She could forget the foolish dream he had reawakened. The dream that it might be possible for a woman to be a reporter and work alongside her man, that there might be something more to love than what she felt toward Jared, that she might be missing something.

Kora stretched and closed her eyes, but a long time passed before she fell asleep.

7

The next two days passed surprisingly smoothly. Kora's decision to accept Jared's proposal acted as a shield against any embarrassment she might have felt around Mace. Mace seemed content to ignore what had almost happened between them, and Kora managed to convince herself that she had blown the whole incident out of proportion. Perhaps he had only been trying to comfort her and had no idea she thought there was anything more going on.

In a strange way, knowing she would marry Jared also allowed Kora to get to know Mace better, to enjoy simply being in his company. She found she liked showing him around Sacramento. Far from scorning the rough-edged, youthful city as she half-expected he would, he found it genuinely fascinating. He seemed to want to explore every block, from the city's beginnings at the confluence of the American and Sacramento Rivers, to its far edges where workmen were putting up new warehouses, schools, stores, and homes as fast as the materials to build them arrived.

Kora took him to Sutter's Fort, the heart of John Sutter's dream of a New Helvetia, which was destroyed by the cursed yellow metal James Marshall had found in Sutter's mill run. The fort had crumbled with the dream, the adobe walls collapsing, the few remaining buildings falling into ruin.

"I still see nobility here," she told him as they surveyed the wreck that had once been an outpost of civilization. "Hardly more than a decade ago this was a near-desolate wilderness. The people who settled this country must have had great vision and courage. But after talking with Diego Amado, I can't help wondering about the price the native people paid to make Sacramento possible."

"It does give you a different perspective," Mace agreed, his pencil flying across his notepad. "Why did Sutter build his fort so far from the river?"

"Our rivers are Sacramento's lifeblood, but they've also been her nemesis. Sutter foresaw the danger from floods, but those who came to cash in on the newfound gold refused to listen to him."

She took Mace down the embarcadero to see where the first merchants had peddled their wares to the miners pouring into gold country. This meager beginning of a city had killed John Sutter's hopes for Sutterville, the city he had planned on higher, drier ground. Kora pointed out where the Eagle Theatre had stood. One of the many buildings destroyed by the flood of 1850, it had nonetheless symbolized the strong public support for the theater and other arts that thrived in Sacramento.

They walked up J Street, which had been raised over four feet after the flood of 1852 and was being raised again now.

"I suppose the flood problem explains these darn sidewalks," Mace commented, stepping down a foot from one section to another.

"Each store has responsibility for raising itself and its street access to the new level," Kora told him. "It should all even out soon. The people of Sacramento refused to move to higher ground, so we're raising the ground itself. Not very practical perhaps, but industrious. With any luck, it should ensure that our commerce won't ever again be halted by such devastating floods."

During their excursions, she and Mace went by the Amados' house, a simple clapboard dwelling hardly more than a shed. The house was deserted, Rosemarie's brother having fled as Kora predicted. The neighbors told them no one had been there in days.

And neither the neighbors nor Diego Amado's co-workers at the livery stable could give them the names of any friends the Amados might have had.

One of the stable hands said bluntly, "Who's gonna be friends with an edyicated Digger?"

Mace's company and their ramblings about town together helped Kora keep the frustration she felt about the murder case back in a manageable corner of her mind. She happily encouraged Mace's insatiable curiosity. It made her see her city in a fresh light and appreciate anew the energy of the men and women who built it.

By Saturday night Kora's back ached and she had a blister on one heel, but she slept more soundly than she had in a long time.

Sunday she spent peacefully with her family, going to church and eating a huge midday meal that left them all pleasantly lethargic for an afternoon of reading, sewing, and quiet chatting in the sitting room.

"Anna, why don't you play us something on the piano," Ellis Hunter suggested during a lull in the already languid activity. "Maybe Kora will sing for us."

"What a good idea." Anna put down her mending to move over to the small piano. As she warmed her fingers with scales and rolling arpeggios, Kora suddenly remembered Mrs. Osborn's baby grand and wondered if anyone ever played it. Thoughts of Rosemarie Amado's life soon overwhelmed her—the young woman living in near poverty, dreaming of better things, while working for a woman who had everything she could possibly want but couldn't possibly appreciate.

Sitting safely in her parents' home, with the rich chords of Wesley's "The Eternal Life" enveloping her, Kora felt her throat constrict. Maybe they could look to God for salvation ultimately, but it didn't ease the pain here on earth of being helpless to save Diego Amado or avenge his wife's murder.

"Are you going to join in, Kora?"

Startled, Kora looked up at her father. "Oh, of course."

She rose to stand beside her mother at the piano and read the hymnal, though she knew the words by heart. She'd never had the patience to learn to play, much to her mother's chagrin, but she had always loved to sing.

As she sang, "O what a blessed hope is ours," she let the music carry her along, washing away her troubles as it always did—though as she got older, her troubles didn't stay away quite as long as they had when she was a child.

A knock on the sitting-room door interrupted her near the end of the second verse.

Troy jumped up to open the door, and Kora's heart stopped for a moment in consternation. It was Jared.

"Sorry. I rang the bell, but no one answered," he explained as Troy ushered him into the sitting room. "I hope I'm not intruding."

Kora recognized the delighted smile he gave at their surprise. It had made her feel warm down to her toes when she had been an unnoticed, tomboyish sixteen-year-old, but today it couldn't unfreeze her suddenly stiff limbs.

Her mother nudged Kora with her elbow, then rose from the piano bench to greet him. "Jared. You know you're always welcome here."

"You're back," was all Kora could think to say. From the odd look Jared gave her, she thought perhaps she shouldn't have said even that much.

"Yes, I am," he replied slowly, as though talking to a simpleton. "I was going to come back tomorrow, but I couldn't wait to see you, so I got on a steamer late last night, and here I am."

"We'd like to hear all about your trip," Anna told him. "But I suppose you and Kora will want to talk first."

Kora shot her mother a look. She wasn't sure she was ready to talk to Jared yet. Maybe she *did* want to hear about his trip to San Francisco first.

"Why don't we go sit out on the front porch," she suggested, knowing it would be too awkward to do anything else.

Jared smiled gratefully at Anna and took Kora's arm as they walked out into the hall.

"I think the parlor would be a little more private," he murmured to her, maneuvering her into the front room.

Kora thought so too, which was why she had suggested the porch. She wanted to be alone with Jared to accept his proposal, but this was all so sudden. She wasn't quite prepared.

"Jared . . ." she began nervously, but he interrupted by pulling her to him and closing his mouth on hers.

"Jared!" She pushed him away, irked by his presumption, but he hung onto her arms.

"Isn't this the way fiancés are supposed to greet each other?" he asked with a smile. "Or haven't you realized you have to tell me 'yes' yet?"

"What do you mean, I have to?" Kora asked. She knew she shouldn't be annoyed, but this wasn't going quite the way she had planned. She had wanted to surprise him, watch his face light up when she told him she'd marry him. She didn't like his thinking it was a foregone conclusion.

But Jared just laughed. "Who else is going to marry a wildcat who's been working as a reporter?" he teased.

"Maybe someone who wouldn't ask me to quit reporting just to marry him," Kora snapped.

She regretted the words instantly when Jared dropped her arms and his smile, but she couldn't apologize for them.

"Are you still all worked up about that?" he asked. "For heaven's sake, Kora, even your parents love the idea. Why are you being so stubborn? How long do you expect me to put up with it?"

She knew she should tell him she'd decided to accept his proposal. She had planned for two days just how she'd tell him and what she'd do to keep herself busy instead of reporting. But now that he stood before her, his handsome face looking arrogant in his impatience, the words wouldn't come.

"Have you thought about your demands at all?" she asked, with renewed certainty that he hadn't, not for a moment. "Have you thought about what you're asking *me* to put up with? Have you even considered that maybe my wish to continue being a reporter isn't just silly and stubborn?"

Jared threw himself down onto one of Anna Hunter's fine, uncomfortable parlor armchairs and sighed. Kora knew he didn't take what she was saying seriously. She had to turn away toward the windows to control her rising frustration.

"Kora, you know I'm right. Just admit it. Have you worked on a story since I've been gone that couldn't be reported just as well by someone else? Probably better? Sacramento doesn't need any more reporters, much less a woman reporter. It's not as though the topics you write about have any real significance. It's time you accept that."

As his words cut into her, she slowly turned to face him. He really didn't understand her at all, because if he did, those words would have been deliberately cruel.

"For your information, there is an important story that no one else is reporting," she said, struggling to get the words past the ache in her throat. "A young Indian woman was killed on Wednesday. The police have arrested her husband, but they've got the wrong man. The real murderer is still at large."

"And I read the piece your brother and Fielding wrote about it. Do you really think they needed your help collecting those meager details?"

Kora opened her mouth, but even now she couldn't tell him she wrote most of Troy's stories. Before, she had been afraid he'd tell her father. Now she realized he simply wouldn't believe her.

Jared shook his head, smiling slightly, and his tone softened to condescension as he turned his irritated slouch into a fatherly lean. "I'm not saying you don't work hard, Kora, or that it's your fault you can't see the facts as clearly as a man would. I simply don't think women should be reporters. They don't have access to all the necessary information, they don't have the stamina, and they're too emotional. Just look at how you're acting now."

Kora could only stare at him as he stood and came over to her. He placed a hand against her cheek. She had to suppress the urge to shy away in revulsion.

"That murder you mentioned is a small, unimportant story. The woman was obviously a prostitute, and her husband got tired of sharing. End of story. Sorry, Kora. Give up reporting and save your romantic outlook for our married life."

"How can you say that?" she whispered, looking into Jared's handsome, uncomprehending face and wondering who he was. "How can you say that?" she asked again, this time her voice coming out too loud.

"What?" he asked, seeming honestly confused.

Kora stepped away from him, the sobs building in her chest. She fought them down, but they caught her breath, making speaking difficult.

"You may not think much of me as a reporter," she said, the words coming in gasps at first, but getting stronger. "But at least I don't judge the importance of every story by how much it could advance my career. At least I still think justice is important."

She had built momentum now and couldn't stop, despite Jared's scowl. "You're not a reporter, Jared. You're just a politician in training. So don't you go around criticizing my instincts. Diego Amado did not murder his wife, and if you think I'm being emotional because I'm only a woman, well, Mace Fielding agrees with me."

He snorted. "Mace Fielding! Well, now, don't I feel silly." Anger and sarcasm dripped from his voice. "I'm sure Mr. Fielding—oh, excuse me, I mean 'Mace'—has a much better idea of what's what in Sacramento than I do, being such a pompous ass from Boston and all."

"That's not fair! He's not like that!" Kora told him, not so upset that she couldn't appreciate the irony of her defending Mace. "He's a better reporter than you'll ever be, because he actually cares about reporting."

"Oh? And is that why he's working for a second-rate weekly paper out here in California?" Jared's voice rose toward a shout as a vein began pulsing at his temple. "Working for a man too stubborn to see when the times have passed him by? If this is the only job he's fit for, I hardly think he qualifies as a journalistic genius."

Kora opened her mouth to defend her father, but shock and fury stole her voice.

"Damn it, Kora, what's got into you? You've been acting crazy this whole past week. I'm beginning to wonder if it's not more than just nerves, if you've completely lost your mind."

"No, Jared, you're the one who's acting crazy!" Kora finally yelled back, trying to break through the barrier of his failure to understand. "Everything was fine until you decided that asking me to marry you gave you the right to tell me what to do. And I was going to do it, too."

She finally had the sobs under control and looked at Jared without a film of tears, seeing him clearly perhaps for the first time. "I was going to accept your proposal today, but you never gave me the chance. And maybe it's just as well, because I got to see what you're really like. I think it's time you left."

"Christ, Kora!" He tried to grab her as she swept past him, but she pulled free and reached the stairs.

"Kora, you *will* marry me!" Jared shouted at her from the parlor doorway, his cool condescension completely gone. "You'll beg me to forgive you for this." The pain in his voice cut her, but his anger only made her back straighter and her step more determined.

"No, Jared. I don't think so."

She reached her room, closed the door behind her, and leaned against it, only then letting herself think about what had just happened. Her family must have heard all the yelling. Her mother would be furious with her for her rudeness, and her father would be even more sure that her reporting was a mistake.

The tears came now. Kora sank to the floor, burying her head in her hands. She wept as though her heart would break, but she didn't know herself whether she cried more for driving Jared away or for the loss of her childhood dreams of him, still more real to her than the Jared who had hurt her so badly today.

Worse than wanting her to quit being a reporter, he simply didn't think she ever had been a real reporter.

Her work meant nothing to him. Any man could have done it better, he had implied. Maybe her father believed that, too. Maybe that was why he was so eager for her to leave the business.

No, that was too much. She couldn't think about that. For a while she couldn't think about anything except that her life, so perfect just a few days ago, had fallen apart around her.

The sobs that shook her offered no comfort, but eventually they exhausted her and she could cry no more. She sat still, trying not to move or think, afraid the hurt would come back. Only silence came from downstairs. Jared must have left.

Then she heard the soft tread of feet on the stairs. Only her mother walked that quietly. The steps stopped before Kora's room, and knuckles rapped gently on the door. When she didn't answer, the knock came again, and the door opened. Kora didn't look up.

"Kora?" Her mother's skirts rustled as she kneeled down to sit beside her. Kora didn't think she'd ever seen her mother sit on the floor before. "What happened?" she asked.

Kora saw the concern in her eyes. "I don't want to talk about it, Mama," she managed to say.

"You decided not to marry him?"

"Oh, Mama," Kora said, her voice choking again. "I was going to accept his proposal. But then he said I wasn't a good reporter, and I wouldn't be missed if I wasn't working. And he . . . he . . ." She couldn't tell her mother what he'd said about her father.

Anna wrapped an arm around her and pulled her close. Kora gratefully leaned her head against her mother's shoulder.

"Shhh. I know it hurts," Anna murmured. They sat quietly, and for a fleeting moment the world felt safe to Kora again.

"I should never have allowed you to work for your father," Anna said finally, as much to herself as to Kora. "It was my responsibility to raise you to be a lady."

Kora sat up sharply and wiped away the last of her tears.

"It's not your fault, Mama. I would have found a way, with or without your permission."

The look in Anna's eyes told Kora her mother thought that highly unlikely. "Don't talk back, Kora," she said automatically. She rose to her feet, giving Kora a hand to help her up. "Did you tell Jared no?" she asked, her tone all business now.

Kora didn't answer.

"Do you still want to marry him?"

"Mama, how could I after what we said to each other?"

"A little argument isn't important. Married people argue. That's how it is. You have to learn to avoid arguing about ridiculous things. Like your reporting. You know, Kora, you can't go on like this. You'll end up an old maid, and if anything happened to your father, you'd have no one to support you. Give up this foolishness and marry Jared, if you have any sense at all. That is your mother's advice. Think about it."

Anna Hunter swept out of the room before Kora could protest.

But for once Kora had no intention of protesting. She walked over to her writing desk and sat heavily in the chair. There was no use in arguing with her mother or, for that matter, with her father. They obviously had their minds made up. But it still hurt that they refused to see her point of view.

She let her head drop to her arms resting on the desk. For once in her life she had no idea what to do. Her mother said to marry Jared. Jared said she *would* marry him. But something inside of her knew she'd be giving up a vital part of herself if she did.

She remembered her father's saying he would have chosen her mother over reporting without hesitation. He loved her that much. But Kora wondered if their love would have been so strong if her mother had been the type of person to insist he give up his life's work.

And suddenly she realized with blinding clarity that she didn't love Jared enough to give up everything for him. The fear of losing him, the fear of ending up a lonely old maid as her mother predicted, had blinded her to that. But she'd learned the painful truth this afternoon.

Now she had lost Jared—not Jared, really, but a dream of Jared she had believed in. And even though the image of herself without the sort of love and family her parents had achieved still frightened her, she nonetheless rejected her mother's notion that she couldn't take care of herself. She hadn't thought much about the nominal salary her father paid her for reporting, but she'd saved all that she hadn't spent on clothes and other necessities. If anything happened to her parents, she could manage to support herself with her writing. She could write dime novels, if nothing else.

She tried to consider the problem rationally, but her head hurt too badly to think. The thought of tomorrow loomed in her mind. When would Jared try to corner her into giving in? Going to work and suffering the disapproval of her mother and father would be awful enough, if they even let her go to work at all.

She tried to reject that possibility, but it nagged at her. Her parents kept saying the decision was hers, but perhaps they meant only if she made the decision they approved of. They hadn't treated her like a child in years, but suddenly they viewed her desire to make her own choices as willful and foolish.

And she felt like a child at the moment. She felt trapped upstairs, alone, as she had as a little girl when she'd been sent to her room to think about something bad she'd done.

She found herself wondering what advice Mace would give her if she asked him. Her reporting didn't seem to bother him. Of course, she couldn't actually ask his advice because he'd be off to gold country tomorrow morning with her grandfather.

Kora's thoughts drifted to her grandfather's claim. The sun beating down on the mountain, sparkling off the creek. No sounds except the gurgle of flowing water, the chirping of a bird or two, and the wind rustling the dry grasses.

That was a place where one could think.

The next morning Kora walked softly down the stairs, treading carefully to prevent the steps from creaking. Dodge made this difficult by twining about her legs at each tentative footfall. He seemed always to know when she was leaving and believed that breaking her neck would keep her safe at home with him.

Fritz's small satchel already sat by the door, and

Kora placed her heavy carpetbag beside it. The grand-father clock read five-fifteen.

She could hear him moving about the dining room, finishing up his breakfast. She heard his voice, speaking to someone.

Damn!

She'd been hoping to avoid a scene with her parents. She prayed they'd understand her need to get away, but no one had acted predictably lately, and she didn't want them to forbid her to go. She would go anyway, and she couldn't bear the thought of the rift it might cause in the family if she was forced to directly disobey them.

Her grandfather's voice came more clearly from the door of the dining room, "Tell the cab I'll be right there."

"I'll take your bag out, too," a cheerful voice replied, and Kora sighed with relief. Troy.

"Kora! I didn't expect you to be up for hours," her brother greeted her with a teasing smile. "You're just in time to see Grandpa off."

He paused as he reached down to lift the two bags by the door.

"Would you carry mine out, too?" Kora asked.

"You're going with Grandpa?"

Kora nodded, grinning at his surprise.

"Because of Jared?" The way he said it let Kora know he understood that Jared was reason enough.

She nodded again.

"Do you want to talk about it, sis?"

"No, but thank you," Kora replied, grateful she could count on Troy not to judge her.

"You know this will mean I'll actually have to write something for this week's paper, don't you?"

Even his comic grimace couldn't bring a smile to Kora's lips. "I know it will mean extra work for you, Troy. I'm sorry. If Mama and Papa have their way, you may have to get used to it."

Troy squeezed her shoulder. "Ma and Pa have never been a match for the two of us, kid. We'll work this out, don't worry. Do you want me to talk to them for you?"

She shook her head. "You stay on their good side. I don't want to cause any more problems than I already have. I do have a favor to ask, though. Feed Dodge for me?"

Troy glanced down at the anxious furball by her feet. "I suppose. Not that he couldn't afford to lose a pound or two. Let's get you out to the cab, then." He bent back down and lifted the two bags with a groan. "What do you have in here?"

"Rocks," she quipped, laughing as he rolled his eyes. She followed him out to the hansom cab to wait for her grandfather.

Mace stood in front of the Orleans Hotel, where the offices of the California Stage Company were located. The smoke from his cigarette burned his lungs and cleared his head of sleep. The sounds of the city echoed in the half-light—the clatter of a door here and there from a store being opened, a horse clopping down a side street nearby, the creaking of the traces of the stagecoach horses as they shifted in anticipation.

Mace looked back at Jessica, who sat on their bags, leaning against the wall of the hotel. She seemed to be only half-awake.

The door to the stage office closed with a bang, and the stage driver appeared. Dust coated his blue jeans, black waistcoat, and red bandanna, as though this were the end of the run instead of the beginning.

"Okay, folks, let's git yer luggage stowed."

Jessica stood, yawning sleepily, and Mace helped the driver lift their bags onto the coach.

"You folks kin have a seat," the driver said. "We'll be ready in a minute."

He proceeded to circle the stagecoach, checking the wheels, tugging the traces, patting the horses.

Jessica looked up at Mace, worry in her eyes. "What about Mr. Kraus, Papa?"

"I'm sure he'll be here any second," he assured her. "If not, we'll just take our things back off and go on the next stage."

They heard the clatter of a horse and carriage.

"There, that must be him now," Mace said, relieved, as the driver of the hansom cab turned onto Second Street and pulled up behind the stage. "Fritz! We were beginning to think we'd have to leave without you!" he called as the old man descended from the cab.

"I never leave a good breakfast before I have to," Fritz told him with a smile.

Mace took the two bags the old miner had lifted from the floor of the cab. He grunted. "What are you taking with you, Fritz? Rocks?"

"*Ach,* no. Something better. My granddaughter."

Mace looked up in time to see Kora step down onto the street. She smiled at him, almost shyly, her hand sweeping away a nonexistent stray hair. Mace wondered how she managed to look so lovely in that simple golden brown traveling outfit. She wore it tailored to her supple form, without hoops, in deference to their travel conditions.

"Kora! You're coming?" Jessica bolted past Mace to throw her arms around Kora, startling both Mace and Kora. "How wonderful! We'll have lots of fun."

"Of course we will." Kora took the girl's hand, and Jessica pulled her toward the stage. She glanced back again at Mace, still looking uncertain.

"Of course we will," he agreed, hardly knowing what he was saying. At the sight of Kora, a rush of conflicting emotions had run through him, foremost of which was a feeling of elation that she would be with them. He hadn't wanted to think of spending a week or more without seeing her.

Yet, his reaction bothered him. He wasn't setting off on a holiday; he had business to attend to. Still, he caught himself whistling as he tossed her bag onto the stage.

By the time they reached Placerville, Mace could hardly wait to get out of the coach and stretch his aching legs. Dust and a rough road had made the ride less than comfortable, and he had spent most of the journey trying not to get bounced forward into Kora's lap.

A bustling frontier town, despite the fact that its gold fields had all but run dry by 1864, Placerville had a life of its own. Not simply a mining town, it functioned as a last outfitting and resting stop for miners heading to their claims in the Sierras or to Nevada and the silver dreams there. It provided traveler, miner, and deadbeat alike with drinking, gambling, and a place to sleep for the night. Not to mention the more refined pursuits of theater and church.

The hot sun beat down on the dusty streets. Mace's lungs felt coated with the fine silt hanging in the air. And he knew the dust could only get worse as the summer arrived in earnest and dragged itself out, hot and merciless on the unsheltered foothills.

While the stage driver changed teams, Mace excused himself from the others to enter one of the town's several bars and get them all something to drink.

The saloon was dark, a cool relief after the blinding heat outside, but also disorienting. He had to pause a moment to let his eyes adjust.

Not one of the finer establishments in town, the place sported plank tables with splinters showing, unpainted walls, and a roof that sagged in places as though tired of its role in life. Only the bar looked cared for; it gleamed, being newly polished, and was clearly a haven for thirsty miners determined to spend a week's earnings in one glorious night.

Few patrons graced the saloon this early in the day. Some old men played cards at a table in the corner and a thin, apparently inebriated gentleman sat at the bar, noticing only the drink in his hand.

Mace approached the bar, watching the bartender size up his new customer.

"What can I get you?" The man's cultured accent surprised Mace.

"A beer, please. You from Boston?" he asked.

"Originally." The bartender slipped into his professionally amiable stance. "You're a Bostonian, too, aren't you? What brings you all the way out to nowhere?"

The man dipped a glass beneath the counter, then

swung it onto the bar, miraculously filled with a suspiciously pale brown liquid.

"I'm looking for a friend." It wasn't strictly true,
but then, a friend of his brother's was close enough to
being a friend of his.

Mace downed the beer. It might have been
watered, but anything was a blessing after that stage
ride.

"Another?"

Mace nodded.

"This friend live here in Placerville?"

Mace took a sip of his second beer and wondered
if the bartender added more water with each drink,
assuming his customers would be too drunk to notice
or too tired to care.

"Near here, I think," he answered, trying to match
the bartender's conversational tone. "Name's Garrett.
I hear he owns a mine now. The Bitter Creek Mine.
He told me to drop by when I got to California. I
don't suppose you could give me directions?"

"Not me," the man answered, "but Rusty sure can.
Hey, Rusty! Get over here and give this man directions to Bitter Creek."

One of the old men in the corner looked up from
the card game.

"Hell, I'm losin' anyway," he grumbled and walked
over to the bar. "You an investor?" he asked as Mace
motioned for the bartender to pour Rusty a beer.

Mace shook his head. "Just a friend."

"Hmph." Rusty took a swig of his beer. "Too bad.
They've struck the big lode, from what I hear."

The drunken man at the bar looked over at them
for the first time. "Somebody's always striking it
rich," he said bitterly. "Never means a damn thing."

Rusty shook his head in disagreement. "I tell ya, I saw one of them nuggets they took right off the ground there. Some fella was showin' it off all over McGillicuddy's Bar. I hear he got sacked, 'cause they didn't want it all public like that. Ain't that right, Abe?" he hollered. "They struck it rich an' lookin' for investors to expand the operation?"

One of his friends from the corner responded without looking up, "Yep. That's so."

"That's good to hear, for my friend's sake. So how do I get out there?" Mace was anxious to be going, thinking of the people waiting for him out in the heat.

"Well, it ain't hard. You got a piece of paper?"

Mace took out his reporter's notebook and Rusty marked down a surprisingly careful sketch of Placerville and the roads in and out of town.

"I'm a miner," Rusty explained. "A miner's got to know his way 'round a map. This here's the road to Washoe, right through town. And not more'n eight miles out, there's the road out to the Bitter Crick. It's out of the way, but the traffic's made the ruts clear 'nough."

Mace thanked the old miner heartily, bought him another beer, then ordered a pitcher of water to take out for the others to share.

Outside, under an awning in front of the post office, Kora downed a glass gratefully and made Jessica drink two.

"Dehydration is nothing to fool around with up in the Sierras," she insisted.

"The mountains back east aren't anything like this," Jessica marveled, hardly able to stand still, trying to take in all the sights around them.

Fritz chuckled. "We haven't hit the mountains yet,

Liebling. Ach, the little hills—they're nothing but babies."

Jessica looked toward Kora and Mace to see if they expected her to believe this.

"You'll see the snow on the peaks when we top this hill," Kora said.

After the relief of their brief rest, the heat and dust of the stagecoach were even more intolerable, but the scenery fascinated Mace as it subtly shifted from the open foothills—smooth slopes broken by stands of oak and nut pine and impenetrable thickets of manzanita, to the majestic forests of the Sierras themselves. Graceful yellow pines set the stage for the first noble sugar pines, towering two hundred and more feet into the sky, but themselves dwarfed by the snowy peaks beyond.

Compared with the morning's leg of the journey, they arrived in Bear Pass in a mercifully short time. Not much more than a stage stop with a general store, Bear Pass was the outpost nearest Fritz's claim. Leaving the stage behind, they followed Fritz to the Gold City Livery Stable to retrieve his mule and buy two more and a pony for Jessica. Fritz explained that they'd sell the animals back, at a substantially lower price, when they made the return trip.

Mace eyed his new mount warily. The pale gray beast had a stubborn set to its legs, and its lip curled above yellowing teeth as he approached.

"Can't we just walk to the claim?" he asked with a grimace when he noticed Kora watching him.

She laughed. "Well, it's a long walk, but you may be walking anyway, if the look in that animal's eye means anything."

She mounted her own dark-haired mule, a fairly

obliging animal as far as mules went. Mace walked around the side of his and had to dodge out of the way when the beast tried to bite his elbow.

"Isn't this fun, Papa?" Jessica asked. She had already established a rapport with her little pony and was eager to be going. "I feel like a miner already."

"All you need is a slouch hat and a gold pan," Kora said.

"Come on, Papa, let's go!"

Mace looked at the animal before him. He had learned to ride when he was three and felt at home in the saddle, but mules were something else again.

He gritted his teeth, grasped the reins firmly, and swung himself quickly into the saddle. The animal's drooping ears pricked up, and it threw its head back, but when the head jerked back down, Mace stopped it short with a heave on the reins. The mule tried to get its head down again, tensing to throw him through the nearest wall, but Mace hung on, pulling up on the reins until the beast snorted and began backing up.

Mace loosened the reins slightly and gave the mule a quick jab in its ribs. It shook its head but stepped forward, following the lead of Fritz and his mule.

Warily taking his eyes off the mule's twitching ears, Mace caught the look of admiration on Kora's face, but all she said was, "I'd keep a close rein on that fellow. He's still got a mean look in his eye."

Mace responded with a wry grin. "What? Prince here? He's just a little high spirited, is all."

Kora laughed and pulled her mule in behind his. "Just in case he tries to run back home," she teased.

Mace shot her a disgusted look over his shoulder but couldn't help returning her grin. That open, honest smile did something to his insides he couldn't quite explain away.

"I'm glad you could come," he told her, unable to make it the light comment he had intended.

Her eyes dropped from his, and he thought he saw her cheeks redden.

"I hope you don't mind," she said, suddenly self-conscious.

Mace knew he should mind, but as long as she was already here and there wasn't a thing he could do about it, he might as well enjoy it.

"Not at all," he answered. He could have sworn she blushed, and his desire for her rushed over him again like a wave. He could only be glad they weren't alone. It was getting too hard to control himself around her.

A sudden jolt made him whip back around and yank the reins to keep his mule from throwing him into a nearby thorn bush. Grateful for the distraction, he concentrated on keeping his seat for the next two hours.

8

Fritz Kraus's cabin sat in a small, flat clearing above a rushing mountain stream. As Kora's mule passed over a low rise and through a stand of scrubby pine trees, she pulled to a stop for a moment to take in the view. The afternoon heat was fading as the sun sank down behind them, and Kora knew again just what had drawn her grandfather to this little spot.

Yellow pine and white fir straggled up the rocky slopes around them, while closer by manzanita showed its ruddy limbs beneath dusty green leaves. Tucked in the shade of a hillside, golden California poppies nodded their bright heads in time to the slow rhythm of the day.

Her grandfather's cabin itself was nothing much to look at. When he'd staked a claim almost ten years ago, he had built it himself out of rough logs now turning gray with age. Even so, shaded by its guardian apple tree, it blended with the scenery, creating a picture of harmony.

The little shed at the edge of the clearing would hold only two of the mules, so Fritz found some wooden stakes and helped Jessica and Kora tie their animals where they could forage for grass.

"We'll keep your mule locked up," he told Mace. "He would love to get into my *garten* and then run back to home."

Kora glanced toward the fenced area downstream from the cabin. Soon the first small onions and carrots would be available for her grandfather's rabbit stew. Fritz had a knack with plants, though he kept the garden small in the vain hope that deer and rabbits would find it not worth raiding.

Kora and Jessica entered the cabin, opening the heavy brown curtains to the late rays of the sun while Mace and Fritz unloaded the mules and brought in their bags.

"Cozy," Mace commented as he paused in the doorway.

Fritz chuckled. "*Ja,* when you build it yourself, you economize."

Kora turned from the curtain she was tying back to glance about the cabin, realizing for the first time that she would be sharing this small space with a man to whom she was not related.

The cabin's main room served as kitchen, dining room, and living room. An iron stove sat near the middle of one wall, an arbitrary divider between the rough dining table and the living area, which consisted of an old couch and two homemade wooden chairs. A worn rug lay between the couch and chairs, and two pictures adorned the rough walls—a photograph of Kora's grandmother and a sketch of Sacramento's embarcadero in 1852.

A doorway next to the stove led into a small addition to the cabin that served as her grandfather's bedroom, containing a bed, a dresser, and a small table with a lamp. The only room with an actual door was the closet lean-to where Fritz kept his gardening tools and extra cots and blankets for when his family visited.

"Where are Kora and I going to sleep?" Jessica asked, immediately perceiving the crucial problem.

"Kora will take my bed, and I have a little cot just your size that used to be hers. I'll show you."

Fritz opened the closet and quickly found what he wanted. He set up the small cot next to the single bed, dropping a pillow and blanket atop it.

"And now for a door." He pulled out a huge red wool blanket, then a hammer and nails, and in no time closed the bedroom off from the rest of the cabin.

"See?" he said to Jessica, stepping back to admire his handiwork. "What do you think?"

"Great!" Jessica exclaimed. Fritz held the blanket aside for her to enter the newly created room.

Kora watched them, trying not to look at Mace. Somehow when she came here with her parents and Troy, that blanket seemed much more substantial.

"So where do Fritz and I sleep?" Mace asked, setting down the bags he'd brought in.

"I expect Grandpa will sleep on the couch and he'll pull out another cot for you," Kora answered, trying to sound matter-of-fact.

"This should be interesting," Mace murmured with a wicked smile at her.

Kora knew he was just trying to needle her, but she blushed anyway. She really hadn't thought this out last night. Being so near Mace twenty-four hours a day might disturb her more than her parents and Jared combined.

Mace raised one eyebrow in mock chagrin. "I had no idea things would be so . . . public. Do you think your grandfather will have a nightshirt I can borrow?"

Kora stared at him in shock at the implication of that comment, then realized he was teasing her again.

"You're awful!"

"You're right, I'm sorry." He almost looked contrite, except for the laughter in his eyes. "But you'd be awful, too, if you'd been the one riding Placerville Pete, terror of the Sierras, all afternoon."

The image of Mace cursing at his stubborn mule as it tried time after time to toss him down a gully or roll him onto a rock made Kora giggle and spoiled her righteous scowl.

Mace laughed, too, a sudden, heartening sound that echoed in the tiny cabin. As Kora released the tension that had gripped her since her fight with Jared, she collapsed onto the couch.

"What's so funny?" Jessica asked, coming back from the bedroom to bounce down beside Kora.

Kora looked at Mace, but he only shrugged and rolled his eyes.

"Nothing," she said finally, but she couldn't stop one last giggle as she said it.

Kora awoke the next morning to Jessica's excited chatter nearby. For a minute the sound disoriented her, but when her eyes focused on the rough wooden ceiling above her, she smiled. She sat up in her grand-father's bed and ran a hand through her hair.

Little light seeped around the heavy wool blanket that served as her wall, so the bedroom remained dim. Kora saw that Jessica's cot was empty and guessed from the clatter in the other room that she and Mace were watching Fritz make breakfast—omelettes, or so she hoped. Her stomach grumbled at the thought and she dressed quickly, wishing she had a mirror to check herself before going out to face Mace, and then feeling disgust at herself at the thought.

She hadn't fallen asleep as quickly as usual last night. The knowledge that Mace slept in the next room, separated from her only by her grandfather's blanket—and Jessica and Grandpa, she reminded her-self—had kept running through her head. And he had evidently not slept well either, the creaking of his cot a constant reminder of his all-too-male presence in the surprisingly hot cabin.

After she and Jessica had retired, Kora had heard him changing in the other room and had been unable to stop herself from wondering what he looked like bare chested, in the dim lamplight. She wondered also what it would be like to touch that chest, the thick curly hair, the skin taut over the hard muscles.

Stop it, Kora ordered herself sharply. The very memory of her thoughts made her blush and caused her breathing to quicken. She shouldn't think such things about a man, any man, but especially not one as dangerously handsome as Mace Fielding.

Whatever protection her childish illusions about Jared had given her against her attraction to Mace, it had begun to evaporate when she stepped out of the cab at the Orleans Hotel yesterday morning. No longer feeling bound to Jared, she was forced to see Mace not as the eastern dandy she had first taken him to be, nor as the fellow reporter she had come to enjoy working with, but as a very attractive single man.

The thought frightened her a little. After her disastrous near-engagement to Jared, she didn't quite trust her feelings, which made it even more difficult to decide just what those feelings were. She couldn't say now exactly when her feelings toward Jared, whatever they were, had changed. She certainly wasn't ready to be hurt again the way Jared had hurt her Sunday. But she found herself not knowing how to act around Mace, and her curious reporter's mind wondered things about him that weren't any of her business.

Of course, it wasn't as though she had anything to worry about. Mace had made it clear enough that he wasn't interested in anything more than friendship with her.

At least that's what he said, a little voice nagged her, *but* . . . She remembered the way he'd looked at her when he'd almost kissed her on her porch. What had that meant?

Kora knew she should put all this out of her mind. If Mace found her attractive, he could let her know, and if not, she wasn't going to make a fool out of herself, acting like a blushing schoolgirl. She had more important things to concern herself with. Her parents wanted her to quit reporting, and she had to decide what she wanted to do. She had no time to waste on self-satisfied, arrogant, irritating men.

Still, she pinched her cheeks to give them a little color before she pulled aside the blanket to step into the main room of the cabin.

Her grandfather and Jessica stood before the stove, concentrating on the golden flapjacks in the cast-iron skillet. Kora's disappointment that breakfast would not be omelette increased when she realized that Mace wasn't there. She supposed he was out enjoying the spring morning. Morning and evening were pure delights at that time of year in the mountains.

"Morning, Kora," Jessica said with her usual good cheer. "We're having real miner's flapjacks for breakfast!"

"Morning, Jess," Kora answered with a smile. She looked at her grandfather. "I know you brought sausages from Sacramento. Are we having them, too?"

"Of course!" He pointed to a plate of sizzling patties already on the table. "And now these are ready, too."

He ran a spatula under each of the four golden circles in the skillet, flipping them onto a pile waiting on a plate nearby. He poured out the last of the batter into four more circles.

"We thought we'd have to drag you out of bed to eat."

"I guess I was tired," Kora admitted.

"We're going to look for gold today," Jessica told her. "Mr. Kraus is going to teach me to use a gold pan."

She left the stove for a minute to fetch a large, shallow black pan from beside the door.

"See those grooves?" She pointed out the ridges curving along one half of the pan, glancing up from under her dark bangs to make sure Kora was watching. "You use those to catch the gold flakes when you swirl the dirt around in the water."

Kora had been just about Jessica's age when her grandfather had taught her to pan for gold. She'd found it terribly exciting for about the first ten minutes, until her back and arms began to ache and her dress got all wet. Making matters worse, she had tilted the pan too far, sending the tiny flakes she'd caught spinning away in the clear stream water.

"The best part of panning is the picnic at lunch, is it not so?" Fritz said.

"But of course," Kora agreed heartily, making her grandfather chuckle.

"I think we're done," he said, placing the last of the pancakes on the plate. He carried them to the table and sat on the bench beneath the window.

Kora sat across from him next to Jessica. Only three places were set for breakfast.

"Should we wait for Mace?" she asked.

"He's gone already," her grandfather said.

"What? Where?" Kora looked up at the door as though she expected Mace to come through it.

"He wanted to go see a real mine," Fritz replied. "It's two or more hours away, so he got started early."

Kora dropped her butter knife to her plate. He'd left to go to a mine, without even telling her. Was he that caught up in the gold fever after all?

But Fritz's words sent suspicion of another kind prickling through her.

"You suggested a mine for him to visit?"

Fritz shook his head. "He already had directions."

"Did he say where he was going?"

"*Nein.*" Fritz looked at her speculatively. "But his notebook was opened on the table."

"And?" she pressed.

"There was a map to Bitter Creek Mine."

A hot coal of anger burned in Kora's stomach. If Mace had a map to a specific mine in his notebook, he must have intended to go there from the moment they began this trip. That could only mean he was pursuing a story. And that he had decided not to include her.

"Can you draw a map for me?" she asked her grandfather.

His expression was dubious, but he took the pad and pencil she offered.

"They say they have hit it rich at Bitter Creek," he told her as he drew.

"Don't you believe it?"

Fritz shrugged. "The mountains aren't so kind," he said. "They are better at taking than giving, *nein?* If Bitter Creek is rich now, tomorrow may they have an avalanche. That is how it goes if you love the mountains only for the gold."

He finished his map and turned it so Kora could see. "You take this road there from Placerville," he explained, pointing to one of the lines he had drawn. "But from here, it is faster. You take this trail around this mountain here. You see? You cut onto the Bitter Creek road there. The owner is a man called Garrett."

Kora nodded. "How long ago did Mace leave?"

"A half hour, maybe an hour."

Kora smiled.

"Kora? Aren't you going to eat your breakfast?"

She looked down at Jessica's anxious face. "Why not?" she said, her spirits rising again. No need to go hungry just because she was angry with Mace. She ate a stack of pancakes and a generous helping of sausage.

"You don't mind if I watch you get rich tomorrow, do you?" she asked Jessica after they'd cleaned up the remains of the meal. She went into their bedroom to get her hat and jacket.

"No, that's all right." Jessica glanced around. Fritz had gone out to the outhouse. Still, she lowered her voice to say, "Don't be mad at Papa for going off without telling us. He's been acting strange since he decided we should come out here."

Kora looked down at the girl by her side. She was eager to be on her way, but something was obviously troubling Jessica.

"Why do you think he's acting strange?" she asked, sitting down on the bed.

Jessica sat down beside her. "I don't know." She glanced up at Kora. "I think it has to do with my mother."

Kora was startled. In the time she'd known him, Mace had never discussed his deceased wife with her, and she knew Jessica had never known her.

"Why do you say that?" she asked.

Instead of answering right away, Jessica got up and pulled her bag from under her cot. She dug through it until she found a silver-framed picture, which she brought over to Kora.

"That's her," she said, as Kora took it from her. "Her name was Cecilia."

The portrait showed a young woman with large eyes, a sharp nose, and a sensuous mouth. Unruly curls framed her oval face, and from the pale scattering of freckles on the woman's nose, Kora guessed the hair to be red.

"She's lovely," she said finally, not sure why that weighed so heavily on her spirits.

Jessica shrugged. "I guess so."

Kora waited for her to continue.

"Papa gave me that picture when I was five. It's the only picture he had of her, but he never asked to see it or anything after that. When Mr. McDougall got sick and asked him to go to California, Papa said no at first. Grandmother didn't want him to, and he didn't know what he'd do with me. But a couple of nights later I was going to the kitchen to get some water, and I found him asleep in the study. This picture was on his lap—he must have gone into my room to get it after I fell asleep. The next day he told me to get packed, we were going to California. The picture must have had something to do with it."

The image of Mace sitting alone with a photograph of his dead wife on his knee struck Kora with sadness, but she couldn't see any connection to his trip west.

"Maybe he just didn't want to leave the house where they'd been happy together," she said, the thought making her stomach tighten strangely. "Maybe it was hard for him to say good-bye."

But the words didn't make Jessica any happier than they made Kora. "Maybe," Jessica said doubtfully. "He never talks to me about her. He'll talk about anything else, but not her. And I can't ask my grandmother about her. Grandmother hated her."

From the troubled look on Jessica's face, Kora guessed that Jessica's grandmother had never tried to hide that hatred from the little girl.

"What about your mother's parents?" she asked.

"They died before I was born."

They fell silent for a moment, but Kora could tell Jessica was struggling with something. She waited for the girl to speak.

"Sometimes I think he doesn't want to tell me about her because she died because of me," Jessica confessed finally, her voice hardly more than a whisper.

"Oh, Jess." Kora wrapped her arms around the girl's shoulders and hugged her tight. "Don't you even think such things. The fact that your mother died in childbirth is not your fault, and your father doesn't think that for a minute. You know how much he loves you."

Much about Mace Fielding remained a mystery to Kora, but there was no questioning his love for his daughter.

"I know it," Jessica said. She wiped the corners of her eyes with the back of her hand. "But I want to know what my mother had to do with us coming to California."

Kora took Jessica's hand, so small next to her own. "Honey, whatever your father's reasons for coming to Sacramento, I doubt it has anything to do with your mother."

"Maybe not, but maybe you could find out? He might talk to you. He likes you."

Kora squeezed Jessica's hand. It couldn't hurt to mention Jessica's concerns to Mace. He probably had no idea his daughter was so curious about her mother.

The thought popped into Kora's mind that Mace could be still so in love with his wife that he couldn't bear to talk about her. That might explain his odd behavior when it came to Kora herself. She'd suspected that Mace hid some kind of pain behind his polite facade.

But the theory that he was pining away after his dead wife didn't sit well with her. It didn't satisfy her reporter's instinct for the story.

But then, maybe that was just because she didn't *want* it to be true . . .

"If your father doesn't want to talk, he sure won't talk to me," Kora finally said. "But I'll see what I can do, okay?"

Jessica nodded.

"I'd better go find him, then. And you'd better concentrate on finding us some gold."

She gave Jessica a reassuring smile. Jessica smiled back, unable to remain too solemn for long. Kora gave her a quick hug and then hurried outside.

Her grandfather was standing down by the stream, smoking his pipe. He looked up and waved to her as she crossed to the mule shed. He must have been intentionally giving her and Jessica time to talk, because he now headed back to the cabin.

Kora wasted no time in saddling her mule, her anger at Mace's desertion of her stronger than the worries that Jessica had raised.

Eating breakfast and talking with Jessica had given Mace a sizable head start, but her map gave her quite an advantage over him, since he had probably gone most of the way back to Placerville to find the road to the Bitter Creek Mine. If she didn't catch him on the way, she would arrive not far behind him.

"Mr. Garrett said to show you into his study. Follow me," directed the heavyset, elderly housekeeper.

Swatting fruitlessly at the dust caked on his blue jeans, Mace followed her down the paneled hallway. He'd worn an old shirt and coat for the ride out to the mine, assuming Garrett's place would be as rough as Fritz Kraus's cabin. He'd been unprepared for this well-built ranch house set in a little yellow valley populated by a small herd of cows.

The miner from the bar had marked "Garrett's Ranch" on his map, and Mace had decided to stop there before going on to the mine. As luck would have it, Garrett hadn't yet left for his daily inspection of the mine's activities.

The housekeeper stopped at the end of the hall and opened the door to Booth Garrett's study.

"Here's Mr. Fielding, Mr. Garrett," she announced, then stood aside for Mace to enter.

Garrett's office looked more as though it belonged in downtown Boston than on a western ranch. Mace's boots sank in the thick red carpet. Two of the dark paneled walls supported polished bookshelves half-full of a variety of practical volumes. The focus of the room was a huge oak desk, covered with curling maps of California and the Bitter Creek Mine.

The man behind the desk rose quickly to cross to Mace and shake his hand.

"Mr. Fielding. What a pleasure. I remember your brother with great fondness."

Booth Garrett appeared to be in his late thirties, though gray already peppered his wiry brown hair. He wore gray tweed and recently polished black boots, the image of a country gentleman. His sharp blue eyes sized Mace up quickly, while his mouth smiled a hearty welcome beneath his drooping mustache.

"Mr. Garrett." Mace shook the man's hand. He wasn't sure how to go on, now that he'd finally found the man he'd been looking for.

"Sit down, sit down," Garrett said, offering the chair before his desk. "Would you like some coffee? Or perhaps something stronger?"

"Maybe a glass of water, if it's not too much trouble," Mace said. His throat ached from the dry ride he'd had this morning.

"Of course." Garrett poked his head out the study door. "Ingrid! Some lemonade for our guest."

He returned to his desk and sat down. Leaning back, he rested his right ankle on his left knee.

"Mr. Mason Fielding," he said again, shaking his head with a smile as though he couldn't quite believe it. "What brings you to California?"

"I came out here to do some reporting for the *Sacramento Valley Times.*"

Garrett's eyebrows rose. "Are you here to do a story on Bitter Creek? I'm flattered, though I must say I didn't expect the news of our good fortune to spread to the city quite so quickly. We've been trying to be discreet. Ah, well, rumors fly fast." He hardly seemed displeased by the idea.

"I would like to visit the mine," Mace said, trying to decide how to continue, "but to be honest . . ."

A knock at the study door interrupted him.

"Your lemonade, Mr. Garrett," Ingrid announced as she entered, carrying a tray with a pitcher and two glasses.

"That's fine, Ingrid." Garrett waved her away as she put the tray down on the desk. Garrett poured lemonade into the two glasses and handed one to Mace.

"You were saying?"

Mace took a sip of the lemonade, letting the sweet-sour liquid soothe his dry throat.

"To be honest," he continued, "I came out here to see you."

Garrett's eyebrows rose even farther and he smiled, though something about his manner told Mace he wasn't as pleased as he sounded. "Again, I'm flattered. What can I do for you?"

Mace steeled himself. He was finally going to learn what he needed to know. It was too late to wonder if he really wanted to hear the truth.

"It's about my brother, Mr. Garrett, about his death."

Garrett shifted in his chair, dropping his right foot back to the floor.

"That was a long time ago, Mr. Fielding."

Mace nodded. "Yes, I know. When we got your letter informing us of Jesse's death, it explained all we wanted to know at the time. But since then, well, some questions have arisen."

Garrett frowned, and his tone hardened. "Mr. Fielding, if this is about your brother's property, I can only say what I said in the letter, which is that our partnership specifically indicated that if either your brother or I died without issue, the other would receive his half of the partnership. Your family is entitled to none of the money I received from that partnership. I have the papers, if you would like to examine them."

Mace felt his intention to like Garrett for Jesse's sake fade. He didn't appreciate the implication that he would follow a man across the country to try to steal his legally gained property. "No, this has nothing to do with money. I'm sure all of that is in order."

"Very well. I'm sorry I jumped to that conclusion. Please go on." Garrett leaned back in his chair, but the air of relaxed goodwill did not return.

"This is very difficult for me to say," Mace began again. "Although we had had a falling-out, I loved my brother, and I find it hard to believe ill of him."

Garrett's eyes met his with guarded curiosity.

"I went out to Kansas when it became a state to report on the violence there," Mace continued. "On my way home, I stopped by Calbert, Missouri, to see where you and my brother had your ranch."

"Not much to see."

Garrett was right. There had been nothing left but some burned-out ruins twenty yards from the railroad tracks. Mace had simply stood there, staring at the scorched earth and crumbling remains of walls, wondering why he'd gone out there at all. Guilt, he supposed, and anger that he hadn't had a chance to make peace with Jesse before he died.

He sighed. "No, not much to see. But I stopped by a bar in Calbert, and I ran into a man who said he used to work for you, an old man called Jackson."

Garrett froze. "Jackson, you say? Yes, I remember him. Bit of a drunk, but I gave him work when I had it."

Mace fixed his eyes on Garrett. "There's no easy way to say this," he said grimly. "Jackson told me you and Jesse had had a disagreement about selling the ranch to the railroad. He said you didn't want to sell, refused to, in fact." He took a deep breath.

"Mr. Garrett, Jackson told me you weren't attacked by Indians at all. He believes my brother made a deal with some unscrupulous railroad men to have you killed so he could get the money from the ranch sale. He thinks the railroad men got greedy and decided it would be cheaper just to kill you both."

While he spoke these words, Mace watched Garrett's face go hard and blank, then fill with surprise. Despite his personal interest in Garrett's response, Mace wondered what the man had been anticipating that had made him so tense. Whatever his expectation,

Mace's words hadn't fulfilled it. Slowly Garrett began to shake his head.

"No," he said tentatively, then more firmly, "No. That's simply ludicrous. Jesse could never have done something like that. I knew that you two had quarreled, though he would never say why, but even so, you must know he would never even have thought of such a thing."

Mace clenched his fist. *Not alone, he wouldn't.* "Jackson said he heard Jesse arguing with Cecilia, that she was adamant that they sell. She said Jesse had to give up his stupid, stubborn pride and do what had to be done."

Garrett shook his head again, relaxing back into his chair.

"I'm sure such words must have bothered you, Mr. Fielding, but Clancy Jackson has never been a reliable source of information."

He took a sip of the lemonade that had sat forgotten on his desk. Absurdly, Garrett's very casualness made Mace suspicious. He could have sworn the man was hiding something.

"I agreed with Jesse that we should sell two days before the attack," Garrett said. "We'd already begun talking with the railroad people. I don't know what stories you've been hearing, Mr. Fielding, but not all railroad men are outlaws."

He chuckled briefly, then his expression turned serious. "Besides which, I was there when we were attacked. I saw those sons-of-bitches close up. Sometimes I still see them in my nightmares. They were Indians all right. As savage as wolves. Bent on nothing more than senseless destruction."

Mace let out a long breath. He felt as though he'd

been holding it since he left Calbert, three years ago.

"Then, in the end, Cecilia told the truth," he murmured, relief flooding through him. Whatever Garrett's hidden agenda, Mace's instincts told him that he'd spoken the truth about Jesse. His doubts about the wisdom of coming to visit Garrett faded away. He'd needed to find this out, both for his own sake and for Jessica's, though she'd never know it.

"Cecilia told the truth about what?" Garrett asked sharply.

Mace looked up, startled. He hadn't realized he'd spoken aloud. "About the attack," he said, and then he remembered that Garrett knew nothing of Cecilia's escape, just as she had never known that Garrett had survived.

"Cecilia Shaughnessey died in the attack that night." Garrett rose, his face darkening.

Mace shook his head. "No. She escaped by crawling into some tall grass. She said she must have passed out, and when she came to, the house was burned to the ground. She assumed both you and Jesse had died. She was afraid, and she ran. She came back to Boston."

Anger and surprise and something else flickered across Garrett's face. His voice came out oddly strained and flat. "For God's sake, why didn't you tell me that when I wrote to you? All these years I thought she was dead."

"I'm sorry." Mace felt the familiar lump of grief and guilt in his stomach. "She died of pneumonia soon after she reached my house, before we even got your letter. I saw no reason to trouble you with that."

Garrett stared at him silently for a moment, an

unreadable expression in his glittering eyes. Mace knew what the next question would be. Cecilia had been pregnant. . . .

A sharp knock interrupted the tension. Ingrid opened the door, disapproval in her face.

"Mr. Garrett, I'm sorry to disturb you. There's a young woman here who says she wants to speak with you. She says she's a friend of Mr. Fielding's."

Mace rose from his chair with a muttered oath as Kora swept through the door with the grace of a queen. Her face looked as lovely and innocent as an angel's, except for the satisfied glint in her golden eyes as they flicked over Mace. He clenched his jaw to keep it from dropping open in surprise.

"Mr. Garrett," she said, her voice sweet and breathless, as she extended her hand. "What a pleasure to meet you."

9

Kora had ridden halfway to the Bitter Creek Mine before her initial burst of anger gave way and doubt set in. She had been so sure back in the cabin that Mace had deserted her because he didn't want to include her on the story he was obviously chasing. After all, Jared certainly wouldn't want her poking her nose into anything he might be working on.

But what if there was no story? Maybe Mace simply wanted to invest quietly in a mine rumored to be the next El Dorado. If that was the case, it would be hard to explain her traipsing out after him. He'd probably think she was following him because of some sort of puppy love. Kora's face burned with mortification at the mere thought.

More than mental discomfort plagued her, however. Her tailbone still hurt from the day before, and the ride today had only made it worse. The fine dust of the mine road not only clogged her lungs but

coated her green-check gingham dress, already dampened by sweat. She'd worn the dress because she
knew it accentuated her trim figure and the gold in
her hair, but her appearance after an hour and a half
on the trail would hardly impress anyone. To top it all
off, she had forgotten her hat, and her nose was well
on its way to burning yet again.

By the time she reached the mine owner's ranch
house, Kora had half a mind simply to give up and go
back. But then she saw Mace's ornery mule in the
paddock, and that had hardened her resolve. She'd
come too far to give up. She'd just have to brazen out
the situation as best she could.

So she'd put on a confident smile and insisted that
the housekeeper take her in to see Mr. Fielding and
Mr. Garrett. And now here she stood in Garrett's
study, with no idea of how to proceed. The atmo-
sphere in the room made her feel distinctly uncomfortable.

"The pleasure is all mine," Booth Garrett replied to
her vivacious greeting as he took her proffered hand,
forcing a smile. His ice-blue eyes glittered. "Miss . . . ?"

"Hunter, Kora Hunter," Kora told him, giving him
a coquettish smile. She glanced at Mace. If looks
could kill, his gaze would have struck her dead right
then and there. Whatever was going on here, it wasn't
as simple as she had supposed.

"I assume Mace has told you he works for a paper
in Sacramento, Mr. Garrett," she said, hoping that
indeed he had. "I'm his partner."

"You're a reporter?" he asked, as though he must
have misunderstood.

"Yes, I am." She shot Mace a sharp glance, warning him not to forget that again soon. "We've heard

that your Bitter Creek Mine has struck it rich. That would be a big story in Sacramento."

"Well, it had to get out sometime," Garrett said with an exaggerated sigh that turned to a smile. "I'd be pleased to have such a lovely reporter be the one to tell the story."

"Why, thank you," Kora said, ducking her head shyly. If he wanted to underestimate her, he was welcome to. She'd learned to turn that irritating, all-too-common attitude to her advantage, and she wasn't ashamed to use it.

"Believe me, Miss Hunter, we haven't had anything so lovely to set our eyes upon out here in months." He turned to Mace. "Mr. Fielding, I assume our conversation is concluded?"

Mace nodded, seeming relieved. Kora's curiosity about what he and Garrett had been talking about pricked at her furiously.

"Then I'm afraid I must really get back to work." Garrett gestured to the maps and papers on his desk. "A prosperous mine is a lot more work than one that's just getting by. I have to post guards, think about investors and investments. . . . Well, I guess I shouldn't complain." He chuckled. "Feel free to ride on out to the mine. Tell the foreman, Pete Shaw, that I said to give you the grand tour."

Garrett came around from behind his desk, and Kora understood that he was ushering them out of his study, though his manner remained amiable.

"Pete can answer your questions even better than I could. Hell, I always look busy—pardon my coarse language, miss—but he's the one who does all the work."

The man's mustache quirked appealingly when he

smiled, but Kora noticed that his eyes never warmed. Their coldness chilled her. Garrett seemed to be a man used to being obeyed, and she guessed that he would be willing to use force to get his way if his considerable charm failed him.

"Thank you for your time, Mr. Garrett," Mace said, shaking the man's hand. "What you've told me eases my mind a great deal."

"Of course. I'm glad I could clear it up for you. You'll have to come see me again sometime, and we'll reminisce some more about Jesse and Cecilia."

Kora couldn't figure out what had passed between the two men, but Garrett's words told her for certain that Mace's reasons for coming here today had to do with more than a mere news story.

"Cecilia? Wasn't that Jessica's mother's name?" she asked, suddenly wondering if Jessica had been more perceptive about her father's motives than Kora had given her credit for.

"Jessica?" The word came from Garrett's lips like an accusation.

"My daughter," Mace said, glaring at Kora.

She looked at him in surprise, wondering at his anger and the possessiveness in his voice.

"And you'll have to tell me all about your daughter as well," Garrett said.

Kora glanced at Garrett. All the congeniality had left him.

"Well, thank you again, Mr. Garrett," she said awkwardly, moving toward the door, which he opened for her.

"It's been a pleasure, Miss Hunter," he said automatically. Then he blinked, focusing on her again. He reached out to take her hand. "I hope you enjoy your tour of the mine. If you and Mr. Fielding are staying at Green's Hotel in Placerville, be sure to have Mrs. Lawrence bake you one of her famous blackberry pies."

Kora's face heated at Garrett's subtle implication. "Mr. Fielding and I are staying with my grandfather, Fritz Kraus, for a few days, out at his claim," she informed him, hoping he would accept the fact that her grandfather was an adequate chaperon for a single young woman.

Standing beside her, Mace had to suppress a grin at her discomfiture. It served her right for following him out here. His anger at her unexpected interruption was fading quickly. Now that he could put away his nagging fear that Jesse and Cecilia had conspired in murder, little could dampen his spirits.

Besides, Kora's presence had effectively prevented him from having to talk about Jessica. Mace had no intention of discussing her with Garrett, no matter what the man might suspect about Mace's motives or his daughter.

"Your grandfather has a claim near here?" Garrett asked with interest.

Kora nodded. "It's not far, back up through those hills over there." She waved vaguely eastward.

Mace rested a hand on her shoulder. "The cabin's a bit rough, but it's cozy."

She wrenched her shoulder from his hand and glared at him.

"We'd better be going, Miss Hunter," he continued, throwing a wicked smile at Kora. "We want to have plenty of time out at the mine. And we don't want to be wandering through the hills after dark."

His tone implied that they might have better things to do.

For a moment, he could tell she wanted to slap him. Instead, she turned away, and stepped into the hall, almost colliding with a thin, dark man hurrying down the corridor.

It took Mace a moment to recognize the dour frown of the startled man.

"Miles Osborn!" Kora exclaimed. "Good afternoon."

The lawyer's beady brown eyes widened abruptly as he recognized her. He looked beyond her, and his mouth pinched when he saw Mace.

"What are you doing here?" he asked Mace.

Kora's back stiffened at Osborn's disregard for her greeting.

"We're guests of Mr. Garrett's," Mace said, some amusement in his voice. "What are *you* doing here, Mr. Osborn?"

Osborn started and glanced nervously over his shoulder, as though he'd been caught contemplating something criminal. Then he seemed to recollect where he was.

"I'm Mr. Garrett's lawyer," he stated loudly, trying to regain the authority he had displayed when he ordered the two reporters out of his house the other night. "I demand to know what you're doing here!"

"We're on our way to tour the Bitter Creek Mine," Mace answered. Osborn annoyed him, and he couldn't resist needling the man, especially since he was acting so oddly. "Did you think we were checking up on you, Mr. Osborn?"

"If you *are* following me around, I'll have you arrested for harassment!" the lawyer snapped.

"Mr. Osborn, how could we be following you when we got here first?" Kora asked, her voice deceptively sweet. "It appears you're following us."

Osborn's frown drooped all the way down his chin. "I am not making an idle threat," he sputtered angrily. "You stay away from me, my wife, and my clients. Do you hear me?"

"Miles, Miles," Booth Garrett interrupted, stepping from his study to place a hand on the lawyer's arm. "Mr. Fielding's brother was an old friend of mine. We were just catching up. Don't get so upset. You work too hard, my friend."

Garrett guided Osborn past Mace and pushed him gently into the study.

"Don't mind Miles. He's a good lawyer, but a little temperamental," he said to Mace. "Remember, ask for Pete Shaw at the mine. Good day, Miss Hunter."

"Good-bye, Mr. Garrett."

Mace offered Kora his arm, but she ignored him, and he followed her down the hall and outside. Mace decided it must be a good five to ten degrees warmer than when he'd arrived a mere hour or so before.

Kora continued to ignore him as they walked over to the paddock to retrieve their mules. He watched her walk, her golden head held high, her long, strong legs carrying her gracefully across the packed earth.

A surge of joy swelled inside him. He had carried such a load of anger, betrayal, and guilt inside him since Jesse and Cecilia had died. Jackson's accusations against them had only made it worse, eating at him until he'd seized the opportunity to come out to California and learn the truth once and for all.

Now, no matter how illogical it was, he felt absolved of the rage he'd felt toward his brother and

Cecilia, the rage that had made him believe they might be capable of something so monstrous as murder.

Coming here, he had cleared their names of that crime, if only to himself. Whatever they had done to him, he had loved them, and he owed them that much. Now that he'd learned the truth, a great burden lifted from his heart.

Still, the interview with Garrett bothered him. The man's suspicious attitude made him look as though he had something to hide. He obviously thought Mace intended to use Jessica to try to get money out of him. Mace supposed that would be enough to make anyone edgy.

He shook his head. Garrett's worries were unfounded. In order to stake a claim to Jesse's money, he'd have to expose Jessica to the very facts from which he'd protected her all her life. Jessica's well-being was his first priority. Garrett would recognize that soon enough when Mace made no move to contact him again.

Still Mace felt a twinge in the back of his neck, a vague feeling of danger. After finally meeting Booth Garrett, he was glad he wouldn't be facing the man in a court battle, or a battle of any kind. He sensed that underneath the civil amiability of the gentleman rancher, ran a current of violence.

He pushed the thought from his mind. Garrett had freely given him the information he sought. He should be grateful to the man. Suddenly, too many possibilities hung in the fresh California air to waste the day on unfounded suspicions.

He increased his stride, overtaking Kora as she reached for the reins of her mule. Brushing past her, he leaned against the animal's side, trying to look forbidding as he prevented her from mounting.

"Well?" he demanded.

"Well what?" she asked, her eyes flashing at him, her lips pressed together in irritation.

Mace had to fight both the urge to laugh and the desire to pull her into his arms and put those lovely lips to better use. Instead he said, "What was that all about? Following me out to Garrett's ranch and interrupting a private discussion? What in hell were you thinking, Miss Hunter?"

Kora kept her gaze steady on his. She knew he had every right to be angry with her, but she would keep her pride and not let him see her flinch.

"What were *you* thinking, Mr Fielding?" she asked, matching his tone. "Sneaking off before daylight like some low-down thief. I don't care how big a story I was working on, I wouldn't run out on *my* partner."

She thought she saw the corner of his mouth twitch. "You can be damn sure I'll never try it again," he said. "For God's sake, Kora, do you really think I'd try to scoop you on a story like that? First of all, I obviously wouldn't get away with it. And secondly, I'm not sure I'd get as much of a story if you weren't along. You have a tendency to keep things interesting." Then he gave a definite smile. "I usually prefer to work alone, but not since I've gotten to know you. You're a damn good reporter."

Kora's lips parted in disbelief. Tears stung her eyes, and she looked away, turning a shoulder to him. She believed he meant that, to the core of her heart.

"Kora? Are you all right?" He touched her shoul-

der and turned her to him. Then he took her chin
with thumb and forefinger and tilted her face so he
could look her in the eye. "I'm sorry. I'm not really
angry. If I'd thought you were trying to scoop me, I'd
have done the same thing."

"I know." Kora tried to sound sassy and failed.

"Then what's wrong?" The gentleness in his voice
made Kora want to sway against him, let him hold
her close. She needed so desperately for someone to
believe in her. And now Mace said that he did.

Her heart swelled at his concern. The touch of his
hands on her arm and her chin made her tremble.

"Thank you," she whispered.

The sound of her voice and the look in her eyes
jolted Mace. His hand flattened out along the curve of
her jaw.

"For what, sweetheart?" he asked, hardly aware
that the endearment had slipped off his lips.

"For telling me that. For saying you think I can be
a reporter."

"And who would have the poor sense to say you
couldn't?" Mace asked, gently teasing. He brushed a
tear off her cheek with his thumb. Then he bent down
and kissed her softly on her forehead.

That light touch sent what felt like a shock of electricity through her. She clutched at her mule's saddle
for support.

"Come along. We'd better get going if we want to
see that mine." Mace forced himself to pull away
from her. His encounter with Garrett had left him
light-headed, but that didn't change who he was. He
had to be careful, because he knew his feelings went
beyond desire with Kora, and he couldn't bear to hurt
her, or to let her hurt him.

But God, all that woman had to do was look at him, and he wanted her. He might as well admit it. Last night, the thought of her sleeping in the next room had tortured him so badly that he'd finally given up and left the cabin, sitting on the splintering front steps and breathing the cool night breezes until the first faint shimmer of dawn.

His thoughts of Kora made him slow, and his gray mule surprised him with a nip, catching his frock coat just above his elbow. Mace kneed him in the belly, and when the animal let go, he quickly tightened the cinch on his saddle. The mule gave him a baleful look. Mace glared right back.

"Behave yourself, or I'll feed you to the coyotes," he growled.

He heard Kora laugh, and he found himself grinning foolishly as he swung into his saddle.

"I'm betting on the mule," Kora teased as he pulled up beside her, but her eyes still shone with gratitude.

"You're on." Mace leaned toward her and lowered his voice suggestively. "What do you have to give me when I win?"

He was rewarded with a blush, but she tossed her head.

"You won't."

Booth Garrett stood at his window, watching them ride up the dusty road away from his ranch.

"I'm telling you, they suspect something," Miles Osborn was telling him anxiously. The lawyer strode up and down beside the bookshelves, pausing now and then to repeat his fears.

"Stop that pacing, you're making me crazy,"

Garrett said. He brushed past Osborn to open his study door.

"Ingrid!" he bellowed. The housekeeper appeared at the end of the hall. "Get me Fred Baker." Baker had worked for him for years, and right now Garrett had need of his ranch foreman's particular talents and discretion.

"Booth, they're checking up on me. We've got to do something."

Garrett turned to glare at his lawyer. He really wanted to hit something right now, and Osborn's nervous mannerisms were making it very difficult to control himself. Perhaps Osborn saw that in his eyes, because he abruptly sat down and shut his mouth.

"Would you quit acting like a hysterical woman?" Garrett snarled. "I've told you, they had no idea you were my lawyer or that you'd be coming to see me. They suspect nothing. Fielding is after only me, so you can shut up and relax."

Osborn frowned, but he picked up the contract lying on Garrett's desk and read through it again.

It was Garrett's turn to pace now. The memory of Mace Fielding's visit made him fume. It occurred to him that the man would have made a good poker player, not letting his real motives show in his face, keeping his cards close to the chest.

Fielding had concocted his ludicrous story to let Garrett know he had certain suspicions about his brother's death without voicing them directly.

Garrett cursed. He should have slit Clancy Jackson's throat when he had the chance. Whatever Jackson had really told Fielding, Garrett felt certain that Fielding intended to use it to blackmail him into accepting

Fielding's "daughter" Jessica as Jesse's daughter, forcing Garrett to turn over her "inheritance." It was all very clever.

Garrett's lips twisted. He played a mean hand of poker himself, and he was even better when he cheated.

He whirled to plant himself in front of Osborn. "Well? You've read that damn thing ten times now. Do I have a case that only legitimate children would count as Jesse's heirs?"

"I don't see why you ever signed this ridiculous thing, Booth. It's not very professional."

Garrett sent him a withering look, and Osborn continued quickly, "It doesn't even say 'heirs.' It just says 'issue.' An illegitimate child issues forth the same as any other."

Garrett nodded. He didn't plan to settle this in court anyway, but he liked to know his options.

There was a knock on the study door, and a rough-looking man in dirty work clothes entered. His eyes were the color of green ice, and his thick black beard couldn't hide the jagged scar across his right cheek.

"Fred, come in." Garrett strode back to his desk. He brushed everything on it to the floor, then pulled a map from one of the drawers and laid it out on top. It designated all of the claims in the area, and though miners came and went every day, it marked the particular claim he looked for clearly enough.

"See here, Fred?" He gestured the man over and circled Fritz Kraus's name with a pencil. "I have a little job for you to do."

Garrett grinned. It was time he got rid of Fielding's ace in the hole.

*   *   *

The Bitter Creek Mine wasn't at all what Mace had expected. He had entertained a vague picture of tunnels dug into the mountains and rail carts bringing ore up from the bowels of the Sierras. The hydraulic technique for mining the ore-bearing deposits—the placers, which had given Placerville its name—was both cruder and more ingenious than he could have imagined.

No mysterious holes bored into the ground. Instead, great flumes or raceways arced from streams high back in the mountains on stilts over seventy feet high. Water from the hoses attached to these flumes poured forth with incredible force, melting away the bank of hard earth beneath. The resulting stream of muddy water was then directed down the sluices—long, specially built troughs for conducting the water.

The foreman, Pete Shaw, a small but wiry man in his fifties, thoroughly enjoyed Mace's surprise at and interest in his operation. He enthusiastically explained the principles of placer mining.

He led Mace to one of the sluices not currently in use. "Ye see these blocks?"

He pointed to the double row of timber ends in the bottom of the sluice.

"Ye fill the bottom o' the sluice with quicksilver. The gold sinks in between the blocks an' the quicksilver dissolves it. Then all ye have t' do is heat away the quicksilver an' ye got yer gold."

He grinned up at Mace, a gold tooth glittering in the sun.

"Impressive," Mace had to admit. He looked around again at the mine, watching the thick brown water flowing through the sluices. The careless water had gouged and savaged the denuded flat where the richest ore lay.

Mace knew where all that dirt had gone. On the steamer trip up to Sacramento, he'd spoken with a former steamship captain who had told him the muddy river had once been as clear as a mountain stream. Now the Sacramento and American Rivers, and even San Francisco Bay, were being clogged by the massive amounts of silt pouring into them from the gold country. He wondered if that soft yellow mineral everyone sought so eagerly really compensated for its cost.

"I worked down near Placerville afore them placers all washed up," Shaw said, interrupting his thoughts. "An' I didn't think much would come of this one here a t'all, to tell the truth. But just over there," he pointed to a hillside where the hydraulics had halted for the moment, "we hit some good ore. We're doin' that slow, 'cause we found some pretty darn big nuggets an' we don't want to wash them away."

"No, I don't suppose you do," Mace said.

He looked around for Kora. Her feet hurt from walking around on the rocky, uneven ground, and she was sitting on the edge of one of the unused sluices, looking out toward the west.

"I think maybe Miss Hunter and I should head back, before it gets too late," he said. He shook Shaw's hand. "Thanks for the tour. It was very informative."

"My pleasure," the old man answered with another of his frequent grins. "Come on back if'n ye got any more questions."

"I'll do that." He picked his way back down the hillside to Kora. "You ready to go?"

She nodded with evident relief. "I know this is all

new to you," she told him as they walked back to the mules, "but if you've seen one placer mine, you've seen them all."

The sun burned miserably hot on their backs as they rode toward Fritz Kraus's cabin. By September the dust on the roads would be inches thick, and the Bitter Creek diggings would be all but shut down for the season for lack of water.

They made the long, hot ride in silence. Kora's stomach had begun to tighten with hunger, and she spent most of her energy trying to find a position on the saddle that didn't aggravate her sore posterior. And Mace's thoughts about what he had learned this morning occupied him too fully to want to talk much.

They followed Kora's shortcut back to the cabin and made good time. They were almost there when Mace's mule stumbled.

Mace cursed and pulled the mule's head back up, but the animal lurched again. He hopped one more step and then stopped, his ears flattened, refusing to budge.

"Damnation." Mace swung down from the saddle. The mule's ears relaxed. Mace looked down at the animal's feet. The beast leaned to the left, touching only the tip of his back right hoof to the ground.

Kora heard the curse and looked back over her shoulder to see Mace standing beside the mule.

"Something wrong?" She dismounted and looped her reins around a manzanita branch. "Looks like I may have won our bet," she teased as she reached Mace and his immobile mule.

"Hold his head," Mace told her, ignoring the jibe. When she'd taken the mule's bridle, he leaned down to lift the tender foot. He grunted and pulled out a pocket knife. A few seconds later, he held up a sharp stone for Kora's inspection.

"He hasn't got the best of me yet," he said, grinning. Then he looked past her and the grin widened. "Can't say the same for you, though."

Kora turned. Her quiet, unassuming mule was gone.

"Damn!" She ran up the trail to where it curved around a boulder. No mule to be seen. The beast was probably halfway to Bear Pass by now.

"Damn!" she said again, and heard Mace's low chuckle as he came up behind her. "It's not funny!" she snapped, but a laugh escaped her anyway.

"Maybe you'll think twice about making fun of other people's problems from now on," Mace said as he swung into his saddle.

"And I suppose it would serve me right to walk the rest of the way?" she asked. "My feet hurt."

She waved her right foot in the air, managing a respectable pout despite her desire to laugh.

"I certainly wouldn't want you to damage such lovely feet," Mace said. He offered her a hand.

Kora looked at it suspiciously.

"You can either ride with me or you can walk," he told her. "It's up to you."

She glanced up and saw the challenge in his laughing eyes. It would be more proper for her to walk, unless he let her ride alone. But he showed no sign of dismounting, and her feet really did hurt. Besides, after the way he'd spoken to her this morning, the thought of being so close to him sent a delicious shiver through her.

"All right," she said. She'd never hidden from a challenge. She gave him her hand.

"Put your foot on my boot. No, the other foot. Okay." He put his other hand on her waist and swung her onto the saddle in front of him. His right arm held her about her middle, and her left thigh pressed against his as her feet dangled over one side of the mule.

Kora pulled her right knee up toward the saddle horn so she didn't twist quite so far sideways, but that only pressed her more firmly against Mace's chest.

The laughter left her abruptly, and she knew she'd made a mistake. Mace's heat ran along her back, her thigh, her stomach, making her feel almost instantly light-headed. Her breathing came faster, and she wondered if he could hear the beating of her heart, it pounded so loudly through her veins.

"You comfortable?" He breathed the low words against her ear. Heat suffused her body, the hot blood rushing to her cheeks. She nodded, glad he couldn't see her face.

What was happening to her? She'd known this man less than a week, and yet her whole body responded to the sound of his voice, his slightest touch. She'd never felt this way before, this turbulent swirl of emotions and desires.

Kora breathed deeply, trying to calm herself, trying to understand what she felt for the man behind her. Her reporter's mind told her that while her emotions might be in turmoil, her behavior certainly suggested she was falling hard for Mason Fielding.

This morning she'd been furious to think he'd leave her out of his work. Then she'd cried when he called her a good reporter and said he liked having her around. She'd almost cried again when he'd stopped holding her, so they could leave for the mine. And now, when she should be making every effort to keep contact with him minimal, she felt herself leaning back against his chest, letting herself melt against him.

Mace's breath caught and his eyes shut briefly as she pressed against him. His head inclined almost against his will and he caught the light, flowered scent of her hair. It brushed against his chin, soft as silk, and he wanted to run his hands through it, lift the shimmering gold of it to his lips.

Beneath his right hand, he could feel the rise and fall of her chest as she breathed. One movement of his thumb and he would feel the curve of her breast above her corset. She shifted, trying to get more comfortable, and her thigh moved against his.

Heat pulsed through Mace's loins, and all the feelings he'd been trying to deny rushed over him. He wanted to tighten his arm around her, but if she moved back any farther, she would press against the hard manifestation of his desire. The thought almost pushed him over the edge.

He brought the mule to a stop.

"Is something wrong?" Kora asked. Her back felt cold despite the sun's heat as he pulled away from her.

"This can't be comfortable for you," Mace said, his voice tight. "I'll walk."

He slipped from the mule's back, leaving Kora grasping the saddle horn to steady herself.

"But I can't ride like this," she said, wondering why he'd dismounted. Did he find having her so near objectionable? "This isn't a sidesaddle. This mule will throw me off in a minute."

Not meeting her gaze, Mace replied curtly, "I'll lead him."

Kora looked down at her hands to hide the fact that his shortness with her stung. A fold of her skirt had caught on the saddle horn. She pulled on it. It didn't budge. In frustration she gave it a ferocious tug. Her skirt came loose, but she lost her balance and slipped off the saddle.

Before her feet touched the ground, Mace had her in his arms. Her skirt slipped along his legs as he lowered her gently to her feet. As she felt her limbs weaken at his touch, Kora wondered briefly if her fall had really been an accident. Because this was what she wanted, his arms around her back, his body pressed to hers. She had wanted it, without knowing it, since their first day together.

She tilted her face up to his and her breath left her. Her brief fear that he would laugh at her drowned in the depths of those compelling blue eyes. He brought his lips to hers, and as they touched, Kora felt a hot lassitude spread from deep within her to her fingers and toes.

Mace lifted his lips from hers. A groan escaped him, and he kissed her again, voraciously this time. Her lips parted beneath his, and he flicked her teeth with his tongue. She gasped, a throaty sound that sent his head spinning.

Kora raised her arms to Mace's neck, and she ran her fingers through the thick hair at its base. When Mace's mouth left hers, she opened hers to protest, but then his lips found her neck. She clutched at him as new waves of sensation flowed down her spine to the core of heat swelling within her.

The arms around her back pulled her to him spasmodically. The buttons of his coat pressed against her chest, and against her lower belly she could feel the surprising hot hardness of him. She shifted against it, and he moaned.

"God, Kora," he breathed against her ear. His tongue flicked her earlobe, and Kora thought she would faint. The world went dim around her. All she knew was Mace and how he made her feel.

She nearly cried out when he shifted back from her, but then his hand ran up her waist to cup her breast. She knew that she should pull away and not let this man who didn't share his secrets touch her in this way. But whatever distance he kept from the world, it was gone now. His body was as taut with need as hers. And she could no more deny it than he.

Mace looked down at her, wonder filling him at her response to his touch. Her eyes looked into his without reluctance or fear, filled only with the heat of her desire. He dimly remembered telling himself to stay away from her, to avoid getting entangled with this slender, headstrong beauty. But the words meant nothing when he was touching her like this, when neither of them could deny the passion that had been threatening to blaze between them since they'd met. His hand found its way to the buttons of her bodice. Slowly her skin appeared beneath his touch. He ran a finger down one breast and around the rosy nipple, which hardened to his stroke.

He had to stop now. What this incredible, innocent young woman offered him was too precious to take here on a rocky path in the heat and the dust, with a malevolent mule watching their every move.

"The damn mule!"

Kora looked at Mace in shock as he dropped his

hands from her and ran past her up the path. She turned in time to see a flicking gray tail round the next bend, and Mace hard on its heels.

For a moment she stood trembling, staring after him. Her hand went to her throat where her pulse throbbed as though she'd been running for her life. She realized her dress still hung open, and she buttoned it as quickly as her trembling fingers would allow. She brushed a hand over her hair, wondering if she looked as tousled as she felt.

Slowly she walked up the trail after Mace and the mule, caught between the recognition that she should feel ashamed of herself for letting things go so far and amazement at the sensations Mace had stirred in her. Kissing Jared had never affected her this way, had never given her this feeling of wanting so much more, of wanting to give so much more.

As she rounded the turn in the trail, she saw Mace a hundred yards ahead. He'd caught the gray mule and stood with his back to her. Kora's face colored as she neared him. Would he think she was a terrible wanton for the way she'd acted? Would he pretend nothing had happened? She didn't think she could bear it if he did.

She came up beside him, looking down at her grandfather's cabin. She'd had no idea they were so close. Her face reddened even more.

"I guess Jess and Fritz are still out panning," Mace said, his sheepish glance informing Kora he was as glad as she that they hadn't been discovered.

He took out a cigarette and lit it. Kora noticed his hand wasn't quite steady.

"Mace . . ." Kora began, not sure of what she should say.

He looked down at her, and she caught her breath at the desire that still shone in his eyes. He reached a hand to her cheek, stroking her temple with his fingers.

"Kora."

And that was enough of an answer. At least for now. She held his gaze for a long moment, and then they moved together toward the clearing.

10

"Mace! Mace!"

The high-pitched screams reached Mace as he shut the door to the shed where he'd settled his mule. The terror in Kora's voice sent him flying across the clearing to her grandfather's cabin. He flung open the door.

"Kora! What's wrong?"

"Oh, Mace!" He saw her then, kneeling on the floor near the old couch. Beside her lay her grandfather, looking small and old, a red stain spreading onto the rug from a gash in his forehead. Kora looked up at Mace, wild-eyed.

He dropped beside her.

"Is he breathing?" he asked as he reached for the old man's arm.

Kora took a shuddering breath and leaned her head down to her grandfather's lips.

"Yes," she said at the same moment Mace found the weak pulse in Fritz's wrist.

Mace gently turned the injured man's head, examining the extent of the wound. Most of the blood had congealed, but the movement started it oozing. He folded his handkerchief and handed it to Kora. "See if you can stop the bleeding. Just press it in place over the wound. I'll start some hot water."

She did as he said, and some of the fear left her eyes, though her hands still shook.

"Will he be all right?" she asked anxiously as he poked the banked fire in the stove and added some kindling.

"In some of the worst battles I saw in the war, I helped the doctors tend the wounded. I saw plenty of head injuries. I don't think this one is too bad." Mace didn't add that he didn't know yet whether or not the skull had been fractured or mention the fact that Fritz's age made any wound more serious than it would be in a younger man.

He filled a pot with water from a bucket next to the stove. Not until he'd set the pot of water on the heating stove did his mind have a chance to catch up with the circumstances.

"Where's Jessica?" he asked suddenly, looking quickly around the cabin.

Kora's eyes widened as she looked at him. She'd been too intent on her grandfather to think of Jessica either.

Mace strode to the bedroom, yanking aside the blanket. Jessica's little cot lay on top of Fritz's wooden bed, blankets tumbling to the ground. Her bag was gone.

His first thought on seeing Fritz lying wounded on the floor was that he must have fallen and hit his head on a chair. Maybe that was still the explanation. Maybe

Jessica had gone into Bear Pass to try to find a doctor. Mace didn't believe it, even as he thought it.

"Jessica!" He reentered the main room and threw open the door to the closet. Nothing had been disturbed.

"Mace?"

He hardly heard Kora as he dashed out the front door and ran toward the creek.

"Jessica!" His voice rang through the late afternoon silence, echoing back to him from the mountainsides. "Jessica!"

He looked up and down the stream bed, praying he would see her dark head bent over a gold pan, unaware of the panic she was causing him. But he saw no sign of her. Only the uncaring quiet of the mountains answered his calls.

A cold ball of fear rose in his throat, a fear greater than any he had felt on any war battlefield. He ran back to the cabin.

Kora met him at the door, and he saw a mirror of his own fear in her eyes.

"Mace, I found this on the table."

She handed him a sheet of paper, folded in two. Printed on it in large, crude lettering, the message read:

> If you wont yor dawter back be at the Eagle Saloon tonite by 11. If we arnt there, come back tomarro nite. We will tell you wat money we wont then.

Mace read the note three times before its meaning sank in. He crumpled the paper in his hand, digging his nails into his palm.

The ice of a mountain glacier ran through his veins. Why? Why would anyone do such a thing?

"I'll kill them." The cold words came through gritted teeth. "If they hurt her, they'll wish they'd never been born."

Kora touched his arm. "They won't hurt her. This is a ransom note. If they want your money, they'll make sure she's all right."

Mace looked at her. She spoke with confidence, trying to give him strength just as he had assured her about Fritz. He stared at her beautiful face, willing away the images of Jessica, terrified and hurt, tied up in some dirty miner's cabin.

"The water should be hot by now," he heard himself saying. "Do we have some rags?"

Kora squeezed his arm, then hurried to the closet, coming back with a sheet. Mace took it from her and tore it into strips. After he dropped some into the boiling water he took down a bottle of whiskey from a shelf near the stove.

Kora sat by her grandfather's head as Mace gently washed away what he could of the dried blood and dirt. The wound began to seep again. He poured some of the whiskey over it, grateful for Fritz's unconsciousness. He quickly covered the area with a dry cloth, then wrapped a strip of sheet around Fritz's head to hold the makeshift bandage in place.

"We have to get him to a doctor," he told Kora as he worked. "He needs something besides the alcohol to keep the wound from festering."

Kora watched him care for her grandfather, recognizing the irony of the situation. When she'd first met Mace, with his fancy clothes and eastern style, she'd been sure he wouldn't last a week in Sacramento.

And here he was, calmly treating her grandfather's injury in a remote, primitive cabin as though it were the most natural thing in the world for him. Suddenly she wanted to tell him how much respect she'd gained for him, how much she cared for him. But now was not the time.

As Mace tied the last knot in the bandage, a groan escaped Fritz's parted lips.

"Grandpa?" Kora put a hand on his forehead and leaned down to him. "Can you hear me? It's Kora. You're going to be all right. Do you hear me, Grandpa?"

Tears misted her eyes as he groaned again. He had to be all right. He just had to.

"Grandpa?"

Fritz's eyelids fluttered and he raised a hand toward his head, only to let it fall back by his side.

"Mmph," he tried to speak. His eyes opened, but it took them a long time to focus on Kora's face. "Annelie?" he murmured. "*Nein? Was ist los?*"

"It's Kora, Grandpa," Kora told him again. "Anna's daughter. You've been hit on the head. Do you remember?"

Fritz's eyes closed again, and his brow furrowed. "*Ach.* Perhaps. It hurts."

He raised his hand again, this time touching the bandage on his temple.

"Fritz." Mace's voice was low, but urgent. "Fritz, it's Mace Fielding. Someone came and took Jessica away. Do you remember anything about that? Please, it's important."

"Jessica!" Fritz's eyes opened wide and he struggled to sit up.

"Grandpa, lie down!" Kora said, but he didn't listen, though he had to hold his head with both hands.

"They got her?" he asked, trying to look around the cabin. He groaned again.

"Yes, they left a ransom note," Mace told him. "Can you describe the men who attacked you? Did you know them?"

"*Nein, ich kenne sie nicht.* I know them not. They were dressed like miners." Fritz frowned with concentration. "We came back here to eat something, and two men was waiting inside. They both had beards. One was blond, mit lots of hair, und red cheeks. He grabbed Jessica."

Fritz's memory seemed to waver here. "I tried to get my rifle." He waved to the corner where his prized Sharps rifle had fallen to the floor. "But the other one hit me. With what, I don't know." He touched his head again gingerly.

"Here, try a little of this." Mace offered him the bottle of whiskey, and the old man took a long swig. He closed his eyes a moment and took another.

"Is better," he said then. "Help me up."

Kora wanted to object, but she knew they had to get him to Bear Pass somehow. She and Mace each took an arm and lifted Fritz into a chair.

"You rest there, Grandpa," Kora said as he seemed about to try to stand. "I'll pack up a few things before we go into town."

"Town?" he asked, startled. "We have to find Jessica."

"You have to see a doctor," she said. "Besides, the kidnappers left a note saying to meet them tonight at the Eagle Saloon. Don't worry, we'll have Jess back in no time."

She glanced at Mace as she said this. His face was expressionless, but the tension showed in the way he clenched and unclenched his fists. She knew he was anxious to be on their way, but they couldn't rush Fritz.

"The Eagle Saloon?" Fritz asked, his brow furrowed in thought. "*Nein.*" He shook his head, frustration apparent in his expression.

"What do you mean, Fritz?" Mace demanded.

"I think . . . I think I hear something. . . ." Fritz said haltingly. Then he seemed to have a flash of memory. "*Ja.* These men, they thought I am dead. I hear them talking. One says now they take the girl back to Argenta. You remember it, Kora. Argenta is that ghost town way out in the mountains. I take you there last summer."

Kora nodded. "Yes, I remember, Grandpa." She turned to Mace. "It's not even a ghost town, really. Just a few half-built and abandoned buildings. It would be a perfect place to go if you didn't want to be found."

She watched Mace digest this information. On the strength of what Fritz had told them, they could ride out to Argenta tonight to try to surprise Jessica's abductors, or they could make the kidnappers' written rendezvous.

Mace ran his fingers through his hair and walked over to the window that looked out over the creek. He stood there silently for a moment.

"I'll meet them at the saloon," he said finally. It galled him to follow the kidnappers' instructions rather than take the opportunity for decisive action. But with his daughter's life at stake, he couldn't take any chances. Besides, he had to get Fritz and Kora safely to Bear Pass before he could do anything else. He couldn't risk the chance that the kidnappers might attack again, that they might hurt someone else who was dear to him.

*   *   *

Mace walked through the swinging doors of the Eagle Saloon at ten-thirty that evening. He had left Fritz resting comfortably in a room at the Union Hotel, under Kora's watchful eye. Bear Pass itself didn't have a resident doctor, but one happened to be staying at the hotel when they arrived. He had examined Fritz's wound and pronounced it not serious, though the headache would last for a while, and he recommended that Fritz stay quietly in bed for the next few days.

Mace stopped just inside the saloon door for a moment, looking around. It was the only saloon for miles and was nearly twice as large as the establishment he'd stopped in at Placerville. Business was heavy.

Mace walked to the bar and ordered a whiskey. He had come early to orient himself before the meeting with Jessica's kidnappers. He sat on a bar stool and tried to relax while he surveyed the activity around him. Groups of men sat at tables around the room, drinking, arguing, and gambling. He reflected wryly that fancy women were about the only vice not represented in the saloon that night.

He'd bought a gun from the general store across the road from the hotel, and the Colt revolver weighed reassuringly against his hip where he'd pushed it through his belt.

He wondered if the men he was supposed to meet had already arrived, if they were already sitting at one of the nearby tables, appraising him as he looked for them. He didn't see anyone who matched Fritz's description of a blond man with a heavy beard. Fritz hadn't gotten a good look at the man's partner.

As his gaze traversed the room, Mace saw a big man with a thick black beard staring at him from a table in the shadowy corner near the door. When he saw Mace notice him, he rose and walked over to the bar. Mace's gut tightened as the man approached. It would take all his self-control not to take a swing at the man before he could find out where Jessica was.

But the man's question was innocuous enough. "Hey, mister, you interested in a poker game?"

Mace felt a wave of disappointment. "No, thanks. I'm not here to gamble."

The man's green eyes narrowed, and Mace noticed he had a jagged scar across one cheek. "What d'ya mean yer not here to gamble?" he asked with false amiability. "Dressed up to the teeth like you are? I figgered you for a cardsharp. I guess I could give you a purty good game, me and a couple of the boys." He gestured back to his table, where three men sat watching their conversation.

Mace's first impulse was to dismiss him. He guessed the man was probably a pretty good poker player himself, trying to con a sucker into a game. Mace didn't need any extra problems right now. But he also wanted to keep a low profile, and sitting at the bar in his tailored clothes, nursing one whiskey for an hour, was not the way to remain inconspicuous. The corner table would give him a good view of the rest of the room. He could afford to lose a little money if it helped him get Jessica back safely.

Mace shrugged. "I guess I'm up for a game or two, but I'm waiting for some friends, so I may not be able to play long."

The man smiled. "Sure you are. C'mon over and meet everybody."

He led Mace back to the table, and the others scooted their chairs around to give Mace room to sit.

"I'm Fred, and this here is Billy, Cap, and Boris. Boris is a Russky from up north."

Mace acknowledged the men's greetings. As he sat down, the Russian started dealing, eager to get the game under way.

They began with five-card stud, then draw, then seven-card stud, as the deal passed several times around the table. Mace's mind focused more on his watch than on the game as the time ticked past ten-forty-five, then eleven, then eleven-thirty. He looked around the room every few moments, straining for any sign that would tell him the men he looked for had arrived.

"Hey, buddy, it's your deal."

Cap's voice brought him momentarily back to the game. Cap was a small man with unwashed red hair and two missing front teeth, and he smiled too much. Mace made no effort to smile back as he began sending the cards sliding across the table.

Mace's glance flicked to the other card players. Billy grinned as he picked up his cards. The thin, wiry man had no talent at poker, but he won and lost with equal good humor. The Russian, Boris, looked over his cards gloomily, becoming more and more morose as he lost hand after hand.

Fred, on the other hand, was becoming belligerent. Mace hadn't seen him drink much of the whiskey he had sitting in front of him, but his speech had begun to slur a little and he glared at Mace across the table.

"Dealer calls." Mace tossed a coin into the pot as the bet came around to him, and then he glanced down at his cards. He should have saved his money. A pair of threes was not going to win this hand.

He checked his pile of coins and odd bits of gold, feeling a mild surprise at the amount of money sitting there. Thinking back on it, he'd won quite a few hands despite his lack of expertise at the game.

"Well, whad'ye got?" Fred growled across the table.

Mace tried not to show his annoyance with the man's ill humor. He tossed his cards to the table.

"I won!" Billy exclaimed with a wide smile, raking the small pile of coins toward him, his three jacks easily the best cards on the table.

Mace pulled his watch from his pocket for what seemed like the hundredth time. It was nearly midnight. The ransom note had said eleven o'clock or return tomorrow. They weren't going to meet him tonight.

He fought down a rush of anger and panic. The fact that the kidnappers hadn't put in an appearance didn't mean anything had happened to Jessica. They just wanted to make him sweat.

Mace pushed down the panic and held onto the anger. He wouldn't let the kidnappers' tactics get to him. He had to stay calm so he could think clearly about what to do next. Staying any longer in the Eagle Saloon would only be a waste of time.

"Gentlemen, it looks like my friends aren't going to show. Thanks for the game, but I'd better be going now." Mace swept his winnings into his handkerchief and knotted it.

"Wait!" Fred slammed a fist down on the table, startling the others. "I knew you was a card sharp. You can't leave now. You gotta give us a chansh to win our money back."

With deliberate slowness, Mace pushed back his chair and stood, dropping his handkerchief into a coat pocket.

"The condition you're in, I hardly think you'd be likely to start winning now," he replied calmly, but his body tensed, ready for anything.

"Aw, c'mon. Don't go now," Billy pleaded. "I just hit my lucky streak."

"Maybe some other time," Mace said. He looked back and forth between Fred and Cap. They would be the ones to start something.

"I'm thirsty," Cap muttered, still smiling. He stood and wandered toward the bar.

"Go on, go on," Boris said, waving Mace away. "You've got enough of my hard-earned gold."

Fred's green eyes glittered, but he made no further objections. Mace warily backed away from the table to the door. His hand itched to rest on the pistol in his belt, but he resisted the urge, keeping his fist clenched by his side as he exited the saloon. No one followed him, and as he stepped into the cool night air, he breathed a sigh of relief.

He stopped to light a cigarette, feeling rather foolish for letting a little animosity over a card game get to him like that. Those men might be rough, but they were miners, not outlaws. Still, there had been something vaguely menacing about that man Fred. Something dangerous lurked behind those cold eyes.

Mace stepped down onto the street and turned toward the hotel, which was separated from the saloon by the stable that served both. As he passed the alleyway that separated the hotel from the stable, he heard a noise. A whimper.

He moved to the mouth of the alley. The night

deepened here, away from the lamps that lit the doors of the saloon and the hotel. Boxes and barrels crowded the narrow space, casting ominous shadows.

"Hello? Is someone there?" He kept his voice low, but it seemed loud in the silence of the alley.

The sound came again, unidentifiable. The hairs prickled on the back of Mace's neck. It might have been an injured kitten or the muffled cry of a baby.

"Who's there?" He raised his voice, but again there was no answer. It must have been a lonely animal or an effect of the wind or even his imagination. But his heart pounded loudly in his ears. Perhaps Jessica's kidnappers had arrived at the Eagle Saloon after all. What if they hadn't had anywhere to leave her? What if they'd simply dumped her in this alley, bound and gagged, until they returned from their meeting with him?

Mace took another step. "Hello? Can you hear me?" Furtive scuffling noises broke the silence of the night, but a rat dashing past his feet quickly explained them. "Is anyone there?"

"Sure there's someone here, buddy."

Mace froze as a hunched shape stepped out of the blackness before him. It was Cap, from the poker game, still grinning like a lunatic. The glint from the pistol he gripped in his left hand held Mace's attention.

"What do you want?" Mace asked, refusing to flinch. He inched his hand down toward his hip, gently pushing aside his coat.

"I don't want nothin'," Cap answered, grinning wider as he looked past Mace, "but my friend does."

Mace spun halfway around only to find himself staring down the barrel of another pistol.

"I don't like people who cheat at cards." Outlined

against the opening of the alley stood the man with the scar, Fred, but now his cold voice showed no trace of drunkenness, and the hand that held the pistol was as steady and sure as death.

Mace cursed himself for being an idiot. These men had set him up. Cap must have sneaked out the back of the saloon to catch him here. Fred had followed Mace to complete the trap, and now it seemed they intended to kill and rob him. If they were ever caught, they'd claim he'd cheated them at cards. They'd get off with their lives and probably their freedom if they got the right judge.

Mace felt overwhelming desperation. He couldn't die now. He still had to rescue his daughter.

"I didn't cheat, and you know it, so let's skip the theatrics," he said, keeping his voice calm, letting his hand edge toward his own pistol. No wonder he'd won so many of the hands. Cap and Fred must have been dealing him good cards on purpose.

"Nobody beats Fred what doesn't cheat," Cap interjected from Mace's left, but his giggle belied the words.

"You just hand over that money in your pocket and no one has to get hurt," Fred told Mace.

"Yeah, no one," Cap echoed, giggling again, "'cept you."

"Shut up, Cap," Fred ordered. "And you, show me your hands."

"I can't give you your gold if I can't take it out of my pocket," Mace said evenly, pulling his knotted handkerchief from his coat with his left hand. He shook it so Fred and Cap could hear it jingle.

"That's it. That's our money, Fred," Cap said.

"And you're welcome to it," Mace told him. "Here."

In one motion he abruptly slung the money at Fred's head and pulled his pistol from his belt. As Fred ducked to avoid the heavy ball of coins, Mace threw himself forward toward an opening between two stacks of crates. Keeping his profile to Cap, he shot at the man from under his left arm as he fell into the narrow gap before him.

As if in slow motion, he hit the wall of the hotel and turned, pistol raised to fire again. Cap's gurgling scream came to him through the ringing in his ears. A fire burned its way up his knee from hitting it against the wall, but he had no time to notice the pain as part of the crate beside him disintegrated at the crack of Fred's pistol.

Mace pressed himself to the hotel wall. He was a sitting duck here. Another shot came through the crate, and Mace imagined he could feel the wind it stirred as it narrowly missed his head. He dropped lower and aimed his pistol in the direction from which the shot had come.

He had his finger on the trigger when an even louder shot roared through the alleyway. It sounded like a rifle blast. Mace looked down, surprised to see himself still in one piece.

"Mace? Mace?"

Mace wondered at the fact that he could hear that sweet voice even through the brittle ache in his ears from the gunshots. He pushed himself fully upright just as a slender shadow appeared in front of him.

"Mace! Are you all right?" Kora's concern was like a blessing.

"Yes," was all he could manage to reply.

The shadow moved again, becoming solid flesh as she threw her arms about his waist, pressing the length of Fritz's rifle against his back. Mace pulled her to him, breathing her scent deeply.

"Where did you come from?" he asked, his head light with the realization that he was no longer about to die. "Are you my guardian angel?" He was only half-joking. As Kora looked up at him, the faint light caught her hair, glimmering almost like a halo.

"I got worried when you didn't come back to the hotel," she told him. She didn't add that she had been waiting in suspenseful agony as the minutes passed and no word came from him. The kidnappers had said eleven, and by midnight Kora had known something must be wrong. "I came looking for you."

"That was a foolish thing to do." He laughed shakily. "But I'm not going to complain. Did you shoot Fred?" He stepped around her into the alley. The two men who had attacked him lay motionless.

"If Fred was the big man shooting at you with a pistol, then yes, I shot him," Kora said, her voice quivering as she realized what she had done.

She had heard an argument in the alley as she came out of the hotel and recognized Mace's voice. When she heard gunfire and saw the huge man near the end of the alley firing away, she had pulled the trigger of her grandfather's rifle without thinking. But now, looking down at the still body, she suddenly realized that she had killed a man.

Mace bent down to feel for the man's pulse. "Definitely dead. You're a good shot," he said with grim satisfaction. He moved down the alley to a second body. "Both dead."

"Oh," Kora said faintly. The rifle dropped to the ground beside her. She felt herself swaying.

"Kora?" Mace's arms closed around her just as her legs gave way beneath her. She was dimly aware of his strong arms lifting her, carrying her out of the alley to the front porch of the hotel.

He set her down gently on the steps. "Kora? Here, sweetheart, lean your head between your knees." His voice soothed her, and she did as she was told, letting the blood flow back into her head.

Suddenly Mace started to chuckle beside her. He broke into a full-blown roar of laughter.

Kora snapped her head up, glaring at him, even though the movement made her dizzy again. "I hardly think it's funny that I feel a little faint at the idea of killing someone."

Mace sobered quickly, but the twinkle remained in his eye. "That's not what I'm laughing at. I was just noticing that you're dressed rather oddly for a guardian angel."

Kora looked down at herself, feeling her cheeks flush. She had on a plaid woolen work shirt tucked into a pair of worn denim pants, which were tucked into her leather boots. She often wore this outfit to work in the garden back home, or to hike, fish, and hunt up at her grandfather's cabin.

"I thought I'd be safer dressed up as a man."

"With hair like this?" he asked doubtfully, running his hand through the thick golden cascade that flowed down her back.

Her hand flew to her head. "My hat! I must have lost it in all the excitement."

"Hang on a minute." Mace stood and disappeared back down the alley. Kora held her breath tensely until he reappeared with her father's old slouch hat and the rifle in his hands. Those two men might be dead, but after today's events, that didn't make her feel safe.

"Thank you." She took the hat Mace offered and tucked her hair up under it. "Is that better?"

He shook his head, letting his eyes wander slowly over her face. "Not at all. I like your hair loose."

Kora looked down, hoping the hat brim would hide the color in her cheeks. His words reminded her of the kiss they'd shared this afternoon, of how good it had felt to be in his arms. It seemed so long ago now.

"Were those the kidnappers?" she asked, suddenly remembering what had taken him to the saloon in the first place. "Did you find out where Jessica is?"

Mace shook his head, his expression returning to the grim set it had held since they'd found the ransom note. "They never showed up."

She could feel the frustration that emanated from him, and it only increased her own fears for Jessica.

"Come on, let's get you inside," Mace said.

Kora took the hand he offered and he pulled her to her feet. She held his arm as they entered the hotel, as much to comfort him as to support herself.

Mr. Kruger, the proprietor of the hotel, greeted them anxiously as they entered the lobby. "What happened out there? We heard shots!" He held a shotgun tightly in his hands. His wife and Dr. Clifton, the physician who had attended Fritz earlier, stood nearby.

Kora wanted to ask why, if they were so worried, they hadn't bothered to come out and offer assistance, but she held her tongue. She couldn't blame them for being frightened. She noticed Dr. Clifton's eyes pass over her, then snap back, staring at her attire. The Krugers, however, were too concerned about the gunshots to notice her odd appearance.

"I was attacked by two cutthroats on my way back here from the saloon," Mace explained wearily. "I think they're beyond your help, Doctor, but I suppose something has to be done with them."

He tossed a knotted handkerchief to the counter beside Mr. Kruger. It clanked heavily.

"That's what they were after. It can be used to bury them."

He put his hand behind Kora's back and guided her to the stairs at the end of the lobby, ignoring the surprised stares that followed them.

"That money . . . where did it come from?" Kora asked, glancing back over her shoulder.

"I won it in a poker game."

Kora looked at him, but he didn't explain further.

"I'd like to check in on Grandpa," she said when they reached the second floor. Mace nodded, and she opened the door to his room.

She had left the lamp burning on the table between the room's two beds. It dimly illuminated the still figure lying beneath a blue-sprigged quilt.

Kora knelt beside her grandfather and felt his forehead, then the pulse at his throat. He was cool and sleeping quietly, the powder the doctor had prescribed making him oblivious to the pain in his head and the noise of the recent gunshots.

"He's fine," she murmured, rising. She turned to look at Mace. "You should try to get some sleep, too. You need it."

He nodded. "I'll try." But Kora could tell he didn't mean it.

"Good night, then." She felt there was something

else she should say, but only silence stretched between them. After a moment he stepped aside, and she walked past him to the door.

As she looked down the hallway to her door, she felt a tingle of nerves. In the dim light from the candle in the one wall sconce, the shadows of the doorways reminded her too much of the alleyway outside.

"Would you like me to see you to your room?"

The low voice sent a shiver of another kind running through her. She quickly squelched it.

"I think I can find it myself, thank you," she said. Hadn't she proved tonight that she could take care of herself?

"It would make me feel better to know there's no one waiting in there for your return." Before she could protest, he had entered the hall and closed his door behind them.

Kora tightened her lips as she followed him. The hall was perfectly empty, and she felt foolish now for letting her nerves show. When they reached her room, Mace held out his hand for the key, but she ignored him and unlocked the door herself.

It wasn't until she'd opened the door into the unfamiliar, dark room that she was glad Mace had come with her after all.

When he passed her into the gloom she saw he held his pistol in his hand, and she shuddered. So much violence had occurred today that even a hotel room suddenly held unknown horrors.

By the dim light filtering through the window across from the door, she watched him move quickly around the small room, checking behind the chest of drawers, inside the wardrobe, under the bed. He opened the window and leaned out, then closed it again, careful to latch it. Finally satisfied, he lit the lamp beside the bed.

The flame highlighted the planes of his face, flickering along his strong jaw made rough from a day's growth of dark beard. His blue eyes remained shadowed, appearing almost black.

Watching the light play across that hard, handsome face, it occurred to Kora that it wasn't exactly proper for Mace to be here in her room, especially at this time of night. She wondered if she should wait in the hall until he left, but that would look absurd. She'd leave the door open, and any busybodies awake this late could make what they wanted of it.

"Thank you for seeing me safely to my room," she said, still a little annoyed at how weak she must seem. She crossed to the window and leaned the rifle beside the bed.

"I don't suppose anyone that handy with a Sharps needs me as an escort, but I'll sleep better knowing you're safe."

Kora heard the teasing in his tone, but also the concern. She turned and parted the curtains, but with the lamp so close, she could see only its reflection in the window. She quickly pulled the curtains shut again.

"I'd better get back to my room. It's been a long day."

She heard Mace move toward the door, his footsteps heavy. Her heart went out to him.

"Don't worry. We'll get Jessica back safely," she said, turning toward him. "They'll come to the saloon tomorrow."

Mace paused, his hand on the door. He shook his head. "Tomorrow we're going to play this game a little differently. I'm going to Argenta."

He looked as though he thought she might object, but Kora felt only relief at his words. A whole day with nothing to do but wait and they might both go crazy. Circumstances had dictated they come to Bear Pass tonight, but tomorrow they could take the offensive.

"Just tell me when you want to leave, and I'll be ready," she told him. "If we go early enough, then even if we don't find them, we can be back here by eleven tomorrow night."

"Oh, no, not we." Mace's face darkened. "I'm going by myself."

Kora placed her hands on her hips, meeting his gaze with her own. If he thought he was going to run off without her again, he was dead wrong. "You have to take me," she said. "You need me to show you how to get there."

"Your grandfather can draw me a map."

"You'll never find Argenta by yourself, even with a map. There's not exactly a highway out there."

"I'll hire a guide!"

"And just whom are you going to hire? One of your friends from the saloon? You could end up tipping off the kidnappers to your plans and get your throat slit in the bargain."

Mace shut the door with a bang and approached her, frustration showing in his face. "I'm not going to put you in any more danger, and that's that," he said fiercely.

In the small room and dim light, he towered over her, power emanating from his lean figure, but she refused to be intimidated.

"What makes you think I'll be in any more danger out there with you than I would be sitting here in this hotel room all day where anyone can find me?"

Mace grabbed her shoulders and she thought he meant to shake her, but instead he sighed in defeat.

"You're right, of course. And stubborn as hell." A grin quirked at the corner of his mouth. "But at least I'll get the opportunity to see you dressed up like this again. Though I still don't know about that hat."

Kora's hands flew to her head, but not quickly enough. Mace snatched the hat from her and sent it flying across the room, laughing as her hair tumbled down her shoulders and across her face.

She glared at him, but she couldn't really be angry. He'd said she could go with him to Argenta. And besides, he was so appealing when he laughed.

Mace reached out to brush the hair away from her face, his eyes still laughing, but something tender also glowed there. A tremor ran through her as his fingers caressed her cheek. Mace must have felt it, too, for his eyes darkened. He brushed his thumb across her lips. Kora's memory conjured up the way his mouth had felt against hers this afternoon. Her lips parted to his touch. In the silence of the night, Kora thought she could hear their hearts beating.

"I think I'd better go," he said finally. The husky quality of his voice caught at her insides, and she shivered again. The strength of her desire to tell him not to leave shocked her into silence.

Mace ran his fingers through her hair one more time, the soft silkiness of it quickening his senses. Her eyes in this light shone a deep golden brown, bewitching him.

"Good night," he whispered, but he couldn't resist bending his head down to hers for just one kiss. Her lips felt like satin against his. She trembled as he pulled her closer, claiming her mouth with his.

Her lips parted, and her tongue touched his lips hesitantly, sending heat blazing through him, pushing away for a moment the anger and fear that had threatened to overwhelm him all evening. He plunged his tongue into her mouth, tasting her sweetness, reveling in the moan that escaped her in response.

As Mace's kiss deepened, Kora pressed closer to him for support. Even as the thought crossed her mind that she shouldn't be letting this happen, that she should be sending him on his way, her hands found their way to his shoulders, and then his neck, her fingers twining in the dark hair curling at its nape. Her breasts flattened against his chest, the nipples stiffening as they brushed the wool of her plaid shirt.

Mace's mouth left hers, and she gasped for breath as he ran his tongue along her jaw, down her neck to the hollow of her throat. His hands tugged her shirt loose from her pants and she felt the warmth of his palms against the bare skin of her back. Everywhere he touched her, her skin responded, sending white hot sparks to ignite a fire deep within her.

Kora knew a proper young lady would stop this now, but as Mace's hands brushed her belly and moved up to hold her breasts, any such thoughts melted away. This was what she wanted, what she needed from this man. He had not only given her his friendship, but also his respect. And she'd never been a proper young lady anyway.

With one hand Mace kneaded her left breast, his thumb rubbing her nipple, sensitizing it to his touch. He pulled the other hand from her shirt to begin unbuttoning it. As he slowly exposed her chest, he ran a string of kisses down her throat, down between the soft mounds. His mouth claimed her right breast, and Kora gasped, clutching at his shoulders, as yet a new wave of sensation rippled through her.

Mace tugged her shirt off down her arms and moved his hands lower, over the soft skin of her belly. He could feel her reaction to his slightest touch, and it was driving him crazy. He found her belt and unbuckled it. As he slowly undid the buttons to her pants, one hand slid between her thighs. She moaned deep in her throat. Even through the heavy denim he could feel her heat.

He rested his hands on her hips, fighting to retain control. He wanted this to be perfect for her, but he didn't know how much longer he could hold back. He wanted her so badly.

When Mace started to pull down her pants, Kora froze. No man had ever seen her naked before. She suddenly felt very unsure of herself.

Mace looked up and saw her expression. He stood and kissed her mouth once more. His hands slipped down to the small of her back and he pulled her close. She felt the hard length of him pressing against her.

"It's all right," he murmured. He pulled her hands up to the buttons of his shirt. "We'll do this first."

Kora looked up into the challenging twinkle in his eyes and felt herself blushing all the way down to the bottoms of her feet. Slowly, she undid his shirt, exposing the curly dark hair and the taut muscles. She had wondered what it would be like to run her hands over that broad chest, and she did so now, gently at first, then more boldly.

As Mace shrugged out of the shirt, she let her fingers trail down his flat stomach to his belly button, and then down the arrow of hair pointing to the waist of his pants.

"God, Kora." He kissed her again, and they clutched each other close, pressing skin to skin, her breasts roughened by his coarse hair. Heat flooded her. Her heart pounded in her ears.

Suddenly Mace lifted her against him and moved forward to deposit her gently on the bed. He leaned down to pull off her boots. When he tried to remove her pants this time, Kora arched her hips to help him get them off, no longer shy.

She watched him as he looked down at her. He trailed his fingers along her breast, then down to her hips.

"You're so beautiful," he said softly.

His fingers moved back down between her thighs, and all thought left her. Delicious tremors shot through her body at his intimate caress. The room began to spin as a hot tension built inside her. She cried out as his fingers slid inside her.

He lowered his mouth to that intimate place and stroked her with his tongue. Kora fought for breath, feeling herself losing control.

"Mace," she gasped, pleading, but not sure what she pleaded for. She gasped again when he stopped, opening her eyes to see him sitting on the bed beside her, pulling off his boots. She watched in fascination as he pulled off his pants, drinking in the sight of his nakedness, her eyes widening at the evidence of his desire.

When he looked up, the heat in his eyes burned her. He moved onto the bed beside her, pulling her close, kissing her deeply.

"Mace," she said again. Her body was desperate

for his. With a will of its own, it writhed against him.

"Kora, sweetheart," he murmured against her neck. His warm hand played across her body.

She touched him in return, marveling at the rough feel of the hair on his chest against her fingertips. She ran a hand down his back and along his hip, then hesitated. Mace reached down and guided her inward, to the surprising heat of his hard shaft. Kora stroked it gently, then, when he groaned in pleasure, she grasped him more firmly. A delighted smile touched her lips as he responded to her.

He moaned, smothering her smile with his lips, thrusting his tongue deep into the warm depths of her mouth. Then he rolled on top of her, and Kora felt the heat within her intensify yet again. With one knee he spread her legs, positioning himself between them. Gently, he guided himself to her, and Kora arched to meet him as he thrust inside her.

"This may hurt a little," he told her, as he pressed against her tightness. He looked into her eyes, dilated with desire, black rimmed with gold. He saw the trust in them and knew he'd do anything to deserve it.

He bent down and kissed her gently, rocking his hips just slightly, the moist heat of her tempting him beyond endurance.

But Kora wanted all of him. "Mace, please," she whispered huskily. She grabbed his buttocks and pulled him closer. He groaned as he thrust into her, and Kora felt a sharp, hot pain that quickly faded as he moved within her, filling her with sensation.

She felt as though she had melted and he was slicing through her, searing her senses. She rocked her hips to him, riding the waves of their passion.

Too aroused to hold back any longer, they came together with the explosiveness of a thunderstorm, and the tenderness of a summer rain. The world disappeared, and only the two of them remained, fused into one. Time stopped, but the sensations swelled. When it seemed as if they could go no farther, rapturous pleasure broke over them in a tremendous wave, wracking their bodies, shattering their senses.

When it was over, Mace eased himself to the side so Kora could breathe, and they lay together for a long moment, savoring what had happened between them.

Kora stared up at the ceiling, her cheek pressed to his, overwhelmed by love and hope and fear. Never in her life had she felt this way before. A sense beyond logic told her that in these moments she had given her heart to this man, without reservation, without knowing if he would give his heart in return.

"Mace . . ." she whispered.

"Hush, sweetheart," he answered gently. He rose to his knees to grab the quilt from the end of the bed and pull it up over them. Then he lay back beside her, his arm across her chest, enclosing her in warmth. "Sleep now. Tomorrow will be soon enough to talk."

A hundred questions spun in Kora's head, but before she could choose one of them to ask, she had fallen fast asleep.

Mace lay awake beside her, listening to the gentle rhythm of her breathing. Guilt curled on the edges of his mind for enjoying her so much while his beloved daughter faced unknown dangers alone. But deeper than that surged the renewed hope and strength that Kora had given him tonight, the faith to believe that he would find Jessica tomorrow and bring her back, safe and sound.

His mind told him that he should regret what had just happened, that caring for a woman this way would only get him hurt. His memory told him that love was fleeting and painful, and that trust in a woman was foolish and naïve.

But with Kora here beside him, her soft body beneath his hand, her scent filling his senses, his memories flickered dim and lifeless, revealing only a hole in his life that Kora could fill. And in that precious, timeless moment, he believed that love could last, maybe a lifetime, maybe forever.

11

Kora slipped out of sleep, a soft noise nudging her to consciousness. Her eyes crept open, and she blinked, trying to drive away the gray fuzziness, but then she realized that it was the room itself that was still dark. With a groan of protest, she rolled over on her side, pulling the covers up over her head.

A faint clatter came from the table next to her bed—the bed she had shared with Mace. Suddenly Kora was wide awake. She moved her hand across the sheet. Except for her, the bed was empty.

The rattling noise came again. Kora's heart leaped to her throat. There was someone in her room. Her mind told her it must be Mace, but the memory of her grandfather bleeding on his cabin floor sent a shiver down her spine.

Through the sheet that covered her, she saw the sudden glow of the lamp. If someone had come into her room to kill her, he certainly wouldn't have lit the lamp first.

Cautiously, she slid the sheet down to her chin.

"Good morning, sleepyhead."

Mace grinned down at her, leaning over the bed. In the instant of remembering what had passed between them last night, Kora had feared that he might regret having made love to her, but the tenderness in his voice made her heart jump with relief.

She noticed that he'd already shaved. He was dressed in old blue jeans and a blue work shirt that caught the sharper blue of his eyes. The clothes gave him a rugged look that made him even more handsome, if that were possible. He raised his eyebrows, and she realized she was staring. Quickly she looked away.

"I brought you some breakfast," he said easily, though doubts were darting through his mind. He had wanted her so badly last night that he hadn't considered the consequences. Did she regret what had happened? "Maybe some hot coffee will wake you up."

Kora's gaze came back to his, and he saw his own uncertainty mirrored there. But she sat up and tossed her head as though it were the most natural thing in the world for a man to bring her breakfast in the morning.

"Is there cream?" she asked, trying to sound nonchalant while stifling a yawn.

Her sleep-ruffled hair fell gently over her shoulders, and Mace let his eyes follow it down the soft curves of her breasts, creamy in the lamplight. He remembered the way they had felt in his hands, and his groin tightened.

Kora followed his gaze, and, suddenly remembering her nakedness, blushed furiously before diving back down beneath covers. She heard Mace's low laugh and felt the bed shift as he sat down on the edge of it. She grasped the sheets tightly in her fists, but instead of trying to pull them down from the top, Mace pulled them up from her feet and tossed them to the side, exposing her nudity.

"Oh!" Kora gasped, furious and embarrassed. She sat up to tug the covers back, but Mace's arms went around her waist, pulling her to him. Kora's hands flew to his chest to push against him.

"Let me go!"

To her surprise, he loosened his grip, but when she pulled away, he caught her wrists.

"Kora, you don't have to hide from me." At the half-pleading note in his voice, she looked up into his eyes. Their blue depths glowed with the embers of the desire she'd shared with him last night, and with another emotion, some gentleness that Kora didn't dare put a name to, lest it be gone. "I didn't mean to embarrass you. You're beautiful, Kora, and there's nothing shameful about your body."

As his eyes roamed over her again, Kora felt her skin prickle with heat, as though he touched her with more than his gaze. It might not be proper, but she didn't feel ashamed when he looked at her like that. He released one of her wrists, running his hand up her arm, over her shoulder, to touch her cheek. Kora lifted her hand to hold it there.

"I . . . I didn't know what you thought about last night," she admitted, watching his face intently for reaction. "Were you . . . are you . . . sorry?"

"God, Kora." Mace took her face in both hands and brought his lips down to hers, almost bruising them with the strength of his kiss. He nudged her lips apart with his tongue, teasing her until her tongue came out to meet his. The heat of that kiss reached deep inside her, rekindling the fire she had felt last night.

Finally, he pulled back.

"Does that answer your question?" he asked huskily. "How could I be sorry that you let me share that with you?"

Happiness swelled within her, but when she reached for him again, he backed away.

"Don't tempt me, sweetheart," he said with a quick flash of a smile. He rose and moved to the tray he'd left on the table. "We have other business to attend to today."

Kora propped a pillow behind her and sat up again, careful to hold the sheet close to her chest this time, while Mace mixed cream and sugar into her coffee.

"Thank you," she said when he handed her the cup and saucer. Somehow she managed to hold the sheet up while sipping the hot beverage. The heat worked its way down to her toes and brushed the last of the cobwebs from her tired brain.

"What time is it?"

"About five-thirty." Mace pushed aside the curtain to glance out into the darkness. "There should be plenty of light by the time you're dressed and we're ready to go. Here, you'll need more than just coffee." He took Kora's cup and handed her a thick slice of bread spread with butter and blackberry jam. "There's some cold ham, too."

"I'm surprised Mrs. Kruger was up so early," she said, taking a large bite of the bread.

"She wasn't. I helped myself to a few things I

found in the kitchen. We've paid for our meals here, after all."

Mace took a long swallow of his own coffee, then glanced back at Kora. Another grin curled at the edge of his mouth.

"As much as I'd love to stay and watch you dress, I'd better go see about the mules. I won't be long." He walked to the door and was gone.

As soon as the door closed behind him, Kora slipped out of bed and dressed, the morning chill spurring her on. Her cold fingers fumbled over the buttons of her shirt, and she shivered as she pulled on her denim pants, which felt as though they'd frozen stiff overnight.

Once dressed, she ate the rest of the food on the tray Mace had left. She found the hat he'd tossed in the corner the night before and pulled it firmly onto her head over her carefully braided hair. She didn't want anything interfering with her sight today. As a finishing touch, she tied a red kerchief around her neck. Finally, she picked up her grandfather's rifle and took a last look at herself in the mirror over the dresser.

She grimaced. She hoped it was her scintillating personality Mace found appealing, because she wasn't going to charm anyone looking like this.

She could almost be mistaken for Troy, she thought. Even her bust was fairly well hidden under the baggy plaid shirt. She tugged a wisp of blond hair down from under the hat brim, then shook her head in defeat and turned away from the mirror.

Kora made her way down to the room where her grandfather and Mace were staying. She paused to knock lightly. When there was no answer, she entered.

A lamp glowed on the table between the beds, and Mace's razor sat beside it, but he hadn't yet returned from the stable. Kora moved over to her grandfather's bed. Even in this dim light, Kora thought he looked better. His face appeared more relaxed, less pale.

He stirred as she reached out to feel the skin around his bandage, relieved to find it cool.

His eyes fluttered open. "Kora?"

"How are you feeling, Grandpa?" she asked softly.

"*Ach*, I've felt worse. And better," he answered. He shifted as though to sit, but Kora put a restraining hand on his chest.

"Don't get up. You need your rest." She waited until he relaxed back against his pillow. "The kidnappers never showed up last night. Mace and I are going out to Argenta this morning. Maybe we'll find Jessica there. If not, we hope to be back before dark."

"I don't like the idea of you going out there with Mace," Fritz said, frowning. "These are dangerous men."

"I know, Grandpa, but I have to," Kora told him. "I'm the only one who can show him how to get there. But I need your help to refresh my memory on the landmarks."

"*Mein Gott.*" Fritz rolled his eyes at her, but he carefully answered her questions about which trails to take. "If you get lost, come back south," he told her finally. "You'll reach the toll road sooner or later."

As she looked over the notes she'd just taken, she could feel her grandfather's eyes still on her.

"Kora, why did you change your mind about coming here with me?"

She wondered why he brought it up now. "It's a long story, Grandpa."

Fritz eyed her speculatively. "Your mama says your young man proposed. But I think you will not marry him, *ja?*"

A faint blush touched Kora's cheeks. Did everyone know Jared had asked her to marry him? "No, Grandpa, I told him no."

"And Mace?"

The blush deepened to a hot red. Could he have guessed about last night? But there was no censure in his eyes, only love and concern.

"He hasn't asked me," she said finally, dodging the question.

Fritz just smiled enigmatically. "I like Mace. He's a good man. You deserve better than that Jared."

Before Kora could ask him what he meant, Mace returned, and Kora had scarcely time to give her grandfather a kiss before Mace hurried her out the door.

Soon they were riding into the mountains in the fresh morning air. Kora's runaway mule had found her way back to her home stable in Bear Pass, and Kora rode her, while Mace rode his belligerent gray.

The farther they rode from Bear Pass, the narrower and rockier the trails became. As the sun rose above them, the day grew hotter, gradually quieting the birds and insects, which were the only creatures they encountered as they rode. Concern for Jessica filled both their thoughts, and neither spoke much.

Noon found them beside a clear-running mountain creek. They stopped to rest the mules and eat some of the sandwiches Mace had brought.

"Shouldn't we be there by now?" he asked her as they finished their quick meal.

Kora knelt down beside the creek to rinse her

hands. "I guess it's farther than I remembered. We're making good time, but it seems to me that we've got at least another hour before we reach Argenta."

She didn't need to look up to know that worry etched Mace's face. They'd known it was a gamble to come out here today, but it wasn't a gamble they could afford to lose.

Kora soaked her kerchief in the creek, pressing the cold cloth to her hot cheeks before knotting it back around her neck.

"I'll try to pick up the pace," she added.

Mace nodded. Without another word they started out again.

Nearly two hours later, Kora pulled her mule to an abrupt halt. They had come through a narrow, boulder-filled pass that their mules had somehow navigated with ease, and now they were winding their way down a mountainside. A break in the trees lay just ahead of them where the trail widened slightly. Her spirits leaped. For the past hour she'd been fighting the fear that she'd gotten them horribly lost, but if she was right, that clearing should give them a view down into Argenta.

"What is it?" Mace asked from behind her.

"Shh." Kora dismounted from her mule. He did the same and came forward to meet her.

"I think we may be able to see Argenta from down there," she whispered. "We'll have to be quiet from here on. Sound travels far in the mountains."

He nodded. "Then let's go see what we can see."

They tied the mules to a tree out of sight and moved forward to the bare ledge that looked over the little valley below. Dropping to their hands and knees, they made their way to the edge. Mace could feel his fear and doubt fade away as the excitement of renewed purpose took its place.

But when he looked out over the valley, all he saw were trees, rocks, and irregular clearings covered in dry yellow grass. No sign of human habitation. They had to be lost. There was no way they could get back to Bear Pass by eleven o'clock tonight to make the kidnappers' second meeting. What was going to happen to his daughter?

"I don't see anything," he said, his emotions lurching dangerously from hope to despair.

"But that's it."

He looked at Kora in confusion. "What's it?"

"See, there's a cabin over there."

He followed her pointing finger down into a stand of white fir trees. He could just make out the jumble of logs that Kora had called a cabin.

"There's another one not far from it. And see those four posts over in the clearing?" Kora gestured back up the valley. "That's where the general store was going to be."

It took him a moment to find the posts she'd mentioned. "This is a ghost town?"

"I guess it's not exactly a ghost town, considering it was never really a town in the first place. A couple of miners thought they'd found good silver ore out here, and speculators jumped in, selling off lots for the 'new Virginia City.' They called the town Argenta and laid out plans for its growth. A few people even began a cabin or two. But nothing ever came of the rumor of silver, and the place was abandoned."

Mace shook his head in amazement. "It really is a sickness, isn't it? This fever for gold and silver."

"Maybe so, but it helped get California her statehood," Kora said. "And it helps keep the newspapers in business. So, where do we start?"

Mace wondered that himself. It didn't look as though anyone had even stopped at this little nothing of a place in years, much less that his daughter might be hidden somewhere nearby.

"I suppose I'll have to go take a look around," he said.

"If I remember correctly, there's only one cabin that's still intact. It should be somewhere in those trees down there." Kora pointed farther down the valley. "Grandpa and I stayed there a couple of nights when we came here last year."

Mace couldn't see much through the pines, but he knew he had to trust Kora's memory. It had brought them this far. He backed up, staying close to the ground until he was sure he couldn't be seen from the valley floor. Kora followed.

"I think it would be best for me to continue on foot from here," he told her as he checked his pistol one more time to make sure it was loaded and ready to fire. He glanced up the trail to satisfy himself that the mules still waited where they'd tethered them. "You keep your eyes open. If someone you don't know comes along this trail, don't hesitate to shoot if it seems necessary."

He saw Kora's jaw set in that stubborn tilt he was coming to know so well.

"I'm coming with you."

Mace pushed his pistol into the belt of his denims and shook his head. "No," he said with finality. "You're staying right here."

Her eyes narrowed. "I won't be in your way, if that's what you're worried about. I'm a pretty good shot with a rifle, as you may remember from last night when I saved your arrogant hide!"

Mace didn't know whether to frown or to laugh. He reached out to touch her cheek instead.

"You're the damned stubbornnest woman I've ever met. But this time, you're going to wait here."

He placed a finger over her lips to forestall the argument she was forming. "Just listen a minute. There's plenty of good reasons for what I'm asking, including the fact that I want to be sure no one sneaks up on us from the back. But aside from that, I need to focus all my attention on rescuing Jessica, if she's down there. I won't be able to do that if I have to be worrying about you."

When she opened her mouth to speak, he continued. "Kora, I would worry. I've lost too many people that I've loved. I don't want to consider the possibility, but I may have lost my only daughter. I couldn't bear it if anything happened to you. Do you understand?"

Her eyes softened, and he saw some of the tension leave her, though he could tell she still wanted to convince him to let her come. But she didn't argue. He bent down and kissed her, savoring the sweet taste of her lips. To his surprise, she wrapped her arms around his neck and pulled him close, kissing him back fervently. He pressed her against him, needing her soft warmth in his arms.

Finally, he backed away, looking down into her face. Her cat's eyes shone with unshed tears as her lips tried to frown at him. Even wearing that silly hat, she was the most beautiful woman he'd ever seen.

"I'll be back in no time," he assured her, his voice rough. Then he turned and began his way down into the valley. He could feel Kora's gaze on his back until he went around a bend, out of her sight.

The rough path dropped sharply toward the valley floor, and as he picked his way around boulders and over minor landslides, he wondered how Argenta's founders had managed to get in the tools to complete the few structures that had actually been built. Everything must have been packed in by mules. After his ride out here today, his respect for those stubborn, odd-looking animals had risen inestimably.

When Mace reached the relatively level ground of the small valley, he realized he must be near the location of the cabin Kora had mentioned. He slowed his pace, his ears pricked for any odd sound. Only a few birdcalls, sounding lazy in the afternoon heat, broke the silence.

As he moved forward, his attention was caught by a shape through the trees. He slipped closer, and the boxy outline of a small cabin became clear.

Mace stepped off the path. The dry grass crackled beneath his feet. He cursed under his breath and placed his feet more carefully, advancing from tree to tree toward the side of the cabin. The wood looked gray and splintery with neglect. A hole for a window had been cut into the wall, but only a square of rotting brown burlap covered it.

Mace stood silently at the window for several minutes, but he heard no sound from within. Moving more quickly now, he walked to the back of the cabin, which was a solid wall. He crept around to the far side, and there he stopped, his pulse jumping.

Someone had built a small, bare corral on this side of the building, apparently using lumber cannibalized from the other abandoned structures. The corral had recently held a large animal, probably a mule, probably as recently as this morning, Mace judged from the freshness of the evidence, wrinkling his nose.

He ducked through the fence in order to stay near the cabin wall. He passed another burlap-covered window, slipped through the other side of the corral, and rounded the front of the cabin to find himself facing the door.

He pulled his pistol from his belt and took a deep breath, trying to control the sudden thundering of his heart. Someone had been there today, but that didn't mean Jessica had. And even if Jessica had been held there, she might have been taken away by the person who had left with the mule.

He took another breath and cocked his revolver. Then he charged the door, hitting it squarely with his left shoulder. It burst open, sending him sprawling across the plank floor. He let his momentum roll him onto his back and raised the gun, moving it with the arc of his gaze as he quickly scanned the cabin.

The room was gloomy, even with the light from the open door, but it took him only a few seconds to see he was in no danger. The cabin was deserted. The room contained only a small table, a chest of some kind, some shelves holding basic food stuffs and a few dishes, and a wooden cot.

Disappointment washed over him, and Mace pounded his fist on the floor, instantly regretting it as a vicious splinter cut into the side of his hand.

"Damn it!" he roared in frustration.

A sharp creak broke the stillness of the cabin, coming from the direction of the cot against the back wall. Mace whirled toward it, rolling up onto his knees with the pistol ready. A brown wool blanket covered the cot, and something moved beneath it. Something small. A muffled whimper rose from under the blanket.

The pistol clattered to the floor as Mace jumped to his feet and stumbled to the cot. He flung the blanket aside and found himself looking down into the frightened blue eyes of his daughter.

"Jess, Jess, honey," he sobbed, dropping beside her. She looked so pale and small, but she was alive. He fumbled with the gag stuffed into her mouth.

"Papa!" Her thin, raw voice tore at his heart.

"Are you all right, kitten?" he asked anxiously, laying a hand against her cheek. It was hot and damp from the oppressive heat of the cabin and the suffocating blanket. "Are you hurt?"

"I'm okay, Papa." Her brave whisper brought tears to his eyes.

"Everything's going to be fine now," he assured her. He could tell her hands were tied beneath her, but he had to untie her feet from the end of the cot before he could turn her over and free her hands. The rope had rubbed her wrists raw, and Mace had to clench his jaw not to voice the curses he wanted to heap on the men who had treated her this way.

As soon as her arms were freed, she turned to him and wrapped them around his neck, burying her face in his shoulder.

"I was so scared, Papa!"

Mace hugged his daughter close. "Are you all right?" he asked again. "Did they hit you or hurt you in any way?"

He felt her shake her head against his shoulder. "He didn't hurt me, but I'm thirsty," she told him.

Mace set her down on the cot. "He?" he asked as

he rose to find her something to drink. "Weren't there two men?"

A bucket of water sat on the table. It was warm, but it would do for now.

"Only one of the men stayed here with me."

Mace found a metal cup on one of the shelves, filled it, and handed it to his daughter.

"Drink it slowly, Jess," he warned. While Mace kept a protective arm around her shoulders, she did as she was told, taking small sips of the stale water until she emptied the cup.

"Is that better?"

She nodded, her eyes dark and serious. "I'm so glad you came, Papa. How did you find me?"

"Fritz heard the kidnappers say they were going to bring you here," Mace told her. He glanced around the cabin, trying to judge the time by the light from the door. He wanted to get Jessica away from there as soon as possible. There was no telling when the man who was supposed to be guarding her would be back.

"Grandpa Fritz is all right?" Jessica's anxious question brought his full attention back to his daughter.

"Yes, he is doing just fine." He was surprised at her affectionate term for the old man.

"I'm so glad!" A smile crossed her face for the first time since he'd found her. "I thought that horrible man had killed him."

Mace waited for an explanation of why she called him "Grandpa Fritz," but none was forthcoming. He experienced a moment of perverse jealousy. She'd never called his father "Grandpa," just "Grandfather." Then again, his father had never paid her any loving attention or made any attempt to be Jessica's friend. Fritz had.

"And that's my father's loss," Mace murmured to himself, looking down at his beautiful, loving daughter.

Too late, the sound of footsteps told him that someone was approaching the cabin.

"Hey! What's going on? Missy!" The anxious shouts were accompanied by a hurrying of footsteps. The kidnapper had seen the open cabin door.

Mace heard Jessica gasp in fear beside him as he reached for his pistol. Just as he remembered he had dropped it on the floor, a tall, thin man with a mane of wild blond hair and a scraggly beard appeared in the doorway.

The man's eyes narrowed as he peered into the dark room, then widened in shock when he saw Mace. Mace dove for his pistol, getting another splinter as he snatched the gun up off the floor. Surprise stunned the blond man for an instant, but he was raising his rifle as Mace fumbled to get his finger on his trigger. Jessica's scream ripped through the cabin.

Mace heard the shot, but wasn't sure he had been the one to fire it until he saw the barrel of the other man's rifle drop to the floor, followed almost unbelievably slowly by the man's body.

"Papa!"

Mace turned in time to catch the small figure hurtling toward him. He caught her to him and felt her sobs against his chest.

"It's all right. It's all right, kitten," he said as he kept an eye on the kidnapper and his gun. A red stain spread across the man's chest.

A frightened moan escaped the kidnapper, silencing Jessica who looked up, saw the blood, and looked away again quickly.

"Help me," the man begged, his eyes on Mace. "Oh, God, don't let me die."

"Why not?" Mace asked, his voice harsh. "It's no more than you deserve for what you've put my daughter through." Then he looked down at Jessica and saw her troubled blue eyes staring up at him.

"I ain't never hurt her, mister," the man said, his voice labored and desperate. "I never hurt you none, did I, missy? I never would hurt a little girl."

"And just what do you call leaving her tied up in a hot cabin without fresh air or water?" Mace asked angrily as he rose to his feet and moved over to examine the man's wounds. It didn't take a medical expert to see that the man was losing blood much too fast. He was going to die with or without Mace's help.

"Don't let me die," the man pleaded again. Mace could see the fear in his eyes, as he had in the eyes of so many men who had fallen on the Civil War battlefields.

"I'll do what I can," he said curtly. He felt a familiar sickness in his stomach at the hope and gratitude in the dying man's eyes.

He strode to the cot and pulled off the dirty sheet. As he came back across the cabin, he saw Jessica watching him, her eyes wide and frightened.

"Go wait outside," he ordered. When she hesitated, he went to her and gave her a quick kiss on the top of her head. "Go on," he said gently, but firmly. "I'll be right here if you get scared, but I want you to wait outside. All right?"

Jessica nodded. Mace gave her a push toward the door, then turned back to the man on the floor. He ripped a large square from the sheet, then knelt down to unbutton the man's blood-soaked shirt.

"I wouldn'ta hurt her," the blond man repeated, wincing as Mace pulled the shirt away from his skin. "It wasn't even my idea. I wish I'd never agreed to it."

Mace grunted. He folded the cloth he held into a thick pad and placed it over the man's wounds. He couldn't use pressure to stop the bleeding, because he was pretty sure the bullet had shattered a rib and, from the sound of the man's breathing, maybe punctured a lung.

"I just really needed the money," the blond man continued, talking to keep from thinking about his wound. "This fella came to me and said if I helped him hold this little girl, I'd get half the ransom. I been mining here in this godless state for near two years now, and I never found even enough gold to live on."

The man's voice quivered with distress as he struggled for air to speak. He grabbed Mace's sleeve, trying to make him understand. "I was all done in. My money's gone, my health was going. I'm sorry now, but I didn't know what to do. I didn't mean no harm. Ma always said my luck's just bad. I guess I won't be seeing her again."

Mace looked down at the bearded, sweating face before him. For a second, instead of a vicious criminal he saw a young man who once had dreamed California would make him rich, one of the hundreds of thousands who, instead of realizing their dreams, ended up broken and penniless. That didn't excuse kidnapping. But Mace couldn't turn away from the plea for some kind of forgiveness in the dying man's pale eyes. And Mace needed the man's knowledge.

"If you're truly sorry, then give me your help," he said, watching the man fight off his pain to listen. "You're the only one who can help me find your partner. Jessica says you brought her here alone. Where's the man who planned the kidnapping? What's his name?"

The man's lips moved, but it took a moment for sound to emerge. He was weakening fast.

"Don't know his name. He wouldn't say. Big man. Black beard. Real cold eyes, I remember. Cold green eyes. And a scar on his cheek." The man's eyes closed.

Mace froze. This man had just described Fred from the Eagle Saloon.

"Was he supposed to get the ransom money from me?" he asked. There was no reply. He leaned forward. "You're lying," he said, his voice rising in anger. "That man tried to kill me last night. He never even said he had my daughter."

The blond man's eyes fluttered open once more. He could hardly breathe now, and Mace felt a sticky dampness beneath his hand where blood soaked through the folded sheet.

"No." The word was hardly more than a whisper, and Mace had to strain to hear the rest. "'S the truth. He was . . . meet you . . . Eagle Saloon. Get money. Said . . . no trouble . . . we get rich. Girl safe."

The pale blue eyes fixed anxiously on his, and Mace knew the man was telling the truth as he knew it. Fred had played this failed miner for a sucker as well. The man's mother had been right. His luck was bad.

12

Kora hurried through the pines, her pounding heart drowning out the sounds of her footsteps. She knew she should slow down and proceed more carefully, but the sound of a single gunshot had sent her running pell-mell after Mace, and she couldn't stop.

If anything had happened to him . . .

Ahead she saw the cabin, partly hidden by the trees. She slowed to a swift walk, gripping her grandfather's rifle in both hands.

She edged through the trees toward the front of the cabin. In the little clearing before the door stood a small figure with long, dark hair, wearing a dusty blue dress.

"Jessica!" She couldn't prevent the excited cry that escaped her.

The girl spun around, a smile on her lips, but

bewilderment and fear replaced the welcome when her eyes found Kora among the shadows of the trees.

Kora suddenly remembered how she must look.

"It's me, honey. It's Kora," she called reassuringly, pulling off her hat, so Jessica could see her golden hair.

"Kora!" Jessica ran toward her, and Kora scooped her up in her arms.

"Are you all right?" she asked, leaning back on her heels to see Jessica better. Then, she remembered why she had run down here in the first place. "I heard a shot. Your father, is he all right?"

"I'm okay," Jessica said. "And Papa's fine, too."

But her eyes remained troubled.

"Where is he? Is something wrong?"

"He's in there." Jessica pointed to the cabin. But when Kora moved toward it, she stopped her with a tug on Kora's sleeve. "He shot the man who brought me here. I think he's dying. Papa said to wait out here."

Kora looked down at the girl beside her. As much as she wanted to run to the cabin and see for herself that Mace was safe and alive, Jessica needed her more.

She bent down to give the girl another hug, relief spreading through her. Mace and Jessica were safe, and by early tomorrow morning they should all be back in Bear Pass, reunited with her grandfather.

As she sat down to wait beneath one of the towering sugar pines, an almost dizzying sense of possibility opened before her. She had fallen in love with a handsome, caring man, who had been willing to risk his life to save his beloved daughter. Not only that, she was coming to love the daughter as well, and was pretty sure Jessica felt the same.

Jessica sat down beside her, and Kora took her hand, letting herself give in to the happiness that shimmered just before her eyes. In sharp contrast to how she'd felt about Jared, she could easily imagine herself as Mace's wife, adventuring together in pursuit of stories, writing by his side, caring for his daughter . . . and any other children they might have together. A smile touched Kora's lips. Right now she saw no reason why her dreams could not come true.

Early evening found Kora, Mace, and Jessica making camp near a small creek about halfway back to Bear Pass. None of them had wanted to stay in the dilapidated Argenta cabin. Whereas once the town had been merely a symbol of false hopes and wasted dreams, now it seemed truly haunted.

Mace had buried the kidnapper in a shallow grave in a clearing near the cabin. They had placed a makeshift wooden cross at the head of the grave but hadn't known what name to put there. The man's soul had joined the ranks of the other miners lost in the harsh wilderness of the Sierra Nevada.

They had brought his mule with them, holding faint hopes that someone in Bear Pass might recognize the beast and thus be able to identify the dead man.

Perhaps the shadow of that death kept Mace from being able simply to enjoy his daughter's safe return to him. Throughout the afternoon's ride, his mind had been unable to let go of the question of why the black-bearded Fred, a man he didn't know, had wanted to kidnap Jessica and kill him. It didn't make sense.

As they sat around a small fire, eating the last of the sandwiches Mace had brought, an idea struck him. Suspicion began to grow in his heart, despite his attempts to dismiss it. After he helped Kora roll out the blankets they had brought and kissed an exhausted Jessica good night, he wandered away from the camp to consider it more carefully.

The pink glow of the evening sky was darkening to purple, the shadows already deep below the jagged peaks of the mountains. Mace went to the edge of the small flat where they were camped and looked out over the short drop to the creek bed.

He took out a cigarette—his last, he noticed—and lit it, enjoying the pungent smoke as it mixed with the clear, cold evening air. Then he heard footsteps behind him. He waited for Kora to speak, but she was silent, listening to the burbling of the creek.

He turned to look at her. Even dressed in an old shirt and blue jeans, she took his breath away. She had left her hat back at the camp, and her braided hair revealed her ears, which were like small seashells above her smooth neck. Wisps of gold hair framed her fine-boned features, and her eyes glinted in the fading daylight.

When she focused those eyes on him, Mace couldn't resist the urge to take her face in his hands and kiss her. Her lips were warm and pliant against his, and the kiss quickly escalated beyond the gentle caress he'd intended. He moved his hands to her shoulders and down her back, loving the way she felt pressed against his chest.

But she pulled back to look up at him with concern. "Mace, something's been bothering you."

He shook his head and bent to kiss her again, but

she pulled farther back. He saw the glint of determination in her eyes and sighed.

"I've been trying to figure out why Jessica was kidnapped," he said.

"Not just for the ransom money?" Kora asked.

"Apparently not." Mace told her what the blond man had said about his partner, the black-bearded man with the scar. "He tried to kill me—not a very practical method of collecting ransom. And even if he had asked me for money, it would still have been odd. Who knew we were out at Fritz's cabin or that my family could afford a large ransom? But he didn't ask for money. He never even acknowledged that he knew who I was. He set me up to look like I cheated at cards, the whole time planning to murder me. I can only assume that Jessica's kidnapping was meant to lure me into a situation where I could be conveniently disposed of."

He felt Kora shiver at the thought, and it tugged at his heart.

"But that doesn't make much sense," she said. "If you didn't know him, what reason could he have had for wanting to kill you? And even if he had a reason, he could have found a less complicated way of doing it. Why bring Jess into it at all?"

Mace looked down at her serious face. She'd cut to the heart of the questions he'd struggled with all day. He liked the sharpness of her mind.

But he didn't like the direction in which the questions led. "The only explanation I can think of, is that whoever wanted me dead also wanted to make sure that if I survived the attack, Jessica would still be out of the way."

"Why?" Kora asked in bewilderment. "Who?"

Mace gazed over her head. Instead of the thickening shadows around them, he saw a figure wrapped in a dark cloak, standing in the rain, holding a small, crying bundle.

He saw again the fear in Cecilia's eyes, her desperation as she begged him to take the child, protect it and care for it as if it were his own. He had never seen Cecilia afraid before. Even after betraying him, she had shown no fear of Mace, only fear that he might turn her baby away.

Her strange terror—combined with the fact that she had run from Missouri, risking giving birth on the way back to Boston rather than looking for help from her Calbert neighbors—had later caused Mace to give credence to old man Jackson's accusations that Cecilia and Jesse had been involved in murder.

But what if Jackson had got it wrong? What if it had been Jesse and not Booth Garrett who had been reluctant to sell his share in the ranch? Perhaps Jackson had been right in thinking the attackers weren't really Indians, that they were hired guns. But maybe they'd been hired by Garrett to get rid of Jesse, and not the other way around.

That would explain Garrett's strange reaction to Mace's visit, the feeling Mace had got that the man was hiding something. And if a man like that—ruthless enough to arrange the murder of his partner and a pregnant woman—truly believed a little girl to be a threat to his fortune, he wouldn't hesitate to take whatever steps were necessary to eliminate that threat. Mace's gut clenched at the thought that Garrett could simply have decided to murder them all, or at least Jessica, instead of concocting such an elaborate scheme. But the man's cleverness had got the best of him this time.

If this speculation had any validity at all, that is. The possibility remained that Mace's own obsession with the past had led his imagination to twist the facts into such a bizarre scenario.

"Mace? Mace, tell me what you're thinking."

He looked at Kora. If his suspicions were unfounded, she might be able to help him see the holes in his theory. But in order to tell her that he thought Garrett might be behind the kidnapping, he would have to tell her everything else.

He looked into her golden eyes, wide with concern and trust. He recalled the night before, and the love and hope she had given him, without asking anything in return. She had never asked for anything from him except his respect, even after what they'd shared. She hadn't asked him for money or clothes or jewels, things Cecilia had expected as a matter of course. But now she was asking for his trust.

And deep in his heart, Mace knew he had to give it to her. If he couldn't share his past with her, he didn't deserve to share her future. But if he told her, would she want to spend the future with him? Would she understand, or would she turn from him, leaving him alone again with those ancient demons?

Looking down at this slender, lovely woman, he could let himself imagine his life was perfect. He had found his daughter, who was now sleeping safely only yards away. He had found Kora somehow, when he least expected to fall in love again. And right now, in the twilight of this clear, fresh evening, he wanted to pretend he had also put the past to rest. He had to tell Kora everything, but not tonight.

"It's probably just anxiety and lack of sleep making me overly suspicious," he said finally, pulling her close again. "I don't want to talk about it until I've thought it through."

She peered up at him, unsatisfied with his response. Despite the warmth in his eyes, she sensed him pulling away again, closing off some part of himself.

"You can't just say you think someone wants to kill you, and then not explain," she insisted.

But instead of replying, Mace bent down and kissed her again. The heat from his mouth and tongue coursed through her body, reawakening the fire she had felt the night before and pushing to one side her misgivings about his secretiveness.

She managed to free her mouth from his. "Mace, talk to me."

But he ignored her, his lips traveling down her jaw to her neck. Kora lifted her hands to his shoulders to push him away, but then his tongue found her earlobe, and a bolt of electricity took her breath away. With a will of their own, her arms slipped around his neck, and she clung to him as a sweet golden fire burgeoned within her.

"We'll talk," Mace promised, his soft words breathed against her ear. "Tomorrow."

His hand found the buttons of her shirt and slipped inside it to cup her breast. Any thought beyond the feeling of his warm hand on her flesh, playing with her nipple, fled from her mind. Mace opened her shirt, letting the cool night air play on her skin as he bent to take her breast in his mouth, moving his hand to massage the other. A moan escaped Kora's throat.

She couldn't believe she was letting him do this to her, out in the open air, with nothing but some flowering dogwood saplings to hide them from Jessica and the trail. But it felt so good to have him touch her, to touch him, to breathe in the musk of his scent under the day's dust. She ran her hands through his hair as he suckled at her breasts, the roughness of his unshaved chin prickling her skin.

But when his hands found the buttons of her blue jeans, she struggled to regain her reason.

"Mace, stop," she pleaded, her voice shaky with desire. She tried again. "We can't do this."

"Can't we?" The husky voice tempted her, while his hand slipped down the front of her pants to the moist heat between her legs. A shudder of pleasure ran through her, and she knew he felt it, because he chuckled deep in his throat as he rose to kiss her again, his hand still rubbing her gently.

"But Jessica," she tried one last time, hardly hearing her own words as the hot fire rose within her.

"Sound asleep."

Kora gasped as his fingers pushed into her, and she knew she was lost. Mace stopped his caress then to help her step out of her boots and then her pants and drawers. He held her close again, his hands pressing against her buttocks. She could feel his desire straining through the denim of his pants. Kora hardly felt the cold air through the heat that crackled between them.

She wanted his skin against hers. She unbuttoned his shirt, letting her fingers run across his chest. Her roving hands found the waist of his pants and boldly unbuttoned them. She slipped a hand around his erect shaft, feeling a pleasing sense of her own power as Mace groaned in response. She stroked him with more authority, wanting to make him as wild as he made her.

"Oh, God, Kora. What you do to me."

Mace pulled off his shirt and spread it on a nearby boulder. He lifted Kora against him and placed her on the shirt. His mouth found her breasts again as his hands spread her thighs. Then his lips moved down, his tongue making lazy circles across her belly. Kora clutched his shoulders as the tension within her became almost unbearable.

He moved down further, and suddenly his tongue found her warm, moist center. Kora bit back her cry of pleasure as waves of sensation rolled through her. Her senses whirled as his tongue caressed her.

When she thought she couldn't take the sweet torture a moment longer, he stopped. He stood, lifting her with him, then turned to sit on the boulder, gently lowering Kora onto his lap. She felt his shaft slip against her, then find her entrance, and she felt Mace shudder as she slid down the length of him.

His blue eyes burned into hers as he moved inside her. He was all she could see, all she could feel, as the movement of their bodies came together, rocking against one another in an ancient rhythm.

As the pleasure she felt rose to a fever pitch, Mace pulled her forward. His lips brushed hers, then moved to her ear.

"Kora," he murmured, almost too low for her to hear. But she did hear, and as the universe shattered around her, she clutched him, wanting him closer, pulling him in. As her senses whirled, she felt Mace shudder within her, thrusting into her until they melded into one. The joy she felt at their union was tempered only by her memory of his earlier evasiveness. But she didn't want to think of that now. She wrapped her arms around Mace and pulled him close, driving away any distance between them with sheer physical proximity.

In the depths of a dreamless sleep, Kora was stirred by a sound. At first her sleep-drugged mind thought she heard the laughter of schoolchildren, but as sleep faded, she realized that if she heard laughter, it was the bone-chilling, unearthly laughter of a fiend from hell. Suddenly fully awake, her ears rang with the horrible cackling that echoed from the mountainsides, the chuckles and shrieks of ghastly demons cutting into her brain.

Her heart pounding, she fought back terror as her eyes tried to pierce the darkness around her. The fire had died, and the myriad stars she could see above her in the clear night sky did nothing to illuminate the dark earth.

As the horrible noise continued, the rational portion of her mind finally realized it must be coyotes playing some game as they chased each other through the night. She swallowed, trying to force her heart back down into her chest, but even as the wild cries faded away into the darkness, part of her still felt as though the hounds of hell had suddenly been loosed on her trail.

Kora pulled her blanket closer around her. Even though she wore her clothes beneath the heavy wool, she felt chilled. She looked around her again, trying to make out Mace and Jessica in the darkness, but she could see nothing. Only the outline of the trees against the stars took form before her eyes.

Just go back to sleep, Kora ordered herself firmly, rolling over and pulling the blanket up to her nose.

She let her mind drift to thoughts of making love with Mace, feeling safe and secure in his arms. She tried to bring back her daydreams of the afternoon, of being Mace's wife, of being with him forever.

But alone in the dark she couldn't get past his silence when she'd asked him why someone would want to kill him. He had closed himself off from her again, and despite the pleasure they had given each other, Kora couldn't help wondering why. He had called her sweetheart, he had made her his lover, but he had never said he loved her. She couldn't bear the thought that he might not. For she knew, with the deep, aching certainty of someone who has finally found what she is looking for but doesn't know if it is hers to take, that she had fallen in love with Mace.

But the calls of the coyotes had sent a chill through her that even the heartrending joy of that knowledge could not dispel. The haunting, unholy sounds conjured up visions of the man they had buried today, of her grandfather lying on his cabin floor, and of poor Rosemarie Amado and her husband, who was waiting to be hanged. She felt helpless, unable to prevent these senseless tragedies. When Kora finally drifted back to sleep, she fell into dreams dark with danger and uncertainty.

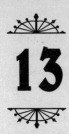

13

Mace found himself whistling as he crossed the road from the Bear Pass General Store, where he'd just bought a fresh supply of cigarettes, to the Union Hotel. He and Jessica and Kora had arrived in town late that morning, exhausted and hungry, to find a worried Fritz all ready to come out after them. But after a hearty breakfast and a catnap, Mace felt as good as new.

Maybe even better. A smile played across his face as he thought of Kora and how lovely she'd looked that morning, her hair coming loose from her braids, yawning like a kitten. He must be in love to find her more beautiful like that than any of the impeccably dressed maidens who had sought his company in Boston. Unexpectedly, incredibly, he had fallen in love.

And if he loved her, he had to share his past with her. He frowned as his thoughts turned to Booth

Garrett. If his suspicions were correct, he had to deal with that man before he could begin planning a future. He couldn't be sure that Jessica and Kora were safe until he knew the truth about Jessica's kidnapping.

"Fielding!"

Mace turned at the sound of his name, halting halfway up the hotel steps. A dour-faced young man pulled his horse to a stop at the foot of the stairs. At first he thought the man a complete stranger, but then he placed the suspicious scowl; it was the fellow he'd met at the Hunters' house the first night he'd arrived. Davy something. Or Davis. Jared Davies. What was he doing here?

"Mr. Davies, this is quite a surprise," he said as the young man swung down from his sweating horse.

The other man's frown deepened as he realized that Mace's position on the stairs forced him to crook his neck to look up at him.

"Where is she?" he asked without preamble.

"Who?" Mace's eyes widened innocently. He suddenly remembered how little he'd liked the man the first time they'd met.

"I'm not here to play games, Fielding." Jared stomped up the stairs to stand level with him. "Where's Kora?"

"Why do you want to know?" Mace leaned back against the stair rail, in a way that said he was in no hurry to cooperate. He made no attempt to hide his dislike of Jared's imperious manner.

Jared's eyes narrowed. "Don't think I don't know what you're up to, Fielding. You think you can turn Kora's head with those slick Boston manners of yours. You've had your eye on her since you got here, and don't think I don't know what's on your mind."

Mace felt his own ire rising, but his voice remained cool. "And what might that be?"

Jared's face reddened. "If you were a real gentleman, you wouldn't push yourself on a girl as confused as Kora is right now. But if you don't have any scruples, let me give you some. You stay away from her."

Mace straightened slowly to his full height. He didn't like the man's attitude, and he wasn't going to tolerate his insinuations. "I don't think you're going to tell me what to do," he said, his voice low but hard as steel.

Jared flinched, but he didn't retreat. "And I don't think you're going to spend any more time with my fiancée," he replied, a note of bravado in his voice.

Mace couldn't possibly have heard right. He found himself struggling to focus on Jared's face, as though he had just been sucker punched. "Fiancée?"

Jared's eyes held a glint of challenge. "Yes, fiancée. We're going to be married next winter."

The world tilted sickeningly beneath Mace's feet. Time spun back ten years, and he was reading a letter. A letter that had turned his life upside down, that had made him swear never to fall in love again. The letter Cecilia had sent him saying she had run away with Jesse, his only brother. Cecilia saying she loved Jesse, had fought that love for months, and was so sorry she had to hurt Mace . . .

"So stay away from her."

Mace stared blankly at Jared Davies, who appeared disturbed by his sudden silence.

"Of course," Mace said dully, only force of habit enabling him to maintain his composure. "I'm not interested in other men's women."

He noticed through the throbbing pain in his head

that Jared looked even more confused than before. But more clearly he saw his brother's face, that carefree, irresponsible smile lighting up his blue eyes. He wondered for the hundred thousandth time how he could have been so blind as not to see in Jesse's face that he'd been sleeping with the woman Mace intended to marry. He also wondered what Jared now saw on his face that he would ignore in order to continue believing in Kora's fidelity.

"Good," the other man said, some of the contentiousness leaving him. He continued with renewed self-confidence, "So, where is she?"

A sudden, intense hatred fired in Mace toward this hot-tempered, cocky young man. If he couldn't erase the message, at least he could misdirect the messenger.

"She's not here," he said. "She left on the stage this morning for Sacramento. I'm sorry, but you've come all the way out here for nothing."

Jared eyed him suspiciously, but Mace's direct look sold him. "Damn," Jared muttered. "That woman needs a husband and children to keep her home instead of larking about like she does."

He looked down at his horse, whose damp neck and lowered head indicated he wasn't going to make it back to Sacramento tonight. But apparently Jared thought he might, because he trotted back down the stairs and mounted, pulling the horse's head up with fierce determination.

"Remember what I said, Fielding," he warned, before turning his horse back toward Sacramento, kicking him savagely in the ribs.

Mace only wished he could forget. Mechanically, he climbed the rest of the steps to the hotel door and made his way upstairs. Rage and pain battled in his chest as he stood in the hallway. Kora had lied to him. How could he have made the same mistake twice, falling in love with an unfaithful woman? He never wanted to see Kora's heartlessly beautiful face again. But he wasn't going to let her off that easily.

Kora stood before the mirror, trying to coax an errant strand of hair into place over her ear. Soft golden curls framed her face, while the rest of her hair fell in a fashionable waterfall from the back of her head. She wore a plain brown muslin dress, not terribly stylish, but clean, and it brought out the golden flecks in her eyes. After her hot bath, courtesy of the efficient Mrs. Kruger, she figured she'd feel elegant in almost anything.

She couldn't help laughing as she gave one last twirl in front of the mirror to make sure everything was in place. Although Mace obviously found her attractive in even the most ridiculous garb, she couldn't help wanting to impress him. She hadn't felt this giddy at the prospect of being with someone since she was a schoolgirl.

And that had been with Jared.

Kora stared at herself in the mirror. She couldn't remember when she had stopped feeling excited at the idea of being with Jared. She hadn't really felt light-headed around him since he'd shown an interest in her, since she'd actually gotten to know him.

Why was it so different with Mace? The answer for which she had been searching for most of the week came to her in a flash. She enjoyed Mace's company, loved being with him, talking with him, even arguing with him. With Jared, she had liked the idea that she was in love, and she had mistaken feeling flattered and pleased by his attentions for love. She suddenly realized she'd never really felt comfortable with Jared, had always felt as though she had to pretend to be the kind of woman he wanted.

The recognition of her mistake sobered her at once. Perhaps it was an understandable one, considering her youth and inexperience, but it was a serious mistake nonetheless. She shivered at the thought of being trapped in a marriage with Jared, each wanting the other to be something they couldn't ever be. By chance she'd met Mace, just in time to recognize her error. Now she had to convince Jared and her parents that she and Jared did not belong together. And despite what Jared had said before she left Sacramento, she was sure he must realize that now.

She squared her shoulders with determination. It was time to face all that she'd left behind in Sacramento—her parents' displeasure, Jared's anger, the questions about her reporting. Despite the fact that her trip up to the mountains had been nothing like what she'd planned, she felt stronger for it. A surge of confidence swelled in her. Not only would she convince her parents to let her continue reporting, she'd prove just how good at it she could be. It was time to stop hiding behind Troy. She'd continue to investigate Rosemarie Amado's death until she had either cleared Diego Amado's name or found proof that he was the killer.

In the midst of these thoughts, she heard the door to her room swing open. She turned to see Mace standing in the doorway. A smile sprang to her lips, but she checked her rush into his arms when she saw the odd expression on his face.

"So, what do you think?" he asked, waving toward the mirror. "Do you look charming enough to entangle me in your web?"

The strange flatness in his voice disturbed her, but she tossed her head to make her curls dance. "What do *you* think?"

A muscle in Mace's jaw jumped, but his expression didn't change. Slowly, he shook his head. "There was a time when I didn't look much farther than a pretty face," he said. "But that was a long, long time ago. Obviously I can still be played for a fool, but once I've seen a black heart, no amount of beauty can hide it."

Kora stared at him. "I don't understand. What are you talking about?"

"What were you thinking, Kora?" he asked. He stepped forward, closing the door behind him. "Were my family's wealth and social standing so much greater than Jared Davies' that you just couldn't resist making a play for them?"

His eyes bored into her, hard and cold. Kora shook her head in bewilderment, trying not to get angry. "Mace, what's wrong? You're not making sense."

"And I suppose you were simply stringing Davies along in case I failed to take your bait." Mace's jaw clenched. Seeing Kora before him, looking so young and sweet, only increased the rage he felt. And if she kept up this innocent act much longer, he wasn't sure he'd be able to hold it back.

"What does Jared have to do with all this?" Kora asked, crossing her arms over her chest. His manner was beginning to frighten her. He wasn't acting like the Mace she knew. "What is going on here?"

Mace stepped toward her, and Kora could feel the

tension radiating from him. The knuckles on his fists turned white as he clenched them; his words were taut with violence.

"Just when did you plan on telling me you were engaged to another man?" he asked.

Kora's jaw dropped. "What?"

"I had an interesting little chat with your Mr. Davies just now," Mace went on, grinding out the words. "It seems he came all the way from Sacramento to see his fiancée. Were you planning on inviting me to the wedding?"

"Jared is here?" Kora's mind raced, trying to assimilate this news. What was he doing there? And what the hell was he up to, telling Mace she was engaged to him? Apparently what she'd said during their last fight hadn't convinced him that she wasn't going to marry him. Well, she would deal with Jared later. First, she had to clear up this misunderstanding with Mace. "He told you we were engaged?"

Mace watched the emotions play across her face— surprise, confusion, anger. But the look in her eyes held no trace of guilt. He might almost have been able to forgive her if it had.

"I can see you weren't counting on that development," he said.

"No, I wasn't," Kora answered sharply. "Because it's not true. I wasn't hiding anything from you about Jared. I just forgot . . ."

"You *forgot?*" He exploded, stepping forward to tower over her. "Is that why you let me make love to you? You forgot you were engaged? God, what a fool I was. This morning I actually thought I was in love with you. Now I can hardly bear to look at you."

A dark pleasure stabbed through him at the look of

pain that crossed her face, though what he'd said wasn't true. He hated her even more because the sight of her made him want to love her all over again. He stepped back, letting a sneer of contempt cross his face. "I could almost feel sorry for that self-important bastard Davies, warning me to stay away from you, not knowing he was just a bit too late."

"What did you tell him?" Kora asked, feeling her world suddenly falling off-kilter. Mace wasn't listening to what she was saying.

"Are you worried I told him the truth about you?"

Mace's face darkened as he stepped even closer. Kora thought he was going to hit her, but instead he spun on his heel toward the door.

"Mace, stop!" she cried out, truly frightened now. "Mace, I never told Jared I'd marry him. I don't love him."

He didn't even turn around. "I pray there is a hell, Kora. I hope each lie returns to torment you for what you've done to me."

She couldn't believe he would say such things to her. All over a stupid mistake. She followed him and grabbed his sleeve.

"Mace, please, listen to me. . . ."

At the touch of her hand on his arm, he whirled, grasping her wrist.

"I've never hit a woman before," he growled, his eyes wild. "But I'll hit you if you touch me again."

He dropped her wrist and Kora stepped back. Tears of confusion and hurt welled in her eyes, but she fought to hold them back.

Mace stepped out into the hall, but he turned before he closed the door. "You needn't worry about Mr. Davies." His voice was brittle with scorn. "He's on his way back to Sacramento, blissfully unaware of what sort of a woman you really are. I suppose he'll find out on his wedding night, but that's no concern of mine."

And then he was gone.

Kora stood for a moment, staring at the door, the pain hovering around her like a cloud for a moment before it hit her full force. A sob rose in her throat as she doubled over, clutching her arms across her stomach.

Her whole body shook as she made her way to the bed, sitting heavily on it just as her legs gave way beneath her. She couldn't understand what had just happened. It didn't make any sense.

It had to be a nightmare. Jared had come after her from Sacramento. He had told Mace that they were engaged. And Mace had come up here raging like a madman, saying he hoped she burned in hell. She didn't know whom to hate more, Jared or Mace—or herself for getting into such a mess.

Tears poured down her cheeks, and she angrily brushed them away. This whole thing was simply ridiculous. She had never agreed to marry Jared. She'd thought she'd made her feelings on that subject clear to him.

She would never have shared what she had with Mace if she'd still planned on marrying Jared. Although she knew now that she didn't love Jared, she owed him that much.

Jared's apparent misunderstanding aside, she had considered herself free to love Mace, and that should have been good enough for him. But he hadn't even given her a chance to explain. He'd assumed the worst, judging from what he'd implied about her being a gold digger.

For the first time he'd said the word *love* in order to inform her that he no longer loved her—but if he really cared for her, he would have given her the benefit of the doubt. He would have given her the opportunity to tell her side of the story. She just didn't understand how he could have acted the way he had. After what they had shared . . .

She reached out to smooth the mattress where they had lain together just two nights before. She sobbed again, this time in humiliation as she flung herself away from the bed. She had given her love to Mace freely and joyfully, and he had called her a liar.

I'll never forgive him for that. Never!

She found a handkerchief and blew her nose, savagely wiping away new tears. What was she going to do now? Her grandfather had invited them all back to his cabin, insisting he would rather risk gangrene than stay cooped up in a hotel a moment longer. But there was no way Kora could return to the cabin with Mace and Jessica now. After what Mace had said to her, she didn't even think she could look him in the face.

As she paced the small hotel room, considering what she should do next, she heard the sound of the stagecoach through the window, pulling up next to the hotel.

She hurried to the window to look down on the coach below. A boy came out of the stable to help the driver change horses. From the direction the coach faced, Kora could see it was heading to Sacramento.

Judging from the haste with which the men were unhitching the sweating horses, Kora understood that they didn't plan a long stop in Bear Pass. Her mind raced. If she could make it downstairs before the stage left, she would be in Sacramento by tomorrow morning. There, she could disabuse Jared of the idea that they were now or ever would be engaged. Once she had that settled, maybe she could make Mace listen to her.

The fact that she had just sworn never to forgive Mace did nothing to dampen her renewed sense of purpose. She threw her nightgown, hairbrush, and other toilet articles into her bag. She didn't have time to get her dresses from the wardrobe.

For a moment she considered leaving without letting the others know where she'd gone. It would serve Mace right if it gave him a scare, but she knew that would be childish, and it would worry her grandfather and Jessica needlessly. Mace probably wouldn't care anyway.

"Gone to Sac. on stage," was all she intended to write, but as always when she put pencil to paper, something else took hold of her. Her feelings poured onto paper in a way she could never seem to equal in speech, and despite her anger and confusion, she let some of that come out now. Even if Mace didn't understand, she couldn't leave him without one last word.

She set the note on the bedside table and stooped to pick up her bag. Her gaze found her grandfather's rifle propped in the corner. It wouldn't hurt for a lone woman riding the stage overnight to have a firearm. But on the other hand, if she ran into Mace in the hall while holding a weapon, she might do something she'd later regret.

She left the rifle and ran out the door.

*   *   *

Mace finished his glass of whiskey with a quick swallow, willing the burning liquid to dull the pain in his head, if not the one in his heart.

"Another," he ordered, pushing the empty glass toward the bartender.

The thin, wiry man behind the bar complied, eyeing Mace speculatively. Mace could tell he was trying to decide if his well-dressed, well-paying customer was going to become disorderly if he had much more to drink. Mace almost laughed. He was hoping to get *too* drunk to be capable of the violence he was contemplating.

He drank half his new glass in one gulp. It wasn't going to work. He didn't think he could ever drink enough to blot Kora's image from his mind.

He remembered the way she'd looked as he left her room, struggling not to cry, her eyes pleading with him to stay and listen to her. He hated himself for hurting her, and that only made him more sick and angry.

Suddenly the image shifted to the last time he had seen Cecilia before her betrayal, her green eyes dancing as he gave her a necklace of silver and diamonds. She'd been excited that day, her moods swinging even more wildly than usual. He'd simply humored her, consumed by his intention to propose to her that weekend. She'd had other plans, however, disappearing the next day with his brother.

He looked down at the amber liquid before him. The damn stuff only made things worse, mixing the pain of the past and present into an even more potent draft.

His only consolation back then had been that his parents had never known that Jesse had taken Cecilia with him when he left. Too wrapped up in their younger son's decision to flee west, blaming themselves for his irresponsibility, they hadn't noticed Mace's moroseness. When they finally became aware that Mace was no longer courting Cecilia, they didn't mention it, simply glad she was gone.

Mace raised his drink to his lips and discovered he'd already finished it.

Back then, he'd thought he'd never get over Jesse and Cecilia's betrayal. But finding out about Kora was even worse. Even after all he had been through, he had let himself trust her. And he wasn't the only one who would be hurt by that. How could he explain to Jessica that they couldn't stay with Fritz and Kora any more? And that they wouldn't be dining at the Hunters' house again.

"Papa?"

He looked down, and for a moment he thought his imagination had conjured up his daughter beside him. But even through the whiskey cloud in his head, he could see that the anxiety on her face was real.

"What th'ell are you doing 'ere?" he growled, vaguely surprised at the slur in his speech.

"Looking for you," Jessica said, shuffling her feet nervously. She glanced around the saloon, wide-eyed.

Mace managed to get to his feet with a minimal amount of help from the bar. He paused a moment to get his balance, then turned his attention to Jessica.

"Out!" he ordered sharply, pointing toward the door. He followed his daughter onto the porch and down to the street, squinting his eyes against the blinding rays of the late afternoon sun.

He took Jessica by the shoulders and turned her to him.

"Jessica Lynne Fielding," he said, taking care to

articulate his words, "you will never, ever enter a saloon by yourself for any reason ever again. Do you understand?"

"How else was I supposed to find out if you were there?"

Once out of the foreign environment of the Eagle Saloon, she was quickly forgetting to be intimidated.

"Two days ago somebody kidnapped you and almost killed Fritz Kraus. So don't you sass me, young lady. I don't want you going anywhere alone, much less some disreputable saloon. Is that clear?"

Jessica's gaze dropped from his and she nodded. "Yes, Papa." She glanced back at him from under dark lashes. "But I did need to find you."

Mace's head hurt too badly for him to stay angry with her. "All right. What's the problem, kitten?"

"It's Kora, Papa. She's gone."

"What do you mean, Kora's gone?" he asked, still having trouble focusing his attention.

"She *left*," Jessica repeated, frustrated by his dense response. "She went back to Sacramento."

"On her mule? That's just the sort of damn fool thing that damn fool woman—"

"On the stagecoach," Jessica interrupted impatiently. "Here, she left this for you."

He took the note she handed him, wishing he felt relief that Kora had gone instead of this irrational sense of loss. He unfolded the note, glaring in irritation at the words that blurred in and out of focus.

Dear Mace,

    Gone to Sac. on stage. Please have Grandfather take my things.

    I have run away from my problems long

enough, and I see now that I have to go back and work things out with Jared. I should have told you that he had asked me to marry him, but my motives were not what you think. Perhaps when you return to Sacramento you will give me a chance to explain. I thought we had become friends, and you owe your friend that.

Kora

The last sentence cut through Mace's whiskey haze like a knife. *She's got a lot of nerve.* But he could feel the pain in her simple signature, alone at the bottom of the page.

Damn it, why should I feel guilty for hurting her after what she's done to me?

"Well?" Jessica's voice interrupted his thoughts.

"Well what?" he asked, not really listening. What had Kora meant when she said that she had to "work things out with Jared"?

"Aren't you going to go after her?"

Mace looked down at his daughter. "Why would I do that?"

Jessica looked away, which usually meant she was going to say something out of line. "I thought maybe you accidentally said something to make Kora upset again," she said, rocking from foot to foot. "I thought maybe you could apologize."

"Apologize?" The word exploded from him, making Jessica jump back in surprise. Mace stared at his daughter in disbelief.

"Apologize?" he asked again, his voice more in control. He looked down at the note in his hand, clearly marked "Mason Fielding" on the outer fold. "Did you read this, young lady?"

Jessica looked down at her feet. "I was worried when I couldn't find her, and I saw her bag was gone."

Mace watched silently for a moment as his daughter squirmed.

"Jessica, look at me," he said finally, waiting until she complied. "You're my daughter, and I love you very much, but whether or not I did anything to upset Kora is none of your business. That's something only she and I can work out. Now, I want you to go to your room and stay there until I come get you, all right?"

She eyed him a moment, and, deciding he was serious, nodded her head. But instead of instantly obeying, she squirmed a moment more. In a rush of bravery, she asked, "You're not going to let her marry that other man, are you?"

Mace didn't know whether to be angry or simply shocked. One thing he did not need was his nine-year-old daughter to play matchmaker. "I don't see that there's anything I can do about it one way or the other."

Jessica looked up at him unhappily, and what she said next went straight to his heart. "Do you think she'd still want to be my friend if she got married?"

For a moment he couldn't answer. After what he'd said to Kora, he wasn't sure she'd want to have anything to do with any part of his family. But he honestly couldn't imagine her turning her back on Jessica.

"I'm sure she will, kitten," he said gently, for the moment forgetting that after what he'd learned about Kora this afternoon he had planned on protecting his daughter from her influence. "She cares about you very much. Otherwise, she wouldn't have wanted to help me rescue you. Now go on up to your room like I told you."

Reluctantly, Jessica turned and made her way back toward the hotel. Mace watched until she'd entered the front door, then he began walking. He needed to stretch his legs and work off some of the alcohol if he wanted to think clearly about what to do next.

The dust rose behind him as he walked, but the air he breathed was fresh and sweet, clearing his head for the first time since Jared Davies had told him he was engaged to Kora.

He knew that Jessica had taken to Kora, liking her almost instantly, but he hadn't quite realized how much Kora's attention had meant to his daughter.

For years his mother had told him that he should marry to give Jessica a mother, but he had thought it worse than foolish to tie himself to someone he didn't love, just to create the semblance of a family. These past few days, though, he had begun to wonder if he might not be able to give Jessica a real, loving mother after all. It had never occurred to him that Jessica might be hoping for the same thing.

He opened the note Kora had left and reread it. It was so damned vague. Just what did she mean that she'd "run away" from her problems? What *was* she going to work out with Jared? Was she intending to go back and marry him?

An hour ago he would have said that was just what she deserved, to marry that ridiculous young ass. But either Kora's note, Jessica's concern, or simply the passage of a little time and the consumption of a little too much alcohol had dampened his initial reaction to Jared's news. At the moment he wasn't so sure exactly what he thought Kora deserved.

He thought back over the time they had spent together—last week as partner reporters, and the past two days as lovers. Never in that time had he found reason to think Kora anything but what she appeared to be—a headstrong, determined young woman, by turns prickly, vulnerable, and passionate.

In her note she had said she deserved a chance to explain her side of things, because she thought they were friends. Mace considered that for a long time. He had never been friends with Cecilia. That simply hadn't been a part of their relationship. Friends. Whatever Kora had done or not done, she was not Cecilia, and it wasn't fair of him to treat her as though she were.

He recalled the scene in Kora's hotel room this afternoon. What if she *had* told the truth about not being engaged to Jared? His mind told him not to believe her, but somewhere deep in his heart, a hope brought to life by his love for her refused to be squelched. Of course, if she had told the truth, then she'd never want to see him again after what he had said to her.

He shook his head. Even this note of hers had to be a ruse, calculated to bring him back under her spell. But he wouldn't know for sure unless he followed and confronted her.

His memory carried him back to that stormy night when Cecilia had returned east, bringing her daughter and the news of his brother's death.

"How dare you ask me to care for your bastard?" he'd shouted at her. "After you deliberately betrayed my love by running off with my own brother!"

She had glared at him, and narrowed her green eyes. "You never loved me. If you'd loved me, you would have come after us and tried to get me back. But no, your pride was greater than your love, and you just let me go, hoping no one would find out I preferred your little brother to you."

At the time, he hadn't understood and hadn't believed her, assuming she was trying to hurt him, something she did so well. But now that he had his love of Kora to compare it to, he wondered if Cecilia hadn't been right. Oh, he'd loved her. But not the way he loved Kora. Even now, he couldn't cut off his feelings for her, and he knew he couldn't just let her go.

But he couldn't go after her, either. Not yet. He had more than just Kora or himself to consider. He had Jessica. Until he determined for certain whether or not Booth Garrett had arranged her kidnapping, none of them would be safe. He had to deal with that first.

And he had to fight down the knowledge that regardless of what he had said and thought about her this afternoon, he would never forgive himself if Kora ended up marrying Jared Davies.

14

Kora stepped out of the hansom cab. She watched as it drove away, wishing for a split second that she had asked the driver to take her home. She could have had a bath, eaten breakfast . . . procrastinated. But she wanted to face Jared first. Before she told her parents, he deserved to know that she did not intend to marry him.

She stood in the early morning sun before Jared's quiet home, wondering if she should have waited to come out here. Last night, or rather quite early this morning, after arriving on the stagecoach, she'd managed to slip up to her room without waking anyone, but she hadn't slept. Thoughts of Mace and Jared had given her no peace, and she had decided to visit Jared as soon as possible.

She took a deep breath, marched up to the front door, and rang the bell. She stood waiting, shivering slightly in the morning breeze. After what seemed an eternity, the door opened. The housekeeper looked out at her in surprise.

"Miss Hunter, what can I do for you this morning?"

"Good morning, Mrs. Sealy," Kora said, pleased that her voice remained calm. "I'm here to see Jared, if he's available."

The housekeeper shook her gray head. "Mr. Jared's already left." Her eyes crinkled with worry. "I don't know what's got into him, Miss Hunter, but he didn't get home 'til after I got here to make bread this morning, and he left again not fifteen minutes ago."

"He's probably working on some big story," Kora said, not in any mood to gossip about Jared's strange hours. "I'll see if I can catch him at the *Union*. Good day, Mrs. Sealy."

"Take care, Miss Hunter. And see if you can't find out what's bothering him," the housekeeper called after her.

Kora found herself back on the street, nonplussed. She had prepared herself to face Jared, and now she wasn't sure what to do next.

A buggy rattled past her, some upstanding citizen at the reins on his way to an office or warehouse or some other thriving enterprise.

Kora sighed. Even if Jared had gone to the *Union* office this morning, she didn't want to talk with him there. She'd have to try again later, hoping her nerves wouldn't snap before then. She might as well go home now. At least she could get something to eat.

She started down the street, feeling the aches from the long stagecoach ride and the effects of not sleeping all night. But that was nothing compared to the pain in her heart. She had tried to keep her mind focused on what she would say to Jared this morning, but she couldn't keep thoughts of Mace at bay for long, and now they came rushing in.

No matter how angry he had made her yesterday, no matter how much she wanted to hate him for what he'd said and for refusing to believe her when she told him the truth, all her heart could tell her was how much she loved him, how much she ached to be with him.

Why had she fallen in love with Mason Fielding? Her life had enough complications already. Now it was in such a mess she didn't know how she'd ever set it right.

"Kora!"

She started at the sound of her name and turned to see Clemency waving at her from the front door of her house.

"Kora Hunter, how dare you march right past me like that without even a 'how do you do'!" Clemency scolded with a smile as she hurried down her walk to catch up with Kora.

"I didn't see you," Kora said lamely.

"Obviously!" Clemency laughed. "What are you doing out here so early if not visiting me? Or do I have to ask?" She raised her eyebrows with a nod at Jared's house up the street. "What is going on with you and Jared?"

Kora hesitated. She didn't want to talk about it, but she didn't want Clemency to hear it from someone else.

"I'm not going to marry him, Clem," she said, wondering how her friend would react.

Clemency's expression was thoughtful. "Are you going home now? Good, I'll walk you part of the way."

Kora had to move quickly to catch up with her as Clemency started down the street.

"It's for the best, Clem," she said, hoping she could persuade her of what she herself now knew with confidence. "We just don't want the same things. He needs a wife who will be an asset to his career, and I need someone who loves the person I am, not the person he wants me to be. We were wrong to think what we felt for each other was love."

At Clemency's continued silence she asked, "You're not mad at me, are you Clem?"

"Of course not, silly." Clemency glanced at her, her pale blue eyes serious. "Jared told me about the fight you two had the other day, and I've been thinking about it a great deal. You know, Kora I thought you two would be perfect together. You're both so attractive and intelligent, you come from good backgrounds. . . . But now I'm not so sure. I mean, even before he proposed, you two had fights. And I can't help wondering if maybe you'd end up like my parents, arguing all the time, resenting everything about each other."

She paused to gauge Kora's reaction. "And I've been thinking that maybe if the two of you could remind me of my parents, then maybe *I* won't end up like them. Maybe their problems are their mistakes, and I'm not going to inherit them. Do you see what I mean?"

Kora looked into her friend's hopeful face and for the first time had some inkling of why Clemency, who so desperately wanted a family of her own, was so wary of marriage. Kora felt a rush of sympathy for her.

"Oh, Clem, you'd never marry someone you couldn't

get along with. You know what to watch out for. I, on the other hand, was foolish enough to think that I could marry any man I pleased and have a marriage like the one my parents have. Don't worry, Clem. I know you'll find the perfect man. After all, they're all crazy about you, so all you have to do is pick him out of the crowd. And I know he'll be handsome, ambitious, and need you to keep him in line."

She barely stopped herself from speaking her next thought aloud: Clemency and Jared would be just about perfect for each other.

Kora scrutinized her friend. Clemency smiled, batting her eyelashes, and an acute jealousy shot through Kora. For a second she wondered if Clemency was agreeing that Jared wasn't right for her so Clemency could have him for herself. Then she dismissed the idea with shame that she'd even let herself think it.

"Look, Clem, I'm really tired. We can talk about this some more later."

"Of course. I'm sorry. You don't look as though you slept much last night. Are you going to be all right?"

How could she answer that? "Don't worry about me, Clem."

Clemency's eyes narrowed. "Something is bothering you besides Jared. You can't keep a secret from me, Kora Hunter. Wait a minute. Didn't Troy tell me you were going up to Fritz's claim for a week? What are you doing back already?"

"Jared followed me up there," Kora said, too tired to invent a better story. "He's harder to convince than you are that we're not getting married."

"I tried to look up Mr. Gorgeous Fielding while you were gone," Clemency murmured, eyes glittering in speculation. "I was hoping he might be lonely. But Troy said he was out of town on a story."

Kora could have warned her brother his discretion would be wasted on Clem. "Let him be lonely, Clemency. You'll be better off."

Her friend's playfulness vanished. "Any time you want to talk about it, you let me know."

Kora cursed the tears that came too easily since yesterday. "Thanks. I'll remember that." She gave her friend a quick hug and went on without her.

During Kora's walk home, images of her warm, comfortable bed swam in her brain, giving way only to thoughts of her mother's biscuits and a hot cup of coffee. When she reached the stairs to her parents' front porch, she could hardly summon the energy to climb them. She stood for a moment at the door, wondering what she would say to her mother and father.

Finally she reached for the doorknob, but before she could touch it, the door swung open. There before her stood Jared, looking almost as shocked and disheveled as she was.

"Jared, what are you doing here?" she asked, the words out of her mouth before she realized how inane they sounded.

"Kora? Kora, baby, is that you?" Her mother, who had apparently been showing Jared out, pushed past him to take Kora in her arms. "Are you all right?" she asked anxiously, then more sharply, "Where on earth have you been, Kora Hunter? You've had us all worried to death. Jared told us you weren't with your grandfather, and we knew you weren't here. . . ."

Tears came to Kora's eyes at her mother's concern, but she couldn't break down now. No matter how much she wanted to have her mother protect her and make everything all right again, things weren't so simple. She had to take control of her life.

"I'm fine, Mama," she said, trying to sound as though she meant it. "I'm sorry I upset you. But I think right now Jared and I have to talk."

Anna Hunter looked from her daughter to Jared and back, resignation on her face. "Of course. I'll just go back to the kitchen and finish cleaning up. When you and Jared are through, then I think you'd better come talk with me."

Kora nodded, but her eyes were on Jared, whose grim expression didn't change as he stepped aside to let her through the front door and into the parlor. She decided that once this was over, she never wanted to have another conversation in that dark, stuffy room. They always seemed to go wrong.

"All right, I'll ask," Jared began, closing the parlor door behind them. "Where the hell have you been?"

Kora's back stiffened as she turned to face him. "I was visiting my grandfather," she replied, meeting his gaze steadily. "I left a message for my parents, so you know very well where I was."

"I mean last night and this morning," Jared growled, his patience worn thin. "That good-for-nothing Yankee, Fielding, said you left for Sacramento yesterday morning."

"Mace . . ." Kora couldn't bring herself to say Mace had lied. That made him sound jealous, and he'd made it clear he no longer cared for her at all. "Mace was mistaken," she said finally.

"That son-of-a-bitch," Jared spat out, slapping the back of a chair. "I knew that bastard was after you from the minute he showed up here. I can't believe you actually followed him up to your grandfather's place. I take it you've finally come to your senses."

Kora's eyes flashed. "Yes, I have. I just wish I had come to them sooner."

"Don't come crying to me about it. After the way you acted on Sunday, I sure as hell don't care one way or the other." But the pain in his eyes said he knew what she'd meant, and that he did care.

"Then why did you follow me all the way to Bear Pass?" she asked, anger overriding her compassion. "Just to tell me you didn't care, I suppose?"

Jared made an attempt at indifference. "I simply thought we ought to get our situation worked out. It's possible I might have forgiven you for your pigheadedness, but I couldn't even find you." His calm gave way once more to hurt anger. "I had to embarrass myself in front of Fielding looking for you!"

"And you told Mace that you and I were engaged! How could you say such a thing?"

He crossed his arms over his chest. "What was I supposed to do?" he asked. "From the expression on his face, you would have thought he owned you. I'd rather make a fool of him than let you make a fool of me."

As she looked into his scowling face, Kora's stomach clenched. She knew now she didn't love him, but she would always care for him. How could things have gotten so out of hand that she had to hurt him and herself so?

She owed it to both of them not to make this any harder than it had to be.

"Look at us, Jared," she said. "We can't even talk civilly to each other any more. I don't know how it happened, but it's obvious we don't belong together.

Can't we just agree to that and put this animosity behind us?"

Jared snorted. "I know exactly how it happened. You refused to accede to my simple, logical request that you quit reporting." But behind the bluster of his tone, Kora heard the hurt and confusion she felt in her own heart.

"You didn't request it—you demanded it," Kora reminded him, but without the rancor she'd felt earlier. "We weren't in love with each other; we were in love with our images of each other. It's best that we found that out before we got married."

She and Jared looked at each other for a long moment. He let out a deep breath.

"Are you in love with Fielding?" he asked, bitterness replacing his anger. "Do you plan to marry him now?"

She took a deep breath of her own before answering. She wanted to lie, to protect Jared's pride and her own. After all, Mace would never contradict Kora if she said she didn't love him. But Jared knew her too well to accept a lie.

"I don't think it matters how I feel," she finally admitted. "He's not interested in marrying me."

"I could have told you so," Jared said. "But I don't suppose you would have listened."

Kora would have smiled at his attempt at concession, but if she had, she would have cried. "I don't suppose I would," she agreed.

"You are an impossible woman, Kora."

For another long moment they stood there, looking at each other, not knowing what to say. Then, surprising herself almost as much as she surprised Jared, Kora stepped forward to take his hand in hers.

"Let's try to go on without hating each other, okay?" she pleaded.

Jared smiled ruefully. "I could never hate you, Kora," he said. "But next time I'm going to fall in love with someone who's not so stubborn, who knows her place is supporting me rather than fighting me."

And Kora felt that nasty pang of jealousy again. She fought it back, knowing she should be more mature than to let her pride be hurt by the fact that Jared planned on finding someone else to marry.

She didn't love Jared; she had no right to be jealous of him. In fact, she would be thrilled if Jared and Clemency—two people she cared about so much—would have a chance at happiness together. But it still hurt. She couldn't help feeling jealousy at that potential happiness, since she had lost her one chance at her own.

Fortunately, Jared didn't notice her inner struggle. "Don't be so stubborn that you wreck your life, Kora," he told her. "Whatever may have happened between us, I don't want you to end up a bitter old maid. I just hope you realize you have to give up your recent behavior before your reputation is ruined and you find yourself completely alone."

Kora decided to take his words in the spirit in which he meant them, rather than waste more of her energy trying to make him understand how much they hurt her.

"I appreciate your concern," she said.

There didn't seem to be anything else to say.

"Good-bye then," Jared said stiffly.

"Good-bye," Kora replied, feeling just as awkward. She followed him to the front door and closed it behind him with the half-relieved, half-regretful feel-

ing that she was closing the door on her childhood
hopes and childish naïveté. She leaned against the
door for a moment, remembering those carefree days
when she had adored Jared from afar. She knew those
times hadn't been as idyllic as they were in memory,
but everything had seemed possible then. Her future
had appeared so exciting, so uncomplicated by sorrow or doubt.

Kora looked down the hall to the dining room
where her mother was waiting. Her parents thought
they had made a mistake in allowing her to follow her
dream of becoming a reporter. Maybe in some ways
they were right. If she had been forced to give up that
dream earlier, perhaps her life would be easier now.
She wouldn't have to face the painful fact that her
gender made her an oddity in her chosen profession,
that her friends and loved ones often didn't understand why it meant so much to her.

Maybe if she'd given up that dream, her fantasy of
being Jared's wife would be coming true. But she
didn't belong with Jared. She didn't know exactly
what had happened with Mace, if he would ever
speak to her again. But for a few incredible days she
had known what real love could be, how much she
could care for another person. And she wouldn't give
that up, no matter how much pain it might cause her.

She sighed deeply, gathering what strength she had
left, and walked down the endless hall to the dining
room. Before she reached it, the door opened and her
mother stepped out into the hall.

"Is he gone?"

Kora nodded.

"You told him you wouldn't marry him?"

Kora nodded again.

Anna shook her head. "I'm sorry." She paused, considering her daughter's appearance. "You're exhausted. Go upstairs. I'll heat some water for a bath."

Kora blinked. "Mama?"

Her mother frowned at her. "I don't have the slightest idea why you would turn down a promising young man like Jared Davies, but you obviously feel you have good reason. You're as stubborn as any Hunter ever was. I may wish it weren't so, but I'm not fool enough to think you'll change just because I tell you to. Now go get ready for your bath." She smiled slightly. "I'll let you know how angry I am afterward."

"Oh, Mama, I love you." Kora hugged her mother tightly, then turned to hurry up the stairs before her tears could start to fall.

Kora struggled to wake from her dream. She was following Mace down the streets of Sacramento, begging him to listen to her. But he wouldn't turn around. He seemed unable or unwilling to hear her, even though she screamed. And she kept tripping on the hem of her dress, because for some reason she wasn't wearing any shoes, and so she fell farther and farther behind.

But she had to catch him. She had to make him listen, because he was in danger and she had to warn him. Something dark was coming after them both. She called his name over and over, but only a moan came from her throat.

"Kora?"

Her eyes opened, and she saw her mother's face leaning over her bed. It took a moment for her to realize she was awake and her heart could stop pounding.

"I brought you some coffee."

Kora sat up, blinking the sleep from her eyes. She took the cup her mother handed her, and sipped gratefully. Sunlight slanted through the window, and she noticed Dodge sleeping by her feet. He had been so glad to see her that he'd tried sleeping on her pillow next to her face, but she hadn't wanted to suffocate in clouds of gray fur.

"What time is it?" she mumbled, stifling a yawn.

"Two o'clock," her mother answered, sitting on the edge of her bed.

Kora yawned again. She had gone to bed after her bath, and must have fallen asleep right away.

"Are you feeling better now?"

"Yes, a little," Kora admitted, though the memory of her dream still troubled her. She took another sip of her coffee.

"Mama," she began, knowing she had to say it sometime, "I know you won't like it, but I intend to continue writing for the *Valley Times.*"

Anna sighed. "I think you should talk to your father about that." She rose. "I hope you understand, dear, I just want for you to be happy."

Without replying, Kora watched her mother leave. No matter what she did, there wasn't much chance of her being happy. Not without Mace. She didn't know quite how it had happened, but loving him had changed her life. Looking at a future without him was looking at a future without her heart.

Kora stood for a moment in front of her father's print shop, gathering her courage. She had always loved this shop, the smell of ink and paper, the feeling of excitement, the sense of camaraderie. She hated standing outside, feeling unsure of her welcome.

She turned the doorknob and stepped in, stopping at the sight of her father sitting behind his desk. He peered at her over his reading glasses.

"The prodigal daughter returns," he commented, taking off his glasses and rubbing the bridge of his nose.

Before he could continue, Kora moved over to his desk, launching into the speech she had been rehearsing on the way over.

"Papa, do you remember when you said that you loved Mother enough to give up the newspaper for her? Well, I don't love Jared that way. Maybe if he hadn't asked me to quit reporting I wouldn't have learned that in time. But I have, and I've told him I won't marry him. You may not approve, Papa, but I can't marry a man I don't love. I hope you can respect my decision and my wish to continue reporting. I'm a good reporter, and I love what I do. I don't want to lose that, too."

She stopped, breathless from trying to get it all out.

Ellis Hunter looked at her, his fingers fiddling with the ear pieces of his glasses.

"And what would you do if I said you're not going to work here at the *Valley Times* anymore?" he asked finally.

Kora's heart dropped, but she had prepared herself for that possibility. She'd thought about it all night, in between worrying about Jared and Mace.

"I'll find a job somewhere else," she said. Jared's comments about her abilities had undermined her confidence for a time, but she knew she was a good reporter and could become even better. "If I can't find work with a Sacramento paper, I'll go on to San Francisco. I'll even write society stories if I have to. I'll find a way."

Her father's eyes searched hers for any sign of wavering.

"Let me make sure I've got this straight. If I fire you, I not only lose one of my most productive, and least expensive, employees, but I also have on my conscience the fact that I drove my only daughter away to live by her wits in San Francisco. Correct?"

"Essentially," she agreed, trying not to let her sudden hope get out of hand.

Ellis Hunter leaned forward abruptly, slapping his hands down on the desk. "In that case, young lady, I think you had better get to work."

"Thank you, Papa!" Kora cried, restraining herself from running over to hug him.

He frowned. "Just don't give me any reason to reconsider, Miss Hunter. For instance, no more running off for days at a time without permission, leaving your employer shorthanded with a newspaper to get out. Troy and Dan Larsen had to stretch to fill in the extra space and worked overtime to help Max with the typesetting. You owe them."

She flushed guiltily. When she left she'd thought he was going to fire her anyway because of the fight she'd had with Jared, but that was no excuse. She'd dropped her responsibilities, and she could face the consequences.

"You can count on me, sir."

Ellis's mouth actually twitched in a brief smile. "I hope so," he said, "because you'll be busy enough that you may regret your decision, at least until Mason comes back from visiting your grandfather. I don't suppose he came back with you?"

Kora hoped her father didn't notice the way her face fell. "No. He didn't say when he'd be back."

Ellis looked at her sharply but didn't comment. "What are you waiting for?" he asked, putting his glasses back on. "Troy could use some help with that darn printing press. It's acting up again. We can't slack off just because we've somehow made it through another week."

"Yes, sir." She gave her father a little salute and hurried back into the print room before he could say anything further.

Max Logan set down a block of advertisements and turned from his workbench to acknowledge her with a wink.

"You came back just in time, missy," he called. "There's nothin' more to do."

Troy stood by the big printing press, which creaked ominously as he turned the drum. "Don't listen to Max, Kora," he advised with a grin. "Run for it while you can."

Kora laughed. "Don't tempt me," she warned. "Or I'll stay away until you get that monster fixed."

The two men laughed as they turned back to their work. For a moment Kora just stood there, in the center of the printing room, everything about it so familiar. She felt so comfortable here, joking with Max and Troy. She belonged here.

But for the first time, as she stood in this familiar, beloved space, she felt there was something missing.

She had gotten through the ordeals of convincing Jared they were not engaged and telling her parents she intended to continue working in the newspaper business. Now all she saw before her was how bleak her life would be without the man who had shown her the nature of true love—and of true heartbreak.

For a dizzy instant she couldn't move from the spot where she stood, knowing she might never discover if Mace had ever felt about her as she felt about him, or why he had reacted so violently to Jared's false claim. She shook herself. She would find out. Mace was a responsible man; he had promised her father to return to Sacramento within the week. She would confront him then.

But as she worked beside Troy that afternoon, trying to submerge her worries in the tasks of oiling gears and cleaning parts, the thought kept returning: even if she managed to convince Mace that she had not tried to deceive him, no amount of persuasion or logical argument could force him to trust her and give their love another chance. Only his own heart could do that. And she had no idea what his heart was telling him.

15

Mace sat with his arm around his daughter's shoulders, trying to hold her sleeping form steady through the rocking and jolting as the stagecoach clattered toward Sacramento.

He was too tense to sleep himself, though he knew his body could use the rest. Returning to Sacramento meant returning to Kora, and he didn't know how he would face that. He'd thought of almost nothing else these past three days. As he'd traveled up and down the toll road, searching for the identities of the men who'd kidnapped his daughter, his mind hadn't been fully on the task at hand. Kora's image rose constantly before him, her golden hair and open smile always lurking in the corner of his eye.

He told himself it wasn't possible that he had fallen so completely in love with her in such a short time. He could find plenty of beautiful women to take her place if he chose. But his heart told him no one could replace her quick wit, sharp tongue, and sweet kisses.

For the hundredth time, Mace forced himself to remember her betrayal, the fact that while she'd been making love with him, she'd been engaged to another man. But no matter how that hurt, it didn't drive Kora from his mind. How could he work with her, be near her—hell, be in the same city with her—unable to forgive her for what she'd done, but unable to stop loving her?

Mace shook his head. He didn't have time to worry about that. He had to concentrate on Booth Garrett, and how he could use what he'd learned against the man.

Over the past three days, Mace hadn't found anyone who knew the identity of the kidnapper he'd killed, though one man he talked to said the description fit a fellow he knew by the name of Slade. The other kidnapper, however, had more than his fair share of aliases. The bartender in Bear Pass called him Fred Baxter, but when Mace found Boris, the Russian from their ill-fated poker game, he'd referred to the man as Fred Shannon. In each of the small way stations Mace visited up and down the road from Bear Pass, he found someone who knew the black-haired man with the scar and the cold green eyes by a different name, though his reputation remained consistent: ruthless and quick tempered.

"We don't keep track too close of a man's name," an old mule driver told him. "'Specially if he's the spittin' image of the devil hisself."

Mace hadn't gotten the link that he'd been looking for until late Saturday afternoon. He'd stopped at the general store in Placerville and asked the young man behind the counter about a Fred Baxter or Shannon or any of the several other last names he'd heard.

A man stocking shelves had called over his shoulder, "Hey, mister, you looking for Fred Baxter who works out at the Garrett place?"

They had matched descriptions, and indeed, the man who had helped to kidnap Jessica and attempted to kill Mace had worked for Booth Garrett, the only man in California who might have a reason to want Mace and his daughter out of the way.

That wasn't proof that Garrett had been involved in the kidnapping. Mace couldn't go to the county sheriff with such slim evidence, but he knew he was on the right track. He had enough information with which to confront Garrett and to judge by the man's reactions whether or not his suspicions were well founded. He wasn't sure what he'd do then, but if Garrett was responsible for hurting his daughter, and perhaps for murdering his brother, Mace did not intend to let him get away with it simply for lack of evidence.

Yes, Mace thought, he was ready for a confrontation with this enemy he hadn't known he had. If only the hunt didn't lead him back to Sacramento and the distraction of a different devil with an angel's face.

He had gone out to Garrett's ranch yesterday morning, knowing it was dangerous but realizing that Garrett probably wouldn't try anything while Mace was on his property. And he hadn't, because he hadn't been there. Ingrid, the housekeeper, had informed Mace that Garrett had gone to Sacramento to conclude some business having to do with opening the Bitter Creek Mine to investors.

The stagecoach tilted suddenly to the right and

then the left, jolting Mace back to the present as the man beside him was thrown against his shoulder.

"Beg yer pardon."

Mace sighed. So here he was, on his way back to Sacramento. And Kora.

"We're almost there."

Mace tried to smile at Fritz's reassurance. Only a small white bandage remained as evidence of the injury the old man had suffered during Jessica's kidnapping. He had wanted to stay on at his cabin when Mace and Jessica left, but Mace had convinced him to return to Sacramento with them. He didn't really think Fritz was in any further danger, but as long as the man behind Jessica's kidnapping was still at large, Mace thought it best not to leave Fritz alone at his remote claim.

On the other hand, riding the stage had its dangers, too. Their driver pushed the horses as if General Lee's entire army were chasing him, and they'd already suffered the delay of a broken axle. They should have been in Sacramento hours ago.

The stagecoach finally slowed from its breakneck speed to the stop-and-start motion of a vehicle in traffic. Jessica stretched beside Mace and sat up with a yawn.

"Are we home?" she asked.

"Almost," Mace told her, wishing he felt as happy about it as his daughter did.

"Good, I'm hungry."

"*Ach,* you must come have breakfast with me," Fritz said. "My daughter makes the best biscuits in the world!"

"Oh, that would be terrific! Can we please, Papa?"

Mace's gut wrenched at the thought of seeing Kora

again so soon. And her family. He wondered what she'd told them. He hadn't wanted to upset Fritz, so he'd merely told him part of the truth: that Jared had come to see Kora and she'd felt she should return to Sacramento to speak with him. Despite Fritz's apparent concern over that news, the explanation had seemed to satisfy him. But now it put Mace in an awkward position.

"It's too early," Mace told his daughter. "Thank you for the invitation, Fritz, but we wouldn't want to intrude."

Fritz waved away his objection. "It's no trouble. No one is expecting me, either. We'll make our own breakfast, if we have to—flapjacks." He wiggled his eyebrows at Jessica.

She laughed. "Grandpa Fritz makes terrific flapjacks," she said, focusing her pleading blue eyes on her father.

Mace fully intended to end this discussion with a firm "No!" but to his surprise he heard himself saying, "I suppose we could have flapjacks with Fritz, but we can't stay long. We have to get you back in school, young lady, before it's too late."

Jessica beamed at him. "Before what's too late, Papa?"

"Before your brain turns to mush," Mace answered, reaching out to tickle her.

At Jessica's shriek, the heavyset woman sleeping beside Fritz awoke with a snort. Her glare ended the horseplay, and Mace suddenly realized what he had agreed to put himself through. He needed to stay away from Kora Hunter, but she drew him like a moth to a flame. He glanced out the window, where the sun was shining brightly now. Maybe she would already be at work. Then he cursed himself for the disappointment he felt at that thought.

Kora sat at the breakfast table, smiling politely through one of Troy's humorous stories. She had no idea what he was talking about; her mind seemed unable to concentrate on anything lately.

"Kora, honey?"

She looked up to see her mother frowning at her.

"Kora, I asked if you wanted some more eggs. You've hardly eaten anything this morning. Or last night. Are you all right, sweetheart?"

Kora forced a smile. "I'm fine, Mama. And I'd love another biscuit if there are any."

She took a biscuit from the basket her mother passed her, noticing that her father and Troy also watched her while she buttered it and took her first bite. The biscuit stuck in her mouth, making it almost impossible to swallow, but she managed, and that seemed to satisfy her attentive family.

Kora set the biscuit down with relief as Troy resumed his story. It wasn't that she didn't want to eat, but nothing tasted good lately. Even her favorite foods seemed drained of flavor. And she hadn't been sleeping well either.

She was back on better, if still tentative, terms with her family. She'd thought she noticed some strain between her parents after her father let her go back to work, but that hadn't lasted. She did worry about what might happen if she succeeded in breaking the Amado case. This morning she planned to visit Diego Amado in jail again—something she'd intended to do as soon as she returned from the mountains, but her father had kept her too busy until today. Despite everything else that had happened, Amado's predicament and his wife's murder continued to haunt her.

In addition to her personal concern that justice be served, this was her story, her big chance to prove herself. She couldn't let Troy's name shield her this time. She knew her rapport with her parents could easily be shattered once more, but there was time enough to cope with that when or if it happened. For now there was peace in the Hunter household.

Other relationships had also improved. She had seen Jared yesterday at church, and not only had he been civil, he had actually smiled at her and wished her well. She couldn't help noticing that he and Clemency had shot each other glances throughout the service.

With her life running so smoothly, it shouldn't bother her that she hadn't heard one word from Mace in three days. But it did. Each day he remained away from Sacramento, her stomach tightened another notch. What if something had happened to him? He had told her he believed that whoever arranged Jessica's kidnapping wanted him dead. What if the killer had finally succeeded? And what about her grandfather and Jessica?

Mace had told her father he would be back to work in about a week, and today marked exactly a week since they'd left for her grandfather's cabin.

Kora crumbled a piece off of her biscuit to make it look as though she'd eaten more. If Mace did not come to work today or send some kind of word, she would go to the telegraph office and contact the law in Placerville. They could send out a deputy to check on her grandfather's cabin.

If it made her look like she might care about what happened to Mr. Mason Fielding, well, she could still tell herself that she didn't. After all, she couldn't help being concerned about her elderly, injured grandfather and a helpless little girl.

A knock on the dining-room door interrupted her thoughts. She looked up to see the very grandfather she had been thinking of, looking hale and hearty as he greeted his surprised family. Behind him stood Mace. Kora's heart stopped, then began to pound.

"Papa, what are you doing back?" Anna exclaimed, jumping up to hug her father. "And what is this bandage? Are you hurt? And here are Mace and Jessica! How good to see you again."

Anna Hunter's hand flew to her hair, patting it into place as she led her father to a seat at the table, frowning at the bandage on his forehead.

"Sit down, sit down," she directed her unexpected guests. Jessica hastily complied, running over to hug Kora. But Mace hung back, staring at her. She could do nothing but stare back as everything else around her faded away. She searched his eyes to decipher his thoughts, but his expression gave nothing away. He looked at her as though she were an interesting piece of statuary sitting across from him.

Kora flushed in confusion and embarrassment, looking down at her hands. But she could feel Mace's presence. She knew when he moved to sit in the chair Anna had indicated to him, knew his eyes still watched her.

Her mother broke into her thoughts again. "Kora? Will you get some dishes for our guests? You're staying for breakfast, of course," she insisted when Mace seemed on the verge of objecting.

Kora went about getting place settings for the newcomers like an automaton, trying not to think or feel. As she placed a plate and silverware before Mace, his physical presence almost overwhelmed her. She didn't look at his face, but the sight of his arms, with muscles tightening under his coat sleeves, and his strong hands clenched on the table reminded her of the way it felt to be held by him, touched by him, loved by him. Her hands shook, and she almost dropped the plate before she got it to the table.

"Now, Papa, what happened to your head?" Anna asked, while Ellis sliced more ham for their guests.

"What? Did Kora not tell you about the kidnapping?" Fritz asked in surprise.

Kora glanced up to see everyone staring at her.

"You were kidnapped?" her mother cried in horror.

"No, no!" Kora shook her head emphatically. "Jessica was kidnapped. I didn't tell you about it, because I knew you'd worry," she added, knowing how inadequate that sounded. "I thought it would be better to let Grandpa tell you about it, so you could see that he's fine and that Jessica's back safe and sound."

Her grandfather's sharp gaze remained on her, and Kora wondered if he suspected the real reason she hadn't wanted to talk about her time in Bear Pass. But she'd managed to turn everyone else's attention from herself to Jessica.

"Are you all right, honey?" Anna asked, reaching out to rest a hand on the girl's shoulder.

"I'm okay," Jessica answered, though her usual vivacity had dropped away when Fritz mentioned the kidnapping. "It was scary, though."

Kora didn't think she could stand being in this

room with Mace for a moment longer, and seeing Jessica's discomfort, she thought of a way out.

"Jess, why don't you and I go mix up some more biscuits," she suggested, plucking the empty basket from the table. "That will give Grandpa and your father time to explain everything."

Jessica nodded gratefully. "Okay." She hopped down from her chair to precede Kora out to the kitchen.

"My goodness, Mace, you must have been so worried!" Kora heard her mother say as she followed Jessica. She didn't glance back, but she could have sworn that she actually felt Mace's gaze follow her from the room.

"Thanks," Jessica said as Kora set the basket down on the kitchen counter and reached for the flour jar. "I don't like thinking about what happened."

Kora smiled at the girl as she handed her an apron. "I don't blame you." She motioned Jessica to hand her the mixing bowl. "I'm just glad you're all right." She stooped to give Jessica another hug. Jessica hugged her back tightly.

They were quiet for a while as Kora mixed the biscuit dough, then rolled it out.

"Want to cut them?" she asked. Jessica nodded, and Kora handed her the round biscuit cutter.

"Kora?"

"What is it, honey?" Kora asked absently as she checked the heat of the oven.

"When you get married, can I still come over and talk with you?"

Kora looked at the girl, startled. Jessica's serious eyes glanced up from her biscuits.

"I mean, even if you and Papa aren't still friends?"

"Oh, Jess. You and I are going to be friends no matter what. All right?"

Jessica nodded with a brief smile. "All right."

Kora felt tears come to her eyes as she watched Jessica lift the biscuits and place them on the baking pan. How she would have loved to marry this girl's father, to help him care for his daughter and watch her grow into a lovely young woman. She hastily wiped her eyes with the back of her sleeve, then took the pan from Jessica and put it in the oven.

Mace stepped through the swinging door into the kitchen to see Kora leaning over the stove, his daughter beside her. Both had put on white aprons. Jessica's swamped her and had to be wrapped all the way around to tie in front. The warm domestic scene broke almost immediately when the two looked up and saw him.

He did his best to sound nonchalant, though his throat tightened at the thought of what could have been. "Jess, you go on back into the dining room and have some ham and eggs. You haven't eaten since last night."

Jessica glanced at Kora, then back to him. "Okay," she said uncertainly. She scooted past him out the door.

Mace hardly noticed her go. Kora filled his senses. He must be imagining it, but he thought he could smell the honey-sweet freshness of her hair. He noticed that she looked pale with dark circles curved under her eyes, but she was no less beautiful for that. She also looked uncomfortable and on her guard, but he saw no fear of him in her eyes.

Kora waited for Mace to speak, her heart thudding in her chest. She had so many things she wanted to say to him, but they had all dispersed at his entrance, leaving her mind empty of everything but the tension between them and the strong desire to rush into his arms and beg him just to love her.

"I haven't told Jessica anything about what happened between us," he said finally, his voice cool and detached. "She thinks of you as a friend, and I don't see any reason to change that."

Kora's face flushed with sudden fury. "How very decent of you," she replied. "I applaud your magnanimity."

"Damn it Kora, I'm being more than fair. After what you put me through, I don't know that I should even let her see you anymore."

His tone cut through her like a knife, leaving her cold despite the heat of the oven behind her. He hadn't come here to listen to her side of the story, and he hadn't changed his mind about her. In fact, he sounded as though he cared even less for her now that he'd had a few days to think about it.

Kora sucked in a deep breath. She would *not* let him see her cry.

"Very well, Mace, have it your way." She turned to pull the biscuits from the oven, moving them deftly to her wicker basket. She hoped he couldn't see her hands shaking and wondered why he didn't just leave. Whirling to face him again, she looked him straight in the eye. "To you, I'm a lying hussy who hurt you terribly. You live with that lie if you want to, but I won't. I'm not going to act guilty for something I didn't do, just to please you. Now, if you'll excuse me."

She brushed past him, and Mace could hardly resist the urge to grab her by the shoulders and shake her—or kiss her, kiss her until she laughed and smiled at him as she had that night in the mountains, when they'd made love beneath the stars. But he let her go. He could never kiss her that way again, not knowing that she'd betrayed him.

As she entered the dining room, Kora breathed a sigh of relief that Mace had allowed her through the door, even as her throat tightened with tears that he hadn't stopped her, asked her what she meant, told her he still loved her.

Her grandfather grinned at her. "Biscuits! I have been dreaming of these all night!" But his eyes questioned hers.

"Enjoy them," Kora told him, her voice sounding thin rather than bright as she'd intended. "I'm sorry I can't stay and share them, but I'd better get dressed for work, before my boss notices I'm late."

Her father frowned instead of smiling at her joke, but Kora hardly noticed his concern. She rushed out of the dining room, taking the steps to her room two at a time.

Kora walked down the row of jail cells, head high, gaze straight ahead. More than a dozen men were in the jail here today, most of them awake, staring at her lewdly. She tried not to wish that Mace were walking by her side.

"Hey, darlin'," one of the men called. "You in here to ease our sufferin'? Lemme show you how you kin ease mine."

The other men laughed. One let out a long wolf whistle. Kora ignored them, stifling her sigh of relief when she reached the end of the corridor. No wonder

Officer Gant had been reluctant to let her come down here alone. But after more than a week, the memory of Rosemarie Amado's face, so innocent and peaceful in death, refused to be banished from her mind. She'd had to come.

She found Diego Amado sitting on his cot, watching her with the same calm stare as he had the first time she had visited him.

"Good morning, Mr. Amado," she said, not knowing how to begin, since the other prisoners were listening to her every word.

Amado almost smiled. "Good morning, Miss—"

"Hunter."

"Miss Hunter. Where is your partner?"

"He's busy." She was not going to tell Amado that she was doing her best to avoid Mason Fielding.

"What can I do for you, Miss Hunter?"

The irony of that question was not lost on Kora. She ignored it. "I understand your trial begins next week."

Amado shrugged as if it meant nothing to him.

"The police fully expect you to be found guilty."

"And so do I."

Kora frowned, but Amado's dark eyes never wavered from hers. She was the one who finally glanced away.

She tried a different tack. "Mr. Amado, Mr. Fielding and I have been investigating your wife's murder. We have been unable to find anyone she knew who might have a motive to kill her or any evidence to suggest that you did not, in fact, do it yourself. And yet, Mr. Amado, foolishly or not, I don't believe you did it. When I listened to you speak last week, you made me think you might be innocent."

She thought she detected surprise on that impassive face, but he said nothing.

She continued, making no attempt to hide her frustration. "If that was mere manipulation on your part, then that's that. But if you are indeed innocent, then you can't simply sit back and tell me the system isn't going to work for you, so you won't bother to fight. You tried to make me feel guilty, you got me involved in your problems, and it's about time you took responsibility for that. Now tell me what you know, or don't expect to see me again!"

This time surprise was evident on Amado's face. He rose to his feet and crossed the cell to stand face-to-face with Kora.

Amado held out his hand, and before she had time to think about it, Kora gave him hers. He shook it firmly.

"Thank you, Miss Hunter," he said with obvious sincerity. "It means a great deal to me that you would think I might be innocent, and even more that you would wish to help me. As long as there are still people who believe in justice, there is hope for others, if not for me."

"Then you'll tell me who you think killed your wife?" Kora prodded. She hadn't come down here with much hope that she could sway him, but now she was sure he—

"No."

"No?" Kora repeated in disbelief.

Amado shook his head. He lowered his voice so that the men in the next cells would not hear.

"I cannot tell you," he said. "As I mentioned before, even if I had proof against the men I suspect, I could not present it in court. An Indian's rights are not equal to a white man's."

"But there's nothing to stop *me* from testifying against a white man. I'm quite prepared—"

"No! You are not prepared. These men have killed once and would not hesitate to do so again, even if you are a white woman and a reporter. I could not put you in such danger."

Kora found herself preferring his resentment and anger to this stoic resignation. Every time she thought of Rosemarie's murderer going free, it made her stomach ache. She had to find a way to convince Amado to help her.

"But think of your wife," she said fervently. "Think of yourself."

"I am thinking of myself," he told her with a slight smile. "I would not like to face the gallows with your death on my conscience."

"Mr. Amado, just because I am a woman does not mean that I'm helpless. I've faced danger before, and I'm not so easy to kill as you might think."

Amado shook his head again, and a wistful look came to his eyes.

"You are so like Rosemarie," he said softly, and Kora felt a strange shiver run up her spine. "She always thought it didn't matter if the world looked down on her because she was an Indian woman. She would simply work twice as hard, and that would earn her the world's respect."

Amado paused. "But it was that attitude—trying to better herself and learning to read despite the obstacles—that got her killed."

His jaw tightened and Kora could see the pain as he remembered his wife.

"What do you mean that learning to read got her killed?" she asked. But she could tell from his expression that he wouldn't answer.

"Take heed, Miss Hunter," he warned instead.

"Forget about my wife, forget about me. If you truly wish to help me, do what I could not, what I would not do while I was free. Help my people. Learn about the Indian people of California, write about them in your paper, criticize the injustices done to them. But forget Diego Amado and his one small problem."

He turned from her then, and Kora knew she would get no more from him.

"I can't give up," she said softly, but clearly. Those words rang in her head as she walked back down the corridor of cells, impervious to the catcalls and lewd comments of the other prisoners. She couldn't give up. Not on Diego and Rosemarie Amado, and not on herself.

Her step quickened. She had given up this morning when she'd run away from Mace. That wasn't her style. She needed to make peace with him, even if he could no longer love her, no matter how painful that was to contemplate. And just maybe she could work things out with him, if only he didn't look at her every time they met as if she had the plague. And maybe the Amado story was just the thing to get them talking civilly. After all, it was as much his story as hers.

If Officer Gant wondered at the determined look in Kora's eyes as she smiled at him on her way out, he didn't let on, though a brief smile touched his lips in return before he bent back to the paperwork on his desk.

Mace paused a moment before opening the door to Ellis Hunter's print shop. He'd dropped Jessica at school, only a little late, and taken their luggage back to Mrs. Johnson's boarding house. He'd had a bath and changed out of his rumpled traveling clothes.

Now he stood here in the street in front of the *Valley Times* office because he couldn't think of a damn thing more he could do to put this moment off any longer. After seeing Kora this morning, he knew he couldn't bear working with her day after day. He would end up killing her or marrying her, neither one a particularly viable option.

On the other hand, he'd promised Ellis Hunter and his editor in Massachusetts that he'd write articles for them over the next year. He could suggest that he spend the time traveling around California getting stories, but he couldn't desert Jessica like that.

He'd simply have to do his best to avoid Kora, and when he couldn't avoid her, he'd ignore her. Though in his heart he knew he couldn't do that. This morning he hadn't been able to keep his eyes off her. Even after she left the room, she occupied his every thought.

Mace shook his head. He was losing his mind. He put out a hand and opened the door to the print shop.

Ellis Hunter stood beside the front desk, looking at a pile of penciled notes. He glanced up as Mace entered, his expression of concentration giving way to a slight frown.

"Mason," he said by way of greeting.

Mace handed him several sheets of paper, covered in the careful script he used when he wanted others to be able to decipher his writing.

"These are a couple of stories I wrote up over the past week on my impressions of gold mining, the mountains, and California gambling," Mace said. "I thought you might want to look them over."

Ellis nodded, glancing briefly at the papers before he set them down on his desk.

Mace continued. "If you don't have anything in particular you'd like me to cover, I thought I'd do some investigation into the management of a mine I visited last week. It seems to be doing well, but I think the man who owns it may have a shady past."

"That's fine," Ellis said, but Mace could tell he hadn't really been listening.

"Is there something wrong?" Mace asked, though an alarm bell in his head said he didn't really want to know.

Ellis considered for a moment, then finally said, "I don't know. Is there?"

Apprehension prickled Mace's neck. Kora must have talked to her father after all. Well, Mace was in the right and damned if he was going to apologize, even if it cost him his job.

"What do you mean?" he asked.

Ellis sighed. "I don't really know, Mason. But if I tell you what I've been noticing, maybe you can tell me what it means."

He looked back at Mace. "My daughter is a very open, honest, and, I must say, outspoken young woman. However, she has been singularly quiet about her trip up to the mountains this past week. Not only did she not tell us about your daughter's kidnapping, but she didn't tell us much of anything at all. That's not like her. And she's not eating or sleeping well, which is even less like my Kora."

Ellis's sharp eyes studied his face, but Mace kept his expression impassive.

"And now it seems that you're no more eager to discuss the subject than she is." Ellis frowned again, obviously uncomfortable. "Kora is an innocent, ideal-istic woman, despite her chosen profession. I don't like to see her hurting, Mason, and I'd like to help. I'd appreciate it if you'd level with me. The impression I get from Fritz is . . . well . . . has Kora fallen in love with you?"

Mace was taken aback by Ellis's direct question. He appreciated the man's honesty, but he didn't have the heart to tell Ellis that his daughter was a deceiv-ing witch.

"I hardly think that's likely, considering her engage-ment," he said finally, managing to sound calm.

"Engagement?"

"To be married." When Ellis's obvious confusion deepened, Mace added, "To Jared Davies."

Mace wondered what was wrong with the man when Ellis shook his head as though he hadn't heard right.

"But Kora and Jared aren't engaged. Where did you hear that?"

"Mr. Davies told me himself."

Ellis's confusion cleared almost instantly. "Jared told you that? I guess I shouldn't be too shocked by that. Jared's always been jealous where Kora's con-cerned. I suppose he thought it was a fair means of chasing off the competition."

"What are you talking about?"

Instead of answering, Ellis asked his own question. "When exactly did Jared tell you about this engage-ment?"

"He mentioned it when he came out to Bear Pass to visit Kora last Thursday," Mace answered stiffly. Ellis could draw his own conclusions about why his daughter hadn't mentioned it sooner.

"And Kora came home the next morning. This is beginning to make sense," Ellis said. "It might interest you to know that Friday morning Kora told Jared she wasn't going to marry him."

Mace's heart jumped with sudden relief that he wouldn't lose Kora to that young cad, but the feeling died just as suddenly. It didn't matter what Kora had done; she'd still betrayed him. Breaking up with Jared was just another ploy to lure him back. He wasn't about to fall for it.

"I don't see what business it is of mine that she broke off the engagement."

Ellis sighed. "Mason, the more I think about it, the more I believe my daughter has fallen for you hard. I don't know what to think about that. I haven't known you very long, but from what I've seen and from what Chester McDougall wrote me about you, you're a good reporter, and, more importantly, an honorable man. Which makes it very difficult for me to understand why Kora didn't explain all this to you herself. She didn't break off an engagement to Jared. There never was one to break. She never accepted Jared's proposal."

Mace's composure finally cracked. "That can't be true!" he said, his voice harsh as he felt his throat constrict. He wanted to believe it so badly that Ellis's words sounded like mockery to his ears. "Are you sure of that?"

Ellis simply nodded.

Mace stared at him, trying to see some sort of duplicity in the man's eyes, but his instincts told him that Ellis wasn't lying. Kora could have been engaged to Jared without her father knowing, but that wasn't likely.

"Why didn't she accept him?" he asked finally.

"He demanded she quit reporting. She wouldn't do it. Not for him. We all tried to convince her to marry him anyway—for her own good, you understand. I wonder now . . . well, it's too late for that."

Mace hardly heard what Ellis said. His mind raced to understand what he had just learned. But all his brain could do was repeat over and over again that Kora hadn't betrayed him. She hadn't been lying when she'd told him that she and Jared weren't engaged.

After the unbelievable impact of that thought came another. She had made love with him freely and honestly, and he had repaid her by calling her a liar.

"Mason?" Ellis asked, concern in his voice. "It's obvious something has happened to set you and my daughter at odds. I hope that what I've said hasn't widened the gap. I'd feel guilty for meddling in my daughter's life again, and hell, I shouldn't have to feel guilty. I'm her father, for heaven's sake."

Mace set his jaw. "I believe I owe your daughter an apology," he said, keeping his voice level despite the emotions boiling inside of him.

Ellis glanced past him out the window. "It looks like you'll get your chance," he said, making his way to the printing room door for a quick exit. "Here she is now."

16

Kora burst through the door to the print shop office and hurried to her father's desk. To convince Mace to work with her on the Amado story, she needed to organize her notes and come up with some new angle they could pursue together.

She had just cleared a spot on the desk when someone cleared his throat behind her. She whirled around to find herself facing the man who had occupied her thoughts all morning long. His chiseled face was more handsome, and his blue eyes more enigmatic than ever. He moved toward her, and Kora instinctively backed against the security of the desk.

"Kora . . ." Mace suddenly didn't know how to continue. She looked so beautiful standing there, her honey-colored hair tucked up under a prim little hat. The sea-green ribbon on the hat brim matched the satin of her dress and brought out the gold sparks of her eyes. He wondered how he could ever have thought such a sweet, honest face capable of deceit and treachery.

"If you're planning to attack my character again, forget it," she said. "I won't be staying in the office long enough for you to get properly started."

She wondered why he was looking at her like that. The heat in his eyes distracted her, making her forget why she had been looking for him in the first place. If only she could make her body forget how he made her feel when they made love. It was humiliating to have his mere presence affect her this way when she knew he hated her so much.

"I'm not going to attack you again," Mace assured her. He meant to say something more pertinent, or at least romantic, but he'd hardly been able to think since she walked in the door. That dress hugged her figure in all the right places, and it reminded him of how that figure felt in his arms.

But pain haunted her eyes, and he knew he was the cause. He wanted to tell her about the new joy that had gripped his heart since he'd met her, how much he loved her, but first he had to take away her pain.

"Kora," he began as gently as he knew how. "I owe you an apology. Your father told me about Jared's proposal to you and that you never accepted it. I know now that Jared lied about you, and you're none of the things I accused you of being. You really are the woman I have come to love so much."

He watched her eyes widen slowly in understanding. But her response took him completely by surprise.

"So now that my father's explained things to you, you know the truth, do you?" she said, moving forward from the desk, her eyes blazing. "How very nice for you, Mace, but you knew the truth last Thursday when *I* told it to you."

"Yes, you did tell me, but at the time, I didn't have any reason to think Jared would lie to me."

Kora's heart pounded with the knowledge that Mace believed in her again, and he was here, telling her he cared for her, that he loved her. It was more than she'd dared hope for. But that didn't calm the fury his words ignited in her veins. "You had some reason to think I would lie? I risked my life to help you find your daughter. I risked my reputation to be with you. And you couldn't even do me the favor of having a little trust in me?"

Guilt swamped Mace. She was right of course, but she didn't know the experiences he had had that had prevented him from trusting her. He should have told her about Cecilia that night on the trail. Maybe this misunderstanding would not have gone so far if he had, but he'd never know. All he could do was tell her now.

"Kora, it seemed to me that you had more to gain from lying than Jared did. You see, you're a woman. . . ."

Kora gasped in disbelief, interrupting him. "This is supposed to be an apology? If so, it's a damn poor one!"

She was shaking with anger now, fueled by the pain she'd lived with since she'd left Bear Pass. "Guess what, Mr. Fielding, I'm well aware that I'm a woman, and I'm quite happy about it, thank you very much. That doesn't make me in any way inferior to you pigheaded, shortsighted, distrustful men."

Mace suddenly realized he'd gone about this all wrong. Now was not the time to reason this out, to make excuses. He stepped forward and pulled her into his arms.

"Damn it, Kora, you couldn't be any happier than I am that you're a woman," he said roughly. Before she could reply to that, he bent down and covered her mouth with his.

She raised her arms, fully intending to push him away, but his kiss overpowered her. Her traitorous body melted against his, reveling in his warmth and the strength of his embrace. She opened her mouth to him, inviting his tongue to enter, meeting it with her own.

The kiss burned deep inside her, setting her ablaze with desire. For a moment, the pure joy of being close to him again swept away all her anger and frustration.

A sound at the door to the printing room caused Mace to let her go. If he hadn't kept a hand on her arm, Kora thought she might have fallen to the floor, she was so dizzy from the kiss. But not so dizzy that she couldn't remember what he had said before the kiss began.

"That doesn't count as a proper apology, either," she hissed before the door behind her opened.

"Mace, there you are," her brother's voice boomed cheerfully. "Can you give me a hand back here? There are some heavy boxes I need to move. Pa and Max are both complaining about their bad backs to get out of helping."

It took Mace a second to compose himself enough to answer. He could still feel Kora pressed against him, making it hard to concentrate on anything else.

"Sure, I'll be there in just a minute," he managed. "Just let me finish this discussion with Kora."

Kora moved past him to the door, and Mace saw

the daggers in her eyes, though she smiled sweetly at Troy.

"I think our discussion is over," she said coolly, despite the tremor in her voice that told him how much his kiss had affected her. "Perhaps you'd better think about what I've said before you try to continue it."

"Kora!"

She was already out the door. Her heart pounded in her chest and she could hardly breathe, but that had nothing to do with her breakneck pace as she hurried down the street.

"Some apology!" she muttered. She thought of the shocked look on Mace's face when she'd rushed out the door.

He probably couldn't believe his kiss didn't make me forget the horrible things he said to me.

But she had to admit it almost had. She could still feel his hands on her back, pulling her close, feel his lips on hers, the heat of his body pressed against hers. Kora blushed at the sensations the mere memory aroused in her. If Troy hadn't come in, she wouldn't have been able to stop that kiss. For days she'd dreamed of Mace kissing her that way.

As the tightness of her corset forced her to slow to a respectable walk, her anger with Mace began to wane. When she'd walked out of the print shop, all she'd wanted was to hurt him with a dose of the rejection and confusion that he'd given her. But now she realized how much her anger might actually cause him to suffer. Just this morning, she wouldn't have thought that possible.

A mere twenty minutes ago she had been plotting how to get Mace to work with her again so that they might have a chance to talk about what had happened between them. The shock of his sudden change of heart and her anger at his bumbling attempt to apologize had thrown her off-balance, but they hadn't changed what was in her heart.

She slowed, confusion enveloping her. Mace had made her so furious just now that she'd felt she actually hated him. And yet neither anger nor pain seemed able to diminish her love for him.

She looked around to discover she'd walked all the way down I Street to the neighborhood where Clemency's and Jared's families lived. Part of her wanted desperately to turn around and run back to Mace, but her father's office was not the place for them to talk. And she needed to work out her own feelings first. Her good sense had a tendency to fly out the window whenever Mace quirked that sexy smile at her.

Her feet found their way up Clemency's walk without any help from her mind.

Clemency greeted her at the door. "Kora! Perfect timing. I'm just on my way to choose the material for my new evening gown. You have to come help me decide. What do you think of the outfit I have on?"

She spun around, her silk skirts ballooning to fill the narrow hallway. The closely tailored jacket matched the broad pink and green stripes of the skirt. She dropped the point of her pink parasol to the floor, leaning lightly on the handle. "Well?"

"Anyone else would look like taffy in that."

"Flatterer."

"Sorry, Clem. You look great."

"Mm." Clemency leaned her parasol against the

coatrack with a long-suffering sigh. "Come on in. I can see my new dress will have to wait."

Obediently, Kora followed her down the hall to the sitting room, a large, airy room made almost uninhabitable by all the knickknacks Mrs. Tate was unable to crowd into the front parlor.

Kora perched on the edge of a sofa that appeared to have given birth to a litter of decorative pillows in a raucous variety of colors and sizes.

"Well?" Clemency demanded, choosing the piano stool as the least cluttered seat in the room.

"Well what?"

Clemency made a face at her. "Haven't we done this before?" She leaned forward, almost knocking over a tiny table covered with porcelain figurines. "You haven't had another proposal, have you?"

"No! Absolutely not!" Kora grimaced at her own vehement denial. She knew Clemency was too sharp to let that pass by.

"This is about Mason Fielding, isn't it? I told you I'd be here to talk to if you needed me, but I'm not going to push you."

"Good, because I don't know what to say." Kora looked down at her hands, noting the rough fingernails, the ink stains. "I don't understand him, Clem. Jared . . . Jared told Mace that he and I were engaged, and Mace went crazy. He wouldn't believe a word I said. Now that Papa's told him Jared lied, he suddenly believes in me again. And I don't know what I feel. Jared could always make me angry, but I felt like murdering Mace this afternoon . . . and I felt like letting him hold me in his arms forever."

She stopped, embarrassed. "I can't believe I'm even saying such things."

"Sounds pretty serious to me," Clemency said. "You're hooked, but good. As an expert opinion, I'd have to say his jealousy isn't necessarily a mark against him." She smiled, deceptively sweetly. "In fact, jealousy can be quite useful on occasion. But you have to be careful. He could be playing on your emotions, hoping to soften you up. Some men are only looking for . . . well, something physical, if you understand me."

Kora blushed. "I don't think that's it." But Clemency's words disturbed her. She had grown up with the warnings—from her mother's injunction against kissing to the admonitions of her less-restrained friends to be sure to have an engagement ring on her finger before she went too far. She hadn't listened. What if *that* was all Mace had wanted all along?

Their lovemaking had seemed so right, though—a fiery extension of the deep tenderness she felt toward him in her heart. And Mace . . . his touch was so intensely honest. She would not repeat his mistake and make hasty conclusions.

"Kora? Are you listening to me? What exactly went on up in those mountains last week?"

"I thought you weren't going to push me."

"I lied." Clemency frowned. "Kora, do you love him?"

Kora saw no point in lying. The damage to her heart was already done. "Yes." She finally knew what love meant. If only that would make everything all right.

"Do you think he loves you?"

Kora remembered their confrontation in the *Valley Times* office. Remembered what she'd seen in his eyes, the words that had burned her heart. A smile began to play about her lips. Just maybe he did. "Today he said he loved me. A bit awkwardly, perhaps . . ."

"That can be changed."

She caught Clemency's eye, and they burst into a fit of giggles. The tension in Kora's shoulders eased, and she laughed until she had to fight for air. As her breathing slowly returned to normal, the worst of her confusion and indecision subsided.

"I don't understand the way he's been acting, Clem, but I owe him the chance to explain himself." After all, that was why she was so angry at him—he hadn't given her that chance.

She stood, and Clemency rose with her.

"So much for my theory that if I find the right man, we won't fight." Her friend sighed.

"This is different from how it was with Jared," Kora said, trying to find the right words. She didn't think telling Clemency that it hurt more would reassure her. "With Mace, it hurts as much to know he's hurting as to be hurt myself. Maybe it means more to work things out between us than to be in the right. I don't know."

Clemency managed a wistful smile. "Maybe if you both feel that way, there's hope after all." She made a face. "You're going to convert me into a pitiful romantic myself if you go on any longer."

She whisked past Kora into the hall. "Are you going to come help me pick out material or not? I'm sure you don't want to catch Mace until you can speak with him in private."

Kora followed her outside. As though washed clean by her lifting spirits, the air seemed to have lost its dust and tiredness. The houses near the Tates' gleamed, their gardens lush with green leaves and early summer flowers. As Kora looked up and down the street, a familiar house, sitting quietly and conservatively behind its wrought-iron fence, caught her eye. It took her only a second to place it as the home of Miles Osborn, lawyer to Mr. Booth Garrett, mine owner, and employer of Rosemarie Amado, murder victim.

She felt a sudden shiver. What was it Diego Amado had said this morning? Somehow Rosemarie's attempt to better herself by learning to read had gotten her killed. Hadn't Dimity Osborn commented on Rosemarie's literacy as well?

Kora pulled her notebook from her pocket and quickly flipped back through it. On the page she'd used for notes during the interview with Mrs. Osborn, she'd written "READ" with a circle around it and an arrow pointing to the heading "ROSE." That both Amado and Mrs. Osborn had mentioned the victim's ability to read was probably just a coincidence, but it couldn't hurt to talk with Mrs. Osborn. Besides, it would annoy the woman's obnoxious husband.

Kora glanced at her watch, noting the early hour. Miles Osborn would probably still be at work this afternoon, and therefore unable to object to a reporter's lending a sympathetic ear to his talkative wife.

"What now?" Clemency asked, glancing up at her from the bottom of the front steps.

Kora tried Clemency's own eyelash-fluttering trick. "Can I catch you next time on the shopping, Clem? I just had an idea for a story I'm working on. . . ."

Clemency pouted. "I'm beginning to sympathize with Jared about your reporting. But I suppose I can manage without you."

Kora came down the steps to give her a hug. "Thanks for the talk, Clem. You're a real friend."

"You sure you won't come with me? They have some lovely ecru silk, perfect for a wedding gown. . . ."

"Clem!"

Her friend smiled, and with a delicate shrug headed down the street in the direction of the dry goods store.

Kora made a face at her retreating figure, then hurried across the street to the Osborn house. She knocked sharply with the lion's-head door knocker.

A large Mexican woman appeared at the door, wearing a sober gray dress covered with a ridiculously frilly white apron. A tiny cap of similar fluff topped her prudent black bun.

"May I help you?" she asked with a musical Spanish accent.

"I'd like to speak with Mrs. Osborn," Kora said. "My name is Kora Hunter, and I'm a reporter. I spoke with Mrs. Osborn last week."

The maid looked at her doubtfully. "Wait here a moment, please."

Kora didn't have to wait long.

"Follow me," the maid commanded when she returned. Kora got the impression the woman didn't understand why her mistress would deign to speak to a person of such questionable status as Kora.

"Señorita Hunter, Señora Osborn," the maid announced as she ushered Kora into the Osborns' front parlor.

"Thank you, Maria," Dimity Osborn said, dismissing her.

"Good afternoon, Mrs. Osborn," Kora said, moving into the room as the maid left. "I wasn't sure you'd see me."

Mrs. Osborn blushed as she waved for Kora to take a seat. "Oh, I'm so sorry about the other day. You mustn't mind Miles." The words tumbled out easily as though she were in the habit of saying them often. "His bark is worse than his bite, as they say. Would you like some tea?"

"Yes, that would be nice," Kora said as she sat down opposite her hostess.

"As you can see, I've finally found a replacement for poor Rose. Do you still have questions about her murder?"

After handing Kora the tea, Mrs. Osborn sat perched on the edge of her overstuffed chair, one hand fluttering over her heart as though to prepare herself for whatever wild thing Kora might say next.

"Yes, I do," Kora admitted, knowing that was exactly what Dimity Osborn hoped to hear. "But I'm afraid I haven't gotten very far in my investigations. I was hoping you might be able to help, even more than you already have."

Kora noticed Mrs. Osborn's flush of pleasure and felt a twinge of pity for this woman whose life was so dull that even a murder provided welcome entertainment.

"Oh, I don't see what more I could tell you," Mrs. Osborn demurred, "but of course, I want to give all the help I can."

"Thank you." Kora took a sip of her tea. "This is very good," she murmured, setting her cup and saucer down on the tea table. Actually, it tasted something like warm dishwater, but she didn't know what else to say.

"Yes, it is, isn't it? Maria is such an improvement over the first woman I tried to hire. That chit ran off to the gold fields with some man she said was her husband, but I'm not so sure." She gave Kora a significant look. "Anyway, I'm glad she left, because Maria is a godsend, though I would prefer a slimmer maid, like Rosemarie."

She shook her head with a resigned sigh. "I'm afraid, though, that replacing Rose would be a vain hope. But at least I don't have to worry about Maria stealing my silver or getting herself killed in an alleyway. These Mexicans are devout Catholics, you know, and whatever you may say about Catholics, they're still better than those heathen Indians."

Kora bit her tongue to keep from saying something that would get her thrown out of the Osborn home. She was quickly remembering how annoying Dimity Osborn's attitudes and prejudices could be. She didn't understand why the woman couldn't see the contradiction between rhapsodizing about Rosemarie Amado's talents one moment and dismissing Indians as thieving pagans the next.

She settled for commenting, "Maria certainly seems competent to me."

Mrs. Osborn nodded, but Kora interrupted before she could elaborate. She didn't want to waste her whole afternoon here. "Mrs. Osborn, one of the reasons I came back to see you was that I noticed in my notes that you mentioned Rosemarie knew how to read and write. That struck me as being unusual in someone of her background. What can you tell me about that?"

Dimity Osborn looked startled. "Do you think that bears on the murder?" she asked. Her hands fluttered as she waved away her own question. "Of course, I suppose you know more about such things than I do."

A slight note of censure tinged her voice as though

she thought it her duty to object to a woman who knew anything about murder, but Kora could see the curiosity burning in her bright blue eyes.

Mrs. Osborn shrugged delicately. "The Shipmans, the people her family was indentured to, did their best to improve the savages in their care. They wanted them to be able to read the Bible, like other Christian folk. I often had Rosemarie read my correspondence to me. My eyes tire so easily, you know."

Kora wanted to ask the woman why she didn't just swallow her pride and get some glasses, but she held her tongue.

"And Miles had no idea," Mrs. Osborn continued with an almost impish smile. "He doesn't care whom I hire or what their qualifications are, you see, as long as everything is clean and supper is on time.

"Rosemarie always dusted his study—it's just across the hall—and one day he found her in there, and, I don't know how, but it came out that she could read." Mrs. Osborn shook her head, a giggle escaping her lips. "You should have heard him yell. He likes to keep his business private—client confidentiality, you know," she said, obviously repeating words her husband had used on that occasion.

Mrs. Osborn's description of her husband's tantrum reminded Kora of Osborn's odd behavior when she and Mace had run into him up at Booth Garrett's ranch. Either the man was extremely volatile and nervous—not necessarily the traits *she* would look for in an attorney—or something was going on that was worth looking into.

Before she could press her hostess for further details, they heard a loud crash from deeper in the house. Footsteps hurried down the hall.

"Señora Osborn!" Maria called from the parlor doorway, her face a mask of disapproval. Excitement thickened her accent. "Is that *loco* giant dog of yours again. He got into the kitchen and made mud everywhere. You come. I must see if I can save the ham for supper!"

"Muffy," Dimity Osborn explained apologetically as she hurried after Maria. "I'll be right back."

It took a moment for Kora to recover from the thought of dainty Dimity Osborn owning anything big and muddy. When she did, she realized she had been left to her own devices, with Miles Osborn's office standing empty across the hall, just waiting to be explored.

Kora felt a brief moment of shock at herself for even considering sneaking through another person's private office, but when she weighed Rosemarie Amado's murder against a little snooping, what she was thinking of doing not only didn't seem so bad, it seemed like her civic duty.

She tiptoed to the parlor door. Down the hallway she heard the excited barking of a dog that, to judge from the depth of its voice, must have been as large as a small bear. Deciding she had several minutes before Mrs. Osborn would have enough peace to remember her guest, Kora dashed across the hallway to the door she assumed led to Mr. Osborn's study.

She didn't even have time to worry that the door might be locked before she'd opened it and slipped through. The room's decor left no doubt that this was Miles Osborn's personal study. None of his wife's lace or flowers had made their way into here. Dark wood paneling matched the formidable bookshelves and the heavy desk. Only the large west window, which let the afternoon light gleam in on the polished wood and the brass of the lamps, mitigated the gloomy effect.

Kora quickly took stock of the room. The bookshelves held nothing the least bit interesting—mostly thick tomes on law and a few dry legal histories. A glass-fronted cabinet along one wall displayed a collection of miniature ships, some of considerable workmanship, but they held no value for Kora's search.

She moved to the desk and began to open drawers. She didn't know what she was looking for, but none of the papers and pamphlets she saw looked incriminating, or even interesting. When she reached the top drawer which held only extra pens, ink, and a rosewood pipe, she heaved a sigh of discouragement. Miles Osborn obviously kept most of his legal papers in an office somewhere downtown. If there had been anything damaging for Rosemarie to find here, he'd long ago removed it.

She turned without much hope to the pile of papers on the desk. They seemed dry enough—listings of gold and silver prices, mining stocks, and such. About to drop them back to the desk, a familiar name caught her eye. She was looking at what appeared to be a documentation of profits and expenses for the Bitter Creek Mine. She glanced over it, then stopped and read through it again.

Apparently Booth Garrett had bought the mine about a year and a half ago. According to the figures on the sheet, it had lost money steadily ever since. Kora looked down to the last months on the list. From what she could make out, the Bitter Creek Mine was on the verge of bankruptcy, destined to go the way of so many of California's mines. There had been no improvement over the past several months, even though the mine had supposedly hit pay dirt.

Kora flipped back through the other papers. She found a sheet with notations indicating that both Booth Garrett and his lawyer, Miles Osborn, had been purchasing large amounts of gold. She stared at the figures for a moment. Why would a man who owned a suddenly productive gold mine need to buy gold?

Her mouth set into a grim line. A man who was salting his claim, that's who. If a man wanted to get rid of a worthless mine by selling it for a huge profit to foolish investors, a few thousand dollars worth of gold carefully planted at his mine was a small price to pay. But such a scheme would be severely compromised if a naïve bystander—such as a maid—got a look at these documents and figured out what was going on.

Engrossed in her own racing thoughts, the sound of the door opening behind her caught Kora completely by surprise.

On the spur of the moment her mind formed a lie about breaking her pencil and coming into the study to find a new one. With elaborate nonchalance, she turned to face Dimity Osborn, but the lie froze on her lips as she found herself face-to-face with Mrs. Osborn's startled husband instead.

"My, my, what have we here?" came a smooth voice from behind the lawyer. Kora glanced past Osborn to see an impeccably groomed Booth Garrett closing the study door behind him. For a moment, no one said a word.

"I was looking for a pencil," she managed at last, lifting her own pencil as though she'd just found it. "I didn't think you'd mind if I borrowed one," she added with a forced smile at Osborn.

"I do mind!" Osborn said. "This is my private desk." Kora could almost see his mind spinning, trying to come to grips with the current situation.

"I'm terribly sorry." She dropped the pencil to the desk. "I'll just be getting out of your way then."

She swept past Osborn, but unfortunately Garrett's brain worked much faster in a crisis than his lawyer's, and he grabbed her arm.

"But you've gone to so much trouble to make sure that you *are* in the way. I'd hate to see all that effort go to waste." Garrett's voice was as smooth and genial as though they had just met at a dinner party, but one look from those cold blue eyes sent a chill down Kora's spine.

"Pardon?" Kora asked, feigning ignorance of the threat in his words. She noticed Osborn frantically flipping through the papers on his desk, making sure they were all there. "I am here to interview Mrs. Osborn. We were having tea when she was called away by an emergency with the dog. I'd better get back to the parlor to finish our discussion and leave you men to your business."

Miles Osborn whirled on her. "That's right. It's our business, not yours. I told you to stay away from me and my wife, and here I find you snooping through my personal papers." His eyes bulged with the indignity of it all, and his voice rose to a near hysterical pitch. "I ought to have you thrown in jail!"

"That wouldn't be such a good idea, since her snooping could get us thrown right in beside her," Garrett said dryly. He hadn't for a moment lessened his iron grip on Kora's arm.

"What could I possibly know that might inconvenience two such upstanding citizens as yourselves?" she asked, wide-eyed, desperately trying to keep up her charade. "I'm quite at a loss as to what you're talking about."

Garrett smiled at her, his white teeth gleaming savagely in his suddenly sinister face. "A gentleman would take a lovely lady like you at her word on something like that," he said. "But I'm afraid I'm not much of a gentleman."

"Oh, God, Booth, what are we going to do?" Osborn asked. He looked about ready to pull out his hair. Kora would have enjoyed the spectacle if she hadn't had a pretty good idea of what Garrett's answer to his question would be.

Garrett's voice crackled with angry impatience. "There you go again, Miles. Getting us into this situation with your carelessness, leaving papers where anyone can find them, and then expecting me to clean up after you."

"But you told me not to keep these documents in my office downtown," Osborn objected with a whine.

Garrett's mouth drooped in scorn. "Obviously I shouldn't have trusted you to keep them anywhere. Well, you needn't worry. I'll get rid of her."

Kora's mouth went dry. From the moment they'd come through the door, common sense had told her they'd have to kill her, but she hadn't really believed it until now. She knew she didn't have a chance against these two men, one of whom, probably Garrett, had already murdered a woman in cold blood. But she couldn't just let them kill her without a struggle.

The argument had shifted Garrett's attention to Osborn. Kora made a fist with her free hand and slammed it as hard as she could into Garrett's stomach.

He grunted, his face twisting in obvious pain, but his grip on her arm never slackened. Instead he jerked her off balance and pulled her arm up behind her back, nearly dislocating her shoulder.

"You can't kill her here!" Osborn squealed as Garrett brought his other arm around Kora's neck and squeezed.

"You bitch," he growled in Kora's ear. He tightened his hold until her windpipe closed, then loosened it slightly. Kora gagged and gasped for air. "You try that again, and it won't be the quick, easy death I had planned."

Kora was stiff with fear, but she didn't plan on letting Garrett know that. "Osborn's right, you wouldn't try anything here," she said with forced bravado.

She was wrong. Dropping his arm from her neck, Garrett pulled a pistol from the shoulder holster under his coat and cracked it smartly on the back of her skull. Kora slumped unconscious in his arms.

Mace usually noticed the smallest details of the environment around him as he walked. It stemmed from the intense curiosity he had felt even as a child about how the world worked, and he had carefully developed it during his years working as a reporter. But today he'd had difficulty concentrating on much of anything since Kora walked out on him at the print shop.

"Mr. Mason Fielding." The greeting caught him completely by surprise.

He halted, noting he'd reached his destination. The Osborn residence sat just up the street to his right. On his left, a pretty young woman waved gaily as she crossed the street to intercept him. She shifted a pink silk parasol to her left arm, reaching out to link her other arm with Mace's. After a moment of utter confusion, Mace recognized her as the young woman he'd met at Kora's house the week before.

"How nice to see you again, Miss . . ."

"Tate. Clemency Tate," she reminded him, her hand on his elbow as she shifted him back into a walk. "How sad. I guess it must be true."

"What's that, Miss Tate?" Mace asked, without much patience. Booth Garrett's housekeeper had told him Garrett was visiting his lawyer. If Mace wanted to surprise him here, he'd have to rid himself quickly of Clemency Tate.

The lady in question sighed sweetly. "You didn't come out here to court me, after all. It seems you only have eyes for Kora Hunter."

"Miss Tate, as charming as I find your company, I do have business to attend to . . ."

As he slowed to a stop beside the Osborns' walk, she turned on him, her soft sky-blue eyes suddenly flashing, all trace of coquetry gone. "You *do* only have eyes for Kora, don't you?"

"Pardon?"

Her cheek dimpled. "I'm asking you what your intentions are, sir." At Mace's obvious consternation, her smile widened. "Kora is a good friend of mine, Mr. Fielding. She can be a trifle naïve. I try to look out for her when I can." Her expression hardened again. "I know how to protect myself from a sweet-talking man, but Kora is liable to take pretty words seriously. I don't want her to get hurt."

"And you're afraid I'll hurt her?" His voice held just a hint of warning.

Clemency met his gaze directly. "I think you are in a position to do so."

Mace struggled to contain his irritation that everyone seemed so willing to assume he'd break Kora's heart. That fact that perhaps he had didn't improve his temper. "I don't believe I have any undue influence on Kora, Miss Tate. She has a mind of her own, and a very willful mind at that."

"I think she would be marrying Jared Davies if it weren't for you."

Mace's stomach lurched, acid fear returning. "Her father told me Kora rejected Mr. Davies' proposal."

"Jared can be quite persistent, and he's a wonderful catch. I know her mother was hoping they'd marry. That sort of pressure could be hard to resist without outside support. For instance, from a man unlike Jared, one who actually valued her reporting."

"If you think Kora would marry a man she didn't love just to please someone else, you don't know her as well as you think you do," Mace said. Just as he knew for certain now that she wouldn't love a man for his money or social position. The question remained, however, whether or not she could love a man as mule-headed and difficult as he'd proved to be. "Are you saying you think Kora would be better off with Mr. Davies?"

Clemency pouted. "I'm trying to bait you, Mr. Fielding, and you're being singularly uncooperative. I'll be honest with you. I think Jared and Kora would make each other miserable. I think Kora is in love with you. Now, I want to know whether you love her."

For a second, Mace held on to his defenses. He had sworn so often never to love again, sworn never to give another woman power over him. But the walls around his heart were so heavy. Kora had broken through them to show him how much lightness love could bring. He was too tired to carry his burden any further, no matter what a refuge it had seemed in the past. Even if Kora could not forgive him, even if he had killed her love, he owed her honesty.

"I do love her."

Clemency nodded. "Then I think you should tell her that. And if you don't mind some advice, I think that's all I'd say to her. Other words can wait." She smiled again, hiding mischievous eyes beneath lowered lashes.

He didn't smile back. "I'll keep that in mind if I can convince her to speak with me at all."

Clemency laid a hand on his arm. "I think she will." She squeezed his arm and turned, making her way back across the street, pirouetting once to blow him a flirtatious kiss.

He shook his head with a resigned smile at her antics, but a small kernel of hope formed in his chest. Whatever Kora had told Clemency since her return to Sacramento, it had convinced Clemency that Kora loved him. There might be a spark of feeling left for him to ignite. Certainly she had warmed to his kiss fervently enough earlier today. His own blood fired at the memory.

But he had to deal with Garrett before he could focus on Kora.

His thoughts were interrupted by the sight of a huge dog hurtling toward him down the street.

"Hey, there!" Mace caught the dog's muddy paws before they ruined his suit. Instead of objecting, the dog wagged its tail happily and tried to lick Mace's face.

"Down!" The order had no effect. The dog, some sort of cross between a sheepdog and a bear, and large enough to pass for a small pony, appeared content to dance with Mace all afternoon, if that was Mace's pleasure. "Down!" Mace dropped the dog's feet to the ground and pushed on the top of its head to keep it there. Big brown eyes looked up at him worshipfully.

Mace glanced around to see if he could spot the dog's owner, but the street was deserted.

The dog's head wiggled out from under his hand, and the animal tried to jump up on him again. Mace slipped past him down the Osborns' walk, but the beast followed him, running its head against Mace's hip until Mace paused to scratch its ear.

"You'd better go home," he warned the dog. "I don't think they'll appreciate your manners here."

But the dog followed him to the door. With one hand holding the animal down, Mace knocked.

A stern-looking maid opened the door with Dimity Osborn right behind her. Mrs. Osborn leapt forward when she saw the dog.

"Muffy!" she exclaimed, dropping down to hug the beast's head. "You bad dog! You know I don't like it when my baby runs away. Now sit."

Mrs. Osborn straightened, and to Mace's surprise, the dog remained sitting obediently by her side.

"Thank you so much for bringing him back to me," she said to Mace. "He likes to chase buggies, and I just know that one of these days . . . Oh!" She peered more closely at Mace's face. "Oh! It's you, Mr. . . . ."

"Fielding," Mace told her, still trying to get over his shock at finding out that the dog belonged to Dimity Osborn.

"Oh, yes, of course, Mr. Fielding." Her hands began fluttering in agitation. "Why, you must be looking for Miss Hunter."

He started in surprise. "Actually—" He intended to say that actually, he had heard that Miles Osborn and Booth Garrett were holding a business meeting here, and he wanted to see Mr. Garrett if that was possible. But Mrs. Osborn interrupted him.

"Oh, it's just awful," she said, her eyes tearing up in sympathy. "And to think, she seemed fine just moments before. I never would have thought she wasn't feeling well."

"Kora was here?" Mace asked, instantly alert. "What happened?"

"They've taken her to the hospital," Mrs. Osborn told him. "But I'm sure she'll be all right."

"The hospital?" His heart began to pound painfully. "Why?"

Mrs. Osborn fluttered again. "Well, you see, she seemed fine to me when she got here. I had to go see about Muffy. He'd gotten mud all over the kitchen, you know, and Maria was in quite a snit about it. So, I went back to—"

"Why did they take Kora to the hospital?" Mace shouted. He wanted to grab Mrs. Osborn by the shoulders and shake the answer out of her.

"She fainted!" Mrs. Osborn yelped, backing away. "As I said, she was fine just a few minutes before. But my husband came home to find her passed out on the sofa in the parlor. He promised he didn't yell at her or anything," she added quickly. "And Mr. Garrett assured me, too, that she'd already fainted before they walked in."

Mace's blood ran cold. "Who took her to the hospital?" he asked, knowing the answer before she replied.

"My husband and Mr. Garrett. I would have gone, but I was in such a state, Miles thought I might swoon myself." She patted a hand over her heart, breathing more deeply at the mere thought. But if she expected a show of sympathy, she was disappointed.

"You're sure it was a faint?" Mace asked her, his voice roughened by his sudden fear. "You're sure she wasn't dead?"

"Oh!" Mrs. Osborn gasped in horror at the question. "No, she was alive. I saw her breathing."

Mace felt a brief reprieve. He turned on his heel to start back up the walkway.

"Mr. Fielding?" Mrs. Osborn called after him. "Mr. Fielding, are you going to the hospital?"

But he no longer heard her. His thoughts churned with anger and trepidation. Where had they taken her? Certainly not to any hospital. No, once again Garrett had resorted to kidnapping to get to Mace. The man was crazier than he'd thought, but this time Mace intended to be a step ahead of him. He would make sure that Garrett never touched another person Mace loved. But first, he would search every building in the city if he had to in order to find Kora, and once he did, he was never going to let her go.

17

Kora's head banged against something, and she felt the sharp pain of hair being pulled from her scalp. She would have moaned, but she didn't have any control over her vocal chords. Someone was carrying her over his shoulder, and from the jerky motion, she surmised they were climbing a stairway. The motion leveled off and stopped, and she heard the sound of a doorknob turning. Then more stairs.

"Booth, what are you going to do with her?" The anxious voice of Miles Osborn rose behind them. The sound came thinly to Kora's ears.

Garrett carried Kora into what she guessed was an attic room and tossed her onto a bed. This time, she had to struggle to stifle the moan that came to her lips. She was beginning to remember the danger she was in, and she thought it best not to let these two men know she had regained consciousness, or something close to it.

"Miles, do you really want to know the answer to that?" Garrett asked. He jerked on Kora's arms, winding a rope about them. He was tying them to the bedpost.

"No, I don't," Osborn muttered. "But I think you ought to do whatever it is as quickly as possible."

Garrett finished with Kora's arms and began tying her feet.

"I'm going to do it when I think the time is right and not before," he growled at his lawyer. "This woman isn't some worthless Digger you can just dump in an alley, in case you hadn't noticed. People are going to wonder where she went, and the police may actually do some investigating if they think she's been murdered. I've got to have time to either make it look like an accident or make damn sure they can't trace her back to us, which means you're going to have to keep your wife's trap shut, do you understand?"

"Yes, of course," Osborn replied.

Garrett snorted.

"What about Fielding?" Osborn asked. "If she's his mistress, he's going to come looking for her."

Garrett laughed, a low, humorless sound. "I'll take care of Fielding," he said in a voice that made Kora's blood freeze. "I was going to have to clear up that situation anyway, and now I have one more card to play."

A hand came down on her neck, and Garrett's fingers ran down between her breasts. Her body shrank from him involuntarily.

Garrett chuckled. "So our little possum is awake. I'm terribly sorry about that bump on the head, Miss Hunter, but it shouldn't trouble you too long."

Kora opened her eyes to glare at him. "You won't get rid of me as easily as you think," she said with a confidence she didn't feel. "Now, get your dirty hands off me!"

Garrett smirked, and his hand moved down to her belly. "I like spirit in a woman," he said with a lecherous grin. "Too bad we don't really have time to get to know each other better."

"One more second in your presence is too much time!" She moved on the bed to try to escape his touch.

Garrett laughed again. "No wonder Fielding lets you follow him around. I guess I'd put up with a woman playing reporter, if she looked like you."

"Garrett," Osborn interrupted. "We don't have time for this."

"Quit your complaining." He took his hand from Kora's waist to pull a handkerchief from his pocket and stuff it in her mouth. She managed to nip one of his fingers, feeling a brief moment of satisfaction at his yelp of pain.

"You bitch," he snarled, slapping her across the face with the back of his hand. Tears sprang to her eyes at the pain, but she didn't make a sound. Garrett grabbed her hair and wrenched her head around to tie the gag behind her head.

"Garrett!" Osborn whined, shifting from one foot to the other at the delay.

Finally Garrett finished and moved away from the bed. "Be good, little girl," he smirked. Kora closed her eyes. She wouldn't give him the satisfaction of knowing how frightened she was. Then she heard him join Osborn. Stairs creaked, then the door below closed behind the two men.

Kora kept her eyes clenched shut, trying to stop

the tears that threatened to come. She had to stay calm, or she'd never get out of here. She tried to breathe evenly through her nose, tried to ignore the thick, choking cloth stuffed in her mouth. She pushed at it with her tongue and tasted blood. Garrett must have cut her lip when he hit her.

She opened her eyes again and looked around her. With her hands and feet tied to the bedposts, she could still roll from one side to the other and get a fairly good view of the room.

It was evidently an attic room, with considerable floor space, but with a sharply sloping ceiling. Apart from the bed, the only furniture was a large scratched chest of drawers with a mirror over it, and a couple of rickety chairs. There were several boxes against the walls. Everything was coated with a thick layer of dust. Tiny motes danced in the light coming in from two small windows.

Kora tugged fiercely on the ropes that bound her to the bed. Every pull only dug them further into her flesh and sent puffs of dust floating into her eyes. A coughing fit seized her as she choked on the dust and her gag.

She sagged limply, feeling the pull of despair. She wasn't going to get out of this scrape. Garrett would get away with it all—fraud, kidnapping, murder, and heaven only knew what else. Diego Amado would hang for a crime he hadn't committed, and she couldn't do a damn thing about it.

She was tied up, completely helpless, in the attic of a murderer, and no one even knew she was missing. Her father would assume she was working on a story, and Mace would think she was still angry and trying to avoid him. No one would worry until she didn't come home for supper tonight. And by then it might very well be too late.

A sob formed in her throat at the thought of never seeing her family again. She'd never write another article or make another visit to her grandfather's cabin. And would anyone remember to feed Dodge?

Most of all, she'd never get a chance to tell Mace how much she loved him. Her anger at him for not trusting her seemed petty and unimportant now, compared to how much she needed him—his friendship, his support, and his love. Never again would he touch her, smile at her, tease her.

She'd never know the joy of being held by Mace again. Garrett planned to kill her, and she didn't see any way to stop him. And what had Garrett said? He would take care of Mace, too.

Ice ran through Kora's veins. Garrett intended to kill him. Mace was in terrible danger, and here she was feeling sorry for herself. She had to calm down and formulate a plan.

Kora looked up toward where the rope that bound her hands looped around a crossbar of the old wooden bedstead. Perhaps if she moved her arms back and forth, the edge of the wood might gradually cut through the rope. Kora clenched her teeth and began to drag the rope across the wood with as much force as she could muster. At this point, anything was worth a try.

Mace looked up at the neat brown house before him and set his jaw. In the next few minutes, he would finally face Booth Garrett, and he had to keep his cool. Mace's slight advantage—his only advantage, as far as he could tell—was that he knew Garrett had kidnapped Kora, and Garrett didn't know he knew.

At least, Mace hoped Garrett didn't know. He'd wanted to come here directly from Osborn's house, but he'd had to go get Jessica from school first. He'd taken her to the Hunters' house, and although Mrs. Hunter was surprised at his request to babysit his daughter, she had happily agreed to do so. He had to know his daughter was safe, so he could devote all of his attention to finding Kora.

Mace took a deep breath, trying to calm his fears. He'd never felt this sense of dread before. Not when he'd followed Union troops into battle, hearing bullets whiz by his ears, seeing men fall dead not five feet away. Not even when Jessica had been kidnapped. He had believed she'd been abducted for ransom, and he had managed to find her before he knew just how much danger they had both been in. But this time he entered the battle fully aware that Booth Garrett was an unpredictable, devious, murderous man who would apparently stop at nothing to get what he wanted. And the thought of Kora in that man's clutches . . .

Mace firmly closed his mind to such thoughts. Now that he'd found a woman he could love with all his heart, there was no way he was going to lose her.

He walked up to the front door and knocked sharply. Moments later Garrett himself answered it, looking every bit the gentleman in his casual dark suit.

"Fielding, what a pleasant surprise," he said genially. "Won't you come in?"

Mace stepped past him into the hall.

"My housekeeper told me you'd been by this morning. She's gone for the day or I'd offer you some coffee. Would some whiskey do?" Garrett ushered Mace down the hall and into his study. He pulled a bottle of whiskey from a desk drawer. Mace shook his head at Garrett's silent offer.

"Garrett, this isn't a social call," he began.

Garrett's brows lifted. "I'm intrigued," he said, settling himself into his desk chair. "Perhaps you're here to invest in my mine?"

Mace resisted the urge to leap across the desk and strangle the man. Garrett's smugness infuriated him, but his cat-who-ate-the-canary smile also told Mace that Garrett thought his abduction of Kora was still his own little secret.

"Cut the games, Garrett," he said, bringing a fist down on the desk. "I didn't know what kind of a man I was dealing with when I first met you, but I do now. And I'm here to tell you to stay away from my daughter!" At this point, the threat was a red herring, but Mace didn't have to feign his anger.

Garrett frowned at Mace's violent manner, but Mace could see his amusement. "What in heaven's name are you talking about, Fielding? I've never even met your daughter, though I'm sure she's quite charming, being Cecilia's child."

"You know damn well what I mean," Mace growled. He leaned farther over the desk. "You hired Fred Baker to kidnap my daughter and to kill me. Baker messed up. He's dead. And that's all the warning you'll get not to try it again."

Garrett pretended shock. "Really, Fielding, your imagination has gotten the best of you, and that's my most generous interpretation of your behavior. Last week you came to me with a story that your brother may have plotted to kill me, and now you accuse me of equally murderous schemes. My advice to you is to have a glass of whiskey and rethink these wild allegations."

"I know it was you, Garrett. Stop wasting my time. You're afraid I'll put Jessica forward as my brother's child and try to take away the property you got from Jesse after you murdered him. I have no proof of this, of course," he admitted. "I'd take the matter into my own hands, but I have my daughter's future to consider. So I'm willing to bargain. I'm going to take Jessica back to Boston as soon as possible. You have my word that I don't intend to go after my brother's money. And I want yours that you won't try to harm my daughter."

Still shaking his head, Garrett rose slowly to his feet. "Look, Fielding, I don't know what you're talking about. You're not making much sense. But what I do gather from your little speech is beginning to make me rather angry."

He came around from behind the desk. Garrett was not quite as tall as Mace, but he was equally physically fit, and he made sure Mace saw his muscles flex beneath his spotless white shirt.

"I think it's time you left my home."

"Not before you give me your word," Mace replied with equal menace.

Garrett grinned. "Your brother was a good friend of mine. I wouldn't want to spoil his memory by breaking your nose. So if that's all it takes to get rid of you, you've got it. On my word of honor, I won't even go near your daughter, much less harm a hair on her pretty little head."

Garrett motioned him toward the study door, and

Mace stepped through it. He walked down the hall, desperately trying to figure out what to do next. He'd hoped that talking with Garrett would give him some clue as to where Kora might be held, but it hadn't.

At their first meeting, Mace had caught him off-guard. Garrett had been nervous and it had shown. But today, Garrett thought he held all the cards, and not a crack had shown in his good-natured facade.

Mace's little act *had* served one purpose. It appeared to have convinced Garrett that Mace was at least two or three steps behind him. But that didn't do Mace much good if he had no idea where to go from there.

Mace stopped near the stairwell before the door. He'd have to attempt a different approach. He didn't like the idea of trying to beat the truth out of Booth Garrett—he suspected they'd match up pretty evenly in a fistfight—but he didn't have much choice. He could pull the Colt from his coat pocket, but Garrett had already insured he couldn't use it, because he couldn't kill the one person who knew for sure where Kora was being held.

Garrett was coming up behind him, and Mace tensed. If he could catch the man by surprise, it would give him a much-needed advantage. But just as he was about to spin toward his enemy, a flicker of gold caught his eye. There, caught on a splinter of the stair balustrade near his hand, hung four long strands of hair, glinting honey-gold in the sunbeams from the door window.

"Are you all right, Fielding?" Garrett asked, obviously concerned by Mace's sudden immobility.

Slowly, Mace turned to face him, forcing himself not to dash immediately up the stairs. "I'm fine," he said, hoping his face didn't reflect his excitement. "I just want to warn you one more time. Leave Jessica alone."

"I gave you my word," Garrett replied, his face darkening at Mace's threatening tone.

"Keep it." He stepped out the front door, hearing the door close behind him as he moved down the walk. He kept going, not pausing until he'd turned the corner around the house next door.

His heart pounded with new hope and purpose. He knew where to go now. He'd have recognized that beautiful golden hair anywhere.

Mace walked to the back of the corner house. No fences ran behind this block of houses, and it was an easy matter to slip down to the back of Garrett's. Kora was so close he could almost feel it.

"Hold on, I'm coming," he whispered, wishing she could hear him.

Now all he had to do was find a way inside.

Kora bit her lip to keep from crying out in pain as she pulled the rope back and forth along the bedstead one more time. She moaned in frustration. Her efforts weren't doing one bit of good. The rope remained as solid as ever, and meanwhile she'd rubbed her wrists raw, and her fingers were going numb. She'd been at this for what seemed like hours, and every time she rested, it was harder to get up the hope to continue.

She lay there for a minute, trying desperately to come up with a new plan. As time dragged on, it became more difficult to get her brain to function clearly.

The creak of the attic door opening chased thoughts

of breaking the ropes from her mind. Garrett was coming back for her. Her heart began to pound.

Kora swallowed. This was it. She would have to watch for her chance and try to escape when he untied her, if he ever did. Her imagination conjured images of what Garrett might have planned for her: he could drown her in the Sacramento River, or throw her under the wheels of a wagon, or stab her in the back and leave her in an alley as he'd done to Rosemarie Amado. Kora shook her head to force the pictures from her mind. She couldn't let Garrett know she was afraid.

One of the stairs creaked sharply, and the footsteps stopped. Kora hoped Garrett had just remembered something pressing he had to attend to, preferably somewhere in China. But then the footsteps began again. Kora lay on her back, staring at the ceiling, and said one last prayer.

Mace cursed the poorly made stairs as another step creaked beneath him. In his ears it rang out like a rifle shot. He figured as long as Garrett remained in his study, it was unlikely he'd be able to hear Mace tiptoeing around the attic, but he didn't want to take any chances. He had to find Kora before Garrett hurt her, and he was beginning to wonder if Garrett hadn't already removed her from the house. He'd searched the entire second floor with no sign of her. The attic was his last hope.

As his head and shoulders rose above the level of the attic floor, Mace peered anxiously through the dim light. At first he saw nothing out of the ordinary, but a splash of sea-green satin on the bed caught his eye. *Kora!*

Mace's heart leaped. He took the last stairs in two giant steps and hurried to the bed. As he moved closer, his fear began to rise again. She wasn't moving. But Garrett had tied her hands and feet. She had to be alive.

He dropped beside her. "Kora," he whispered, his mouth dry.

Her eyes flew open and her head turned toward him. She made a noise through the gag in her mouth, and Mace recognized his name.

"Oh, sweetheart, are you all right?" he asked, relief flowing through him. He reached up to undo the gag, letting his fingers run along her cheeks, needing to touch her.

"Mace," she said, clearly this time, as he tossed away the bloodstained handkerchief. "Thank God. How did you find me?"

"It's a long story," he told her, as he unbound her hands. He would have moved to her feet next, but she threw her arms around him.

"Oh, Mace, I'm so glad you're here," she whispered against his neck, and he felt the tears on her lashes as they brushed his skin. He clutched her to him, letting his fears drain away as he felt her vibrant and alive in his arms.

"Don't worry. Everything's going to be fine," he assured her, and he knew it would, as long as she was with him.

Kora ran her hands along his back and to his neck, tilting his head down to hers to kiss him. She needed to feel his mouth on hers, to know his being here wasn't just a dream. Her tongue touched his lips, and she felt an explosion of heat as his tongue met hers and plunged into her mouth. The chill of her terror melted beneath the flame of his kiss and the warmth of his embrace.

She felt his lips curve on hers. "And I was afraid you'd never want to speak to me again." The featherlight brush of his words against her mouth, half-teasing, half-beseeching, made her heart flutter so she forgot to breathe.

"Who said anything about speaking?" she whispered back. Her tongue met his, and she heard him groan with the same hunger that fired her.

"Oh, Kora. I was so afraid. The thought of never holding you like this again—"

"I know." She laid her hand along his cheek, loving the roughness under her fingertips.

He placed his own hand on hers. "You're shaking."

Her voice was less than a whisper. "Not from fear."

Their eyes locked, and she thought the power would engulf her. Then his mouth found hers again and nothing else mattered.

Reluctantly, he pulled away. "I'd love to leave and come back in again to be welcomed like that one more time, but we've got to get you out of here." He grinned at her, the devastating grin that sent jolts of electricity down to her toes.

"By all means," she agreed, rather breathlessly.

He released her to untie the ropes around her feet. "Do you think you can stand?" he asked in concern, as he rubbed the red marks on her ankles.

"My feet are asleep." She grimaced at the sharp prickles as her circulation began to flow again.

"That bastard's going to pay for this," Mace growled, helping her to her feet and placing a supporting arm around her shoulders.

Kora shivered at the fierce determination in his voice. "I'm just glad you found me, or it would have been worse."

Mace glanced at the stairs. "We'd better get going, or it still may."

He helped Kora across the room, and she followed him down the stairs, her feet slowly returning to normal.

"Watch that one; it squeaks," Mace warned her as she neared the bottom. He grabbed her by the waist and lifted her down the last few steps. For a moment they held each other, their hearts pounding a rhythm between them, then Mace stepped back and led her down the upstairs hall to the master bedroom.

"You climbed in the window?" Kora asked as he leaned out through the open curtains.

"Don't worry, I'll help you out."

Now that she was free to move, Kora found her thought processes freed up as well. And suddenly, Mace's rescue made very little sense to her.

"Mace, how did you know I was here?" she asked, resisting his pull on her hand. "I didn't even plan on running into Garrett today, much less coming over for tea."

He frowned impatiently. "As soon as we get the hell out of here, I'll explain everything, all right?"

She frowned back. "You're not very good at explanations," she reminded him.

Mace didn't know whether to laugh or shake her. Here they were, standing in a killer's bedroom, on the verge of making a run for safety, and she wanted to know how he'd known where to find her.

He put a hand under her chin, tilting it up until her golden eyes locked with his.

"As soon as we're safe, I'll explain it to you, I promise. Okay?"

Kora nodded. He kissed her.

"Now, let's go."

He moved back to the window and slipped out feet first. Kora leaned out after him and saw that he stood on the roof of a shed next to the house. He waved for her to follow.

She put a foot on the windowsill. She realized immediately that she had a problem. Her hoops were not going to fit through the window.

"Hurry!" she heard Mace whisper from down below.

"Hold on to your horses!" she hissed back. She lifted her skirt and petticoat until they bunched under her elbows, and fumbled with the tapes of her hoops.

"What's taking so damn long?"

Finally she got the hoops undone and they collapsed to the floor with a soft whoosh. Kora looked up to see Mace standing at the window, grinning despite himself at the picture she presented. She dropped her skirt.

"Ready?" Mace was still grinning, and Kora felt herself beginning to blush.

"Certainly," she replied haughtily. Mace helped her get seated on the windowsill and eased her to the roof of the shed. He had left a ladder from the shed leaning against the wall, making it a simple matter to climb to the yard.

Over Mace's shoulder, Kora saw movement behind a curtain in the house across the yard. She caught a glimpse of white hair and glasses.

"Mace," she whispered as he lifted her to the ground, "there's an old lady over there watching us.

She probably thinks we're robbing the place. What if she goes to get the police?"

He grinned at her, but instead of letting her go, he crushed her to him, bringing his lips down on hers in a demanding kiss. For a second, Kora struggled against him. They were still in terrible danger, after all, but the feel of his mouth on hers was too much. She opened her lips to him, and ran her hands up to the back of his neck, pulling him closer to tease his tongue as he tasted the sweetness of her mouth.

Warmth invaded her limbs. The sensations his touch caused continued to surprise her, even as she yearned for more. She sagged against him, loving the feel of his hard-muscled body against her own. Everything around them dimmed in the heat of his embrace.

Finally, he broke the kiss, and she looked up into eyes as blue as the ocean, sparkling with desire and laughter.

"Now that dear old lady won't go to the police," he said in a voice deep with hunger. "She'll think we're eloping."

Mace laughed, and Kora swatted his shoulder indignantly, even as her heart fluttered at the thought of running off with him, to be his forever.

"Now, let's get going." He led her away from the refuge of the shed. The minute they were visible to the windows of Garrett's house, he broke into a run, pulling Kora behind him. She held up her sagging skirts with one hand, barely able to keep up with his long strides. They passed through the yard of the next house and didn't stop moving until they reached the street.

"We made it," Kora gasped as Mace gave her a

moment to catch her breath before continuing down the street.

"You'll have to learn not to wear a corset to a kidnapping," he teased her, but his attention was focused behind them, listening for any sign that Garrett knew Kora was gone. But he thought she was right—they had gotten away. As his tension receded, however, his anger surged. Garrett would not get away with what he'd done, not this time.

As they hurried down the street, putting as much distance between themselves and Garrett as possible, Mace waved down a hansom cab.

"Where to?" the hack driver asked cheerfully. Mace gave him Kora's address.

"But we can't go home yet," she said as Mace opened the door for her. "We've still got to take care of Garrett."

Mace shook his head. "Not *we*. I'm going to go get the police, and you're going back home where you'll be safe." Mace saw her jaw set stubbornly. "Don't argue. I need to get the police to Garrett's house before he finds out you're gone. Otherwise he may try to run. A kidnapping charge could send to him to jail for longer than he'll want to contemplate."

But Kora didn't budge. His mention of jail brought another image to her mind: Diego Amado waiting to be hanged for a crime he hadn't committed. "No!" she protested. "We don't have time. We have to get to Miles Osborn's house as quickly as possible. We have to get the papers on the mine."

He looked at her as though she'd lost her mind. "What are you talking about?"

"The mine," she repeated, then saw that he still didn't understand. "Garrett's been salting his mine with gold that he and Osborn have been buying. They're planning to trick investors into paying more than the mine is really worth, which is almost nothing, as far as I could tell. That's why Garrett kidnapped me. Didn't you know that?"

Clearly he hadn't. "We have to go back to Osborn's house and find those papers, if he hasn't already destroyed them. I doubt we could prove they were salting the mine without them."

Mace's eyes lit up with understanding. "Things are beginning to make a bit more sense. I thought there was something odd going on between Garrett and Osborn, but I was too distracted by Jessica's kidnapping to guess what it could be."

"Driver, we're changing the address," Kora called up to him, but Mace grabbed her shoulder.

"Look, I'd hate for Garrett and Osborn not to be tried for fraud or for any other crime they've committed, but we don't need those papers. They've definitely committed kidnapping, which should put them away for quite some time, and we need to move fast so they don't get away. Now, get in that cab, and go home."

"No." She put her fingertips to his lips to hush him so she could explain. "We *do* need to prove that those two were planning fraud, because that was Garrett's motive for killing Rosemarie Amado. We need those papers to save Diego Amado's life. And as far as I'm concerned, that's worth the risk of letting Garrett and Osborn escape."

She waited with bated breath, hoping Mace would agree. She could see his desire for revenge warring with the logic of her plea. And when his eyes locked with hers, and he nodded once, she knew again just how much she loved him.

He gave Osborn's address to the driver.

"Will you make up your mind?" the man called back, less good-natured than before. "I haven't got all day."

"Just get us there as quickly as possible, and there'll be a bonus in it for you," Mace told him.

"Can do," he responded, cheerful once more. Mace barely had time to hop into the cab behind Kora before the driver cracked his whip and they were off, dashing down the street at a speed too great to be considered completely safe. Both Kora and Mace wished it twice as fast.

"Booth! Booth!"

Garrett frowned at the man puffing on his front doorstep. Miles Osborn was red faced and panting, though presumably not from exertion, as his horse and gig stood serenely just across the street.

"Calm down, Miles, or you're going to have a stroke."

Osborn shook his head. "Booth, we've got trouble," he managed to get out, his voice crackling with anxiety.

"Well, out with it!" Garrett barked, stepping back into the hall so Osborn could enter. He closed the door.

"It's Dimity," Osborn told him. "She was all upset about that girl when I got home—"

"I thought you said you could handle her," Garrett interrupted, menace in his voice.

"Of course I can," Osborn assured him hastily, stepping back a pace. "But it's that fellow Fielding. She told him what happened."

Garrett snorted. That was unfortunate, but not completely unexpected. "So Fielding just left your

house?" he asked, trying to decide how to turn this
new development to his advantage. Fielding would
probably rush back over here. . . .

Osborn shook his head and took another step
back. "Fielding came by over two hours ago."

He winced as Garrett leaned close to him, his voice
thunderous. "Two hours ago? Damn it, Miles, why
didn't you tell me sooner?"

"I didn't know. I went to the office before I went
home—I had some things I had to take care of. That
McCloskey deposition had to be finished today. I do
have other clients, you know!"

"You won't have any clients at all if we're both
thrown in jail for kidnapping," Garrett growled.

His first impulse was to wring the little weasel's
scrawny neck, but he might need Miles. It didn't take
much figuring to realize that if Dimity Osborn had
spilled her guts to Fielding two hours ago, then
Fielding had known all about the kidnapping when
he'd come by the house. Which meant the threats
about his daughter had all been a smokescreen. And
Garrett didn't like the implications of that, not one
bit.

"Come on," he snapped and turned to the stairs.
Fielding had left him nearly an hour before, and
Garrett doubted he'd been spending his time having
an early supper. Since the bluff hadn't gotten him any
information, he should have been back by now, with
a gun or a posse, demanding to know where his darling little partner was. But he hadn't come back.

The more Garrett thought about that, the less he
liked it. He took the stairs two at a time.

"Booth! Wait!" He heard Osborn complaining
behind him, but he didn't slow down until he'd reached

the attic. A sea-green hat sat abandoned on the pillow of the bed, and slack ropes lay haphazardly on the floor.

"Where is she?" Osborn cried in alarm, coming up behind him.

Garrett turned on him, his eyes blazing. "You stupid son-of-a-bitch!" he shouted. "You just had to go to your office instead of going back to shut up your wife like I told you to. You've gotten us into one hell of a mess. If they've gone straight to the police, there's not much we can do but run—but maybe they haven't."

"This mess is not my fault! The whole thing was your idea—salting the mine, killing that Indian girl. All of it."

"You tell that to the police. Maybe they'll realize you're not worth the rope it would take to hang you," Garrett said. "Now let me think."

He forced his mind to click along coolly. It was no good letting your thinking fall apart just because a good plan had done the same. If Fielding and the girl had gone for the police immediately after their escape, they'd be back by now, almost certainly. Which meant they were after something else.

"Did you take those papers on the Bitter Creek Mine back to your office with you?" Garrett asked, focusing his attention back on the lawyer.

Osborn blinked, then shook his head. "They're still at home," he answered. "I hid them!" he added as Garrett's face turned purple.

"Idiot!" Garrett snarled as he brushed past the man and hurried back down the stairs. "And your wife's still at home?" he called behind him.

"No." Osborn was puffing again as he struggled to

catch up. "No, tonight's her night out with those old biddies from the church."

"That's too bad," Garrett muttered grimly to himself as he fingered the pistol tucked into the holster under his coat. Osborn was too winded to ask him what he meant.

18

The breakneck speed of the hansom cab didn't last long. Evening was settling over Sacramento, and people crowded the streets, either going home to supper or finishing up that one last errand that stood between them and a quiet evening. The cab's progress slowed to a crawl, and Mace wondered if it wouldn't be faster for them to get out and walk.

"Mace?"

He turned to look at the woman sitting beside him. She'd fixed her hair, but strands still fell across her forehead and touched her cheek. He couldn't resist the temptation to brush them away. She was so beautiful. But one side of her mouth puffed slightly from where Garrett had struck her, and every time he saw it, he wanted to rush back the way they had come and take care of Garrett personally.

"Mace?"

"Yes?" He wanted to kiss those lips until all she'd

been through in the past few hours was washed from her mind, like the dust washed from flowers in a warm summer rain.

"Don't you have something to tell me?"

"About what?"

She crossed her arms over her chest and frowned at him. "You promised to explain how you knew I'd been kidnapped. As soon as we were safe."

"This is hardly the place."

"Mace! You promised," she insisted, her eyes darkly serious. "We've had enough misunderstandings between us, and I get the feeling there's more going on than you're telling me. If I'd stayed and talked with you this afternoon, maybe I wouldn't have been kidnapped. So I think we ought to get everything out in the open before something else happens."

She was right. He should have told her everything he knew as soon as he began to suspect that Garrett had organized Jessica's kidnapping. But now that he'd found her again, now that she looked at him with eyes shining with love and trust, his heart quailed at the idea of risking losing her again.

Still, if he couldn't tell her the truth about himself, he didn't really have her to lose in the first place.

"It's a long story," he began reluctantly.

"It looks like we'll have plenty of time," Kora prodded with a smile as the cab lurched to a stop yet again.

"I should have told you this before, but it's a story I'm not very proud of," Mace said. He frowned down at his knuckles. "It started a long time ago."

Kora watched him intently. She'd never seen him so hesitant and unsure of himself.

It took him a moment to continue.

"When I was eighteen, I fell in love with a woman," he said at last. "Her name was Cecilia, and she was beautiful. Her hair was red as flame, and her green eyes always looked as though she were up to some sort of mischief. I'd never known anyone like her, and I adored her."

Kora felt a sudden flash of jealousy and immediately felt foolish. The poor woman was dead. If Mace still hurt over it, well, that was only natural.

"I saw her picture," Kora told him. "Jessica showed it to me."

"Mm." The interruption seemed to have jumbled Mace's thoughts, and he had to put them back together. "I intended to marry Cecilia, despite the fact that my parents couldn't stand her and thought she was beneath me."

He stopped, and Kora wondered if he was waiting for her to comment, but suddenly he rushed on, the words coming quickly.

"But the day I planned to ask her to marry me, she ran away. She'd fallen in love with another man, and instead of telling me herself, she wrote me a letter, telling me not to follow, that I'd never find them."

Kora's flash of surprise and confusion was overwhelmed by her sympathy for his obvious pain. "Oh, Mace." She touched his arm, but he brushed her hand away.

"The man who took her away was my brother," he continued in a harsh voice, not looking at her face. He didn't want to see the pity there. "My baby brother Jesse. I couldn't believe it. I think I went a little crazy. But I didn't go after them. I was afraid that if I did, I'd kill them."

The memory still brought a cold sweat to his brow,

and he clenched his fists until his knuckles turned white. But he couldn't stop now, because that wasn't the worst of it, and he had to tell her the worst.

"They went to Missouri. I found that out later. Jesse took his trust fund and started up a ranch with a man he met out there, Booth Garrett."

"I remember he said he knew your brother."

Mace nodded. "Not a year later, though, the ranch was attacked, supposedly by Indians. I now believe the Indians were actually men Garrett hired to kill my brother so he could make a lucrative deal with a railroad company planning a line through the area. But whatever the truth, my brother was killed, and Cecilia escaped, making the long journey back to Boston on her own."

He still marveled at that. For all her weaknesses, Cecilia had possessed a core of great strength. That was one of the things that had attracted him to her.

"On the way, she gave birth to the child she had been carrying," he continued, his voice as level as though the fact were of small consequence, but he heard Kora's indrawn breath. "She and the baby arrived on my doorstep late one evening. There was a terrible storm that night, and she was soaked. The baby was dry, though, and so tiny.

"Cecilia never even blinked when she asked me to take the baby. She wanted me to make sure it was well cared for, whatever became of her."

"And you did," Kora whispered, looking at him in wonder. "You took her child."

"No!" Mace denied it, unable to accept her admiration. She'd realize it was misplaced soon enough. "I told her to take the baby and get out of my sight, that I'd see her burn in hell before I took in her bastard. I told her I thought the child would be better off dead than living with the shame of her birth."

He couldn't look at Kora, couldn't bear to see the horror on her face. "I went to get myself some brandy, because I couldn't stand being in the same room with her, and I couldn't stand the way I was acting around her. And when I came back, the baby was asleep in my favorite chair, and Cecilia was gone."

The scene still shone vividly before Mace's eyes. Cecilia hadn't even bothered to make sure the door was shut. The wind had blown it open, the sudden burst of thunder waking the baby, making her cry for her mother.

"I went after Cecilia," he continued, more softly. "Renner, my butler, and I searched the night for her. She hadn't gone far. We found her under a tree alongside the road not a mile from my house, unconscious. We brought her back and called for a doctor."

He shook his head, wishing he could drive the memory away. "The doctor said she had pneumonia. She'd probably contracted it shortly after giving birth. The wet and cold and emotional stress I put her through didn't leave her a chance. She died before morning."

He remembered sitting with her all night, praying for a second chance. He hadn't got it.

"But I did tell her I'd take her baby and care for it as my own. I told everyone that Cecilia and I had married in secret, and the doctor agreed to go along with my story that she'd died in childbirth."

"So Jessica is your brother's daughter?" Kora asked softly.

"Probably. Even Cecilia wasn't sure if she was his or mine. That was the reason she never married Jesse. She wasn't completely without a sense of honor."

The words tasted bitter on his lips, and he stopped. He no longer had any right to be bitter. Cecilia was dead, and she had given him the greatest gift she could—the daughter he loved so much.

"When Garrett heard that Cecilia had survived to give birth to a daughter, he assumed the child would be a threat to the fortune he'd taken from my dead brother. That's why he kidnapped her. When I went by Osborn's house today looking for Garrett, and found that he and Osborn had supposedly taken you to the hospital after a fainting spell, I assumed he had taken you to get to me. You're not exactly the fainting type. That's why I went looking for you." He paused, gathering a deep breath. "Now you know everything."

Kora watched him, her eyes following his strong profile. He finally turned to face her. His polite, detached facade was gone completely, and she saw years of pain and anger reflected in the blue depths of his eyes.

Her heart swelled with compassion, and she reached over to take his hand.

"I should have told you this before," he said, the words stiff and awkward. "But I didn't want you to despise me."

"Despise you?" Kora said in surprise. "Why should I do that?"

Mace's face darkened, but she could see that his anger was directed at himself. "Why? I killed the woman I loved, because I was too proud to give her shelter when she asked for it. And I haven't changed. When Davies told me you were engaged to him, I didn't give you a chance to explain. I hurt you and chased you away, and you were completely innocent."

Kora shook her head, hardly trusting herself to

speak. His anguish brought a lump to her throat. "No, I wasn't totally innocent," she managed to get out. "Jared *had* asked me to marry him, and I should have told you about it. Besides, it's not all that easy to drive me away. I hadn't given up on you."

Mace stared at her in amazement. "You don't hate me then?"

Kora laughed, releasing her tears. "No, you idiot, of course I don't hate you," she scolded him. "I'm proud of you."

Mace reached over to wipe the tears from her cheeks, still gazing at her in wonder. "Proud of me? Why?"

Kora sniffed, and straightened her back. "Because," she said firmly, "in spite of what Cecilia and your brother put you through, you took their daughter in. And not only did you raise her as your own, you love her as though she were."

A half-grin twitched the edge of Mace's mouth. "You'd better be careful," he told her, his voice deep and rough, "or I'll think you're just saying these things because you've been blinded by love."

Heat flushed Kora's cheeks, spreading up to the top of her head and down all the way to her toes. She dropped her gaze from his.

"I doubt that." She intended to sound self-confident, but the words came out as a whisper. "I think I fell in love with you before I knew you had any good qualities at all."

She felt his fingers under her chin, tilting her head until she had to look at him. His eyes blazed with a heat that burned down into her soul. His mouth found hers in a surprisingly gentle kiss that made her bones melt within her. When he pulled away, she found herself panting for breath.

"I knew you were trouble from the moment I set eyes on you," Mace said. "And here you've gone and made me break my solemn oath never to fall in love again."

Kora flushed even deeper, and her heart fluttered with a happiness she'd never known before.

"Hey! You ever coming out of there?" The driver's voice came through the trap door in the roof into the intimate world of the cab. "You said you were in a hurry."

Kora hadn't noticed they had halted once more, but apparently this stop had nothing to do with traffic. They'd reached their destination.

"I think you ought to wait here. You can go for the police if anything goes wrong," Mace said. The look in his eyes still told her he loved her, making it distinctly difficult for her to think. But she wasn't going to let him do this alone.

"I know where the papers are and what they look like. Besides, I've developed a certain rapport with Mrs. Osborn."

Mace frowned at her. He didn't want to put her in any more danger, but he didn't particularly relish the idea of leaving her alone in the cab, either. In addition, if Miles Osborn happened to be at home, the surprise of seeing Kora alive and free could work to their advantage.

"All right," he agreed reluctantly. "But fix your hair again while I pay the driver. You look like a kidnap victim."

Kora made a face at him, but he'd already stepped out of the cab. She combed her hair with her fingers and pinned it behind her in a loose bun. There wasn't much she could do about her lost hat and hoops, but

Dimity Osborn's eyesight was just bad enough that she might not notice.

Mace came back to the cab door and helped her to the street.

"If Osborn shows up, I want you to get to safety and go for help," he told her in a low voice as they made their way up the walk. The only reason he was letting her come with him at all was that he didn't really believe the lawyer was dangerous on his own, but if Osborn felt cornered, there wasn't any telling what he might be capable of.

Kora shrugged off his concern and rapped the door knocker sharply. Nothing happened. She tried it again. Again no one answered. Mace tried, making the knocker echo dully in the interior of the house.

"It appears Mrs. Osborn is out, and the maid must be as well," he said.

"What do we do now?" Kora asked, her anxiety rising. "We have to get those papers before Garrett finds out I've escaped. We'll have to break in like you did at Garrett's place."

"With that hack driver watching us like a hawk?"

"He already thinks we're eccentric."

Mace ignored her and reached out to try the front door. It opened.

"Trust Dimity Osborn to leave the front door unlocked," he said with a wicked grin. He stepped into the front hall, and after a brief hesitation Kora followed.

The intense quiet of the house gave her a chill as Mace closed the door behind them. Although she knew Miles Osborn was a criminal, she didn't like intruding into Mrs. Osborn's house without her permission.

"Where to?" Mace asked after a moment had passed and no one had jumped from the shadows to ask them what the hell they thought they were doing.

"The study. Over there." Their voices barely rose above a whisper, even though no one was there to hear them.

Kora led Mace into Osborn's study. The evening light filtered faintly into the dark room, making it seem gloomy and forbidding. She went to the desk, but it was bare, except for a bottle of India ink and a large paperweight in the shape of a functional ounce scale.

"They were right here," she said, crestfallen. "Osborn must have taken them with him."

"We might as well make sure."

She nodded. They began pulling open desk drawers, but the contents were as uninspiring as they had been earlier in the day.

Kora's heart sank. She'd been so sure the papers would still be there. If Osborn had taken the proof of his and Garrett's fraud away with him, it was unlikely she and Mace would ever find it.

"What do we do now?" she asked as she closed the last drawer. There had to be something. She wasn't going to let Amado hang for Garrett's crime.

Mace put an arm around her shoulders and pulled her close. "Don't worry. We'll—"

He was interrupted by the sound of the front door being flung open so hard it slammed into the side of the house.

"Down!" Mace ordered.

Her heart frozen by the unexpected noise, Kora allowed him to push her to the ground. She disappeared under the desk just as the door to the study burst open.

"Don't move!" Booth Garrett's barked order set her pulse racing with fear. "Hands in the air, Fielding. I'm sure you've got a gun, so let's not test my marksmanship at this close range. I'd hate to get a mess all over this fine carpet."

Mace's boot moved forward to nudge Kora's skirt farther under the desk. Then his legs disappeared from her view as he moved away.

"Why Garrett, what a pleasure to run into you again," Mace drawled.

"Very amusing, Fielding, but I doubt you'll be laughing much longer," Miles Osborn said, his voice reedy with nerves but gaining confidence in his own home. "Breaking and entering. Outrageous!"

Kora heard noises coming from the bookshelves across the room.

"I suppose this is what you were looking for?" the lawyer asked smugly. "You don't think I'd just leave these out on my desk after your little paramour saw them there. Ha! You're not as clever as you think you are, Fielding."

"Shut up, Miles," Garrett snarled. "I, for one, can't really blame him for thinking you'd be so stupid."

Kora's heart pounded so that she could hardly think. Osborn had the papers, and Garrett was going to kill Mace. She couldn't let that happen. But she had no idea what she was going to do without a weapon and unable to go for help.

"It's not in your best interest to kill me, Garrett," Mace said. His own danger seemed unreal to him. All he could think of was Kora. "Miss Hunter is on her way to the police at this moment to get you arrested for kidnapping. If you run now, they'll hunt you for a while, but if you murder me, you'll never be able to stop running. Even if the police get tired, the men my family will hire won't."

Kora bit her lip in frustration. Mace was trying to protect her and buy time, but he needed help. She had never felt so powerless in her life.

"Killing a burglar is hardly murder," Garrett said. "And I doubt the police will believe any wild stories Miss Hunter has to tell once it becomes clear that the two of you were out to rob Osborn. Besides, I doubt a jury would have much sympathy for a whore calling herself a reporter."

"You don't have the guts to say that without a gun in your hand," Mace growled, vowing to himself that Garrett would pay for that remark, as well as all his other crimes.

Garrett just laughed. "Miles, go get his gun. It's probably in a coat pocket or his waistband. Turn around, Fielding, and keep your hands in the air."

Kora heard Osborn move past the front of the desk with tentative steps. There wasn't any more time. The odds could only get worse from here. She had to do something. Anything. If they were going to kill Mace, she didn't want to be safe.

Crouching, she slipped from under the desk.

"Go on, Miles, he won't bite."

Peeking around the edge of the desk she saw Garrett standing just inside the study doorway, pistol in hand, all his attention focused on the two men in front of him. Kora wished she could let Mace know what she intended to do without giving herself away to Garrett, but she had to act now.

In one swift motion she leaped to her feet and

reached across the desk. Even as Garrett's peripheral vision caught the motion, she had the bottle of ink in her hand and sent it flying at his head.

"Mace!"

Garrett raised an arm to ward off the missile, and it bounced off his elbow, sending black ink spilling into his face.

At the same time, Kora heard Osborn gasp, and she turned to see the lawyer doubled up on the floor, clutching his stomach. In a second Mace had crossed the room to Garrett, throwing himself at the arm with the gun.

Garrett fired, but the ink still blinded him, and the shot struck only the desk. Mace collided with him, the two of them slamming into the door. Garrett's hand hit the door frame and the gun went flying, but with the solid door behind him he managed to push Mace to the floor. He wiped an arm across his eyes and dived for the gun.

But Kora saw it, too, and her fingers grasped it first. Garrett's hand came down on hers, but he lost his grip when Mace's fist found his jaw.

Garrett grabbed Mace's sleeve, and the two men rolled away from Kora, too close to each other to strike a good blow. Kora held the gun in her hands, but she couldn't shoot Garrett without risk of hitting Mace.

Mace stood, pulling Garrett up with him, and the fight continued. What Mace had in height, Garrett made up for in weight, and though each landed several heavy punches, neither gained the advantage.

Kora glanced briefly at Osborn, but he was still curled up on the floor, moaning to himself.

Garrett landed a glancing blow on Mace's shoulder, and Mace retaliated with a ferocious hit to Garrett's jaw. Garrett staggered back, falling against the wall. When he moved forward, Mace hit him again, and he collapsed to the floor.

"That's for maligning Kora's honor," Mace growled savagely. Still panting for breath from exertion and anger, he pulled his pistol from his coat pocket. All of the things Garrett had done were now so clear in his mind: murdering Jesse, kidnapping Jessica and Kora, framing Diego Amado for Rosemarie's murder. In that moment he actually saw red, and he took dead aim at the center of Garrett's forehead.

"Mace?" Kora's soft voice came dimly through the haze of blood lust in his head. He turned to see her still kneeling on the floor, Garrett's pistol dangling from her hand, anxious eyes focused on his face. "Did he hurt you?"

The concern in her voice washed through him like a balm, and his finger loosened from the trigger of his gun.

"Are you kidding?" Mace asked, giving her a slight but reassuring grin through the sudden recognition of pain in his ribs and a swelling in his lip. He looked down at Garrett, whose eyes were focused on Mace's gun.

"Don't worry," Mace said, taking a step back from his murderous rage. "I'm not going to shoot you, unless you decide to make me. I'd miss the pleasure of seeing your face when you're sentenced to hang."

A noise in the hallway caught their attention. "Mrs. Osborn?" a male voice called. "This is the police. Is everything all right?"

Kora and Mace glanced at each other. "In here!" Mace called, lowering his gun, but keeping it where Garrett could see it.

The study door opened, and a uniformed officer looked in. His partner stood behind him. At the sight of the chaos in the room, the officer put a hand on his gun. "What's going on here?" he demanded.

The officer looked familiar to Kora, and she finally placed him. He was the one who had shown her and Mace to Diego Amado's cell the first time, the one who had first told them there was more to the case than there seemed.

"Officer Brady?" He glanced at her and recognition set in.

"Miss Hunter," he acknowledged, and she thought he would have tipped his hat to her but for the fact that he didn't want to move his hand from his gun. "Are you all right, miss?"

"Yes, we're fine," she assured him, trying to rise to her feet and finding her legs about as sturdy as jelly. "These men—"

But a cry from Miles Osborn, still on the floor, interrupted her. "Oh, thank God, officers. Arrest these people. They tried to rob me!"

"Officer Brady," Mace began, calmly putting his revolver back into his pocket, "Mr. Osborn and Mr. Garrett here conspired to commit fraud, murder, and kidnapping. I think you'll find some of the proof you need in these papers." He lifted the pile Osborn had left on the bookshelf and handed them to Brady. "Any other confirmation you need can be found in Garrett's home, where Miss Hunter was bound in the attic after her abduction."

"That's a ridiculous story!" Osborn wailed, struggling to his feet. "I'm an upstanding citizen! I don't know what he's talking about!"

Kora moved closer to Officer Brady and held out

her wrists. His eyes widened at the sight of the red welts there.

"Mark, handcuff these two men," he said to the officer standing behind him. The second officer, even younger than Brady, came into the room, taking his handcuffs from his belt.

"Come on over here," he ordered Osborn.

"This is criminal!" Osborn cried, his eyes dancing wildly about the room as if looking for an escape. "You can't do this to me. I haven't done anything. We never salted that mine, and it was that Digger who killed his wife. You know that."

"Shut up, Miles!" Garrett shouted from his position against the wall. "Just shut the hell up!"

His blazing eyes silenced Osborn, who shrank away from his partner in crime as the young officer handcuffed them together.

"How on earth did you know we needed help?" Kora asked Brady in wonder. "Did the cab driver call for you?"

Brady smiled, making his face seem more boyish than ever. "Actually, we came by because of the dog."

"Muffy?" Mace asked in disbelief. At the sound of his name, Muffy shouldered his way into the study. Wagging his tail, he trotted over to Mace, who instantly placed a restraining hand on the dog's head.

"I see you two are acquainted," Brady observed. "Muffy got into Mr. Waber's store again and was causing quite a commotion. He broke open a flour sack, and so on. Officer Coxe and I just happened to be there getting a cup of coffee. We're old friends of Muffy's, so we brought him on home. It was the open front door that suggested there might be trouble."

Officer Coxe prodded his prisoners toward the

door. "Stupid dog," Osborn snapped at Muffy, and aimed a kick at the dog's side.

Muffy dodged the blow, snarling at Osborn. Mace's fondness for the dog rose a notch.

Brady stepped aside to let the little procession file past him.

"Look," he said to Mace and Kora, "there's no need for both of you to come down to the station. Why don't I have Mark escort Miss Hunter home, and Mr. Fielding can come down and file a report."

"That sounds good," Mace said, before Kora could protest. "We'll be out in just a moment."

Brady nodded and went back outside.

Kora turned to him. "Mace, I want to go with you."

He came over to her, taking her by the shoulders. "Listen to me," he said. "For once. Less than a week ago you shot a man who was trying his best to kill me and would probably have succeeded. You led me out to Argenta to find my daughter, despite the obvious danger. Today, you got yourself kidnapped researching a story that meant a great deal to you. And you've just helped me round up two confirmed felons. All before suppertime."

He cocked an eyebrow at her. "Enough! This time you're going to give in to my desire to protect you. Osborn and Garrett are not going to be pleasant once they get to the police station. Let me take care of it."

What could she say to that? Kora put her arms around Mace's middle and leaned against his chest. His arms encircled her in his protective warmth, and she became conscious of the exhaustion in her limbs. She closed her eyes and felt his strength.

"As long as you don't get the idea that it will

always be this easy to get rid of me," she said finally, with a smile.

"Easy?" Mace rolled his eyes. "You never do anything the easy way, sweetheart."

"I should hope not!"

Mace laughed. "Then we're perfectly suited."

Kora laughed, too, with a full heart.

19

"*Kora, there's someone* in the parlor to see you," Anna Hunter said, leaning through the sitting-room door.

"Thanks, Mama," Kora replied, returning her mother's smile. Once more she wondered at her mother's mood. Her parents had insisted on her staying home from work today to recover from yesterday's excitement, but they seemed surprisingly cheerful this morning, almost exuberant.

Kora set down her notebook. As long as they didn't suggest again that she quit reporting, she wasn't going to complain about staying home for one day. Besides, she could use the time to write about her adventures of the past week. The only problem was trying to get the whole story into one edition of the *Valley Times*.

"Get up, cat," she ordered Dodge, dumping him unceremoniously to the floor when he refused to comply. She brushed some gray hairs from her lap and straightened her skirt.

She wore a simple dress of pale blue silk that set off her complexion and hair to perfection. The skirt hitched at the bottom to show the lace of her best petticoat, and the bodice dipped just low enough to accent her other assets. She'd worn this particular dress because she'd expected Mace to come by this morning to see her, but so far she hadn't heard a word from him.

She'd fallen asleep last night almost as soon as she'd explained to her family what had happened, so she'd missed him when he'd come by to pick up Jessica.

Kora stepped out into the hall toward the parlor. She'd already had a visit from Jared and Clemency. Jared had apparently been by the police station early this morning and heard all about Kora's kidnapping. She'd teased him about coming over to get the inside scoop on the story, but it had meant a lot to her that he'd cared enough to check in on her.

It had pleased her to realize that seeing Clemency and Jared together hadn't bothered her in the least. Each had taken pains to explain that their visiting together was purely for convenience's sake, but she knew them both well enough to see that a mutual attraction was growing. She sincerely hoped that concerns about her feelings wouldn't keep those two apart if they discovered they belonged together.

Kora reached the parlor door and looked in. She hoped Diego Amado didn't notice her eager smile fade slightly when she saw it was he who waited for her and not Mace. After all, she *was* very glad to see him.

"Mr. Amado!" she exclaimed, hurrying over to shake his hand. "I'm so glad *you* could come to see *me* this time."

Diego Amado took her hand and shook it warmly, though he looked stiff in the black suit he wore in place of his denims and work shirt. The suit was a bit out of style but well cared for—obviously his Sunday best—and his black hair was slicked back, though it had been disturbed by the top hat he held in his left hand.

"I've come to thank you, Miss Hunter," he said solemnly. "You not only believed in my innocence, you saved my life—you and Mr. Fielding. I can't repay you, but I will never forget what you have done."

Kora flushed at his gratitude. "I couldn't bear to watch you hang while Rosemarie's murderer went free," she said simply, though her feelings about the case had never been simple.

Amado nodded. "I know. When I learned my wife had died, and I was thrown in prison, I thought there was no justice left in our world. I think now that I was wrong. Perhaps justice is there, just waiting for us to fight for it."

Kora's heart went out to this dignified man who had lost his wife to a white man's greed and had almost lost his own life to white men's prejudices, but who still had the courage to hope for justice. "Some of us have to fight harder than others," she said.

Amado smiled, the self-deprecating smile she knew from seeing him in prison, but this time it reached his eyes. "So I've learned. But that's no excuse to give up fighting. That is why I've decided to go to Round Valley, to the reservation there. I think with my education and my knowledge of the white man, I can help the Indians there. And there is much they can teach me, now that I am willing to listen."

"That could be painful," Kora warned. She knew that ranchers and settlers often treated Indians on reservations as badly as they treated the so-called wild Indians who refused to be corralled where the white man demanded.

"That's why I have to go," Amado replied.

She nodded. "Perhaps after you've been there a while, I could come visit and do a story on the Indians and the reservation." She was no more able to shy away from a challenge than Amado was.

He smiled again. "I'm counting on it."

Kora laughed. "I wish you the best of luck."

He shook her hand again. "And I wish that for you." He placed his hat back on his head, and Kora showed him to the door.

She wandered back into the parlor then, her thoughts moving back over the past two weeks. She remembered her first meeting with Mace on the embarcadero, when she'd hated him instantly. She almost laughed out loud.

She should get back to her writing, but it was so hard to concentrate when every nerve in her body tingled with the anticipation of seeing Mace again. She began to wonder if he felt the same way. Why hadn't he come by? Yesterday he'd said he loved her, but perhaps that had been the heat of the moment. What if he'd changed his mind?

Kora knew she was being silly, but she felt sixteen again, gangly and unsure of herself.

Suddenly a pair of hands came down on her shoulders.

"Oh!" She jumped and then whirled to find herself

in Mace's arms. His eyes danced with mischief. "You scared me!" she scolded, but she let him keep his arms around her.

"I saw you through the window, and I couldn't resist," he said, still grinning wickedly. "What were you thinking about, that you didn't even hear me come through the door?"

Kora laughed. "I was thinking about you."

"About how wonderful I am?"

"About why you were taking so long to come see me this morning!" She punched him lightly on the shoulder.

"Oh, that." He let her go and stepped back. "I saw this in a shop back when you were showing me around Sacramento, and it reminded me of you. I thought maybe you should have it."

He reached into his coat pocket and then took her hand to place a necklace in it. From the delicate gold chain hung an oval pendant, and in the center glowed a dark brown stone shot with a glimmering streak of gold.

"It's lovely," she said softly, turning it in her hand to catch the light.

"It's cat's-eye," Mace told her, lifting the chain from her hand to fasten it around her neck. "The first thing I noticed about you was how golden your eyes were, like a cat's."

"Thank you," Kora said, touching the pendant that hung just below the hollow of her neck. She glanced up at Mace shyly. "You didn't have to get me a gift."

"That's just to soften you up," he teased, but his blue eyes were suddenly very serious. "Kora, until I came to California, I thought I was content with my life. I have a beautiful daughter, I make a comfortable living, and I'm doing work that I love."

He reached out to brush her neck and cup her jaw with his hand. His eyes bored into hers.

"But when I met you, I discovered what my life had been missing. I never thought I'd fall in love again after what happened with Cecilia. And I had no intention of falling in love with you. But I have. And now life without you sounds more bleak than I can bear."

He paused, gathering courage. Kora's heart beat so loudly that she could hardly hear him. "Kora, will you marry me?"

"Oh, Mace," she whispered, love filling her heart. She didn't know how, but this man she had known for so short a time had entered her soul, and she knew she wanted only to spend the rest of her life with him.

Suddenly her eyes caught the brown-sprigged paper of the parlor walls. Her mind flew back to Jared's proposal, in this very room, and the disastrous fight that followed. "No!" she exclaimed in horror, then seeing Mace's shock, added, "Not here."

She grabbed Mace's hand and pulled him into the hall. Not the sitting room; her mother might be there. She opened the front door and led an utterly confused Mace onto the porch.

"There," she said, satisfied. "Now you can ask me."

"Ask you what?" Mace asked warily. "In all the excitement, I've forgotten."

Kora stamped her foot, though the effect was dampened by an irrepressible giggle. "I promised never to have any more important discussions in that parlor," she explained. "They have a tendency to end badly."

Mace's jaw tightened. "Jared?"

Kora nodded. "I couldn't be the woman he wanted, Mace. Are you sure I'm what you want?"

She swallowed tightly. She remembered her father's telling her he would have given up the newspaper business to please her mother. She couldn't have done that for Jared. Somewhere, deep in her heart, a voice told her she could do it for Mace. She knew now what true love was.

"Kora," Mace said, his voice deep and full of love. "You're exactly what I want, what I need in my life. We make quite a team, partner."

"Partner?"

"You seem to me ready to move on from society fluff," he said, a sly twinkle in his eye. "With a little direction from an older, more experienced reporter."

"You?"

"Mm."

Kora raised an eyebrow at him. "You think I'm ready for politics, crime, and corruption?"

"I think the politicians and the criminals had better watch out."

"Good." She smiled sweetly. "Did I ever mention to you how much Troy hates reporting?"

"You told me he prefers the business end of things, but I don't think you ever actually said he hated it. I . . ." He stopped, his eyes narrowing.

"It's a bit late to be warning the crooks and the hacks," Kora confirmed, hoping her cocky tone hid her anxiety over his reaction.

"Your parents?"

"They think Troy takes terrible advantage of me, making me do so much of his background research."

Mace laughed, a low, delighted sound. "You're a wonder, Kora Hunter. You've come into my life and turned it upside down." His voice turned serious. "And every day I will give thanks that you have. You've brought love and hope back into my life, sweetheart."

For a moment Kora's heart was too full to reply. Tears pricked her eyelids.

She blinked and said matter-of-factly, "All right, now. You were asking me to marry you."

"Are you certain? Why would I do something like that?"

"Because I'm such an irresistibly attractive, intelligent, thoughtful, and *patient* young woman," Kora teased back, not sounding patient at all. Excitement suffused her cheeks with pink.

"Ah, yes, I remember," Mace said, his voice suddenly low and intense. "You are lovely, intelligent, and unbelievably tempting." He bent down to brush her lips with his. "Now are you going to tell me yes, or do I have to compromise your honor right here on the porch to make you mine?"

His arms slipped around her, and he pulled her close. His lips found her neck, and moved their way up to her ear. Kora's entire body responded to their touch.

"Mace," she said, but she didn't pull away.

"Don't worry about your parents," he murmured against her ear. "I told them last night I intended to propose. And by the way, Jessica thinks it's a terrific idea, too. So what do you say?"

Kora laughed, a laugh suddenly cut off by his lips on her mouth. She knew the whole world could see them there on the porch, but she didn't care. After all, he loved her, and she was going to marry him. She'd just let him persuade her a little while longer before she agreed.

Comanche Magic by Catherine Anderson

The latest addition to the bestselling Comanche series. When Chase Wolf first met Fanny Graham, he was immediately attracted to her, despite her unsavory reputation. Long ago Fanny had lost her belief in miracles, but when Chase Wolf came into her life he taught her that the greatest miracle of all was true love.

Separating by Susan Bowden

The triumphant story of a woman's comeback from a shattering divorce to a fulfilling, newfound love. After twenty-five years of marriage, Riona Jarvin's husband leaves her for a younger woman. Riona is in shock—until she meets a new man and finds that life indeed has something wonderful to offer her.

Hearts of Gold by Martha Longshore

A sizzling romantic adventure set in 1860s Sacramento. For years Kora Hunter had worked for the family newspaper, but now everyone around her was insisting that she give it up for marriage to a long-time suitor and family friend. Meanwhile, Mason Fielding had come to Sacramento to escape from the demons in his past. Neither he nor Kora expected a romantic entanglement, considering the odds stacked against them.

In My Dreams by Susan Sizemore

Award-winning author Susan Sizemore returns to time travel in this witty, romantic romp. In ninth-century Ireland, during the time of the Viking raids, a beautiful young druid named Brianna inadvertently cast a spell that brought a rebel from 20th-century Los Angeles roaring back through time on his Harley-Davidson. Sammy Bergen was so handsome that at first she mistook him for a god—but he was all too real.

Surrender the Night by Susan P. Teklits

Lovely Vanessa Davis had lent her talents to the patriotic cause by seducing British soldiers to learn their battle secrets. She had never allowed herself to actually give up her virtue to any man until she met Gabriel St. Claire, a fellow Rebel spy and passionate lover.

Sunrise by Chassie West

Sunrise, North Carolina, is such a small town that everyone knows everyone else's business—or so they think. After a long absence, Leigh Ann Warren, a burned out Washington, D.C., police officer, returns home to Sunrise. Once there, she begins to investigate crimes both old and new. Only after a dangerous search for the truth can Leigh help lay the town's ghosts to rest and start her own life anew with the one man meant for her.

Tame the Wildest Heart by **Parris Afton Bonds**

In her most passionate romance yet, Parris Afton Bonds tells the tale of two lonely hearts forever changed by an adventure in the Wild West. It was a match made in heaven . . . and hell. Mattie McAlister was looking for her half-Apache son and Gordon Halpern was looking for his missing wife. Neither realized that they would find the trail to New Mexico Territory was the way to each other's hearts.

First and Forever by **Zita Christian**

Katrina Swann was content with her peaceful, steady life in the close-knit immigrant community of Merriweather, Missouri. Then the reckless Justin Barrison swept her off her feet in a night of passion. Before she knew it she was following him to the Dakota Territory. Through trials and tribulations on the prairie, they learned the strength of love in the face of adversity.

Gambler's Gold by **Barbara Keller**

When Charlotte Bell headed out on a wagon train from Massachusetts to California, she had one goal in mind—finding her father, who had disappeared while prospecting for gold. The last thing she was looking for was love, but when fate turned against her, she turned to the dashing Reade Elliot to save her.

Queen by **Sharon Sala**

The Gambler's Daughters Trilogy continues with Diamond Houston's older sister, Queen, and the ready-made family she discovers, complete with laughter and tears. Queen Houston always had to act as a mother to her two younger sisters when they were growing up. After they part ways as young women, each to pursue her own dream, Queen reluctantly ends up in the mother role again—except this time there's a father involved.

A Winter Ballad by **Barbara Samuel**

When Anya of Winterbourne rescued a near-dead knight she found in the forest around her manor, she never thought he was the champion she'd been waiting for. "A truly lovely book. A warm, passionate tale of love and redemption, it lingers in the hearts of readers. . . . Barbara Samuel is one of the best, most original writers in romantic fiction today."—Anne Stuart

Shadow Prince by **Terri Lynn Wilhelm**

A plastic surgeon falls in love with a mysterious patient in this powerful retelling of *The Beauty and the Beast* fable. Ariel Denham, an ambitious plastic surgeon, resentfully puts her career on hold for a year in order to work at an exclusive, isolated clinic high in the Smoky Mountains. There she meets and falls in love with a mysterious man who stays in the shadows, a man she knows only as Jonah.

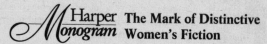

LORD OF THE NIGHT
by Susan Wiggs
A Venetian lord dedicated to justice suspects a
lucious beauty of being involved in a scandalous plot.

ORCHIDS IN MOONLIGHT
by Patricia Hagan
Caught in a web of intrigue in the dangerous West,
a man and a woman fight to regain their
overpowering dream of love.

A SEASON OF ANGELS
by Debbie Macomber
Three willing but wacky angels must teach their
charges a lesson before granting a Christmas wish.
National Bestseller